BART SIMPSON™ BREAKS OUT

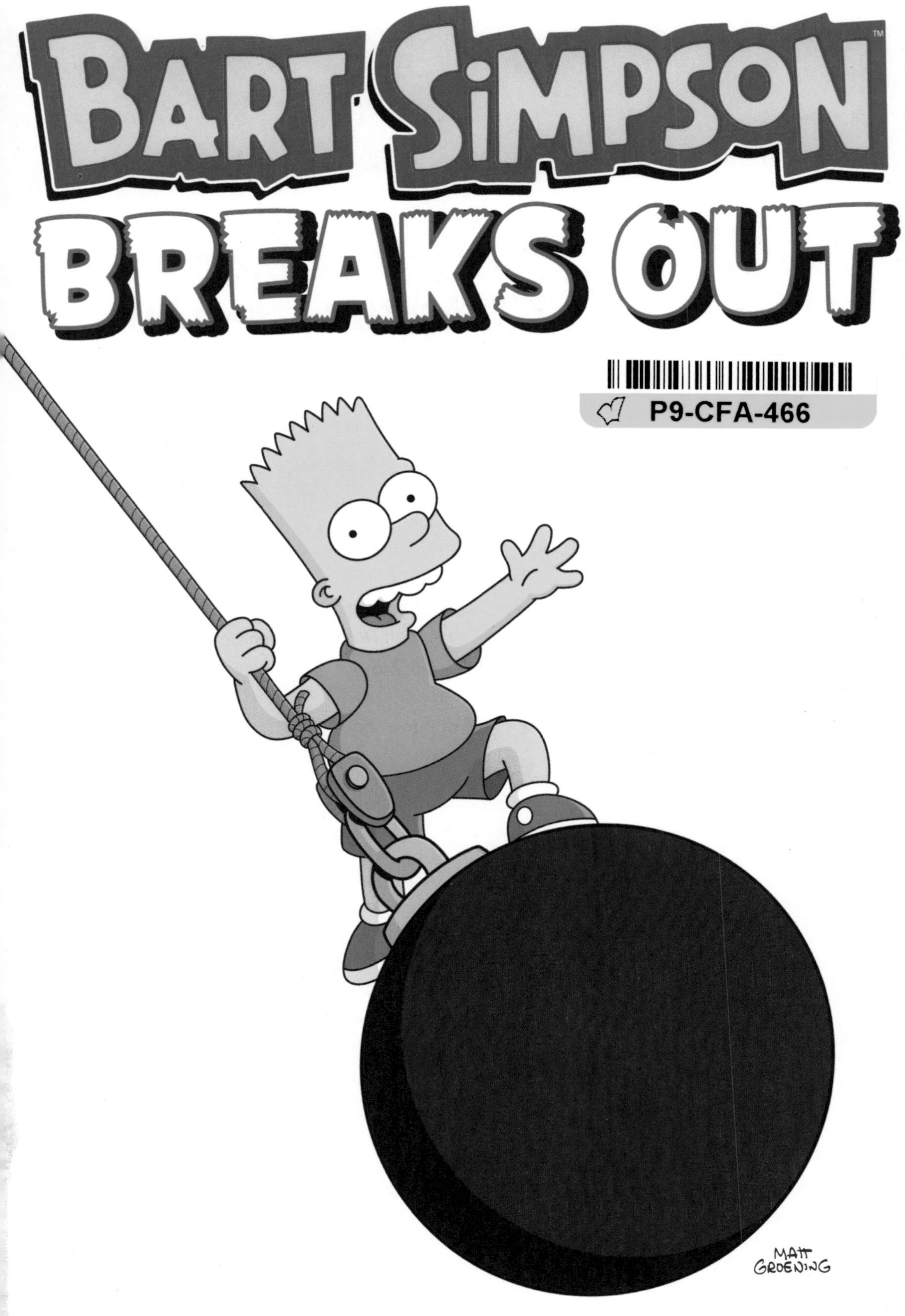
MATT GROENING

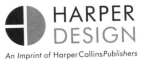

HARPER DESIGN
An Imprint of HarperCollinsPublishers

BART SIMPSON BREAKS OUT

Bart Simpson #78, #79, #80, #81, #82, #83

Copyright © 2019 by
Bongo Entertainment, Inc. All rights reserved.
No part of this book may be used or reproduced in any manner whatsoever
without written permission except in the case of brief quotations
embodied in critical articles and reviews. For information address
HarperCollins Publishers,
195 Broadway, New York, New York 10007.

FIRST EDITION

ISBN 978-0-06-287873-1

Library of Congress Cataloging-in-Publication Data has been applied for.

19 20 21 22 23   10 9 8 7 6 5 4 3 2 1

Publisher: Matt Groening

Creative Director: Nathan Kane
Managing Editor: Terry Delegeane
Director of Operations: Robert Zaugh
Art Director: Jason Ho
Production Manager: Christopher Ungar
Assistant Editor: Karen Bates
Production: Art Villanueva
Administration: Ruth Waytz
Legal Guardian: Susan A. Grode

Printed in China, 2019

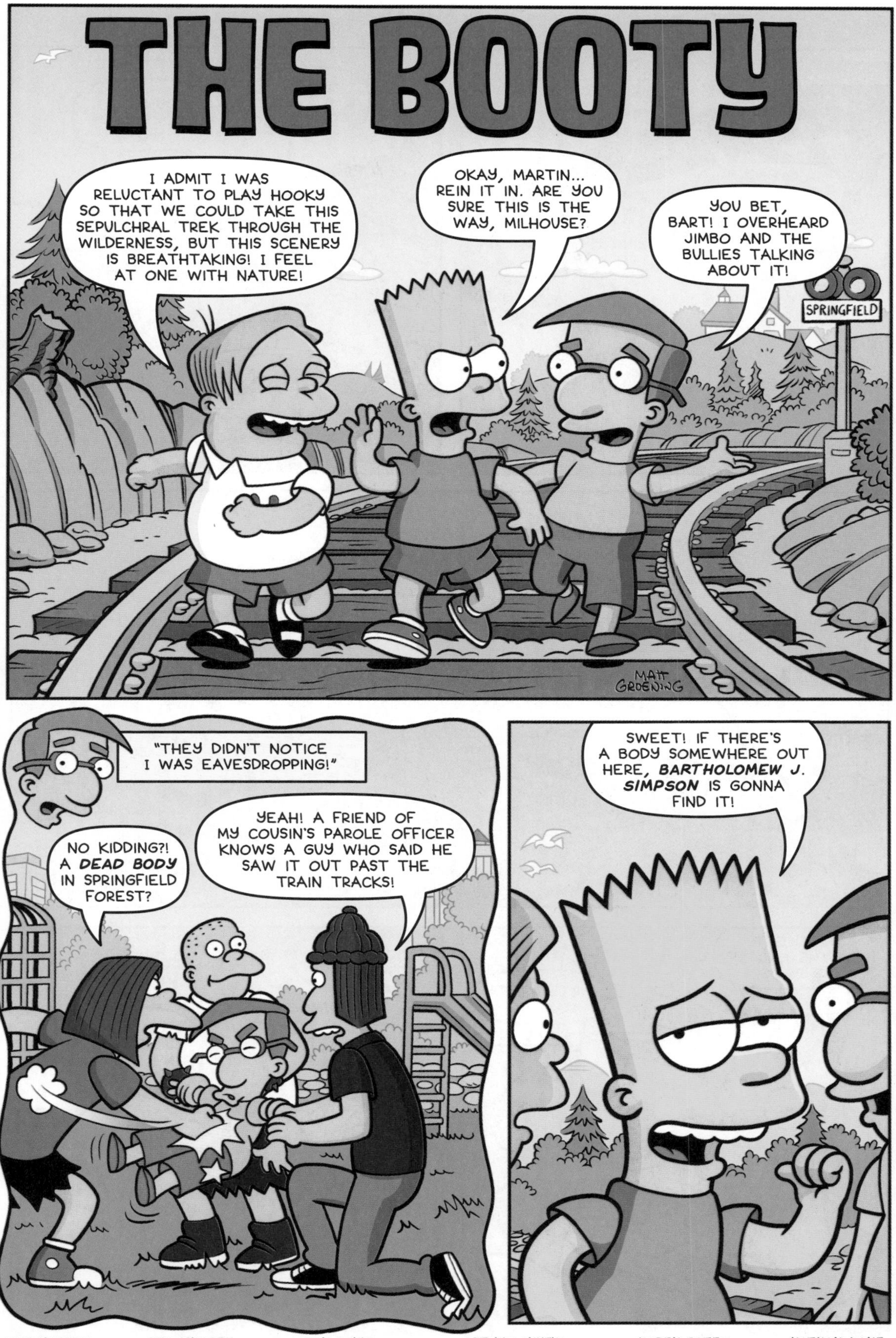
THE BOOTY
I ADMIT I WAS RELUCTANT TO PLAY HOOKY SO THAT WE COULD TAKE THIS SEPULCHRAL TREK THROUGH THE WILDERNESS, BUT THIS SCENERY IS BREATHTAKING! I FEEL AT ONE WITH NATURE!
OKAY, MARTIN... REIN IT IN. ARE YOU SURE THIS IS THE WAY, MILHOUSE?
YOU BET, BART! I OVERHEARD JIMBO AND THE BULLIES TALKING ABOUT IT!
SPRINGFIELD
MATT GROENING
"THEY DIDN'T NOTICE I WAS EAVESDROPPING!"
NO KIDDING?! A **DEAD BODY** IN SPRINGFIELD FOREST?
YEAH! A FRIEND OF MY COUSIN'S PAROLE OFFICER KNOWS A GUY WHO SAID HE SAW IT OUT PAST THE TRAIN TRACKS!
SWEET! IF THERE'S A BODY SOMEWHERE OUT HERE, ***BARTHOLOMEW J. SIMPSON*** IS GONNA FIND IT!

PAT MCGREAL SCRIPT | ***REX LINDSEY*** PENCILS | ***DAN DAVIS*** INKS | ***ART VILLANUEVA*** COLORS | ***KAREN BATES*** LETTERS | ***NATHAN KANE*** EDITOR

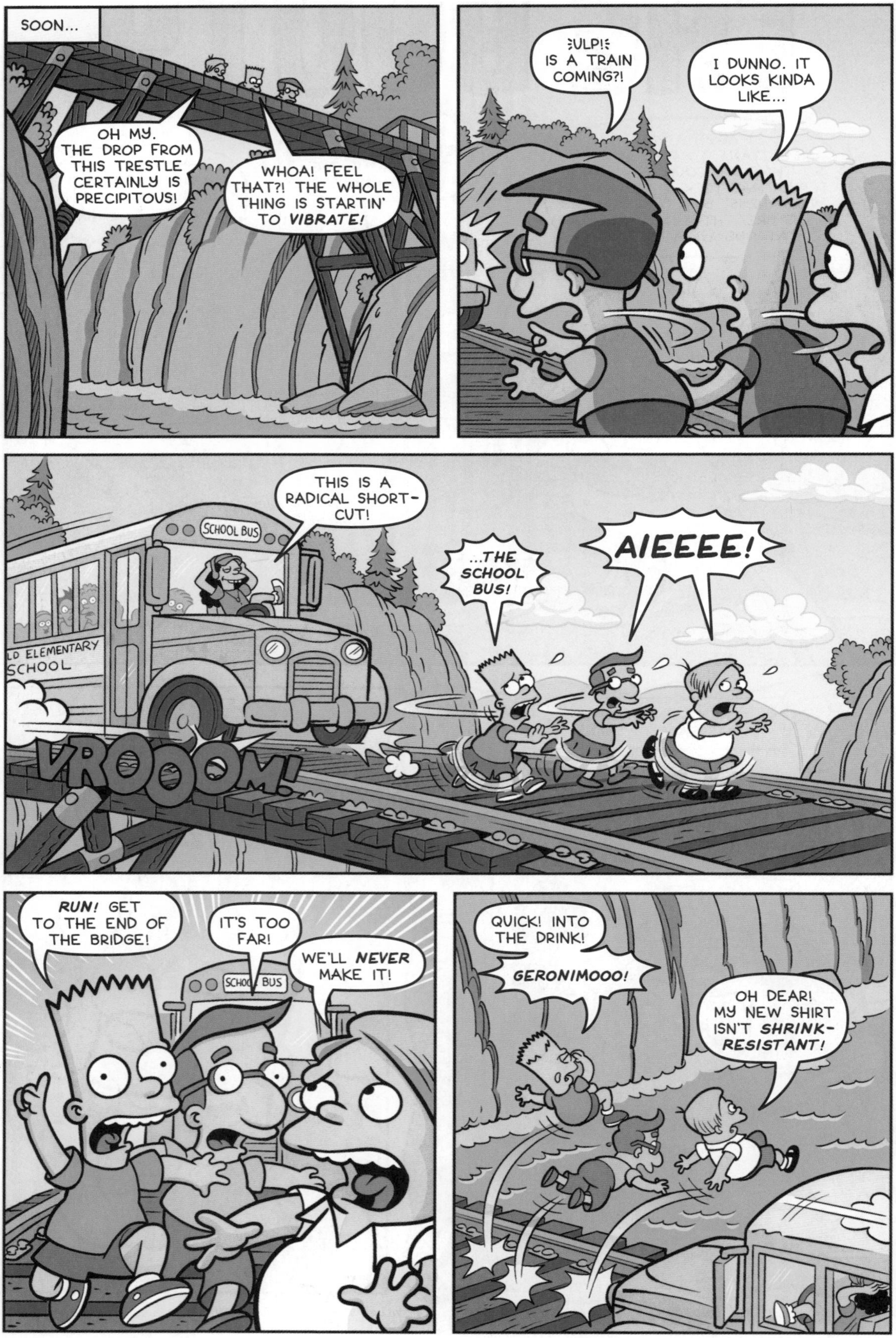
SOON...
OH MY. THE DROP FROM THIS TRESTLE CERTAINLY IS PRECIPITOUS!
WHOA! FEEL THAT?! THE WHOLE THING IS STARTIN' TO *VIBRATE!*
ULP!! IS A TRAIN COMING?!
I DUNNO. IT LOOKS KINDA LIKE...
THIS IS A RADICAL SHORT-CUT!
SCHOOL BUS
LD ELEMENTARY SCHOOL
...*THE SCHOOL BUS!*
AIEEEE!
VROOOM!
RUN! GET TO THE END OF THE BRIDGE!
IT'S TOO FAR!
WE'LL *NEVER* MAKE IT!
SCHOOL BUS
QUICK! INTO THE DRINK!
GERONIMOOO!
OH DEAR! MY NEW SHIRT ISN'T *SHRINK-RESISTANT!*

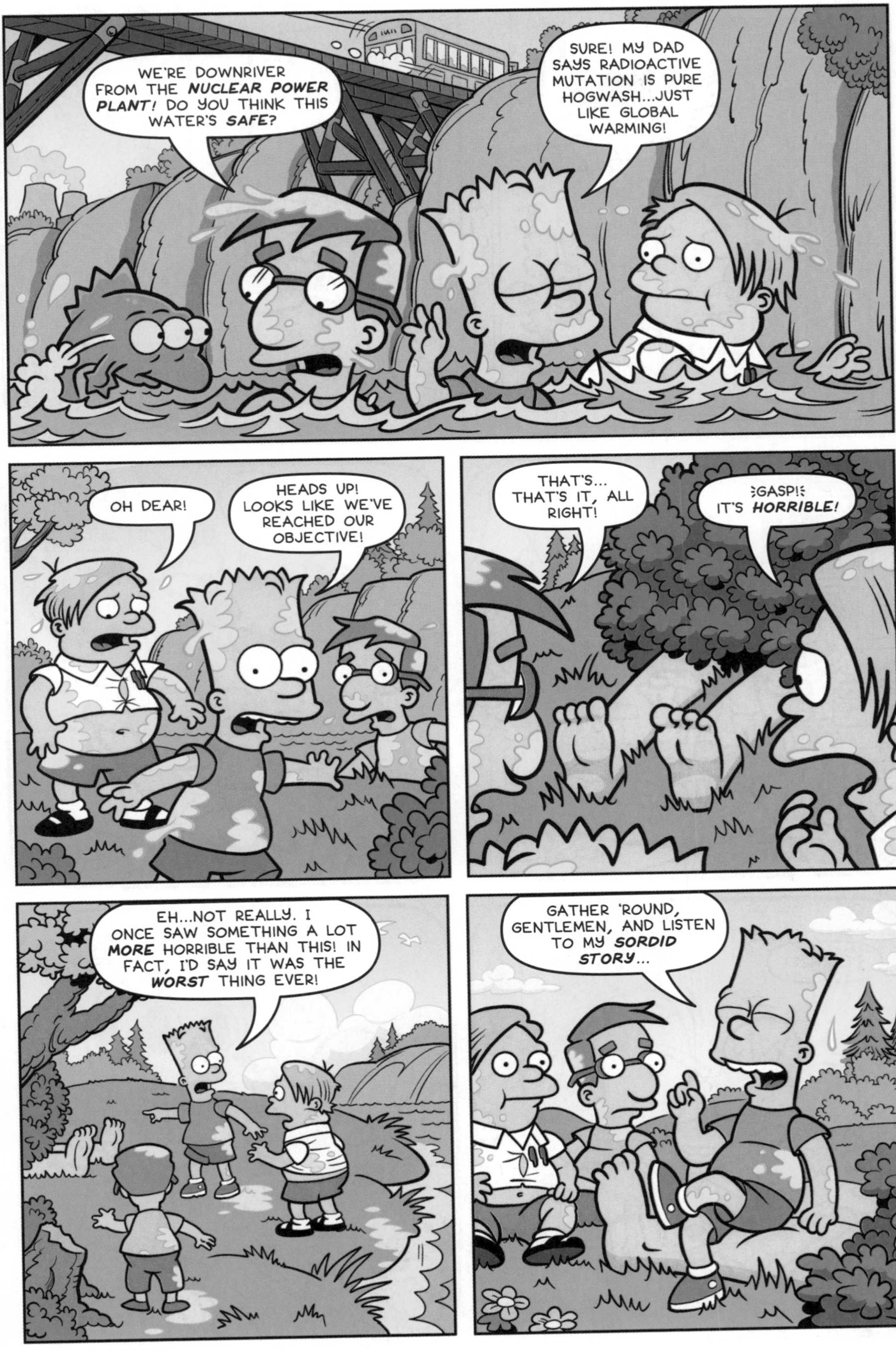
WE'RE DOWNRIVER FROM THE **NUCLEAR POWER PLANT!** DO YOU THINK THIS WATER'S **SAFE?**
SURE! MY DAD SAYS RADIOACTIVE MUTATION IS PURE HOGWASH...JUST LIKE GLOBAL WARMING!
OH DEAR!
HEADS UP! LOOKS LIKE WE'VE REACHED OUR OBJECTIVE!
THAT'S... THAT'S IT, ALL RIGHT!
GASP! IT'S **HORRIBLE!**
EH...NOT REALLY. I ONCE SAW SOMETHING A LOT **MORE** HORRIBLE THAN THIS! IN FACT, I'D SAY IT WAS THE **WORST** THING EVER!
GATHER 'ROUND, GENTLEMEN, AND LISTEN TO MY **SORDID STORY...**

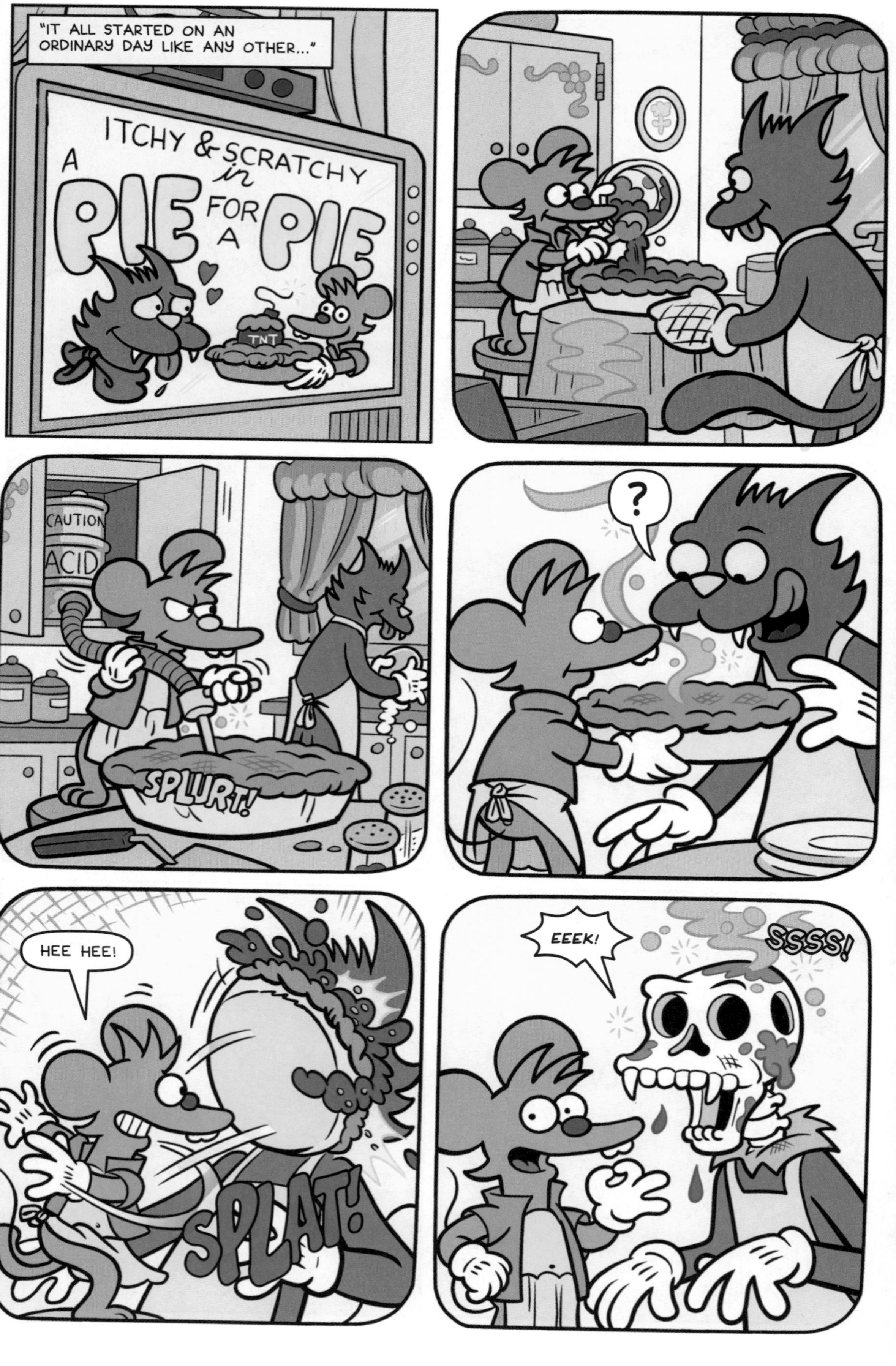
"IT ALL STARTED ON AN ORDINARY DAY LIKE ANY OTHER..."
ITCHY & SCRATCHY in
A PIE FOR A PIE
TNT
CAUTION
ACID
SPLURT!
?
HEE HEE!
SPLAT!
EEEK!
SSSS!

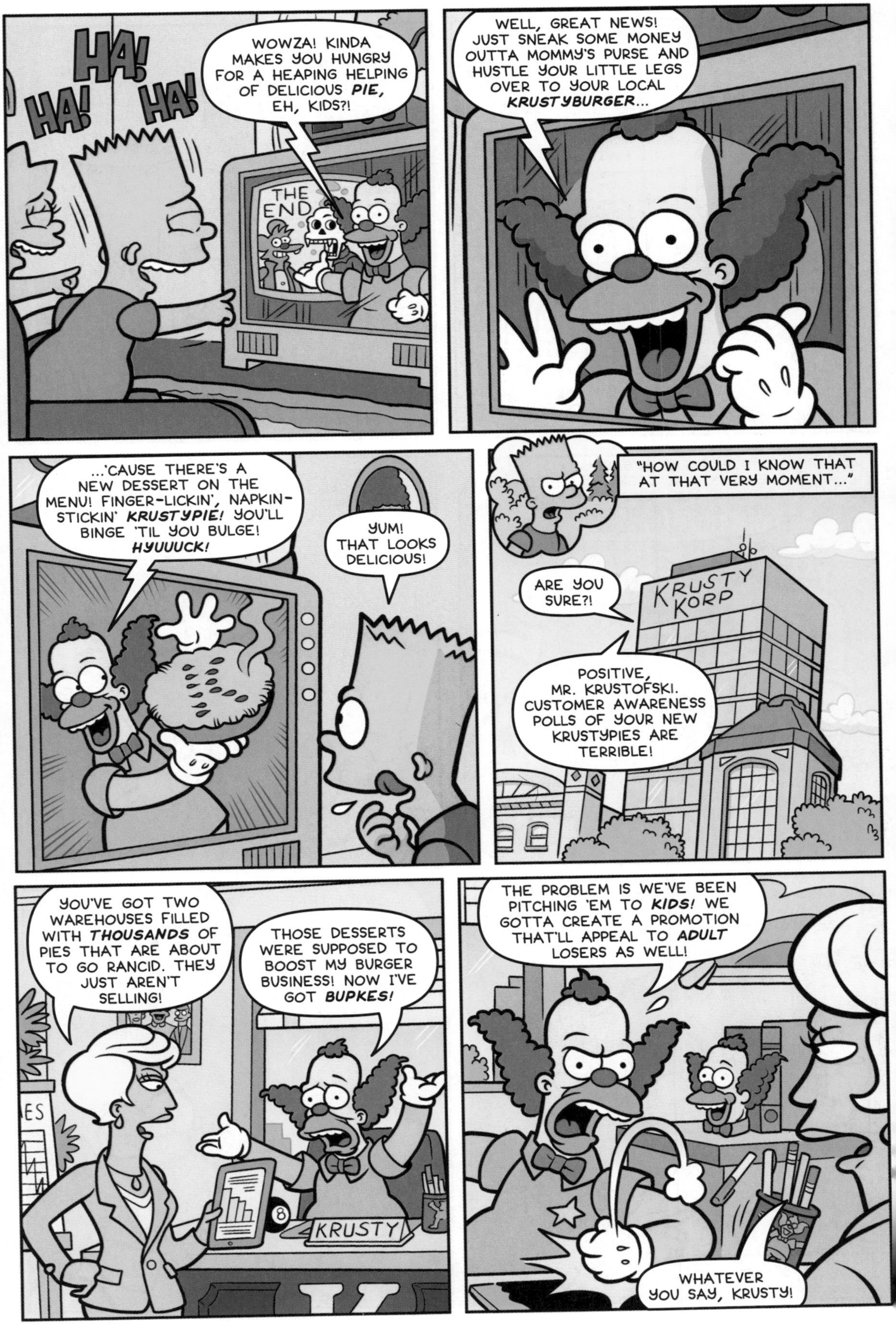
HA! HA! HA!
WOWZA! KINDA MAKES YOU HUNGRY FOR A HEAPING HELPING OF DELICIOUS PIE, EH, KIDS?!
THE END
WELL, GREAT NEWS! JUST SNEAK SOME MONEY OUTTA MOMMY'S PURSE AND HUSTLE YOUR LITTLE LEGS OVER TO YOUR LOCAL KRUSTYBURGER...
...'CAUSE THERE'S A NEW DESSERT ON THE MENU! FINGER-LICKIN', NAPKIN-STICKIN' KRUSTYPIE! YOU'LL BINGE 'TIL YOU BULGE! HYUUUCK!
YUM! THAT LOOKS DELICIOUS!
"HOW COULD I KNOW THAT AT THAT VERY MOMENT..."
KRUSTY KORP
ARE YOU SURE?!
POSITIVE, MR. KRUSTOFSKI. CUSTOMER AWARENESS POLLS OF YOUR NEW KRUSTYPIES ARE TERRIBLE!
YOU'VE GOT TWO WAREHOUSES FILLED WITH THOUSANDS OF PIES THAT ARE ABOUT TO GO RANCID. THEY JUST AREN'T SELLING!
THOSE DESSERTS WERE SUPPOSED TO BOOST MY BURGER BUSINESS! NOW I'VE GOT BUPKES!
KRUSTY
THE PROBLEM IS WE'VE BEEN PITCHING 'EM TO KIDS! WE GOTTA CREATE A PROMOTION THAT'LL APPEAL TO ADULT LOSERS AS WELL!
WHATEVER YOU SAY, KRUSTY!

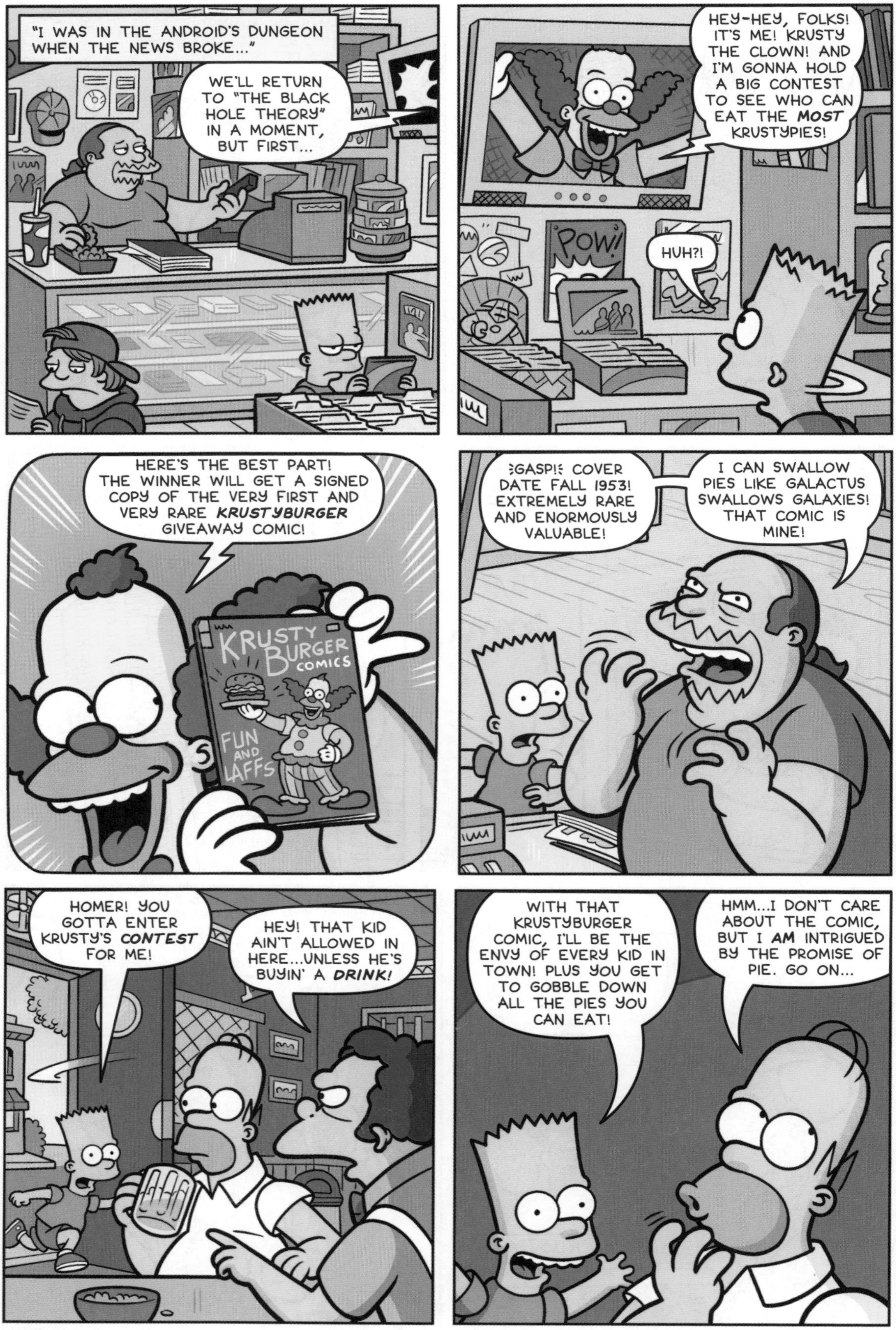

"I WAS IN THE ANDROID'S DUNGEON WHEN THE NEWS BROKE..."
WE'LL RETURN TO "THE BLACK HOLE THEORY" IN A MOMENT, BUT FIRST...
HEY-HEY, FOLKS! IT'S ME! KRUSTY THE CLOWN! AND I'M GONNA HOLD A BIG CONTEST TO SEE WHO CAN EAT THE ***MOST*** KRUSTYPIES!
HUH?!
POW!
HERE'S THE BEST PART! THE WINNER WILL GET A SIGNED COPY OF THE VERY FIRST AND VERY RARE ***KRUSTYBURGER*** GIVEAWAY COMIC!
KRUSTY BURGER COMICS
FUN AND LAFFS
:GASP!: COVER DATE FALL 1953! EXTREMELY RARE AND ENORMOUSLY VALUABLE!
I CAN SWALLOW PIES LIKE GALACTUS SWALLOWS GALAXIES! THAT COMIC IS MINE!
HOMER! YOU GOTTA ENTER KRUSTY'S ***CONTEST*** FOR ME!
HEY! THAT KID AIN'T ALLOWED IN HERE...UNLESS HE'S BUYIN' A ***DRINK!***
WITH THAT KRUSTYBURGER COMIC, I'LL BE THE ENVY OF EVERY KID IN TOWN! PLUS YOU GET TO GOBBLE DOWN ALL THE PIES YOU CAN EAT!
HMM...I DON'T CARE ABOUT THE COMIC, BUT I ***AM*** INTRIGUED BY THE PROMISE OF PIE. GO ON...

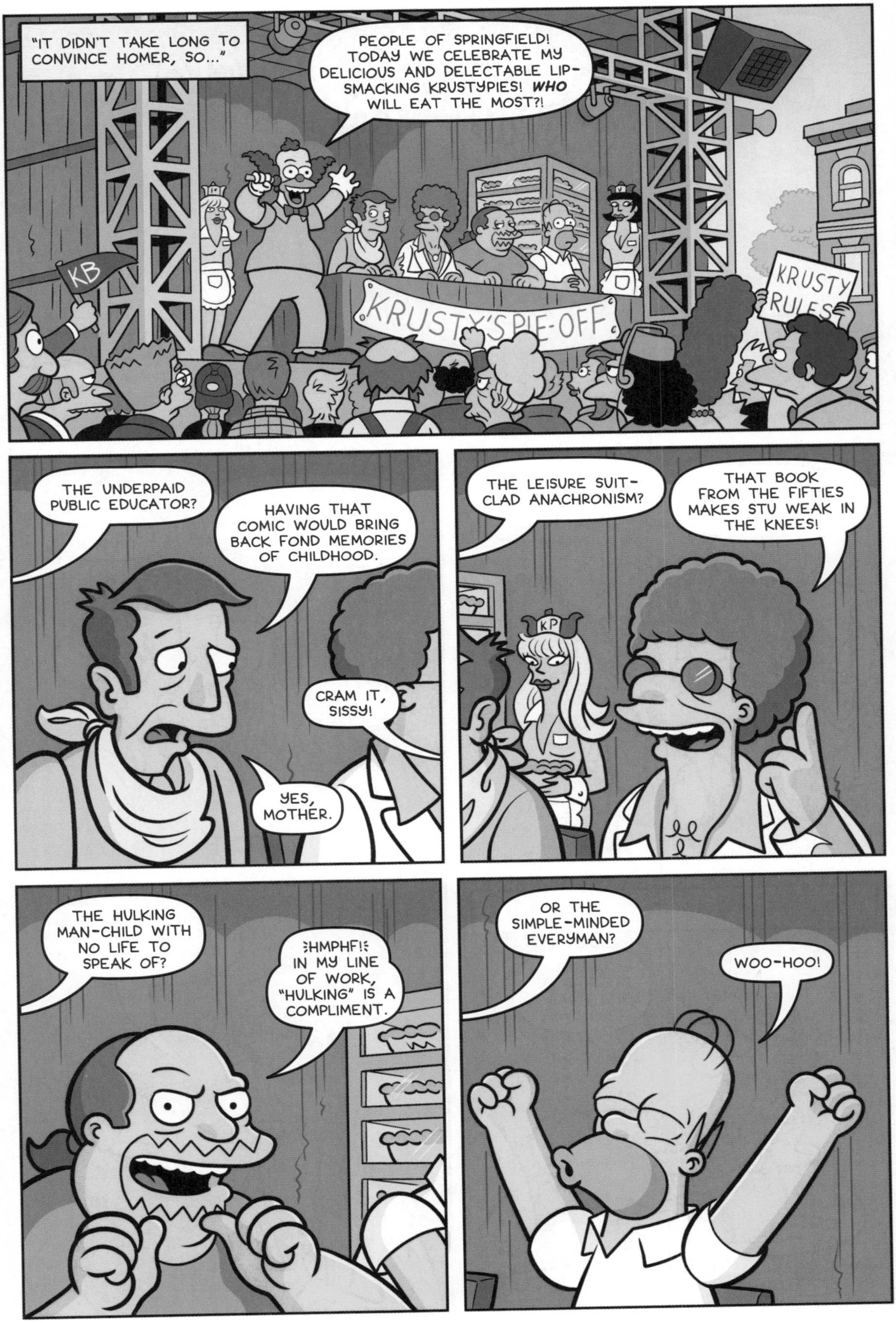

"IT DIDN'T TAKE LONG TO CONVINCE HOMER, SO..."
PEOPLE OF SPRINGFIELD! TODAY WE CELEBRATE MY DELICIOUS AND DELECTABLE LIP-SMACKING KRUSTYPIES! WHO WILL EAT THE MOST?!
KB
KRUSTY'S PIE-OFF
KRUSTY RULES
THE UNDERPAID PUBLIC EDUCATOR?
HAVING THAT COMIC WOULD BRING BACK FOND MEMORIES OF CHILDHOOD.
CRAM IT, SISSY!
YES, MOTHER.
THE LEISURE SUIT-CLAD ANACHRONISM?
THAT BOOK FROM THE FIFTIES MAKES STU WEAK IN THE KNEES!
KP
THE HULKING MAN-CHILD WITH NO LIFE TO SPEAK OF?
HMPHF! IN MY LINE OF WORK, "HULKING" IS A COMPLIMENT.
OR THE SIMPLE-MINDED EVERYMAN?
WOO-HOO!

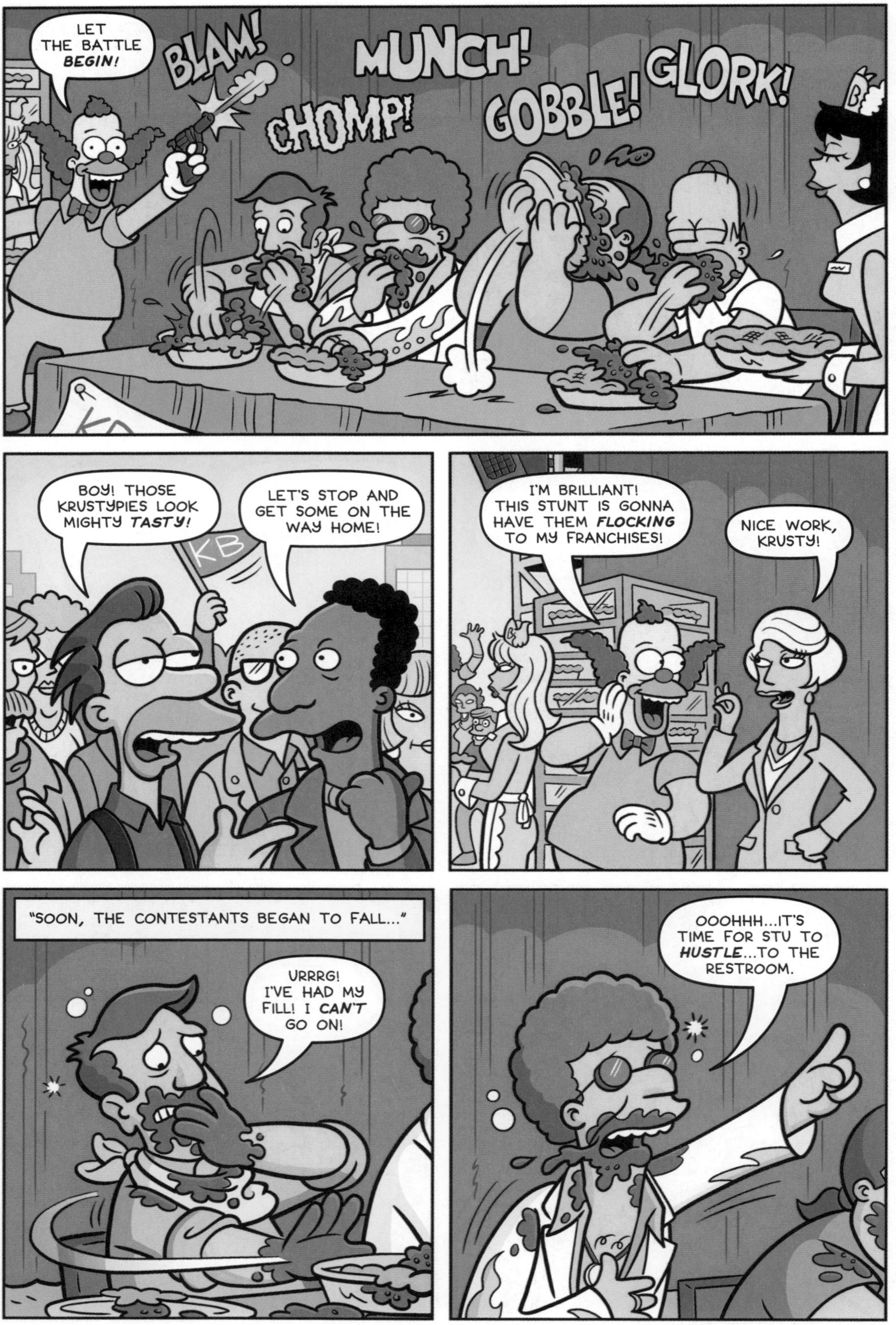
LET THE BATTLE BEGIN!
BLAM!
MUNCH!
CHOMP!
GOBBLE!
GLORK!
BOY! THOSE KRUSTYPIES LOOK MIGHTY TASTY!
LET'S STOP AND GET SOME ON THE WAY HOME!
KB
I'M BRILLIANT! THIS STUNT IS GONNA HAVE THEM FLOCKING TO MY FRANCHISES!
NICE WORK, KRUSTY!
"SOON, THE CONTESTANTS BEGAN TO FALL..."
URRRG! I'VE HAD MY FILL! I CAN'T GO ON!
OOOHHH...IT'S TIME FOR STU TO HUSTLE...TO THE RESTROOM.

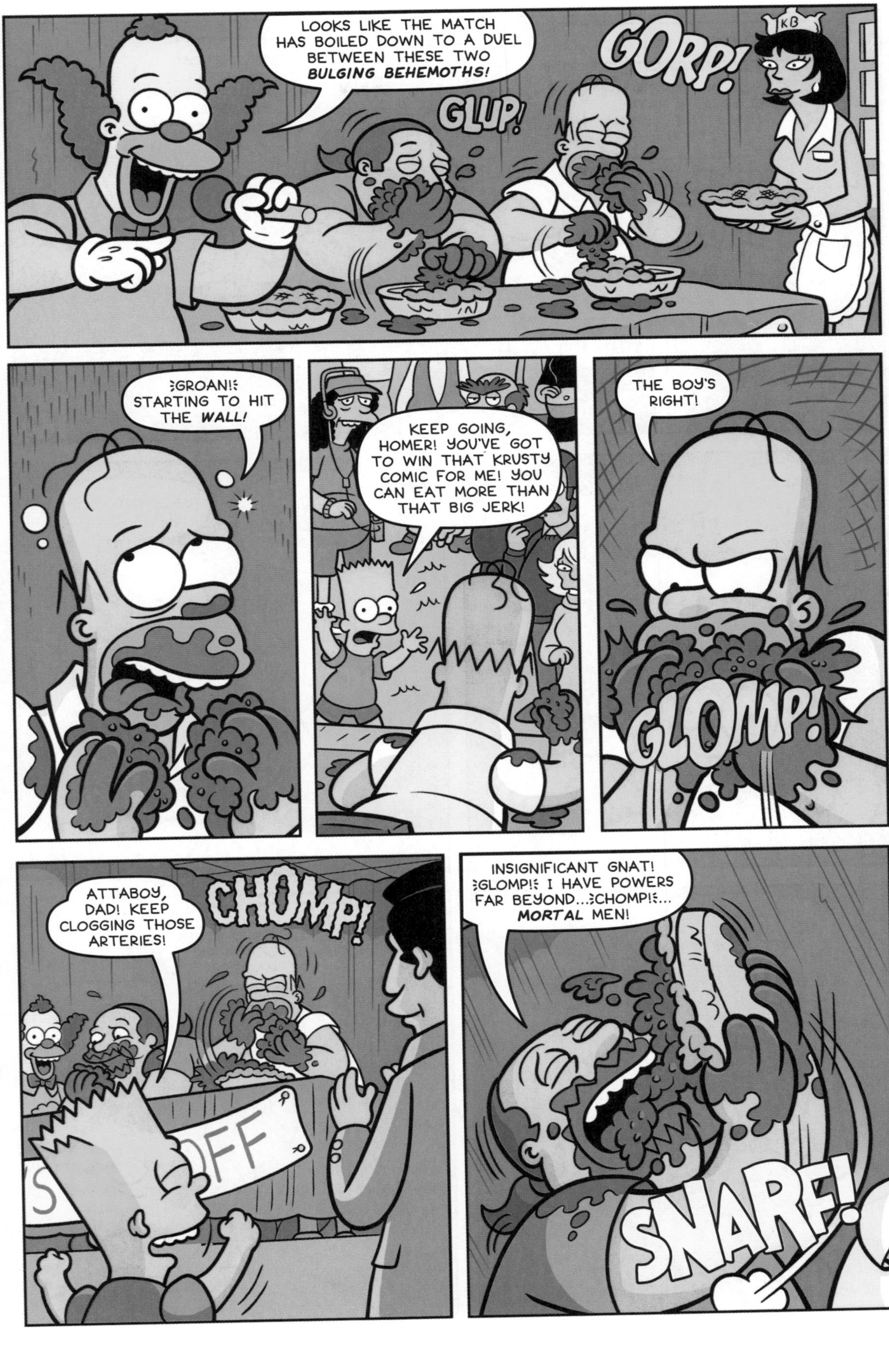
LOOKS LIKE THE MATCH HAS BOILED DOWN TO A DUEL BETWEEN THESE TWO *BULGING BEHEMOTHS!*
GLUP!
GORP!
KB
GROAN! STARTING TO HIT THE *WALL!*
KEEP GOING, HOMER! YOU'VE GOT TO WIN THAT KRUSTY COMIC FOR ME! YOU CAN EAT MORE THAN THAT BIG JERK!
THE BOY'S RIGHT!
GLOMP!
ATTABOY, DAD! KEEP CLOGGING THOSE ARTERIES!
CHOMP!
INSIGNIFICANT GNAT! GLOMP! I HAVE POWERS FAR BEYOND...CHOMP!... *MORTAL* MEN!
SNARF!

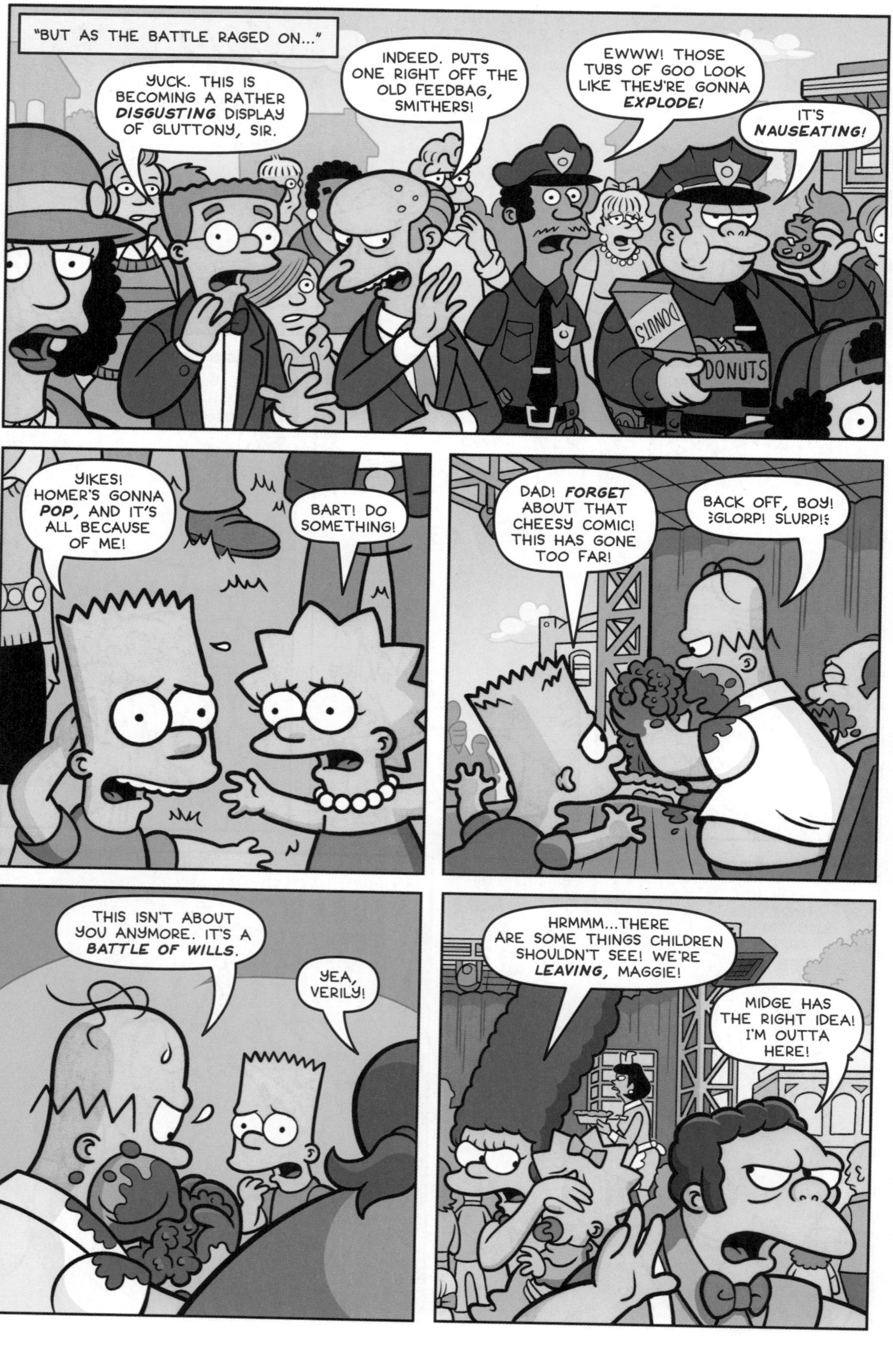
"BUT AS THE BATTLE RAGED ON..."
YUCK. THIS IS BECOMING A RATHER DISGUSTING DISPLAY OF GLUTTONY, SIR.
INDEED. PUTS ONE RIGHT OFF THE OLD FEEDBAG, SMITHERS!
EWWW! THOSE TUBS OF GOO LOOK LIKE THEY'RE GONNA EXPLODE!
IT'S NAUSEATING!
DONUTS
DONUTS
YIKES! HOMER'S GONNA POP, AND IT'S ALL BECAUSE OF ME!
BART! DO SOMETHING!
DAD! FORGET ABOUT THAT CHEESY COMIC! THIS HAS GONE TOO FAR!
BACK OFF, BOY! ⁝GLORP! SLURP!⁝
THIS ISN'T ABOUT YOU ANYMORE. IT'S A BATTLE OF WILLS.
YEA, VERILY!
HRMMM...THERE ARE SOME THINGS CHILDREN SHOULDN'T SEE! WE'RE LEAVING, MAGGIE!
MIDGE HAS THE RIGHT IDEA! I'M OUTTA HERE!

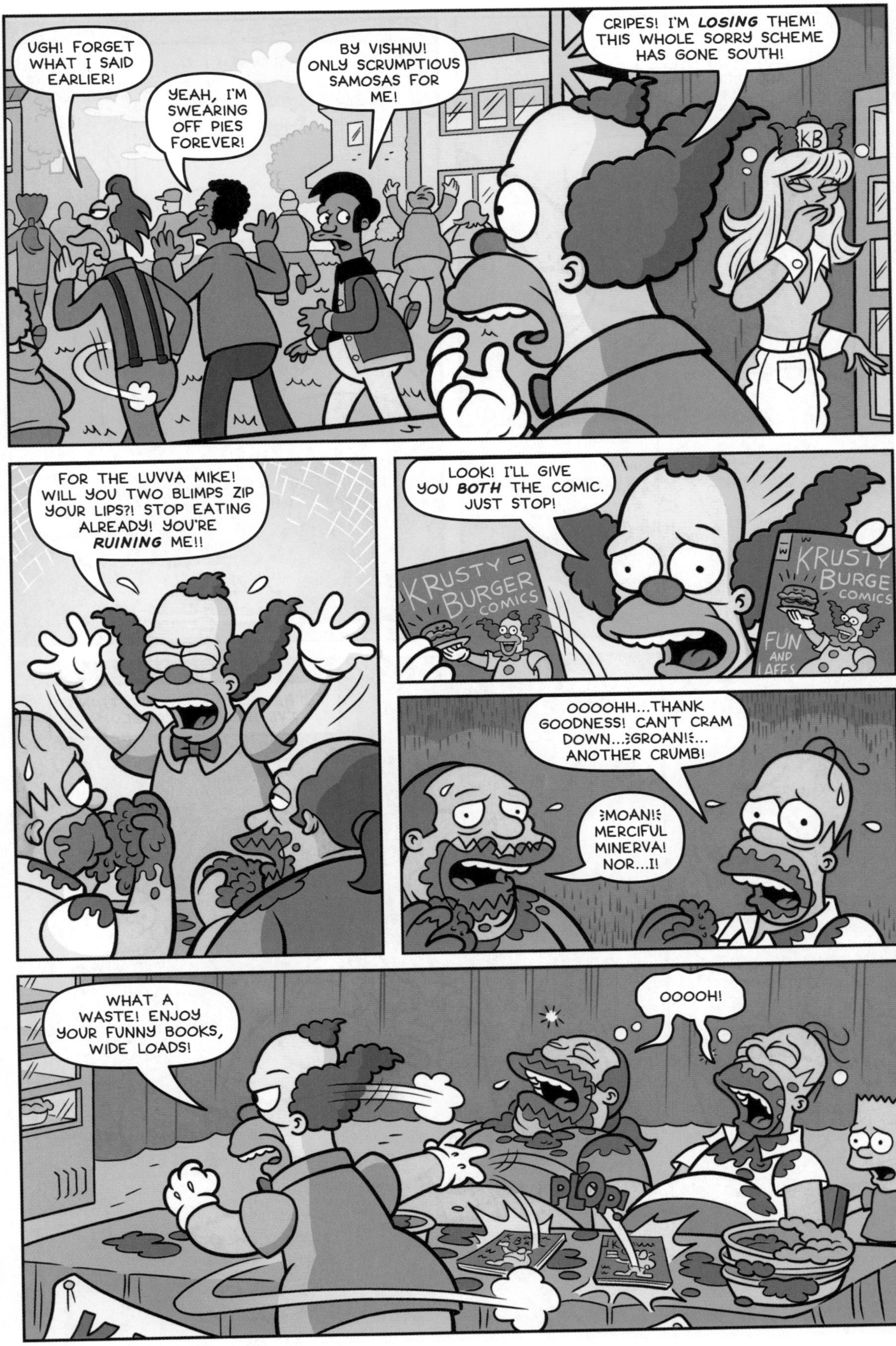
UGH! FORGET WHAT I SAID EARLIER!
YEAH, I'M SWEARING OFF PIES FOREVER!
BY VISHNU! ONLY SCRUMPTIOUS SAMOSAS FOR ME!
CRIPES! I'M **LOSING** THEM! THIS WHOLE SORRY SCHEME HAS GONE SOUTH!
KB
FOR THE LUVVA MIKE! WILL YOU TWO BLIMPS ZIP YOUR LIPS?! STOP EATING ALREADY! YOU'RE **RUINING** ME!!
LOOK! I'LL GIVE YOU **BOTH** THE COMIC. JUST STOP!
KRUSTY BURGER COMICS
OOOOHH...THANK GOODNESS! CAN'T CRAM DOWN...GROAN!...ANOTHER CRUMB!
MOAN! MERCIFUL MINERVA! NOR...I!
WHAT A WASTE! ENJOY YOUR FUNNY BOOKS, WIDE LOADS!
OOOOH!
PLOP!

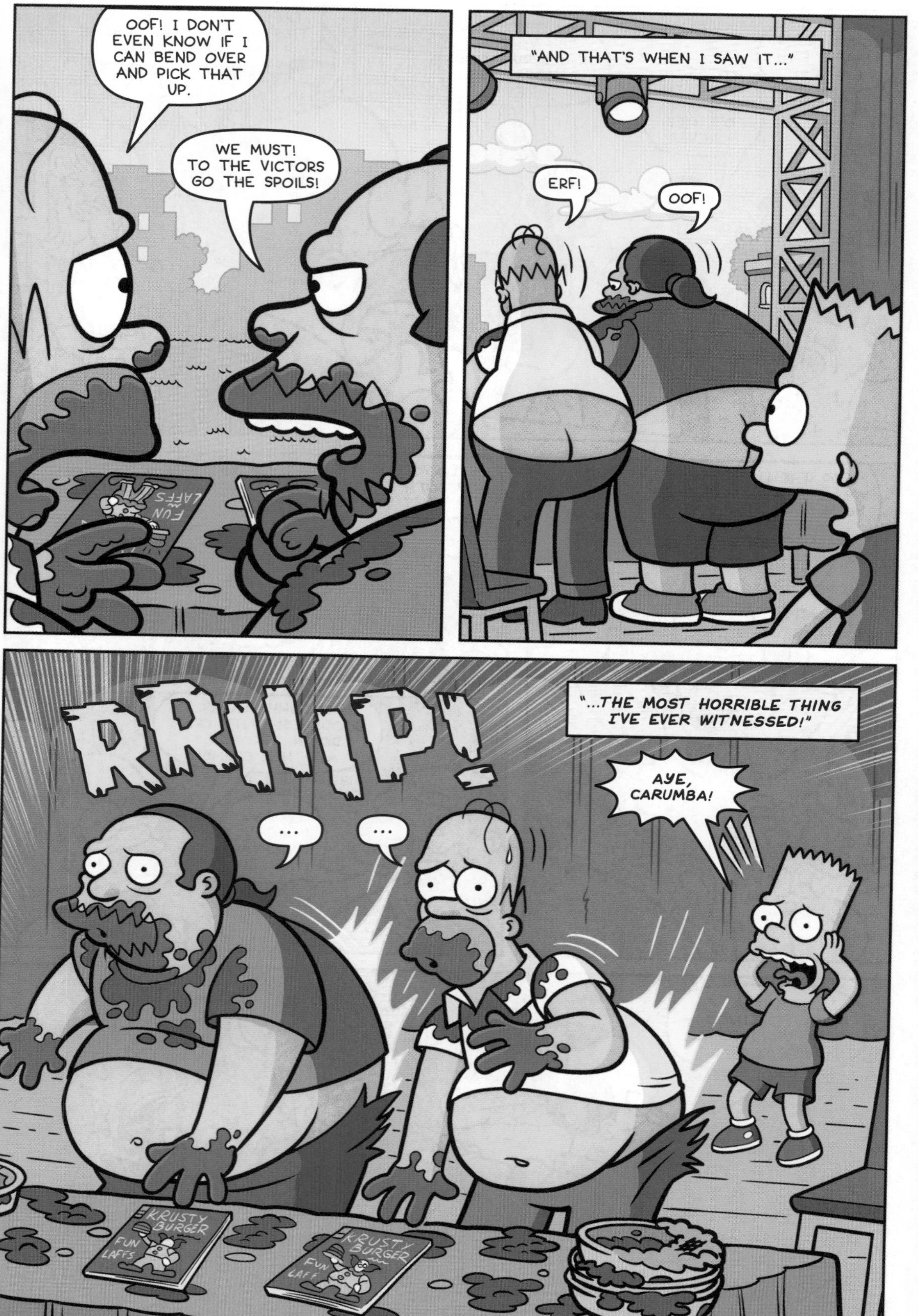
OOF! I DON'T EVEN KNOW IF I CAN BEND OVER AND PICK THAT UP.
WE MUST! TO THE VICTORS GO THE SPOILS!
FUN LAFFS
"AND THAT'S WHEN I SAW IT..."
ERF!
OOF!
RRIIIP!
"...THE MOST HORRIBLE THING I'VE EVER WITNESSED!"
AYE, CARUMBA!
...
...
KRUSTY BURGER FUN LAFFS
KRUSTY BURGER FUN LAFF

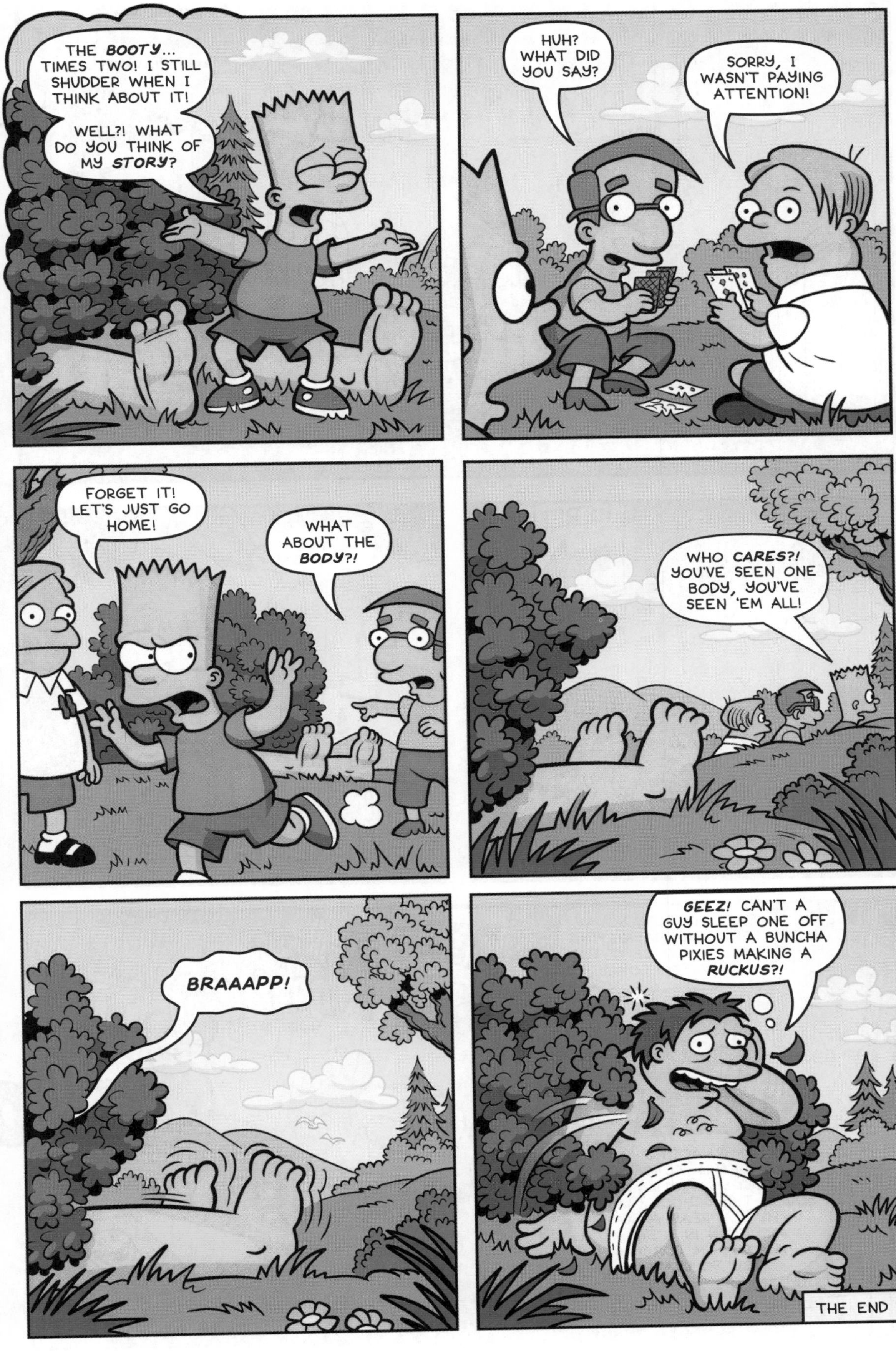
THE BOOTY... TIMES TWO! I STILL SHUDDER WHEN I THINK ABOUT IT!
WELL?! WHAT DO YOU THINK OF MY STORY?
HUH? WHAT DID YOU SAY?
SORRY, I WASN'T PAYING ATTENTION!
FORGET IT! LET'S JUST GO HOME!
WHAT ABOUT THE BODY?!
WHO CARES?! YOU'VE SEEN ONE BODY, YOU'VE SEEN 'EM ALL!
BRAAAPP!
GEEZ! CAN'T A GUY SLEEP ONE OFF WITHOUT A BUNCHA PIXIES MAKING A RUCKUS?!
THE END

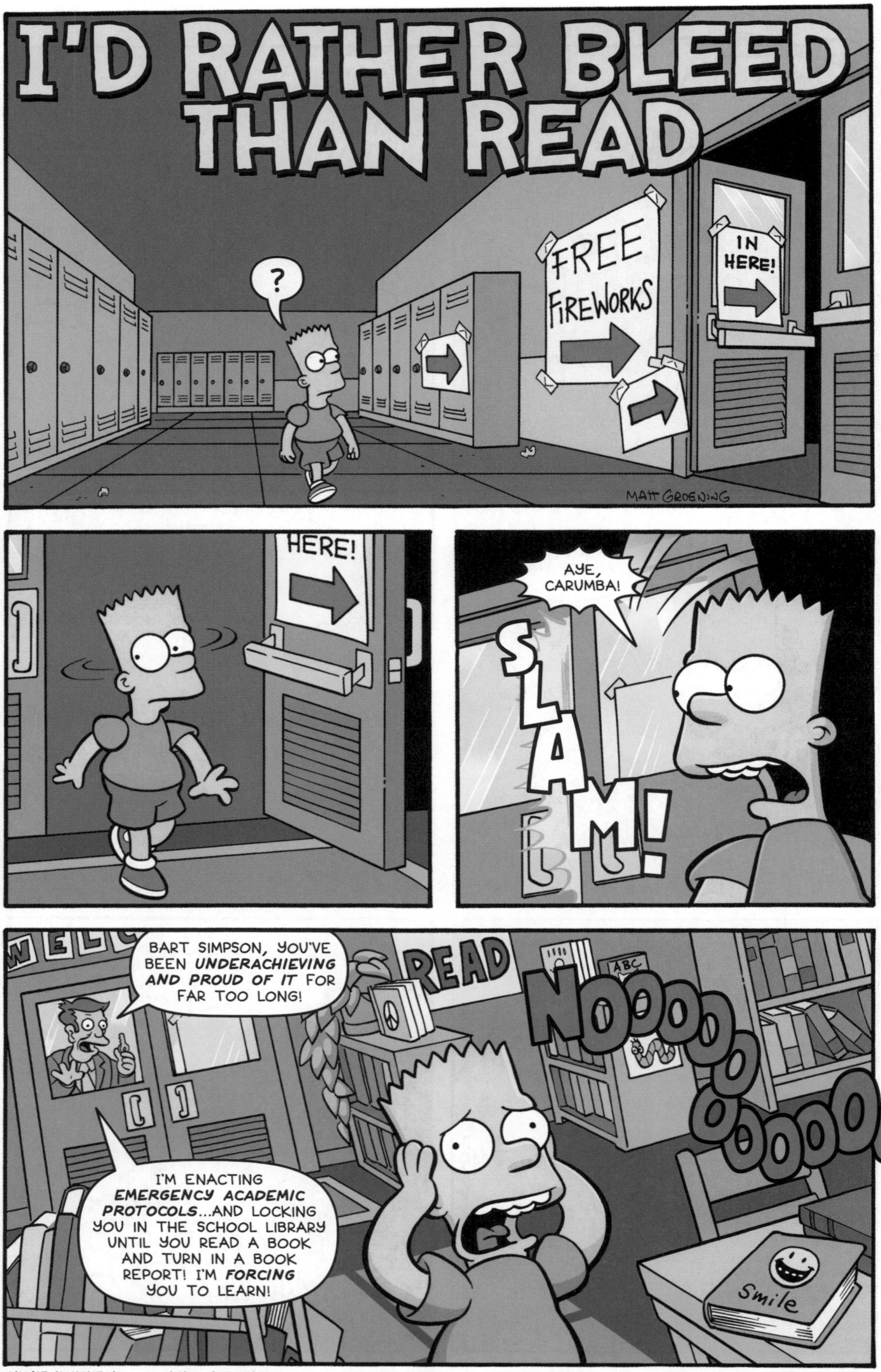
I'D RATHER BLEED THAN READ
?
FREE FIREWORKS
IN HERE!
MATT GROENING
HERE!
AYE, CARUMBA!
SLAM!
BART SIMPSON, YOU'VE BEEN *UNDERACHIEVING AND PROUD OF IT* FOR FAR TOO LONG!
I'M ENACTING *EMERGENCY ACADEMIC PROTOCOLS*...AND LOCKING YOU IN THE SCHOOL LIBRARY UNTIL YOU READ A BOOK AND TURN IN A BOOK REPORT! I'M *FORCING* YOU TO LEARN!
READ
ABC
NOOOOOOOOOOOO
Smile

SHANE HOUGHTON SCRIPT
NINA MATSUMOTO PENCILS
ANDREW PEPOY INKS
ART VILLANUEVA COLORS
KAREN BATES LETTERS
NATHAN KANE EDITOR

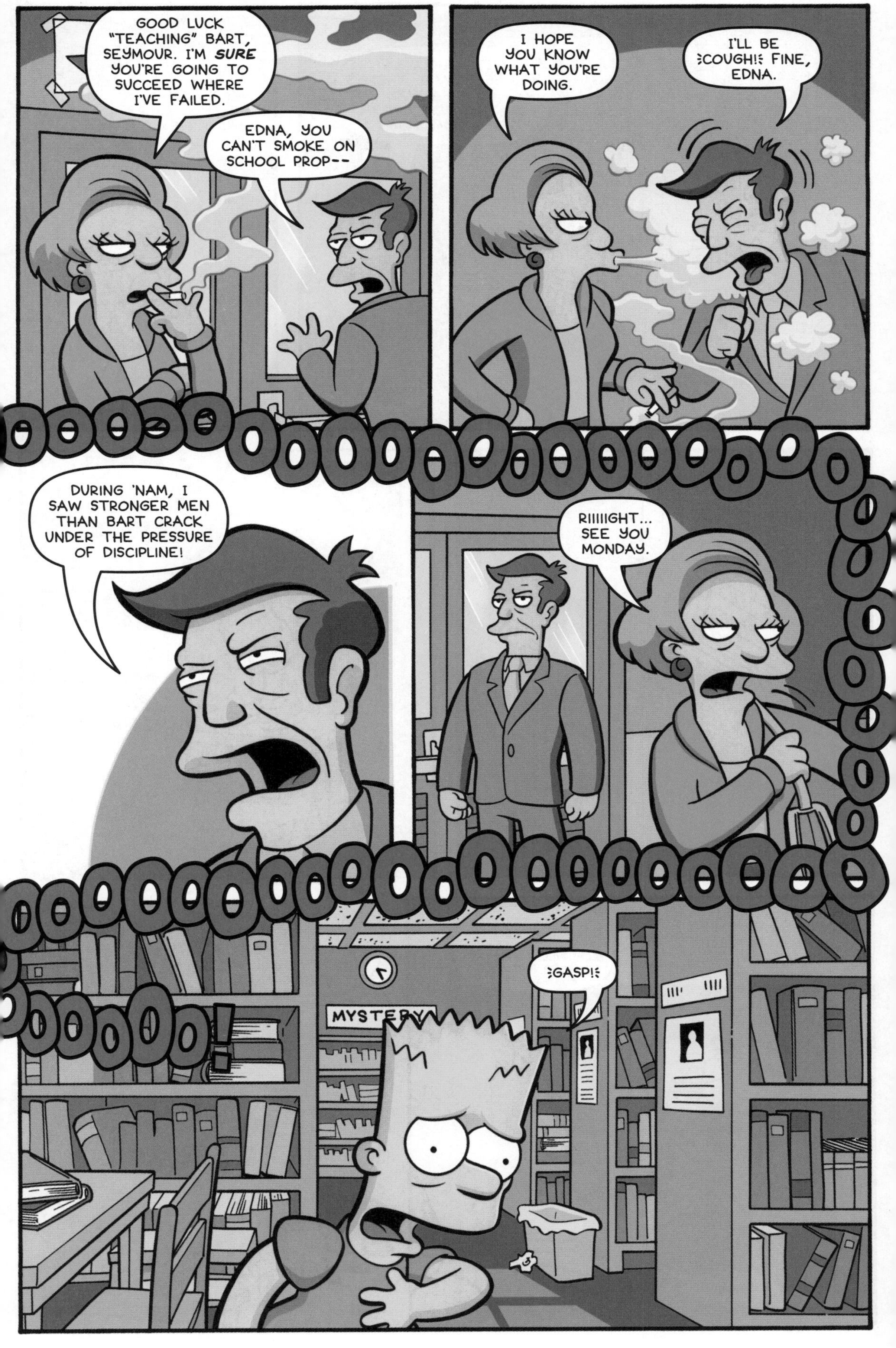
GOOD LUCK "TEACHING" BART, SEYMOUR. I'M *SURE* YOU'RE GOING TO SUCCEED WHERE I'VE FAILED.
EDNA, YOU CAN'T SMOKE ON SCHOOL PROP--
I HOPE YOU KNOW WHAT YOU'RE DOING.
I'LL BE *COUGH!* FINE, EDNA.
OOOOOOOOOOOOOOOOOOOOOOOOOOOOOOOOOOOOOOOOOOOOOOOOOOOOOOOOOOOOOOOOOOO!
DURING 'NAM, I SAW STRONGER MEN THAN BART CRACK UNDER THE PRESSURE OF DISCIPLINE!
RIIIIIGHT... SEE YOU MONDAY.
MYSTERY
GASP!

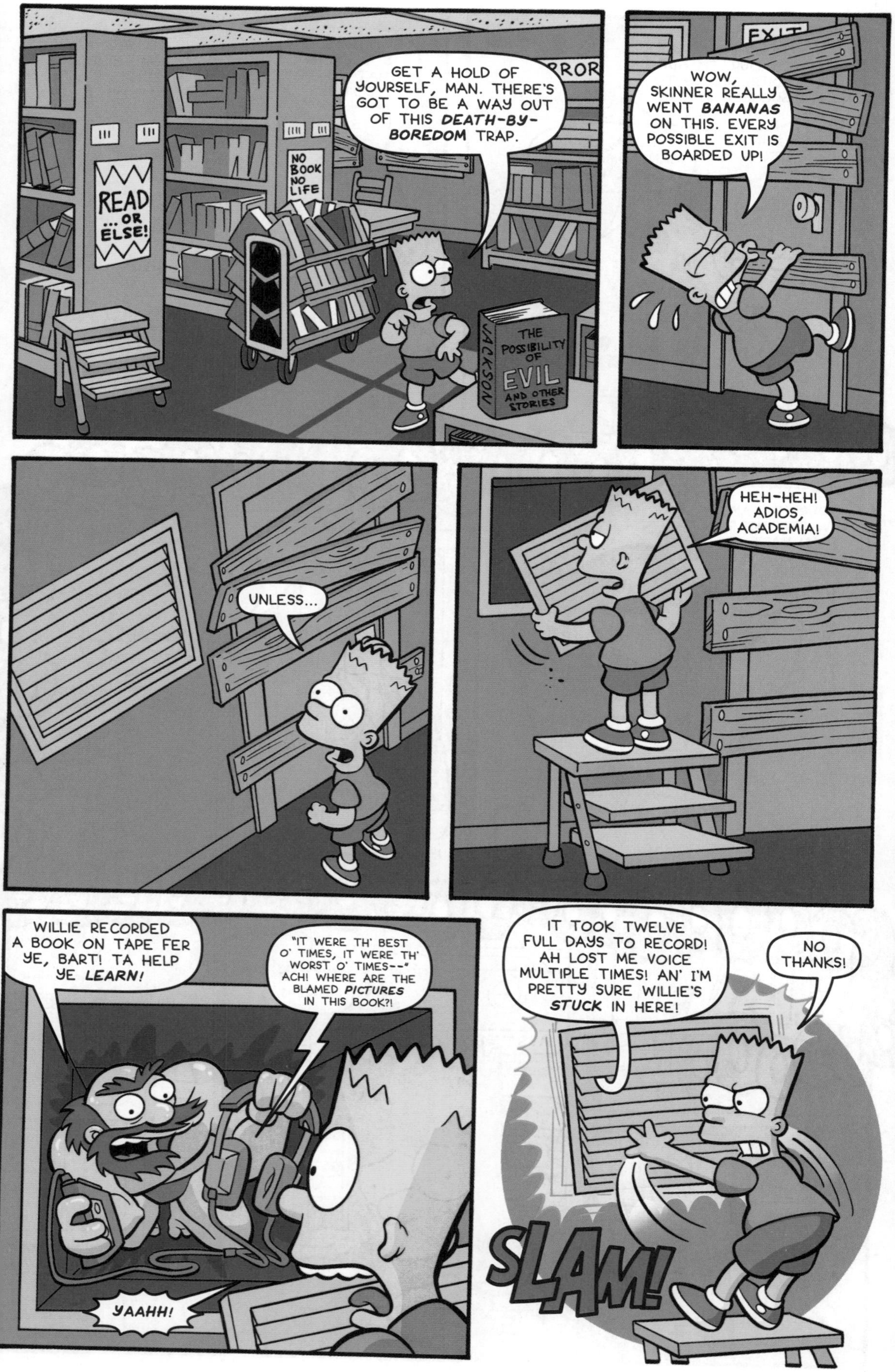
READ ...OR ELSE!
NO BOOK NO LIFE
GET A HOLD OF YOURSELF, MAN. THERE'S GOT TO BE A WAY OUT OF THIS *DEATH-BY-BOREDOM* TRAP.
JACKSON
THE POSSIBILITY OF EVIL AND OTHER STORIES
WOW, SKINNER REALLY WENT *BANANAS* ON THIS. EVERY POSSIBLE EXIT IS BOARDED UP!
UNLESS...
HEH-HEH! ADIOS, ACADEMIA!
WILLIE RECORDED A BOOK ON TAPE FER YE, BART! TA HELP YE *LEARN*!
"IT WERE TH' BEST O' TIMES, IT WERE TH' WORST O' TIMES--" ACH! WHERE ARE THE BLAMED *PICTURES* IN THIS BOOK?!
YAAHH!
IT TOOK TWELVE FULL DAYS TO RECORD! AH LOST ME VOICE MULTIPLE TIMES! AN' I'M PRETTY SURE WILLIE'S *STUCK* IN HERE!
NO THANKS!
SLAM!

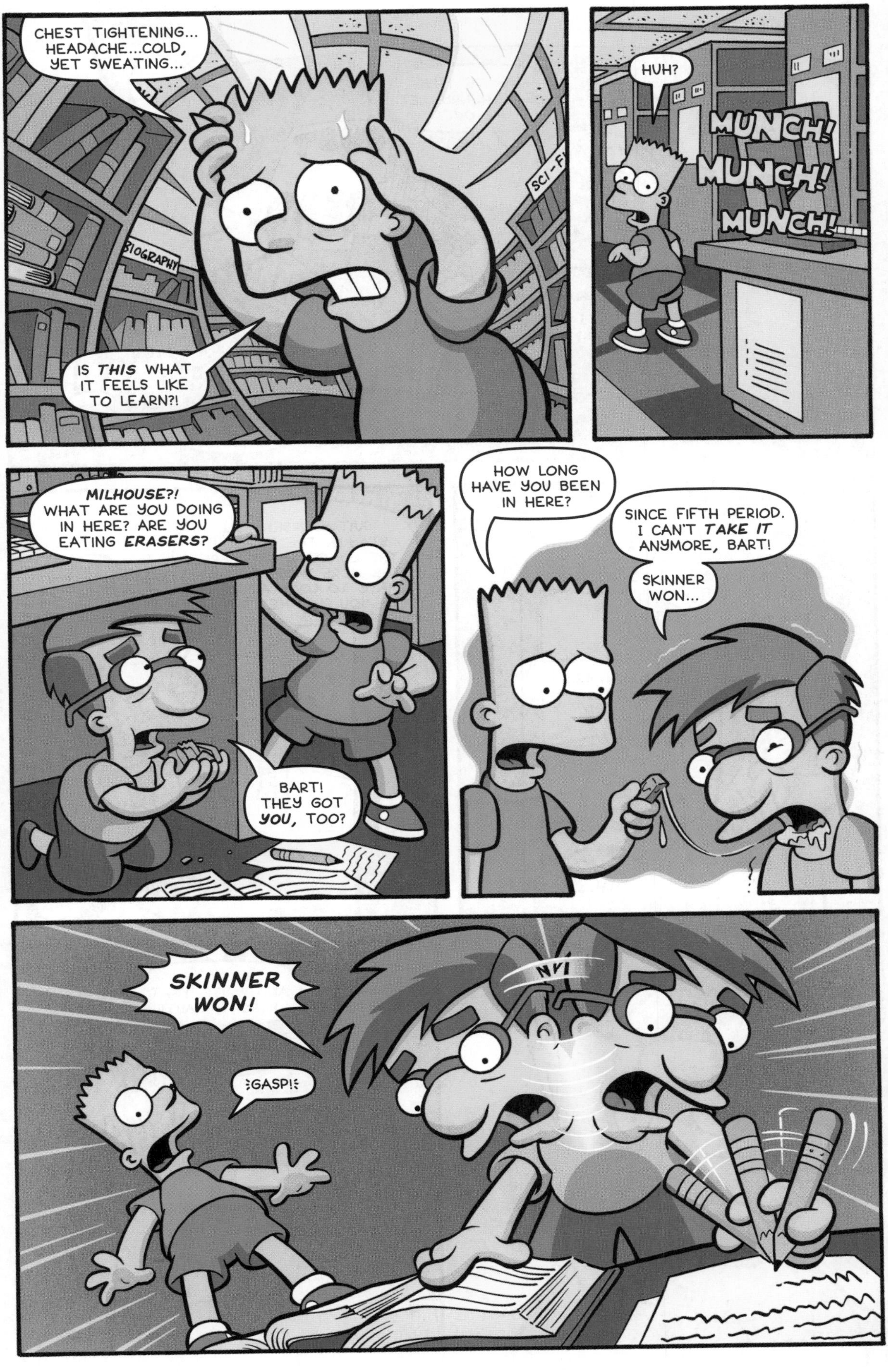
CHEST TIGHTENING... HEADACHE...COLD, YET SWEATING...
BIOGRAPHY
IS *THIS* WHAT IT FEELS LIKE TO LEARN?!
HUH?
MUNCH! MUNCH! MUNCH!
MILHOUSE?! WHAT ARE YOU DOING IN HERE? ARE YOU EATING *ERASERS*?
BART! THEY GOT *YOU*, TOO?
HOW LONG HAVE YOU BEEN IN HERE?
SINCE FIFTH PERIOD. I CAN'T *TAKE IT* ANYMORE, BART!
SKINNER WON...
SKINNER WON!
GASP!

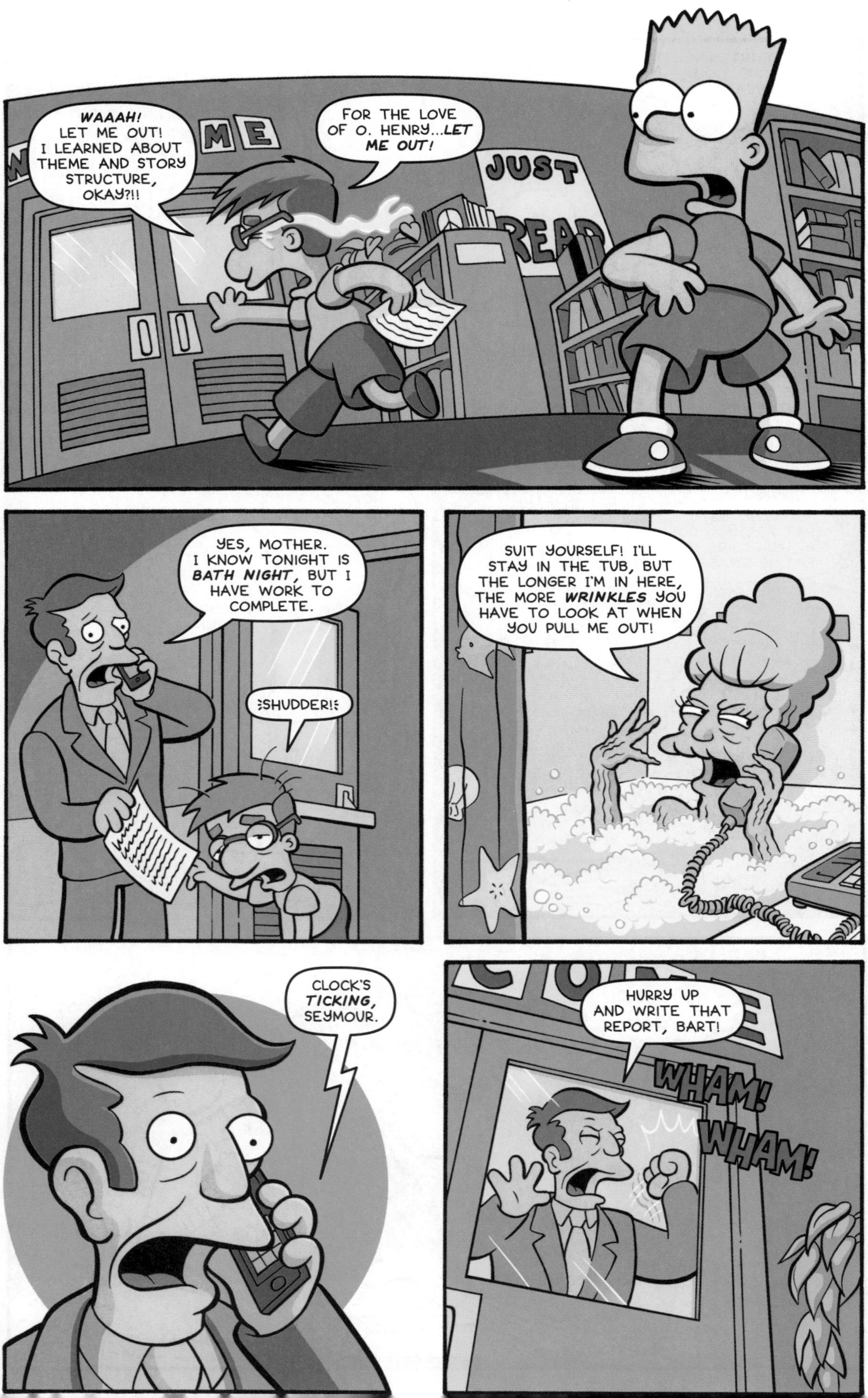

WAAAH! LET ME OUT! I LEARNED ABOUT THEME AND STORY STRUCTURE, OKAY?!!
FOR THE LOVE OF O. HENRY...LET ME OUT!
JUST READ
YES, MOTHER. I KNOW TONIGHT IS BATH NIGHT, BUT I HAVE WORK TO COMPLETE.
SHUDDER!
SUIT YOURSELF! I'LL STAY IN THE TUB, BUT THE LONGER I'M IN HERE, THE MORE WRINKLES YOU HAVE TO LOOK AT WHEN YOU PULL ME OUT!
CLOCK'S TICKING, SEYMOUR.
HURRY UP AND WRITE THAT REPORT, BART!
WHAM!
WHAM!

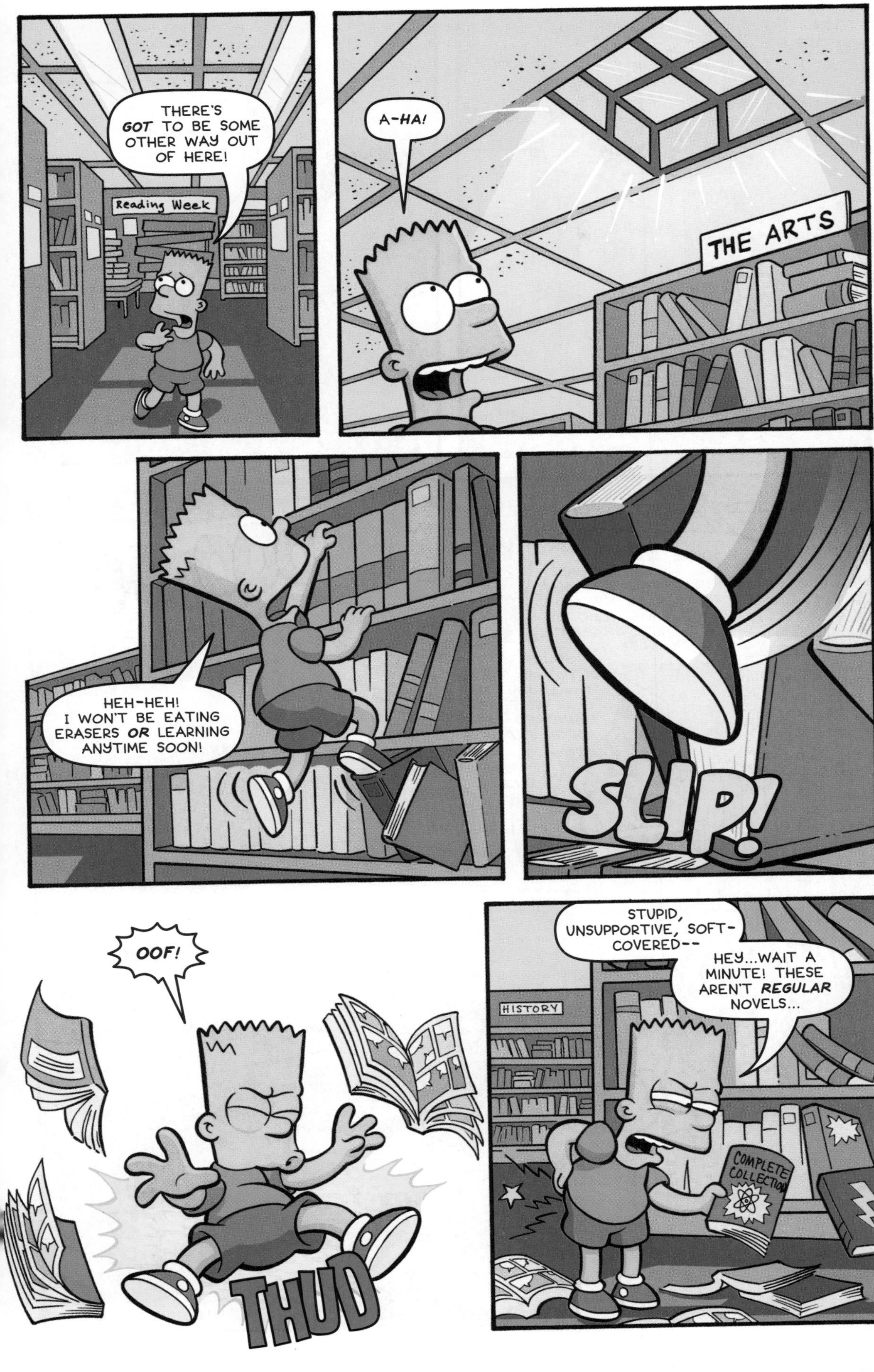
THERE'S GOT TO BE SOME OTHER WAY OUT OF HERE!
Reading Week
A-HA!
THE ARTS
HEH-HEH! I WON'T BE EATING ERASERS OR LEARNING ANYTIME SOON!
SLIP!
OOF!
THUD
STUPID, UNSUPPORTIVE, SOFT-COVERED--
HEY...WAIT A MINUTE! THESE AREN'T REGULAR NOVELS...
HISTORY
COMPLETE COLLECTION

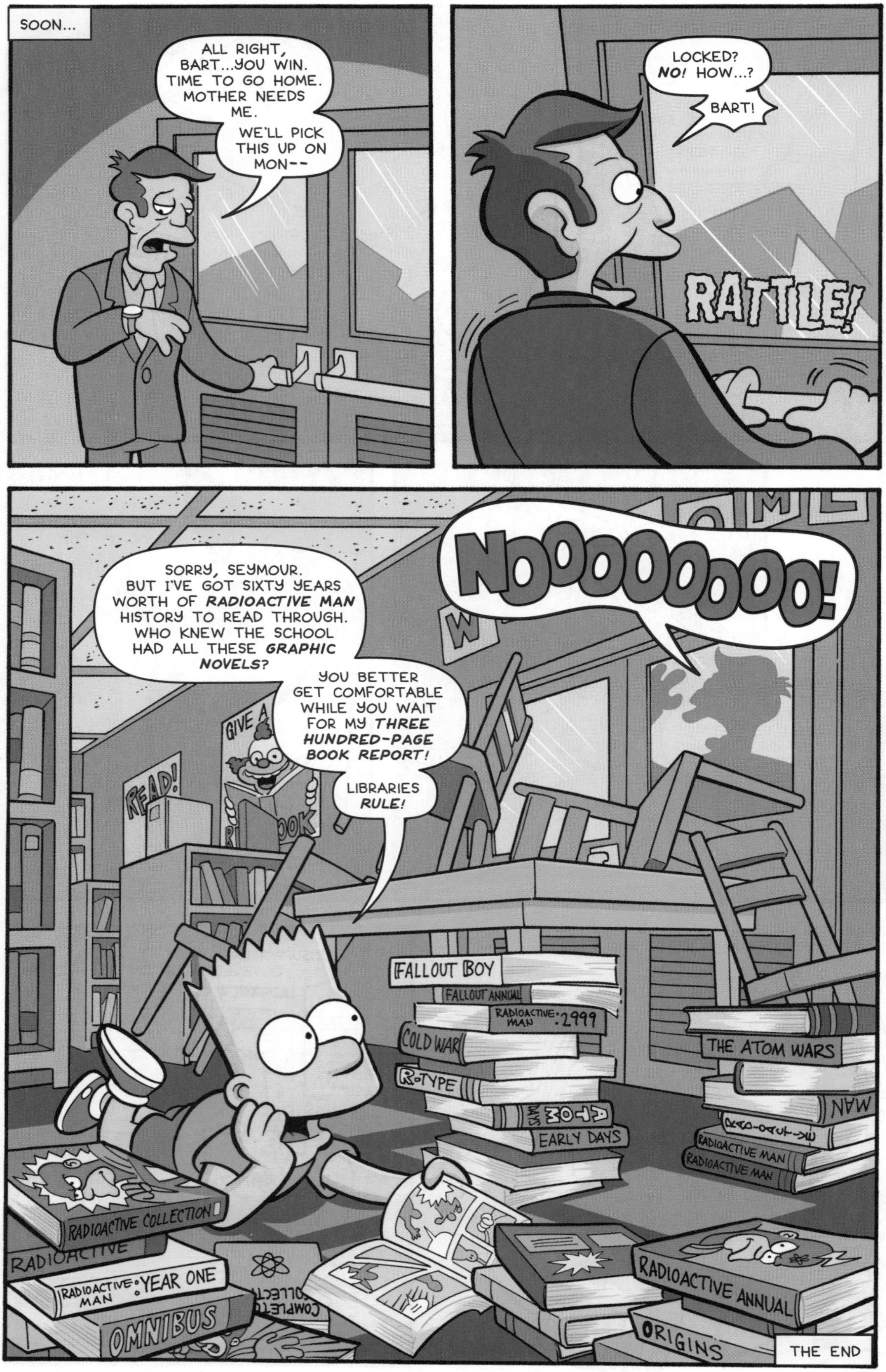
SOON...
ALL RIGHT, BART...YOU WIN. TIME TO GO HOME. MOTHER NEEDS ME.
WE'LL PICK THIS UP ON MON--
LOCKED? **NO!** HOW...?
BART!
RATTLE!
NOOOOOOOOO!
SORRY, SEYMOUR. BUT I'VE GOT SIXTY YEARS WORTH OF ***RADIOACTIVE MAN*** HISTORY TO READ THROUGH. WHO KNEW THE SCHOOL HAD ALL THESE ***GRAPHIC NOVELS?***
YOU BETTER GET COMFORTABLE WHILE YOU WAIT FOR MY ***THREE HUNDRED-PAGE BOOK REPORT!***
LIBRARIES ***RULE!***
READ!
FALLOUT BOY
FALLOUT ANNUAL
RADIOACTIVE MAN 2999
COLD WAR
R-TYPE
EARLY DAYS
THE ATOM WARS
RADIOACTIVE MAN
RADIOACTIVE COLLECTION
RADIOACTIVE
RADIOACTIVE MAN YEAR ONE
OMNIBUS
RADIOACTIVE ANNUAL
ORIGINS
THE END

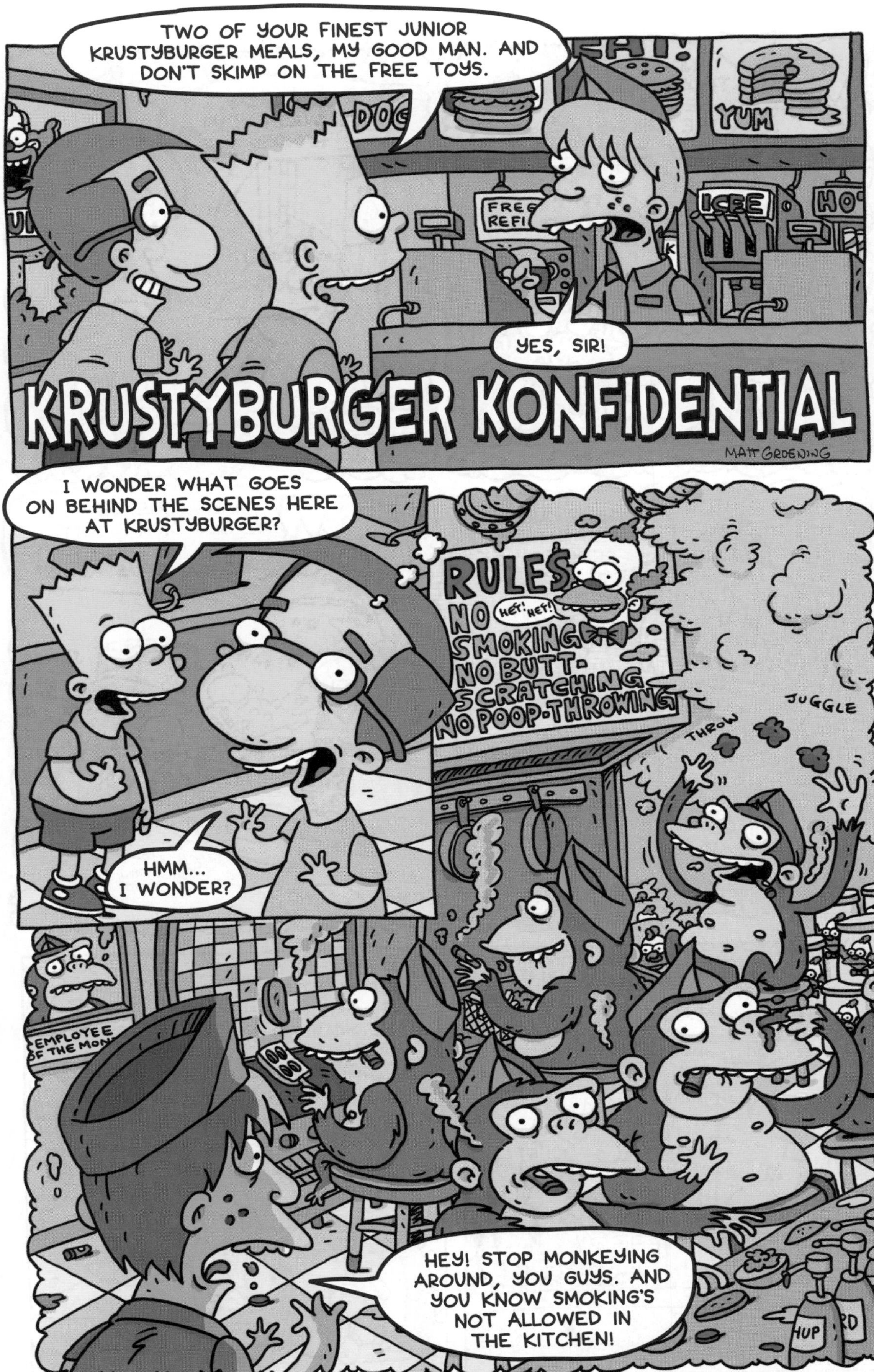
TWO OF YOUR FINEST JUNIOR KRUSTYBURGER MEALS, MY GOOD MAN. AND DON'T SKIMP ON THE FREE TOYS.
YES, SIR!
KRUSTYBURGER KONFIDENTIAL
MATT GROENING
I WONDER WHAT GOES ON BEHIND THE SCENES HERE AT KRUSTYBURGER?
HMM... I WONDER?
RULES
NO SMOKING
NO BUTT-SCRATCHING
NO POOP-THROWING
HEH! HEH!
THROW
JUGGLE
EMPLOYEE OF THE MON
HEY! STOP MONKEYING AROUND, YOU GUYS. AND YOU KNOW SMOKING'S NOT ALLOWED IN THE KITCHEN!

DEAN RANKINE
STORY & ART

KAREN BATES
LETTERS

NATHAN KANE
EDITOR

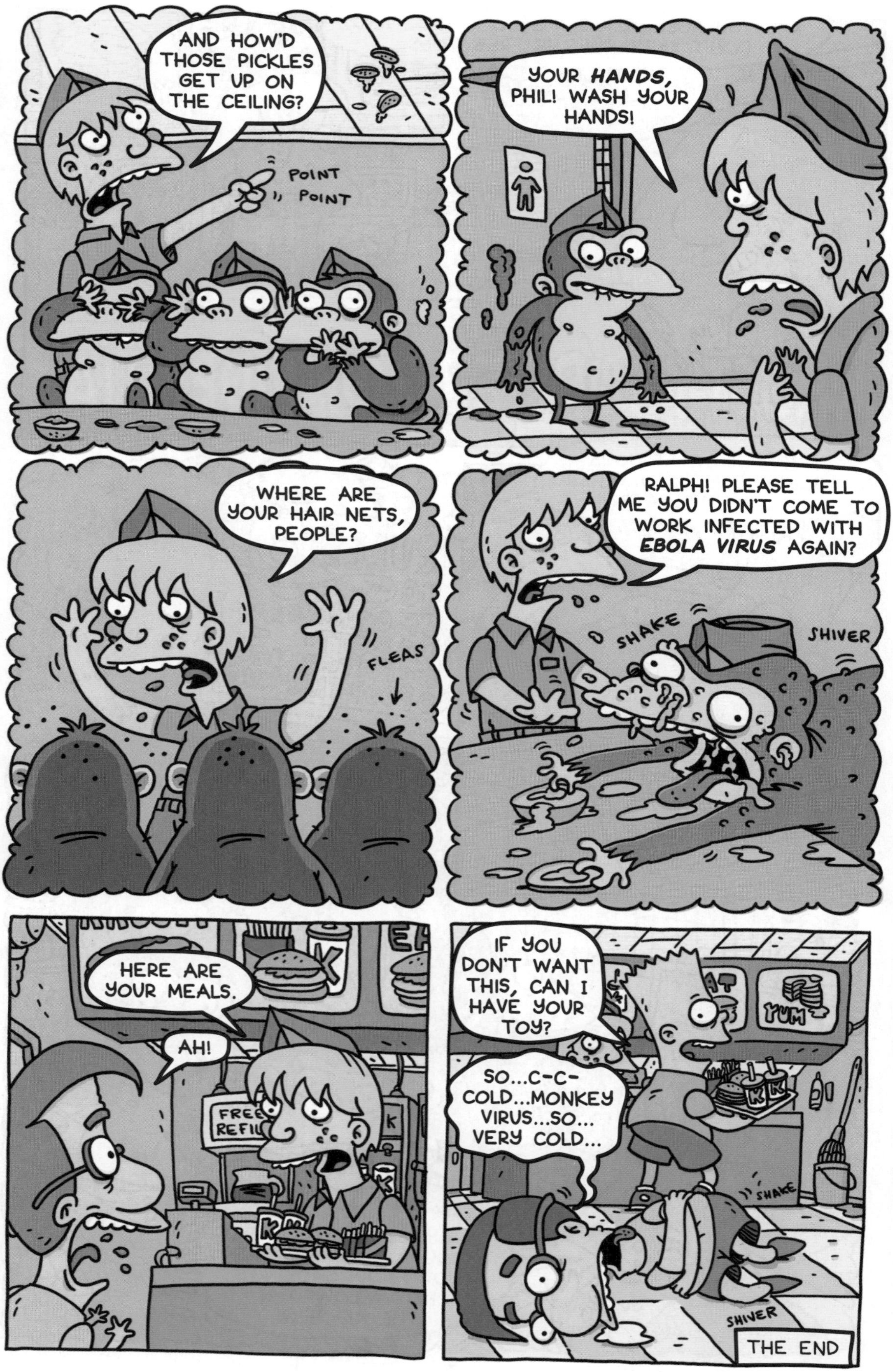
AND HOW'D THOSE PICKLES GET UP ON THE CEILING?
POINT
POINT
YOUR **HANDS,** PHIL! WASH YOUR HANDS!
WHERE ARE YOUR HAIR NETS, PEOPLE?
FLEAS
RALPH! PLEASE TELL ME YOU DIDN'T COME TO WORK INFECTED WITH **EBOLA VIRUS** AGAIN?
SHAKE
SHIVER
HERE ARE YOUR MEALS.
AH!
FREE REFI
IF YOU DON'T WANT THIS, CAN I HAVE YOUR TOY?
YUM
SO...C-C-COLD...MONKEY VIRUS...SO... VERY COLD...
SHAKE
SHIVER
THE END

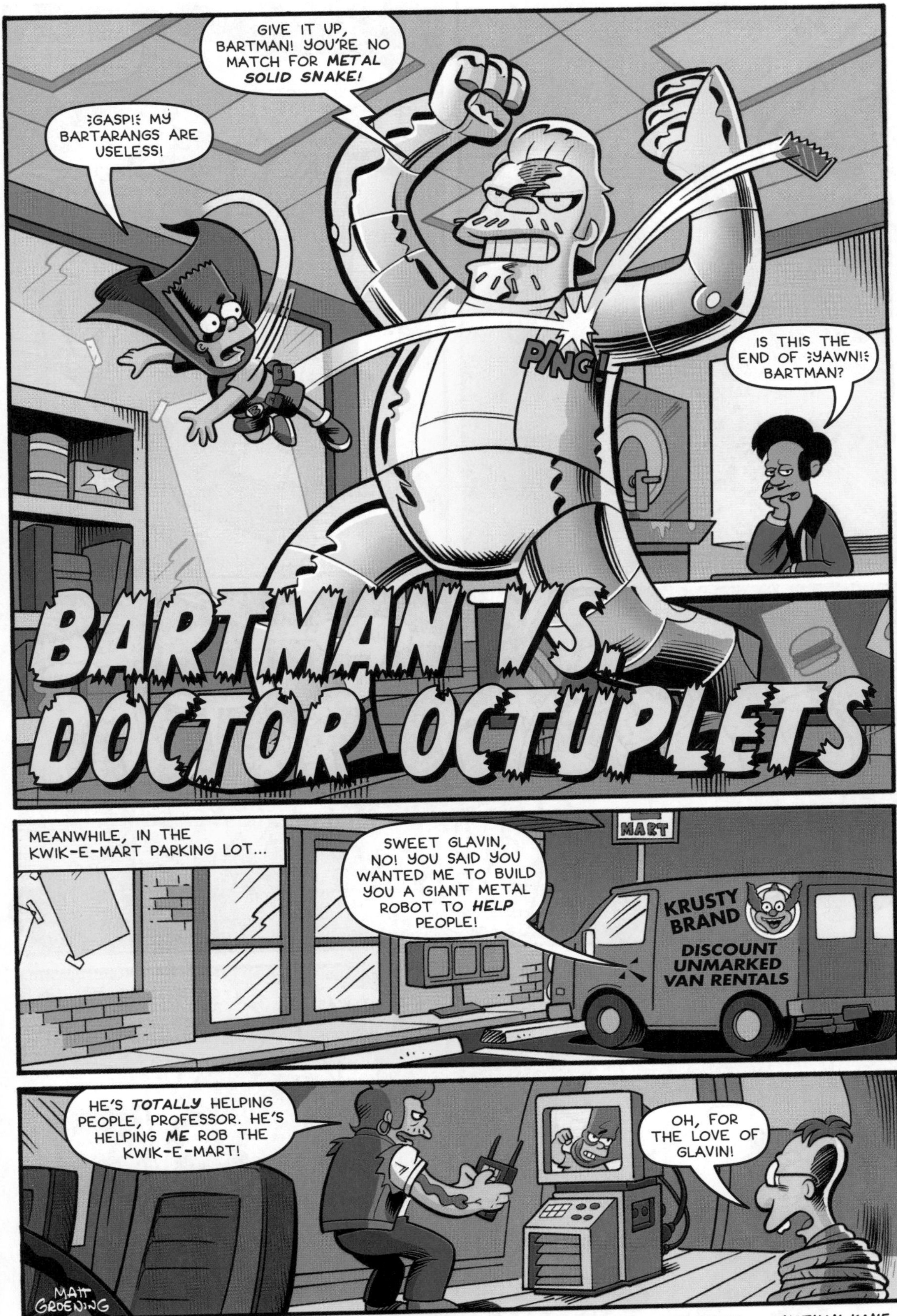
GIVE IT UP, BARTMAN! YOU'RE NO MATCH FOR METAL SOLID SNAKE!
:GASP!: MY BARTARANGS ARE USELESS!
PING!
IS THIS THE END OF :YAWN!: BARTMAN?
BARTMAN VS. DOCTOR OCTUPLETS
MEANWHILE, IN THE KWIK-E-MART PARKING LOT...
MART
SWEET GLAVIN, NO! YOU SAID YOU WANTED ME TO BUILD YOU A GIANT METAL ROBOT TO HELP PEOPLE!
KRUSTY BRAND
DISCOUNT UNMARKED VAN RENTALS
HE'S TOTALLY HELPING PEOPLE, PROFESSOR. HE'S HELPING ME ROB THE KWIK-E-MART!
OH, FOR THE LOVE OF GLAVIN!
MATT GROENING

IAN BOOTHBY SCRIPT | ***JOHN DELANEY*** PENCILS | ***ANDREW PEPOY*** INKS | ***NATHAN HAMILL*** COLORS | ***KAREN BATES*** LETTERS | ***NATHAN KANE*** EDITOR

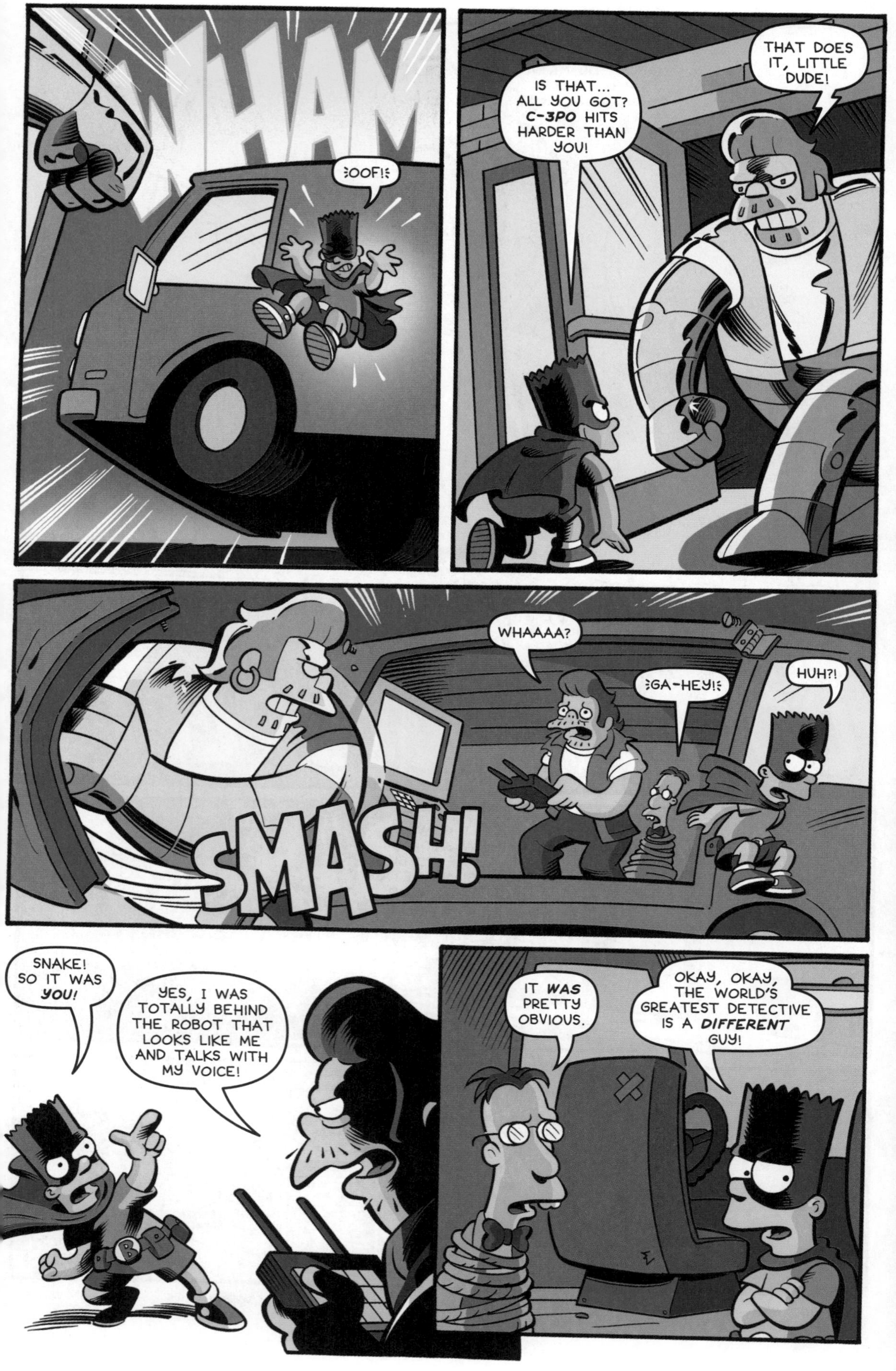
WHAM
OOF!
IS THAT... ALL YOU GOT? C-3PO HITS HARDER THAN YOU!
THAT DOES IT, LITTLE DUDE!
SMASH!
WHAAAA?
GA-HEY!
HUH?!
SNAKE! SO IT WAS YOU!
YES, I WAS TOTALLY BEHIND THE ROBOT THAT LOOKS LIKE ME AND TALKS WITH MY VOICE!
IT WAS PRETTY OBVIOUS.
OKAY, OKAY, THE WORLD'S GREATEST DETECTIVE IS A DIFFERENT GUY!

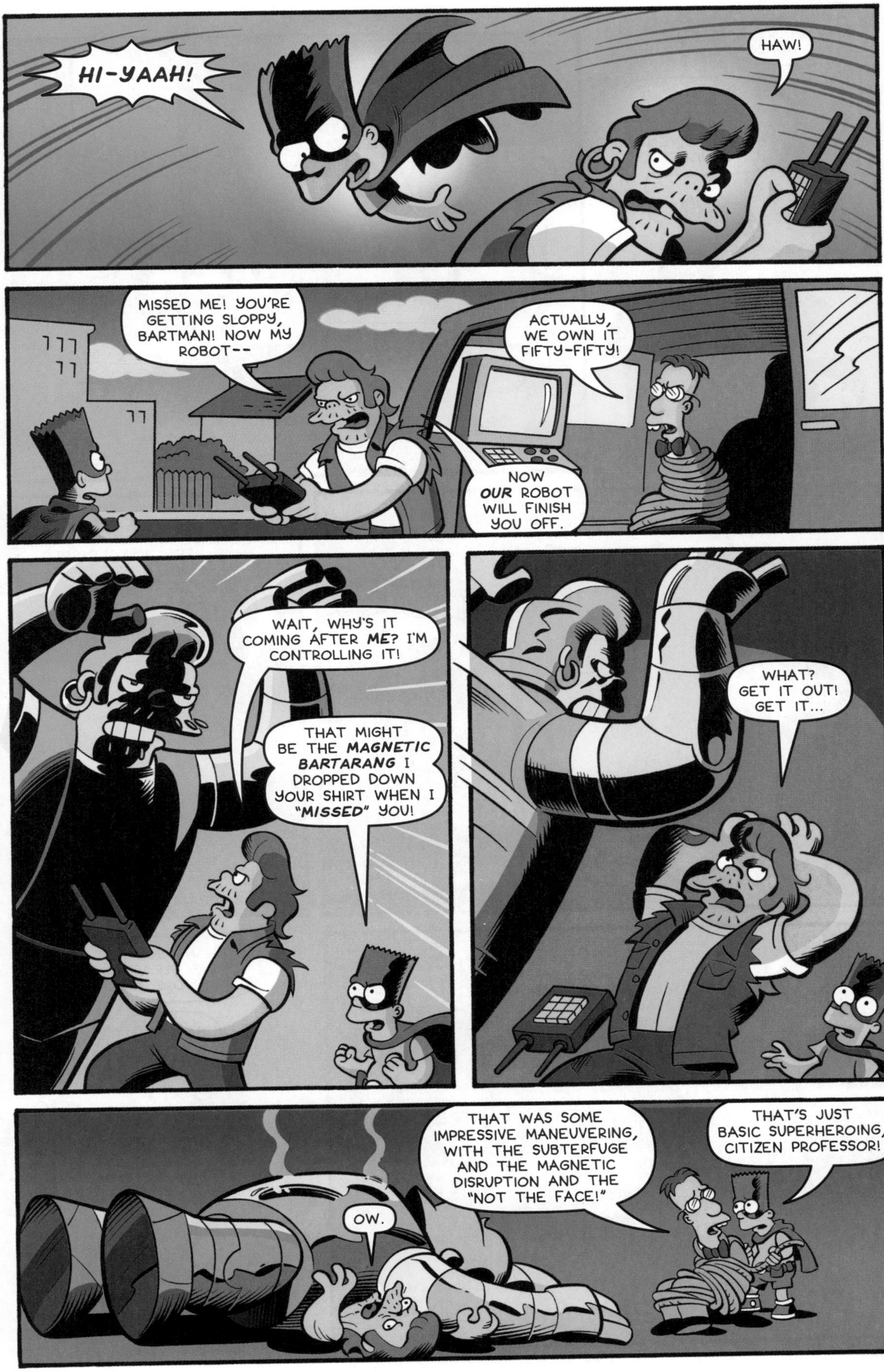
HI-YAAH!
HAW!
MISSED ME! YOU'RE GETTING SLOPPY, BARTMAN! NOW MY ROBOT--
ACTUALLY, WE OWN IT FIFTY-FIFTY!
NOW OUR ROBOT WILL FINISH YOU OFF.
WAIT, WHY'S IT COMING AFTER ME? I'M CONTROLLING IT!
THAT MIGHT BE THE MAGNETIC BARTARANG I DROPPED DOWN YOUR SHIRT WHEN I "MISSED" YOU!
WHAT? GET IT OUT! GET IT...
THAT WAS SOME IMPRESSIVE MANEUVERING, WITH THE SUBTERFUGE AND THE MAGNETIC DISRUPTION AND THE "NOT THE FACE!"
THAT'S JUST BASIC SUPERHEROING, CITIZEN PROFESSOR!
OW.

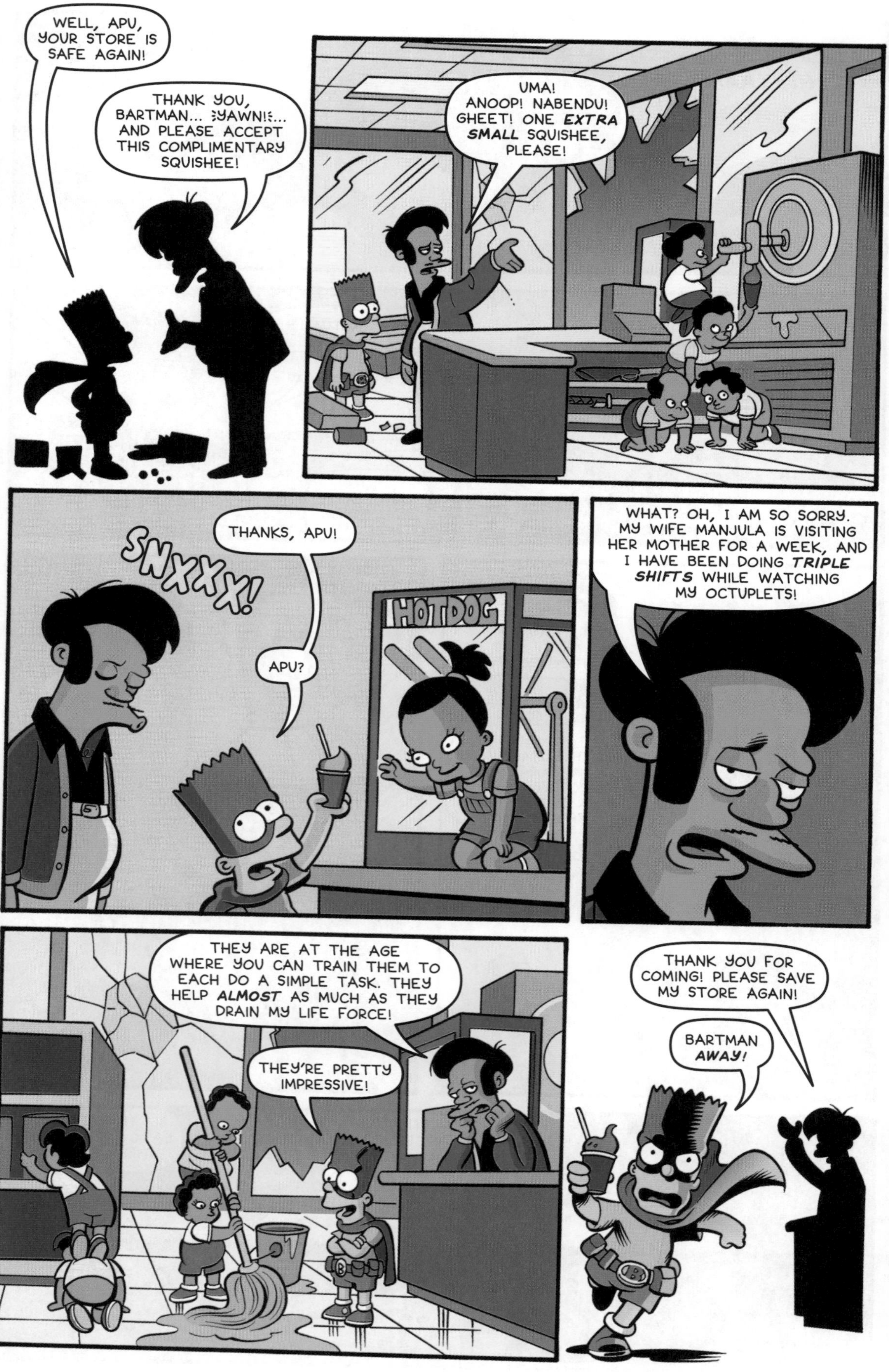
WELL, APU, YOUR STORE IS SAFE AGAIN!
THANK YOU, BARTMAN... ƐYAWNƐ... AND PLEASE ACCEPT THIS COMPLIMENTARY SQUISHEE!
UMA! ANOOP! NABENDU! GHEET! ONE EXTRA SMALL SQUISHEE, PLEASE!
THANKS, APU!
SNXXX!
APU?
HOTDOG
WHAT? OH, I AM SO SORRY. MY WIFE MANJULA IS VISITING HER MOTHER FOR A WEEK, AND I HAVE BEEN DOING TRIPLE SHIFTS WHILE WATCHING MY OCTUPLETS!
THEY ARE AT THE AGE WHERE YOU CAN TRAIN THEM TO EACH DO A SIMPLE TASK. THEY HELP ALMOST AS MUCH AS THEY DRAIN MY LIFE FORCE!
THEY'RE PRETTY IMPRESSIVE!
THANK YOU FOR COMING! PLEASE SAVE MY STORE AGAIN!
BARTMAN AWAY!

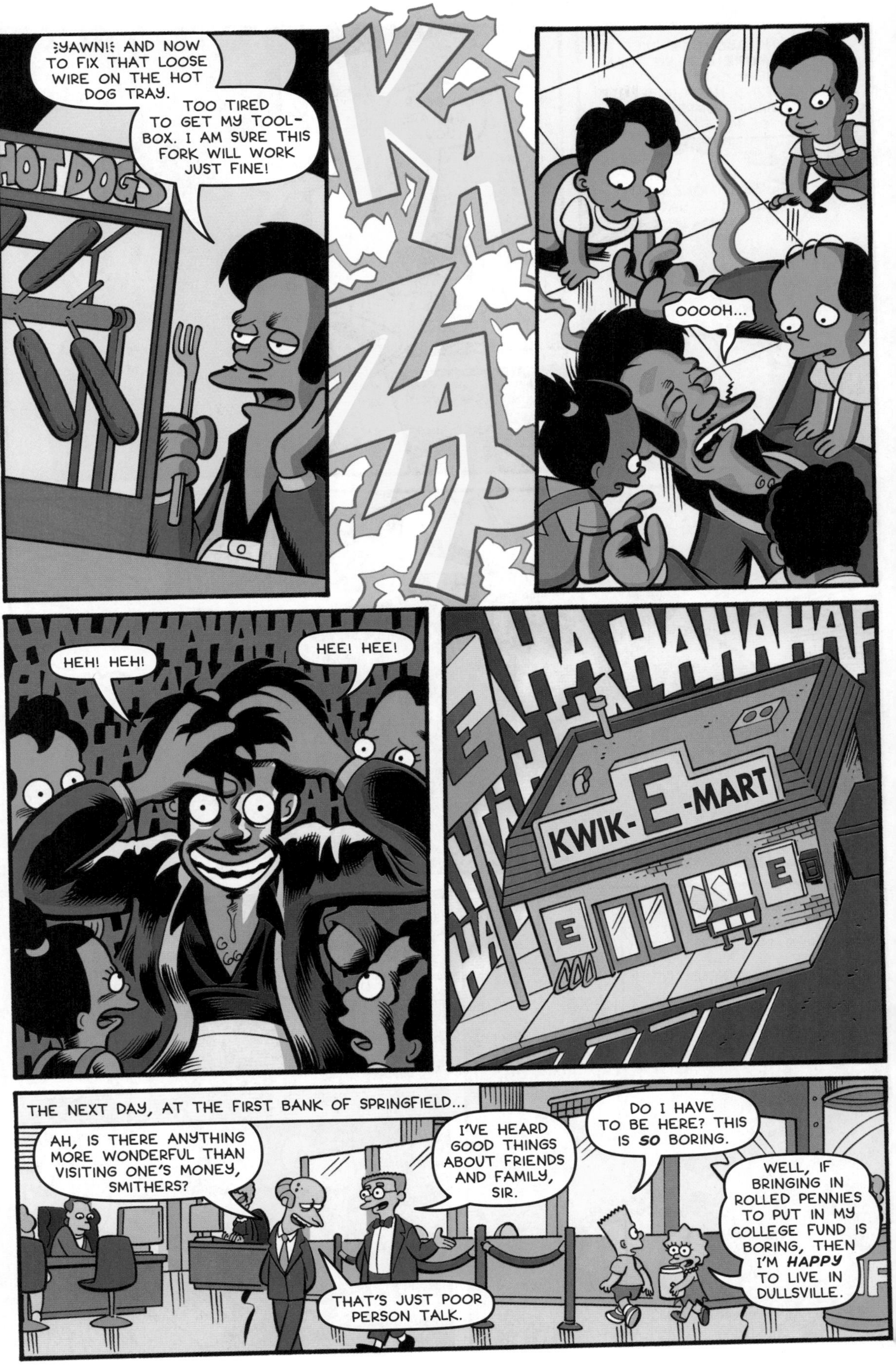
:YAWN!: AND NOW TO FIX THAT LOOSE WIRE ON THE HOT DOG TRAY.
TOO TIRED TO GET MY TOOL-BOX. I AM SURE THIS FORK WILL WORK JUST FINE!
HOT DOGS
KA ZAP
OOOOH...
HEH! HEH!
HEE! HEE!
HAHAHAHA
KWIK-E-MART
THE NEXT DAY, AT THE FIRST BANK OF SPRINGFIELD...
AH, IS THERE ANYTHING MORE WONDERFUL THAN VISITING ONE'S MONEY, SMITHERS?
I'VE HEARD GOOD THINGS ABOUT FRIENDS AND FAMILY, SIR.
THAT'S JUST POOR PERSON TALK.
DO I HAVE TO BE HERE? THIS IS ***SO*** BORING.
WELL, IF BRINGING IN ROLLED PENNIES TO PUT IN MY COLLEGE FUND IS BORING, THEN I'M ***HAPPY*** TO LIVE IN DULLSVILLE.

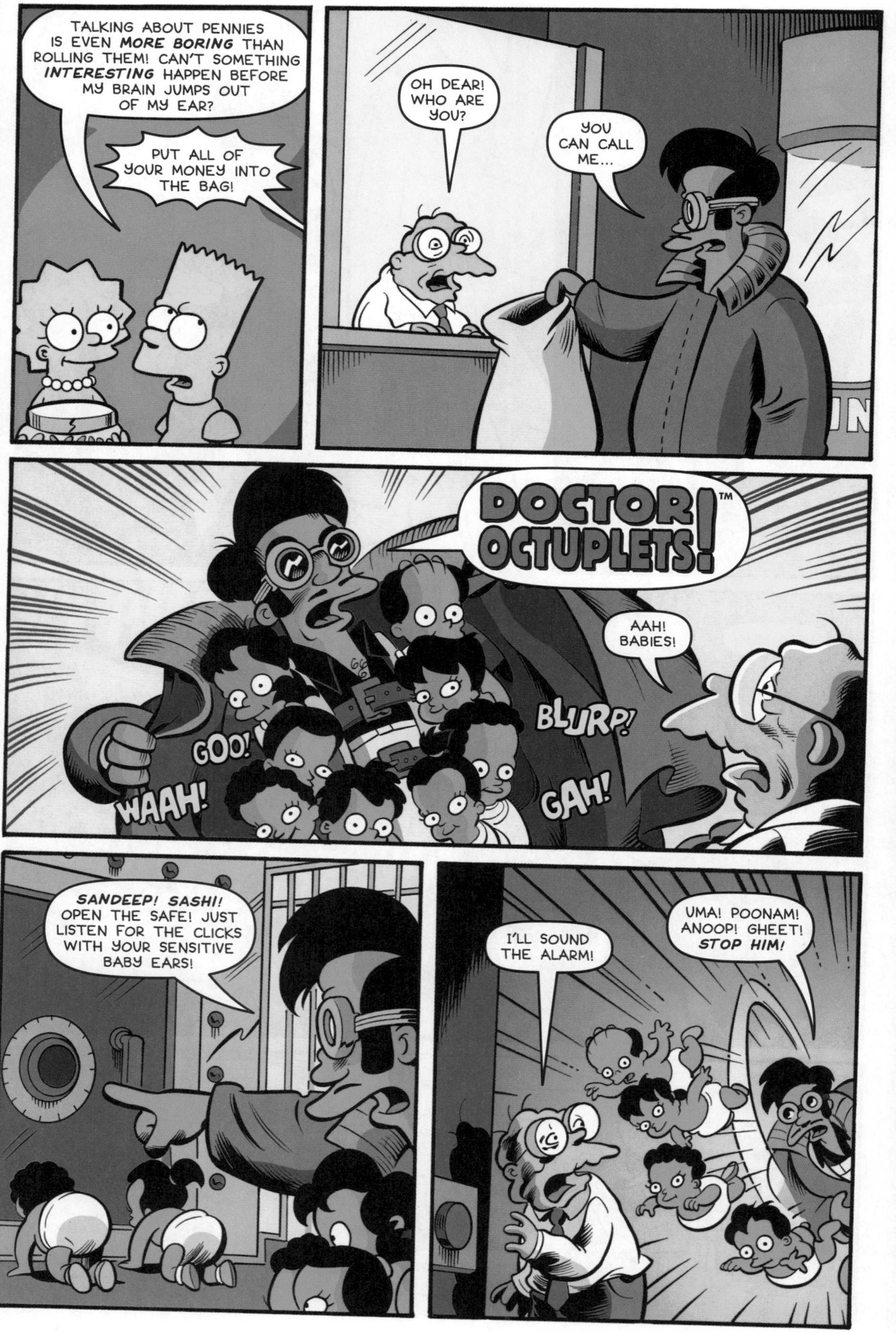

TALKING ABOUT PENNIES IS EVEN **MORE BORING** THAN ROLLING THEM! CAN'T SOMETHING **INTERESTING** HAPPEN BEFORE MY BRAIN JUMPS OUT OF MY EAR?
PUT ALL OF YOUR MONEY INTO THE BAG!
OH DEAR! WHO ARE YOU?
YOU CAN CALL ME...
DOCTOR OCTUPLETS!™
AAH! BABIES!
BLURP!
GOO!
WAAH!
GAH!
SANDEEP! SASHI! OPEN THE SAFE! JUST LISTEN FOR THE CLICKS WITH YOUR SENSITIVE BABY EARS!
I'LL SOUND THE ALARM!
UMA! POONAM! ANOOP! GHEET! ***STOP HIM!***

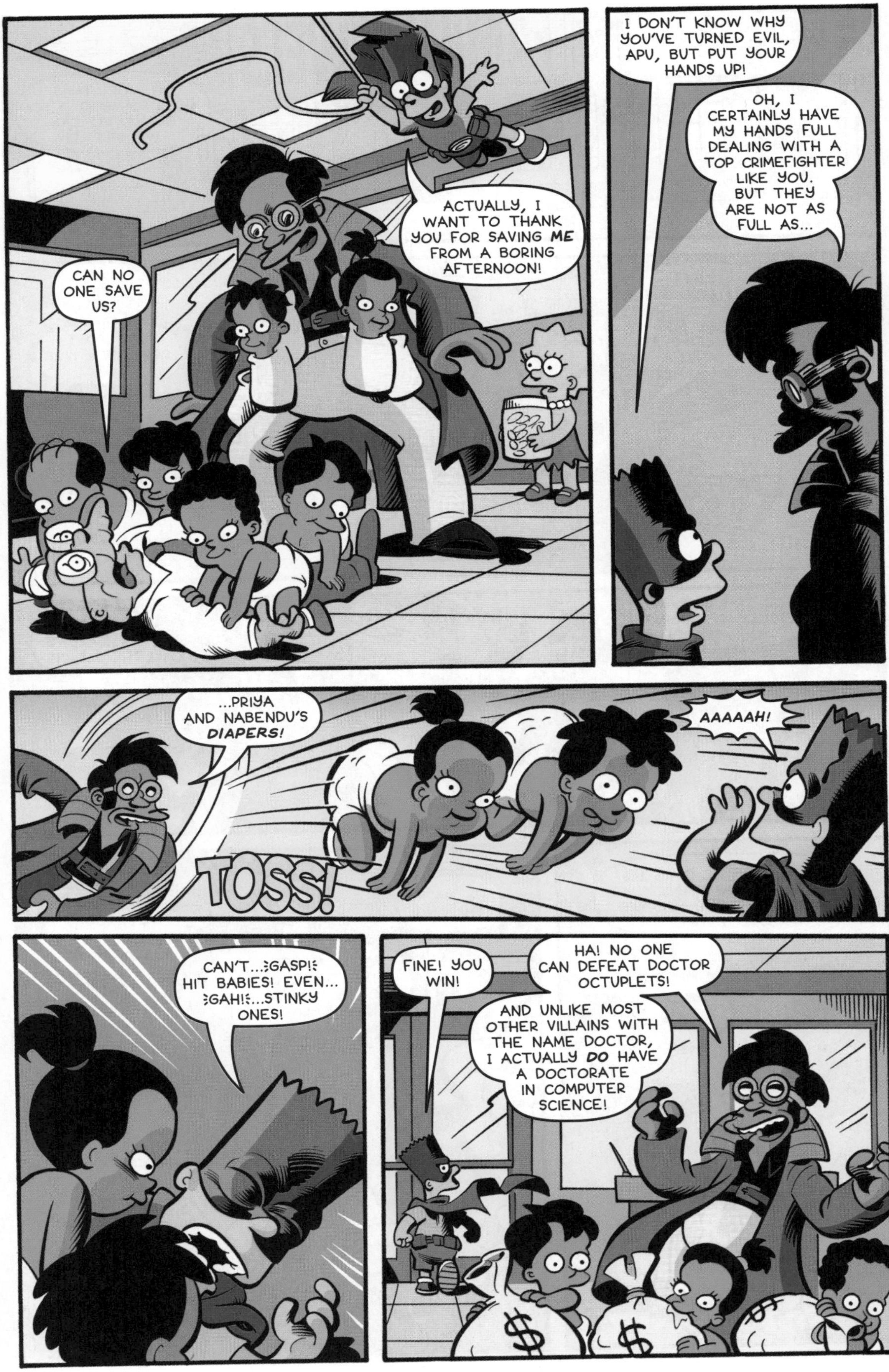
CAN NO ONE SAVE US?
ACTUALLY, I WANT TO THANK YOU FOR SAVING **ME** FROM A BORING AFTERNOON!
I DON'T KNOW WHY YOU'VE TURNED EVIL, APU, BUT PUT YOUR HANDS UP!
OH, I CERTAINLY HAVE MY HANDS FULL DEALING WITH A TOP CRIMEFIGHTER LIKE YOU. BUT THEY ARE NOT AS FULL AS...
...PRIYA AND NABENDU'S *DIAPERS!*
AAAAAH!
TOSS!
CAN'T...GASP! HIT BABIES! EVEN... GAH!...STINKY ONES!
FINE! YOU WIN!
HA! NO ONE CAN DEFEAT DOCTOR OCTUPLETS!
AND UNLIKE MOST OTHER VILLAINS WITH THE NAME DOCTOR, I ACTUALLY **DO** HAVE A DOCTORATE IN COMPUTER SCIENCE!

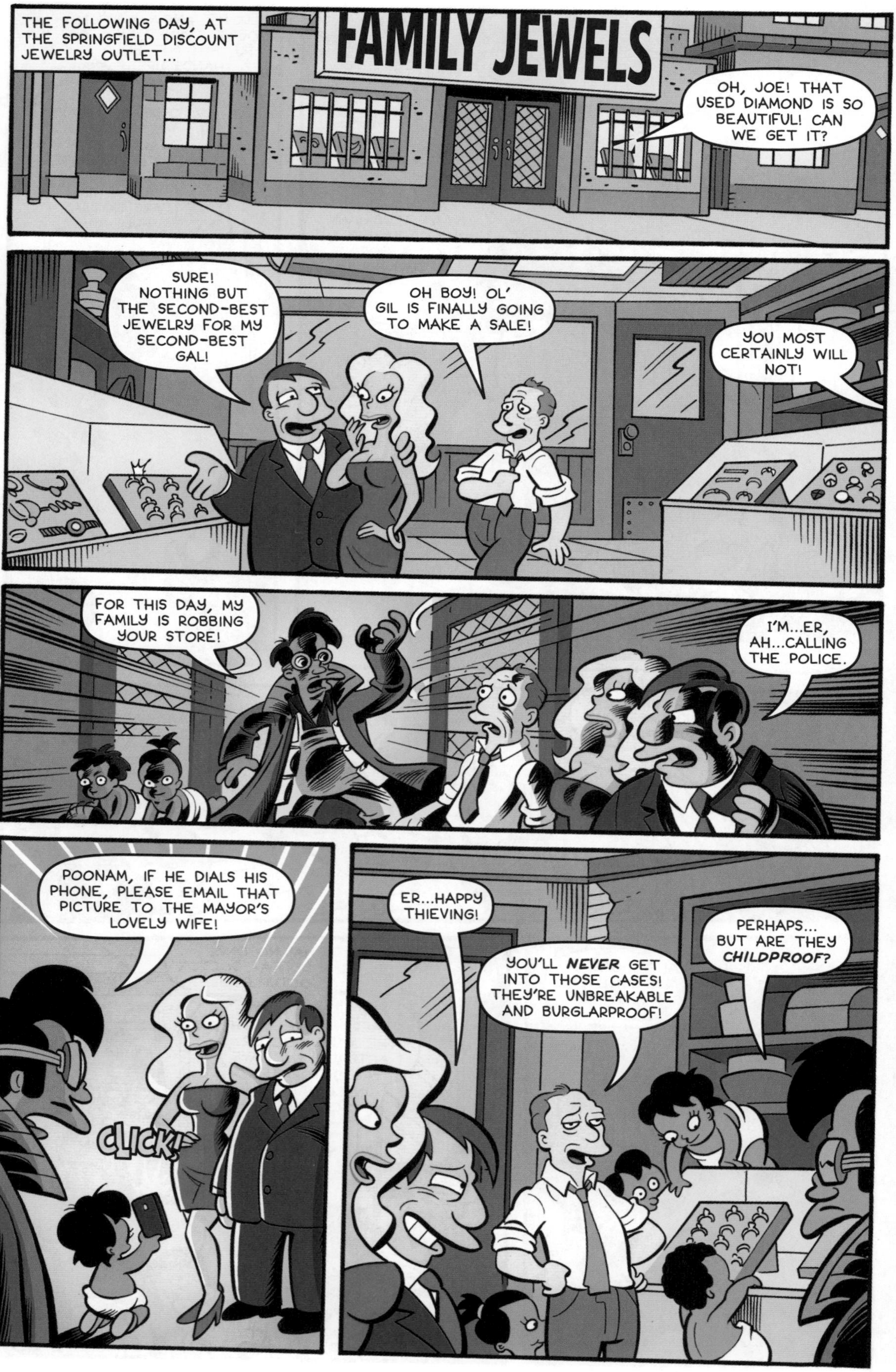
THE FOLLOWING DAY, AT THE SPRINGFIELD DISCOUNT JEWELRY OUTLET...
FAMILY JEWELS
OH, JOE! THAT USED DIAMOND IS SO BEAUTIFUL! CAN WE GET IT?
SURE! NOTHING BUT THE SECOND-BEST JEWELRY FOR MY SECOND-BEST GAL!
OH BOY! OL' GIL IS FINALLY GOING TO MAKE A SALE!
YOU MOST CERTAINLY WILL NOT!
FOR THIS DAY, MY FAMILY IS ROBBING YOUR STORE!
I'M...ER, AH...CALLING THE POLICE.
POONAM, IF HE DIALS HIS PHONE, PLEASE EMAIL THAT PICTURE TO THE MAYOR'S LOVELY WIFE!
CLICK!
ER...HAPPY THIEVING!
YOU'LL **NEVER** GET INTO THOSE CASES! THEY'RE UNBREAKABLE AND BURGLARPROOF!
PERHAPS... BUT ARE THEY ***CHILDPROOF?***

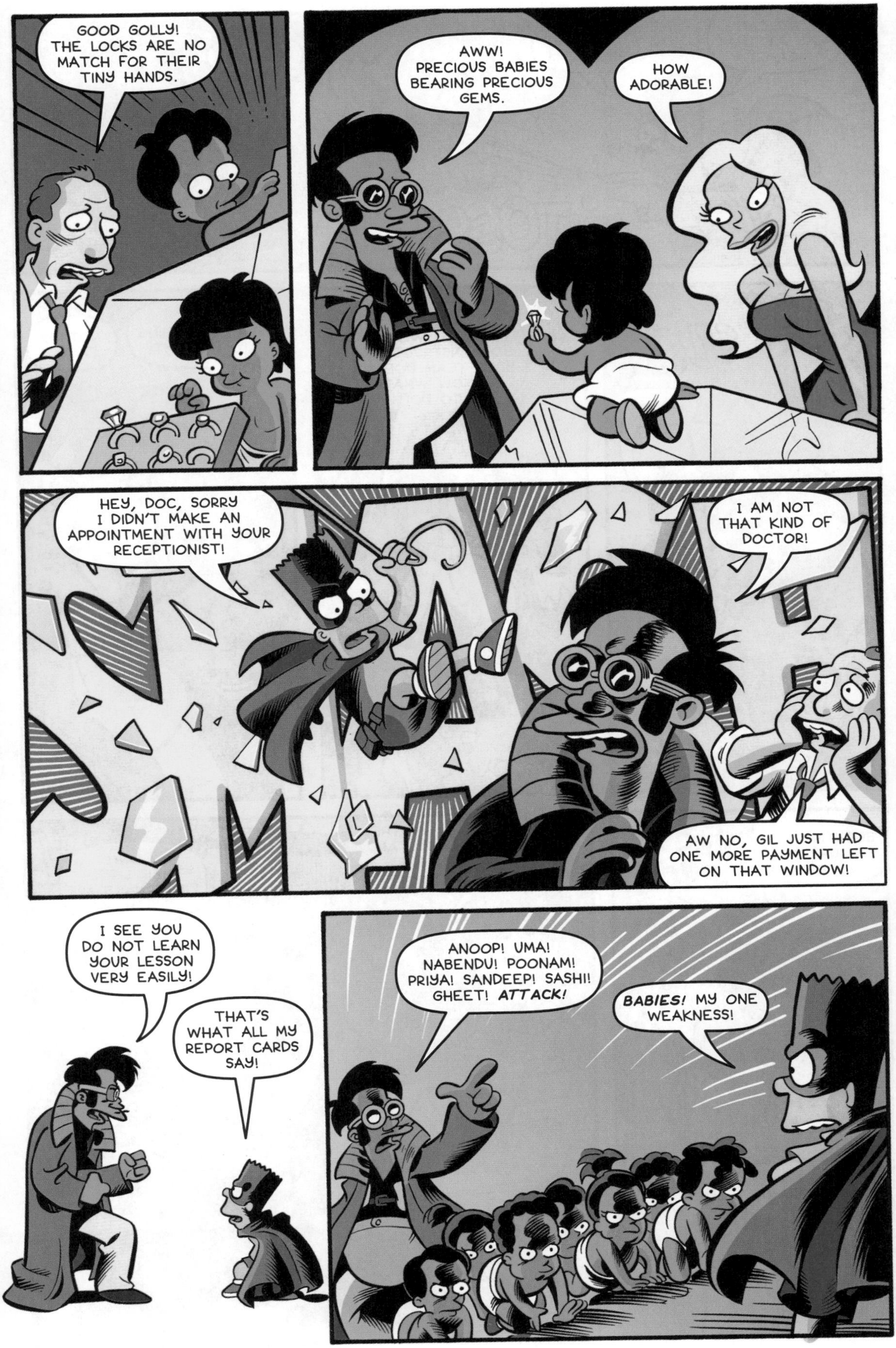
GOOD GOLLY! THE LOCKS ARE NO MATCH FOR THEIR TINY HANDS.
AWW! PRECIOUS BABIES BEARING PRECIOUS GEMS.
HOW ADORABLE!
HEY, DOC, SORRY I DIDN'T MAKE AN APPOINTMENT WITH YOUR RECEPTIONIST!
I AM NOT THAT KIND OF DOCTOR!
AW NO, GIL JUST HAD ONE MORE PAYMENT LEFT ON THAT WINDOW!
I SEE YOU DO NOT LEARN YOUR LESSON VERY EASILY!
THAT'S WHAT ALL MY REPORT CARDS SAY!
ANOOP! UMA! NABENDU! POONAM! PRIYA! SANDEEP! SASHI! GHEET! ATTACK!
BABIES! MY ONE WEAKNESS!

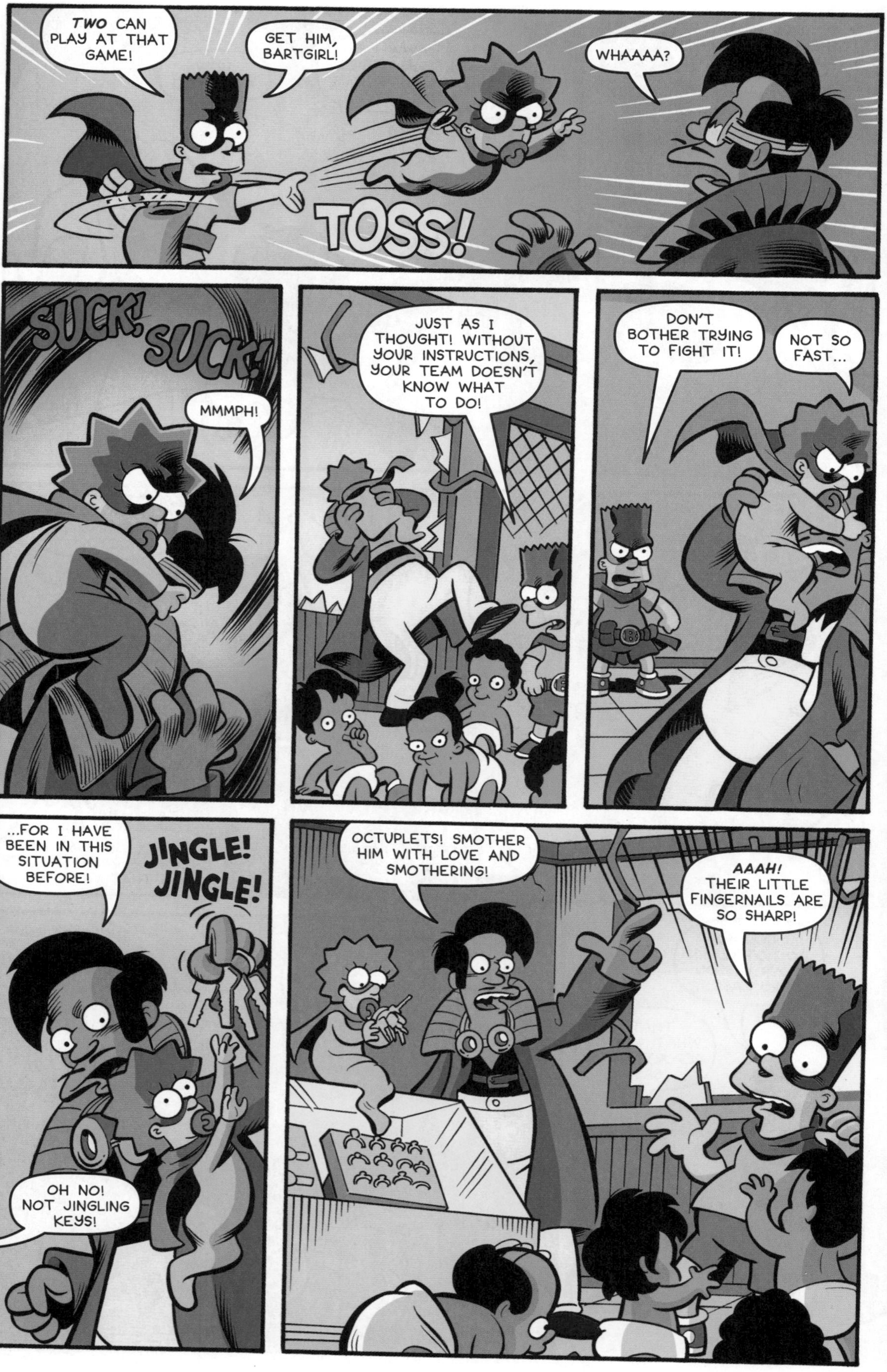
TWO CAN PLAY AT THAT GAME!
GET HIM, BARTGIRL!
WHAAAA?
TOSS!
SUCK! SUCK!
MMMPH!
JUST AS I THOUGHT! WITHOUT YOUR INSTRUCTIONS, YOUR TEAM DOESN'T KNOW WHAT TO DO!
DON'T BOTHER TRYING TO FIGHT IT!
NOT SO FAST...
...FOR I HAVE BEEN IN THIS SITUATION BEFORE!
JINGLE! JINGLE!
OH NO! NOT JINGLING KEYS!
OCTUPLETS! SMOTHER HIM WITH LOVE AND SMOTHERING!
AAAH! THEIR LITTLE FINGERNAILS ARE SO SHARP!

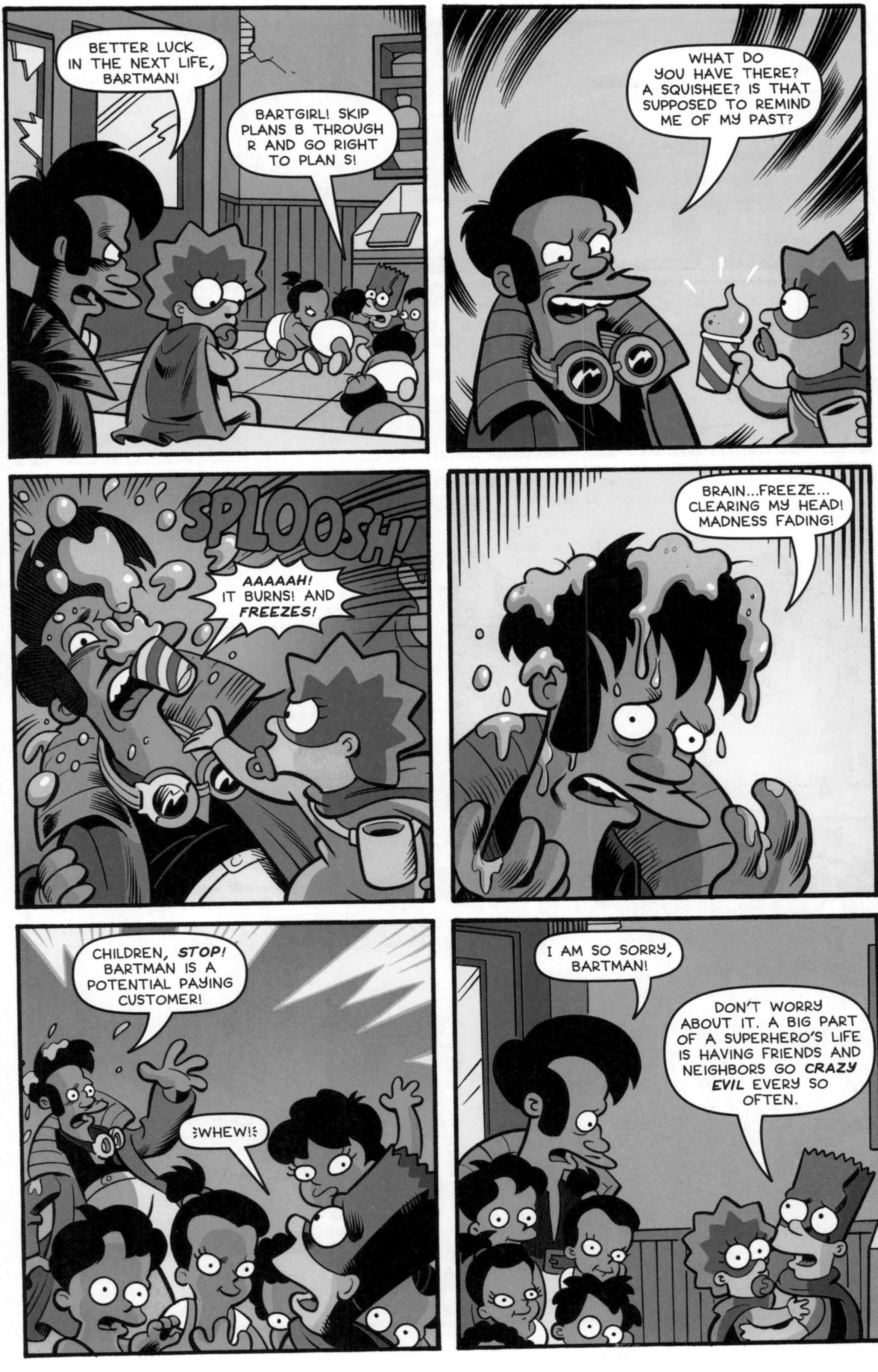
BETTER LUCK IN THE NEXT LIFE, BARTMAN!
BARTGIRL! SKIP PLANS B THROUGH R AND GO RIGHT TO PLAN S!
WHAT DO YOU HAVE THERE? A SQUISHEE? IS THAT SUPPOSED TO REMIND ME OF MY PAST?
SPLOOSH!
AAAAAH! IT BURNS! AND FREEZES!
BRAIN...FREEZE... CLEARING MY HEAD! MADNESS FADING!
CHILDREN, STOP! BARTMAN IS A POTENTIAL PAYING CUSTOMER!
WHEW!
I AM SO SORRY, BARTMAN!
DON'T WORRY ABOUT IT. A BIG PART OF A SUPERHERO'S LIFE IS HAVING FRIENDS AND NEIGHBORS GO CRAZY EVIL EVERY SO OFTEN.

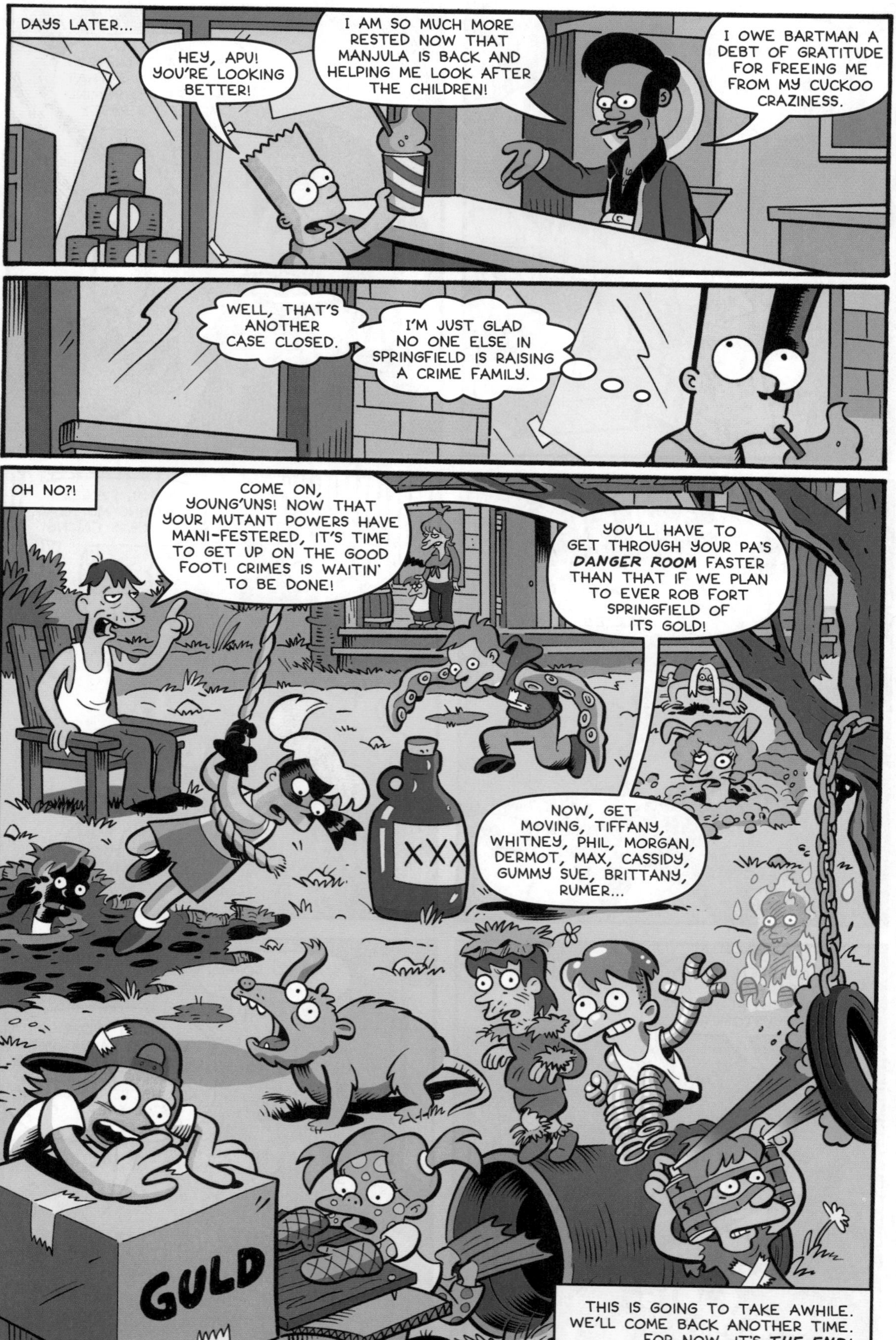
DAYS LATER...
HEY, APU! YOU'RE LOOKING BETTER!
I AM SO MUCH MORE RESTED NOW THAT MANJULA IS BACK AND HELPING ME LOOK AFTER THE CHILDREN!
I OWE BARTMAN A DEBT OF GRATITUDE FOR FREEING ME FROM MY CUCKOO CRAZINESS.
WELL, THAT'S ANOTHER CASE CLOSED.
I'M JUST GLAD NO ONE ELSE IN SPRINGFIELD IS RAISING A CRIME FAMILY.
OH NO?!
COME ON, YOUNG'UNS! NOW THAT YOUR MUTANT POWERS HAVE MANI-FESTERED, IT'S TIME TO GET UP ON THE GOOD FOOT! CRIMES IS WAITIN' TO BE DONE!
YOU'LL HAVE TO GET THROUGH YOUR PA'S ***DANGER ROOM*** FASTER THAN THAT IF WE PLAN TO EVER ROB FORT SPRINGFIELD OF ITS GOLD!
NOW, GET MOVING, TIFFANY, WHITNEY, PHIL, MORGAN, DERMOT, MAX, CASSIDY, GUMMY SUE, BRITTANY, RUMER...
XXX
GULD
THIS IS GOING TO TAKE AWHILE. WE'LL COME BACK ANOTHER TIME. FOR NOW...IT'S ***THE END!***

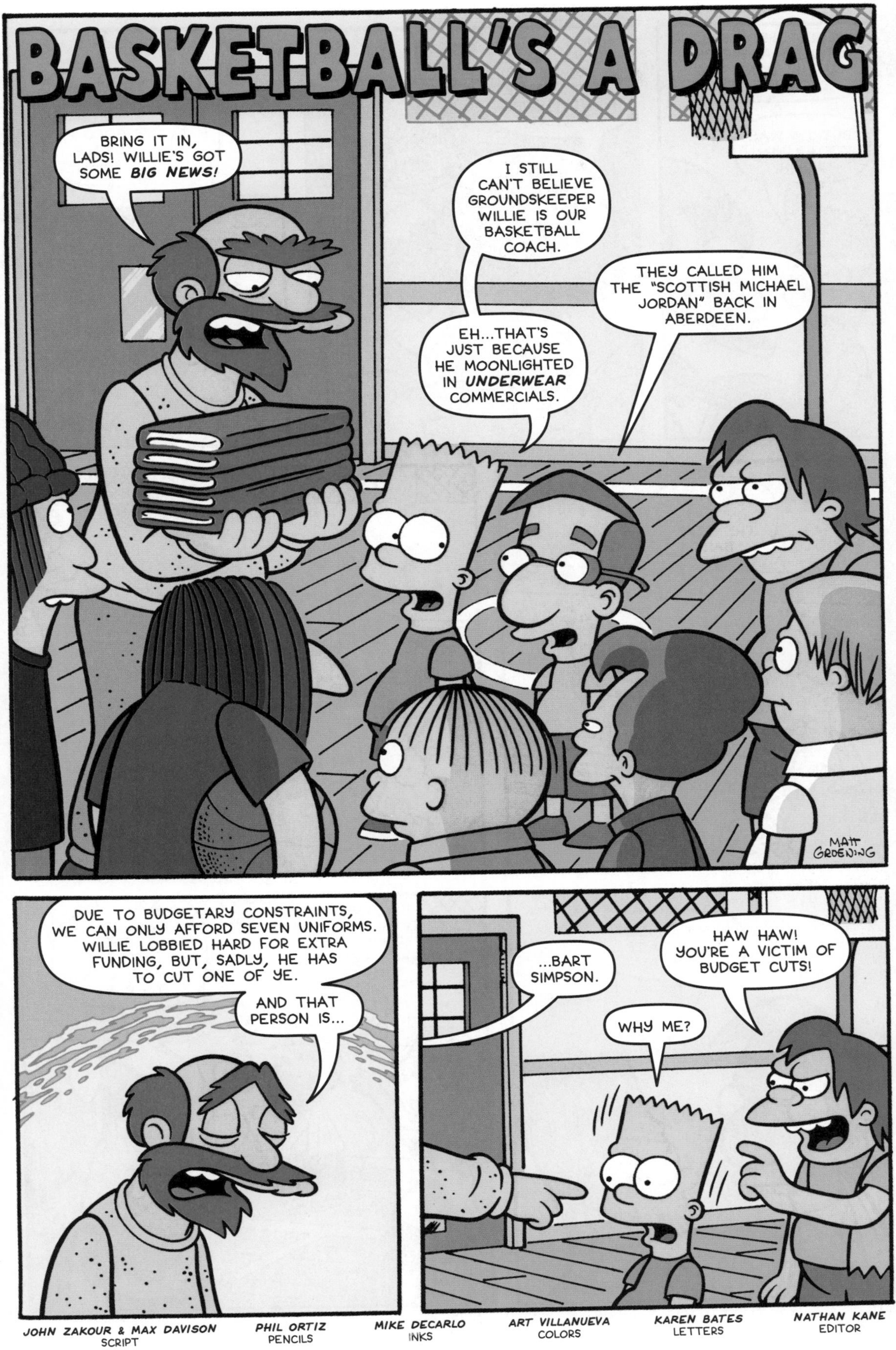
BASKETBALL'S A DRAG
BRING IT IN, LADS! WILLIE'S GOT SOME BIG NEWS!
I STILL CAN'T BELIEVE GROUNDSKEEPER WILLIE IS OUR BASKETBALL COACH.
EH...THAT'S JUST BECAUSE HE MOONLIGHTED IN UNDERWEAR COMMERCIALS.
THEY CALLED HIM THE "SCOTTISH MICHAEL JORDAN" BACK IN ABERDEEN.
MATT GROENING
DUE TO BUDGETARY CONSTRAINTS, WE CAN ONLY AFFORD SEVEN UNIFORMS. WILLIE LOBBIED HARD FOR EXTRA FUNDING, BUT, SADLY, HE HAS TO CUT ONE OF YE.
AND THAT PERSON IS...
...BART SIMPSON.
HAW HAW! YOU'RE A VICTIM OF BUDGET CUTS!
WHY ME?

JOHN ZAKOUR & MAX DAVISON SCRIPT | **PHIL ORTIZ** PENCILS | **MIKE DECARLO** INKS | **ART VILLANUEVA** COLORS | **KAREN BATES** LETTERS | **NATHAN KANE** EDITOR

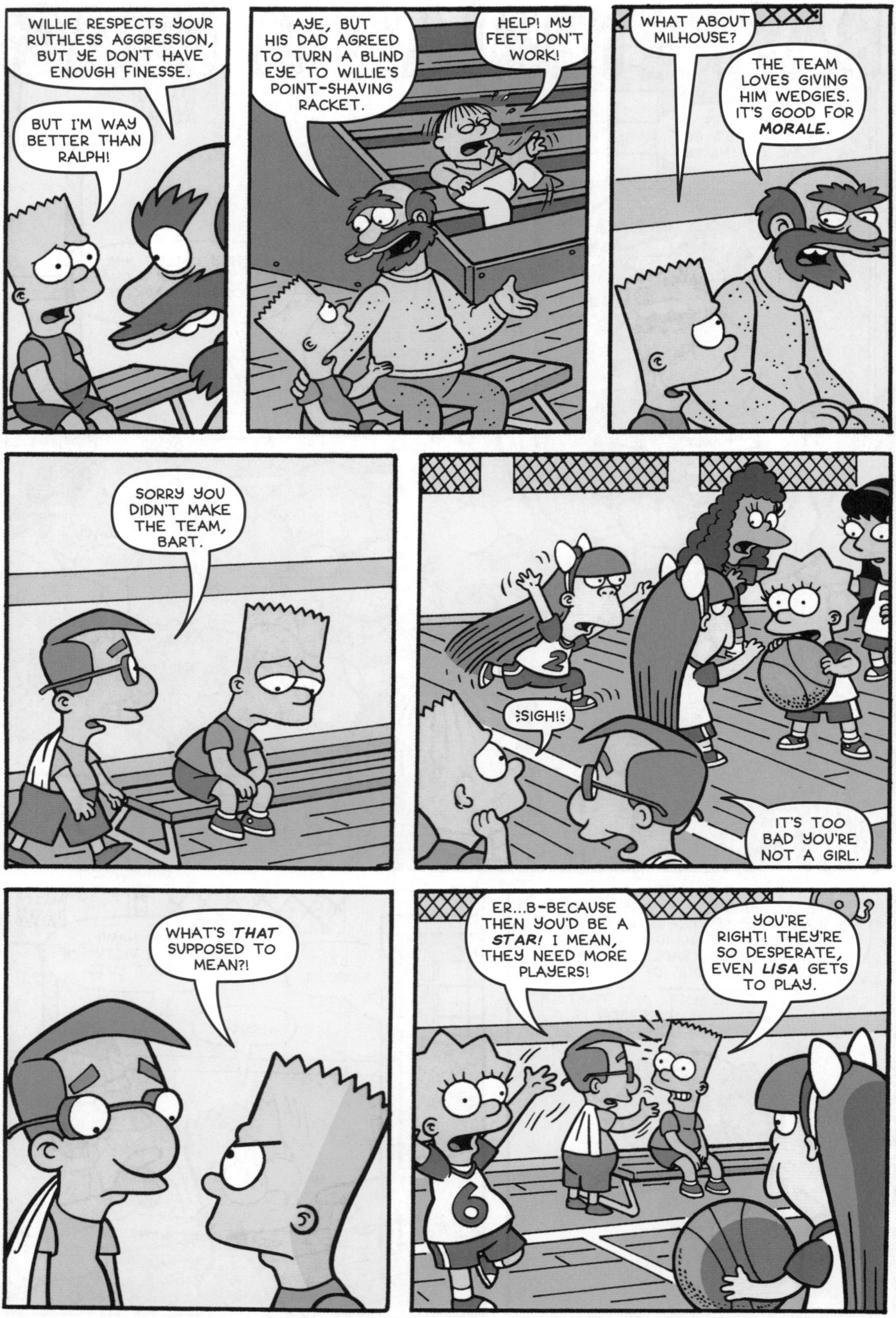
WILLIE RESPECTS YOUR RUTHLESS AGGRESSION, BUT YE DON'T HAVE ENOUGH FINESSE.
BUT I'M WAY BETTER THAN RALPH!
AYE, BUT HIS DAD AGREED TO TURN A BLIND EYE TO WILLIE'S POINT-SHAVING RACKET.
HELP! MY FEET DON'T WORK!
WHAT ABOUT MILHOUSE?
THE TEAM LOVES GIVING HIM WEDGIES. IT'S GOOD FOR **MORALE**.
SORRY YOU DIDN'T MAKE THE TEAM, BART.
SIGH!
IT'S TOO BAD YOU'RE NOT A GIRL.
WHAT'S ***THAT*** SUPPOSED TO MEAN?!
ER...B-BECAUSE THEN YOU'D BE A ***STAR!*** I MEAN, THEY NEED MORE PLAYERS!
YOU'RE RIGHT! THEY'RE SO DESPERATE, EVEN ***LISA*** GETS TO PLAY.

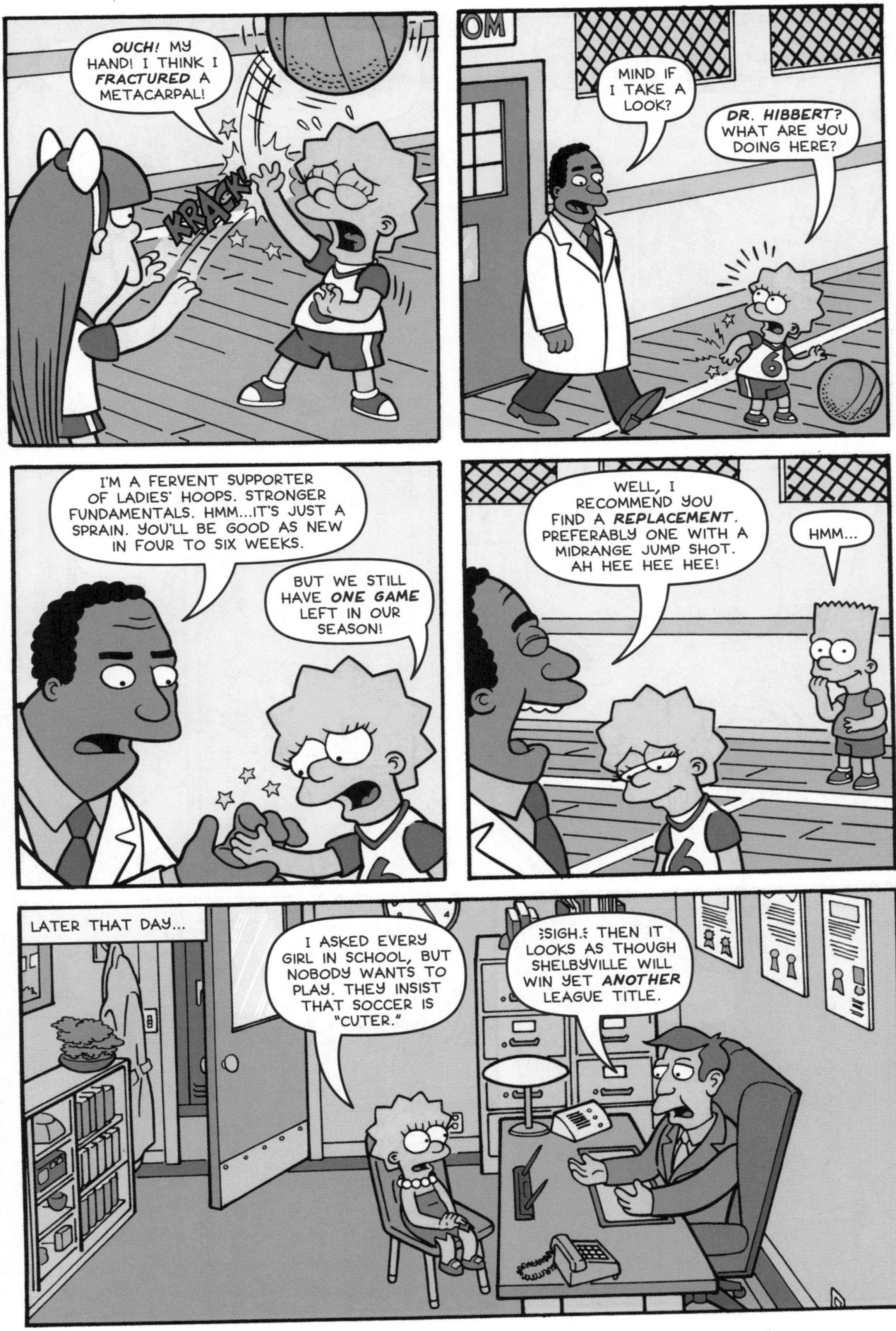
OUCH! MY HAND! I THINK I FRACTURED A METACARPAL!
KRACK!
MIND IF I TAKE A LOOK?
DR. HIBBERT? WHAT ARE YOU DOING HERE?
I'M A FERVENT SUPPORTER OF LADIES' HOOPS. STRONGER FUNDAMENTALS. HMM...IT'S JUST A SPRAIN. YOU'LL BE GOOD AS NEW IN FOUR TO SIX WEEKS.
BUT WE STILL HAVE ONE GAME LEFT IN OUR SEASON!
WELL, I RECOMMEND YOU FIND A REPLACEMENT. PREFERABLY ONE WITH A MIDRANGE JUMP SHOT. AH HEE HEE HEE!
HMM...
LATER THAT DAY...
I ASKED EVERY GIRL IN SCHOOL, BUT NOBODY WANTS TO PLAY. THEY INSIST THAT SOCCER IS "CUTER."
:SIGH.: THEN IT LOOKS AS THOUGH SHELBYVILLE WILL WIN YET ANOTHER LEAGUE TITLE.

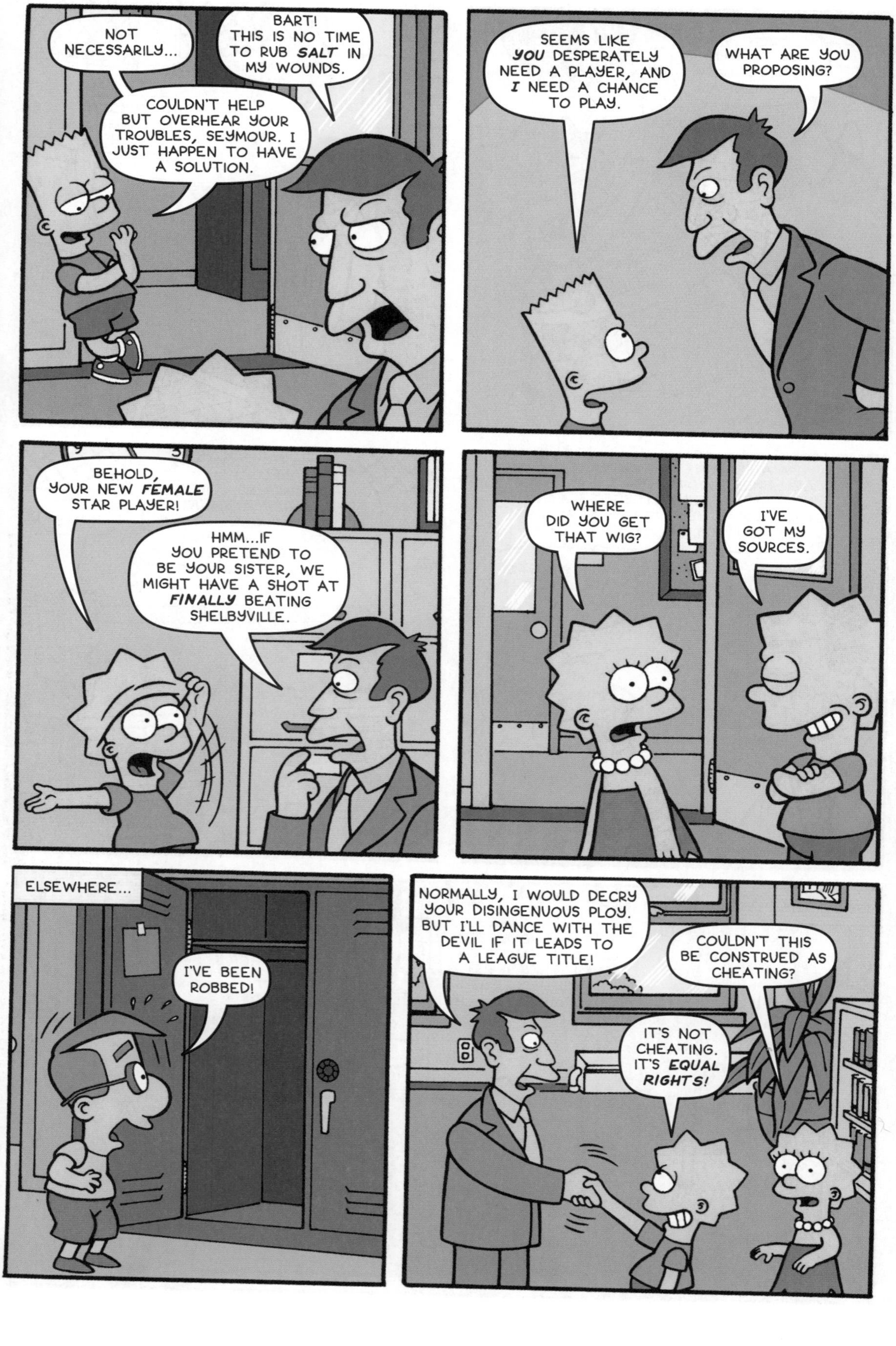
NOT NECESSARILY...
BART! THIS IS NO TIME TO RUB SALT IN MY WOUNDS.
COULDN'T HELP BUT OVERHEAR YOUR TROUBLES, SEYMOUR. I JUST HAPPEN TO HAVE A SOLUTION.
SEEMS LIKE YOU DESPERATELY NEED A PLAYER, AND I NEED A CHANCE TO PLAY.
WHAT ARE YOU PROPOSING?
BEHOLD, YOUR NEW FEMALE STAR PLAYER!
HMM...IF YOU PRETEND TO BE YOUR SISTER, WE MIGHT HAVE A SHOT AT FINALLY BEATING SHELBYVILLE.
WHERE DID YOU GET THAT WIG?
I'VE GOT MY SOURCES.
ELSEWHERE...
I'VE BEEN ROBBED!
NORMALLY, I WOULD DECRY YOUR DISINGENUOUS PLOY. BUT I'LL DANCE WITH THE DEVIL IF IT LEADS TO A LEAGUE TITLE!
COULDN'T THIS BE CONSTRUED AS CHEATING?
IT'S NOT CHEATING. IT'S EQUAL RIGHTS!

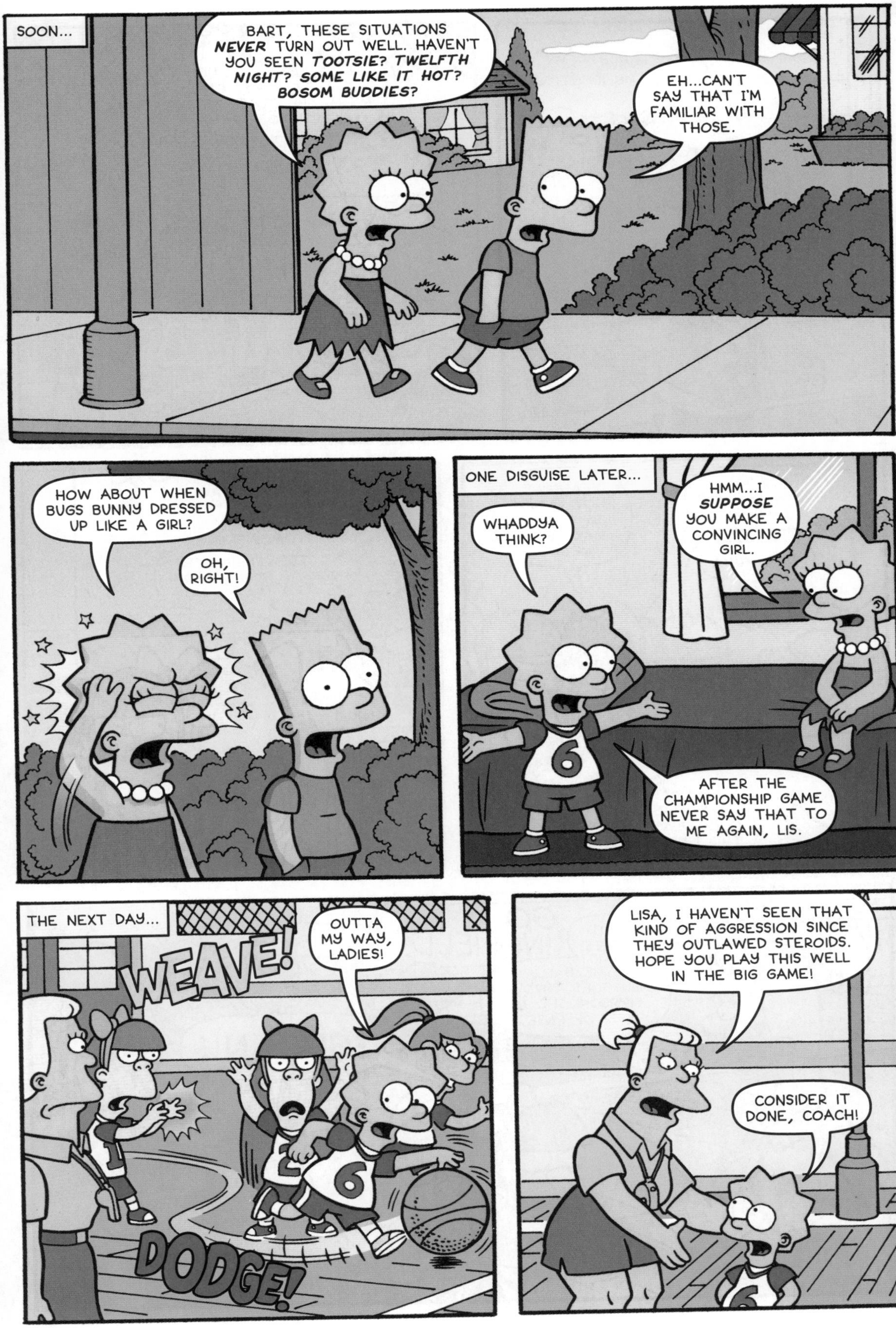
SOON...
BART, THESE SITUATIONS NEVER TURN OUT WELL. HAVEN'T YOU SEEN TOOTSIE? TWELFTH NIGHT? SOME LIKE IT HOT? BOSOM BUDDIES?
EH...CAN'T SAY THAT I'M FAMILIAR WITH THOSE.
HOW ABOUT WHEN BUGS BUNNY DRESSED UP LIKE A GIRL?
OH, RIGHT!
ONE DISGUISE LATER...
WHADDYA THINK?
HMM...I SUPPOSE YOU MAKE A CONVINCING GIRL.
AFTER THE CHAMPIONSHIP GAME NEVER SAY THAT TO ME AGAIN, LIS.
THE NEXT DAY...
WEAVE!
OUTTA MY WAY, LADIES!
DODGE!
LISA, I HAVEN'T SEEN THAT KIND OF AGGRESSION SINCE THEY OUTLAWED STEROIDS. HOPE YOU PLAY THIS WELL IN THE BIG GAME!
CONSIDER IT DONE, COACH!

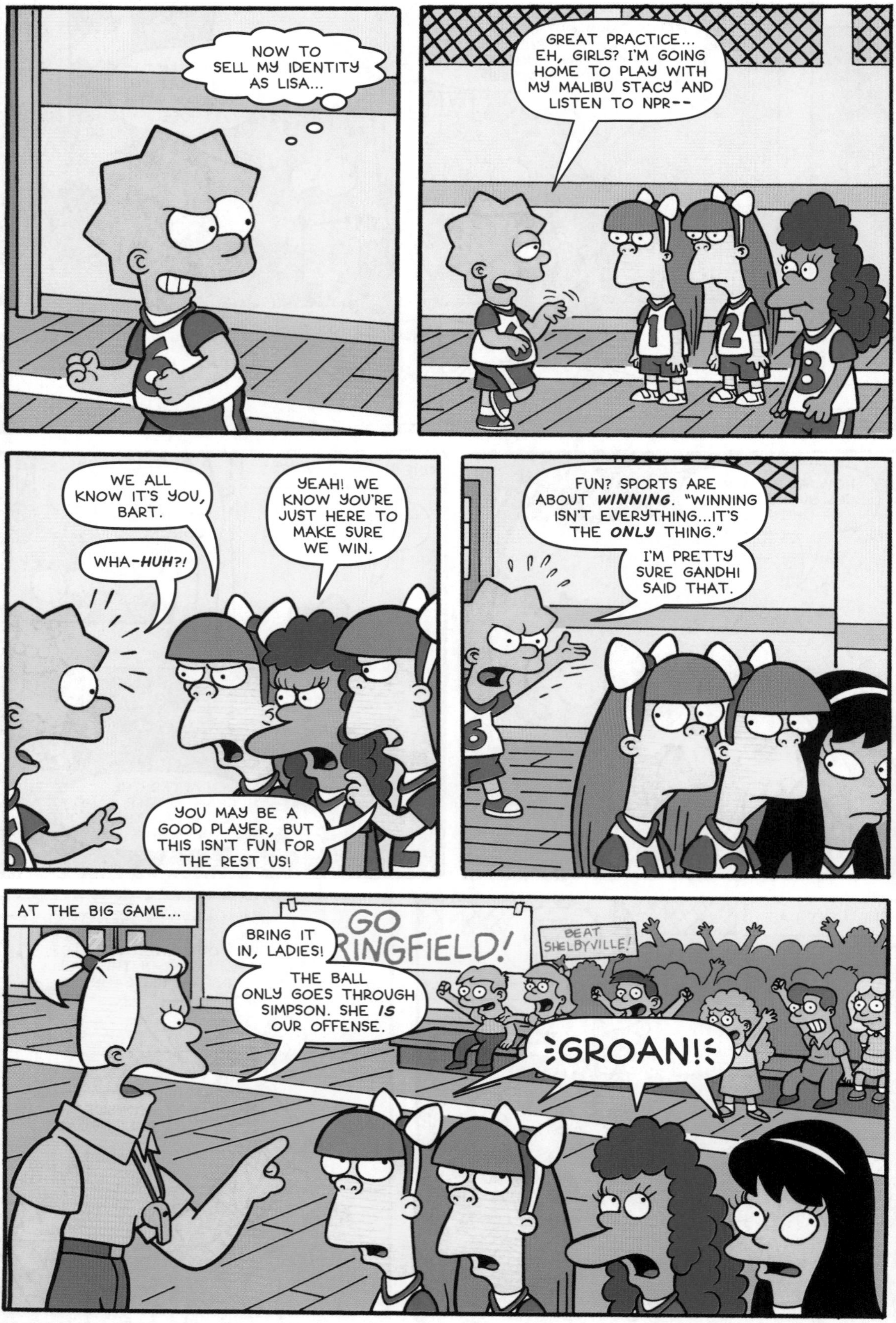
NOW TO SELL MY IDENTITY AS LISA...
GREAT PRACTICE... EH, GIRLS? I'M GOING HOME TO PLAY WITH MY MALIBU STACY AND LISTEN TO NPR--
WE ALL KNOW IT'S YOU, BART.
WHA-**HUH**?!
YEAH! WE KNOW YOU'RE JUST HERE TO MAKE SURE WE WIN.
YOU MAY BE A GOOD PLAYER, BUT THIS ISN'T FUN FOR THE REST US!
FUN? SPORTS ARE ABOUT **WINNING**. "WINNING ISN'T EVERYTHING...IT'S THE **ONLY** THING."
I'M PRETTY SURE GANDHI SAID THAT.
AT THE BIG GAME...
GO ...RINGFIELD!
BEAT SHELBYVILLE!
BRING IT IN, LADIES!
THE BALL ONLY GOES THROUGH SIMPSON. SHE ***IS*** OUR OFFENSE.
GROAN!

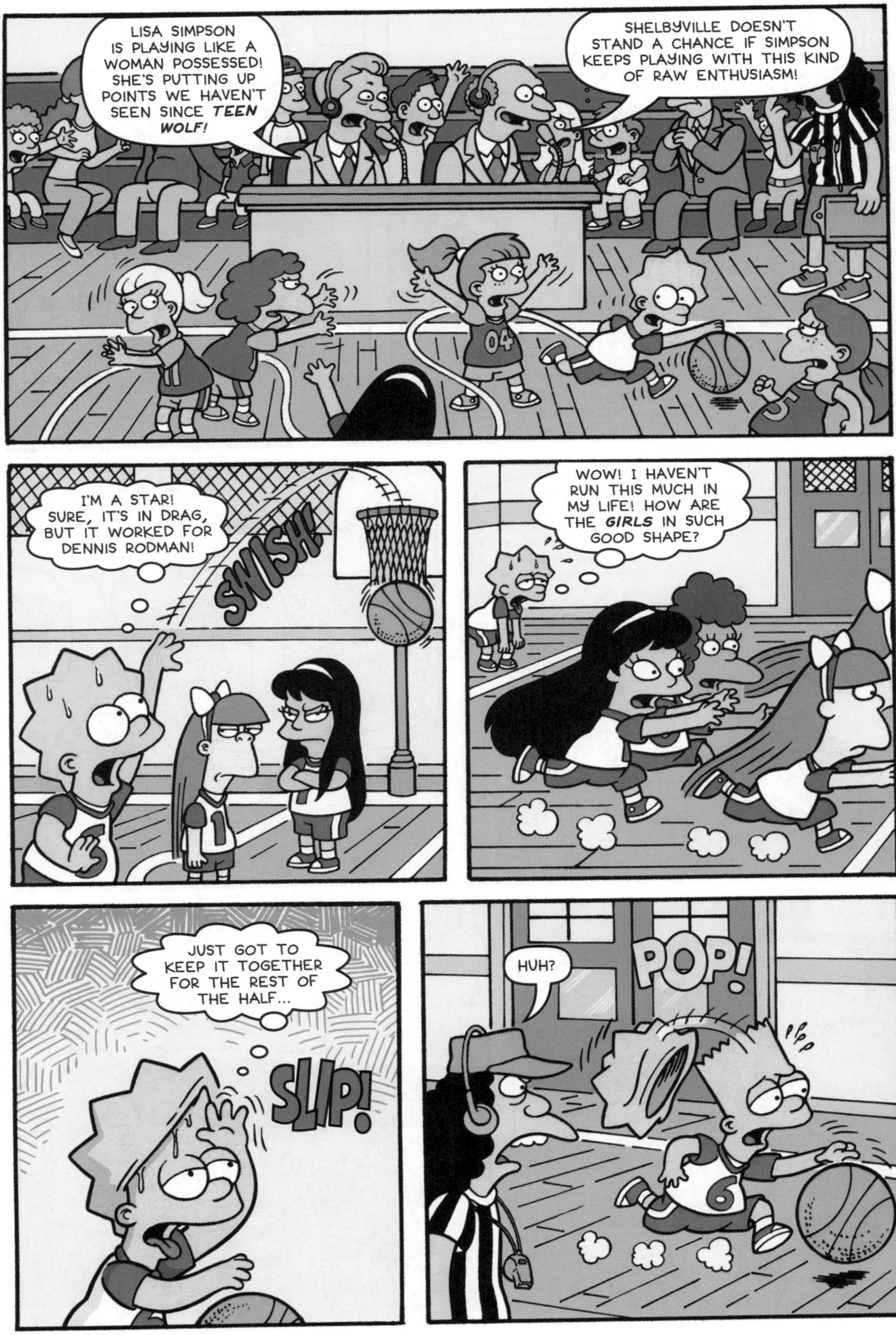
LISA SIMPSON IS PLAYING LIKE A WOMAN POSSESSED! SHE'S PUTTING UP POINTS WE HAVEN'T SEEN SINCE TEEN WOLF!
SHELBYVILLE DOESN'T STAND A CHANCE IF SIMPSON KEEPS PLAYING WITH THIS KIND OF RAW ENTHUSIASM!
I'M A STAR! SURE, IT'S IN DRAG, BUT IT WORKED FOR DENNIS RODMAN!
SWISH!
WOW! I HAVEN'T RUN THIS MUCH IN MY LIFE! HOW ARE THE GIRLS IN SUCH GOOD SHAPE?
JUST GOT TO KEEP IT TOGETHER FOR THE REST OF THE HALF...
SLIP!
HUH?
POP!

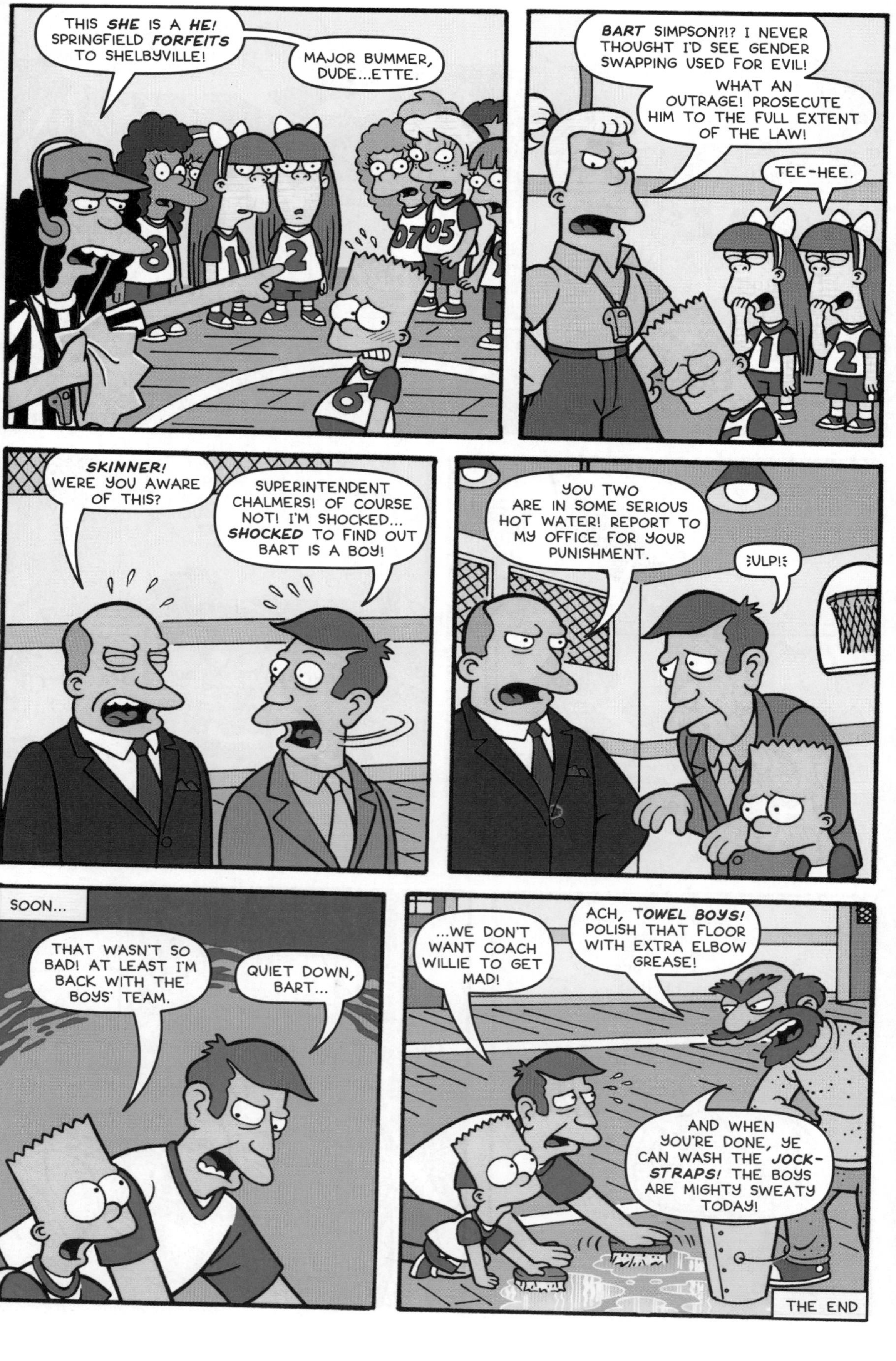

THIS SHE IS A HE! SPRINGFIELD FORFEITS TO SHELBYVILLE!
MAJOR BUMMER, DUDE...ETTE.
BART SIMPSON?!? I NEVER THOUGHT I'D SEE GENDER SWAPPING USED FOR EVIL!
WHAT AN OUTRAGE! PROSECUTE HIM TO THE FULL EXTENT OF THE LAW!
TEE-HEE.
SKINNER! WERE YOU AWARE OF THIS?
SUPERINTENDENT CHALMERS! OF COURSE NOT! I'M SHOCKED... SHOCKED TO FIND OUT BART IS A BOY!
YOU TWO ARE IN SOME SERIOUS HOT WATER! REPORT TO MY OFFICE FOR YOUR PUNISHMENT.
ULP!
SOON...
THAT WASN'T SO BAD! AT LEAST I'M BACK WITH THE BOYS' TEAM.
QUIET DOWN, BART...
...WE DON'T WANT COACH WILLIE TO GET MAD!
ACH, TOWEL BOYS! POLISH THAT FLOOR WITH EXTRA ELBOW GREASE!
AND WHEN YOU'RE DONE, YE CAN WASH THE JOCK-STRAPS! THE BOYS ARE MIGHTY SWEATY TODAY!
THE END

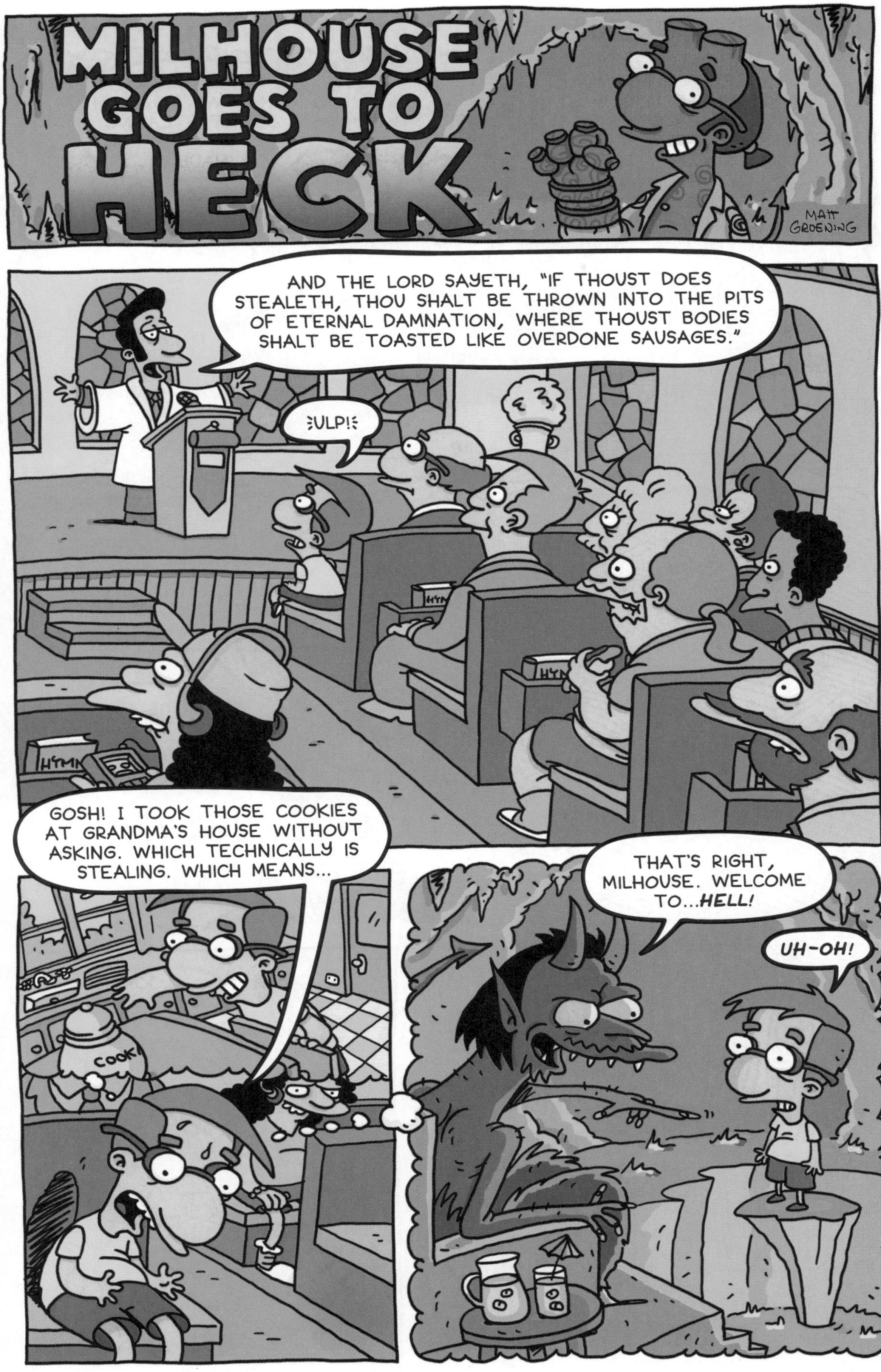
MILHOUSE GOES TO HECK
MATT GROENING
AND THE LORD SAYETH, "IF THOUST DOES STEALETH, THOU SHALT BE THROWN INTO THE PITS OF ETERNAL DAMNATION, WHERE THOUST BODIES SHALT BE TOASTED LIKE OVERDONE SAUSAGES."
ULP!
GOSH! I TOOK THOSE COOKIES AT GRANDMA'S HOUSE WITHOUT ASKING. WHICH TECHNICALLY IS STEALING. WHICH MEANS...
THAT'S RIGHT, MILHOUSE. WELCOME TO...**HELL!**
UH-OH!

DEAN RANKINE
STORY & ART

KAREN BATES
LETTERS

NATHAN KANE
EDITOR

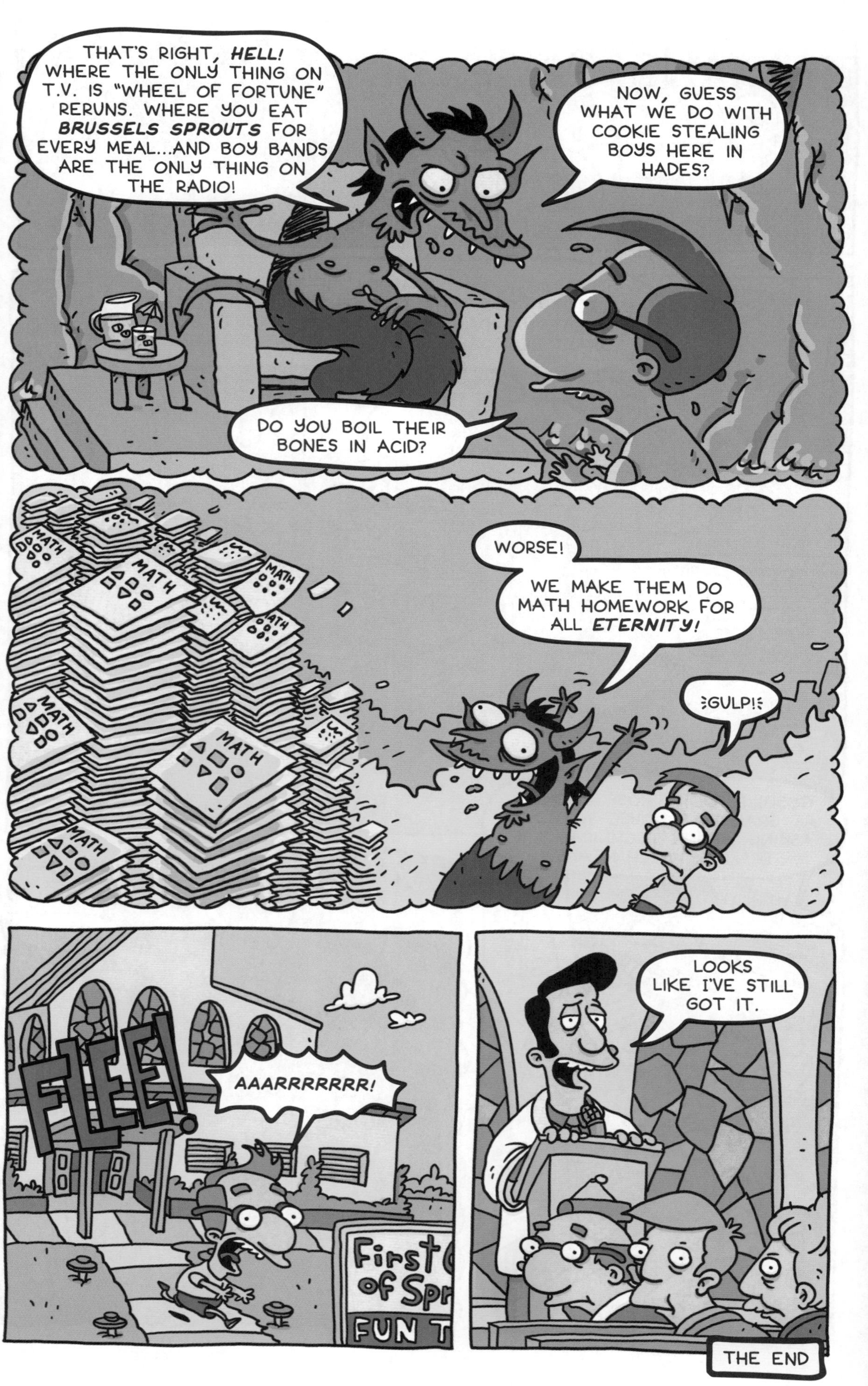
THAT'S RIGHT, HELL! WHERE THE ONLY THING ON T.V. IS "WHEEL OF FORTUNE" RERUNS. WHERE YOU EAT BRUSSELS SPROUTS FOR EVERY MEAL...AND BOY BANDS ARE THE ONLY THING ON THE RADIO!
NOW, GUESS WHAT WE DO WITH COOKIE STEALING BOYS HERE IN HADES?
DO YOU BOIL THEIR BONES IN ACID?
MATH
WORSE!
WE MAKE THEM DO MATH HOMEWORK FOR ALL ETERNITY!
GULP!
FLEE!
AAARRRRRRR!
First
LOOKS LIKE I'VE STILL GOT IT.
THE END

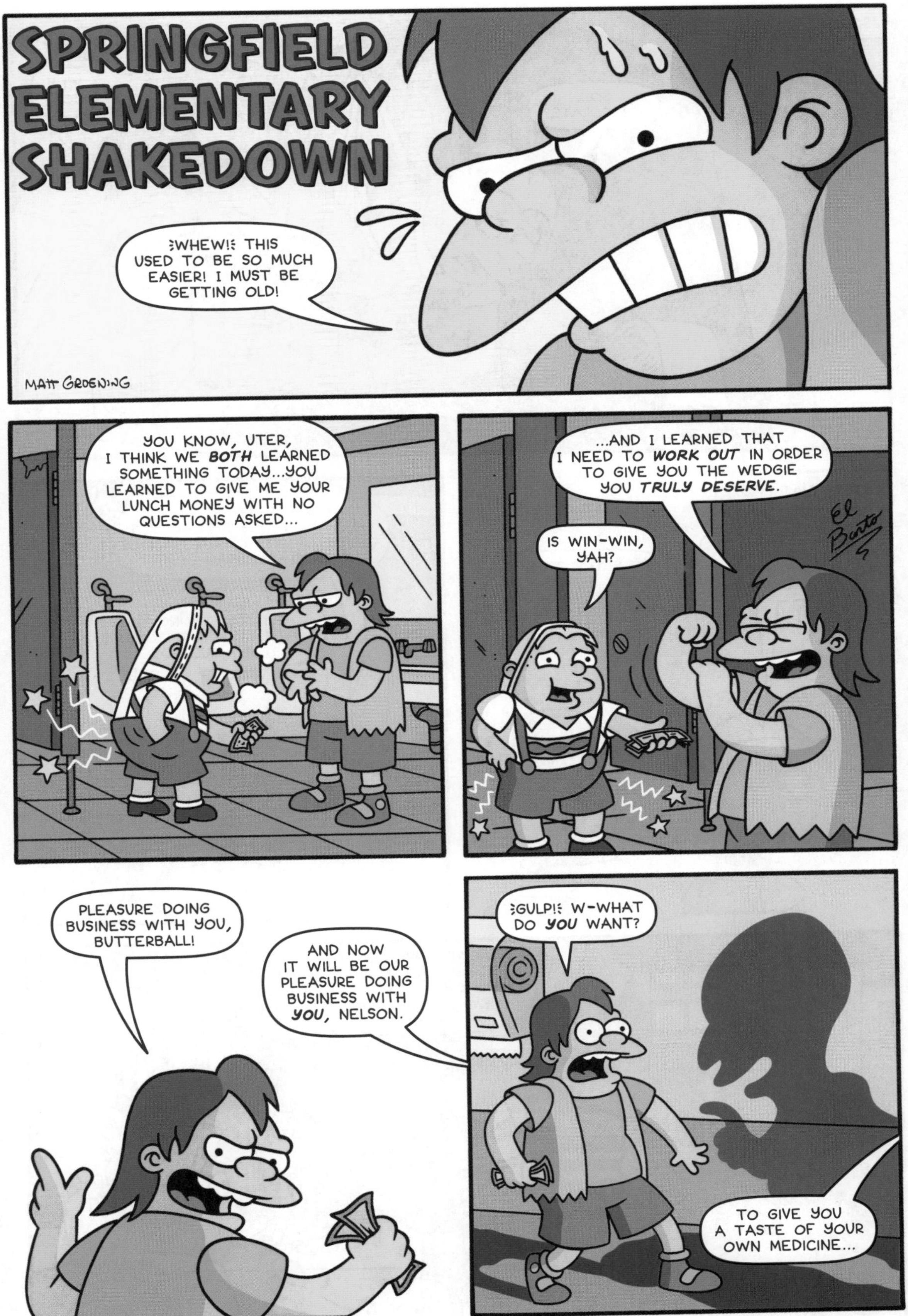
SPRINGFIELD ELEMENTARY SHAKEDOWN
MATT GROENING
WHEW! THIS USED TO BE SO MUCH EASIER! I MUST BE GETTING OLD!
YOU KNOW, UTER, I THINK WE **BOTH** LEARNED SOMETHING TODAY...YOU LEARNED TO GIVE ME YOUR LUNCH MONEY WITH NO QUESTIONS ASKED...
...AND I LEARNED THAT I NEED TO **WORK OUT** IN ORDER TO GIVE YOU THE WEDGIE YOU **TRULY DESERVE**.
IS WIN-WIN, YAH?
El Barto
PLEASURE DOING BUSINESS WITH YOU, BUTTERBALL!
AND NOW IT WILL BE OUR PLEASURE DOING BUSINESS WITH **YOU**, NELSON.
GULP! W-WHAT DO **YOU** WANT?
TO GIVE YOU A TASTE OF YOUR OWN MEDICINE...

ERIC ROGERS SCRIPT | **NINA MATSUMOTO** PENCILS | **MIKE ROTE** INKS | **NATHAN HAMILL** COLORS | **KAREN BATES** LETTERS | **NATHAN KANE** EDITOR

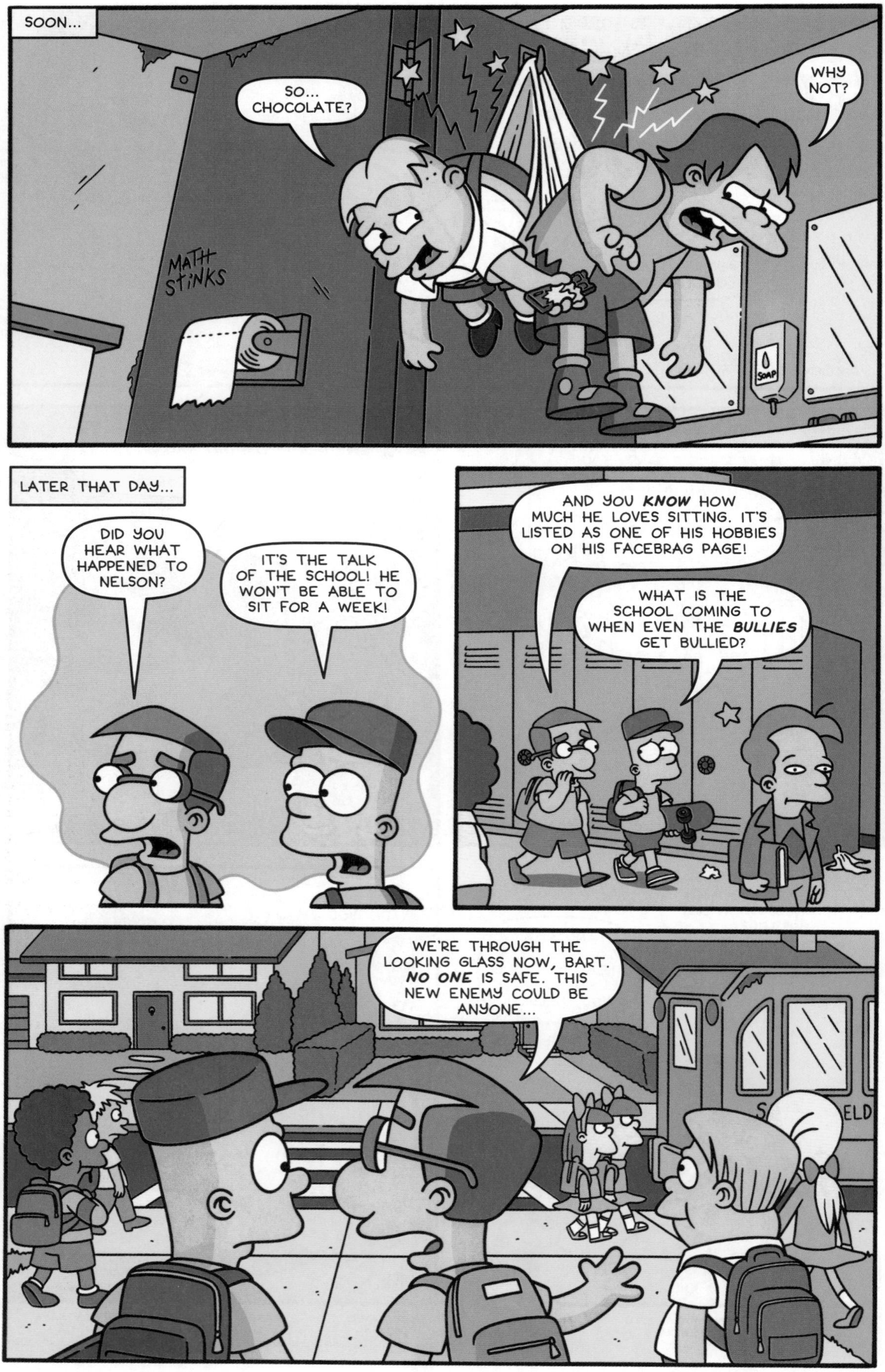
SOON...
SO... CHOCOLATE?
WHY NOT?
MATH STINKS
SOAP
LATER THAT DAY...
DID YOU HEAR WHAT HAPPENED TO NELSON?
IT'S THE TALK OF THE SCHOOL! HE WON'T BE ABLE TO SIT FOR A WEEK!
AND YOU **KNOW** HOW MUCH HE LOVES SITTING. IT'S LISTED AS ONE OF HIS HOBBIES ON HIS FACEBRAG PAGE!
WHAT IS THE SCHOOL COMING TO WHEN EVEN THE ***BULLIES*** GET BULLIED?
WE'RE THROUGH THE LOOKING GLASS NOW, BART. ***NO ONE*** IS SAFE. THIS NEW ENEMY COULD BE ANYONE...

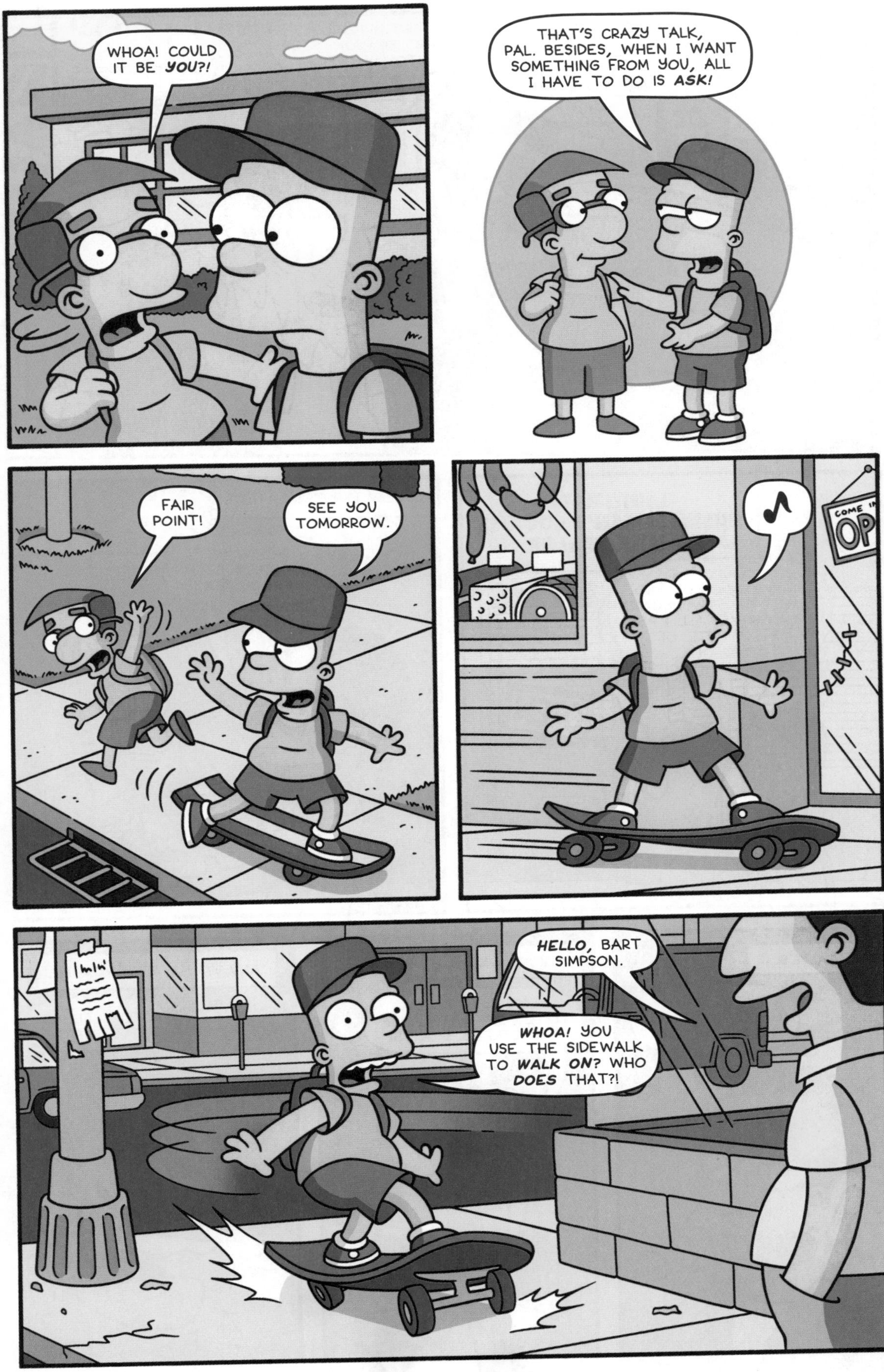
WHOA! COULD IT BE YOU?!
THAT'S CRAZY TALK, PAL. BESIDES, WHEN I WANT SOMETHING FROM YOU, ALL I HAVE TO DO IS ASK!
FAIR POINT!
SEE YOU TOMORROW.
HELLO, BART SIMPSON.
WHOA! YOU USE THE SIDEWALK TO WALK ON? WHO DOES THAT?!

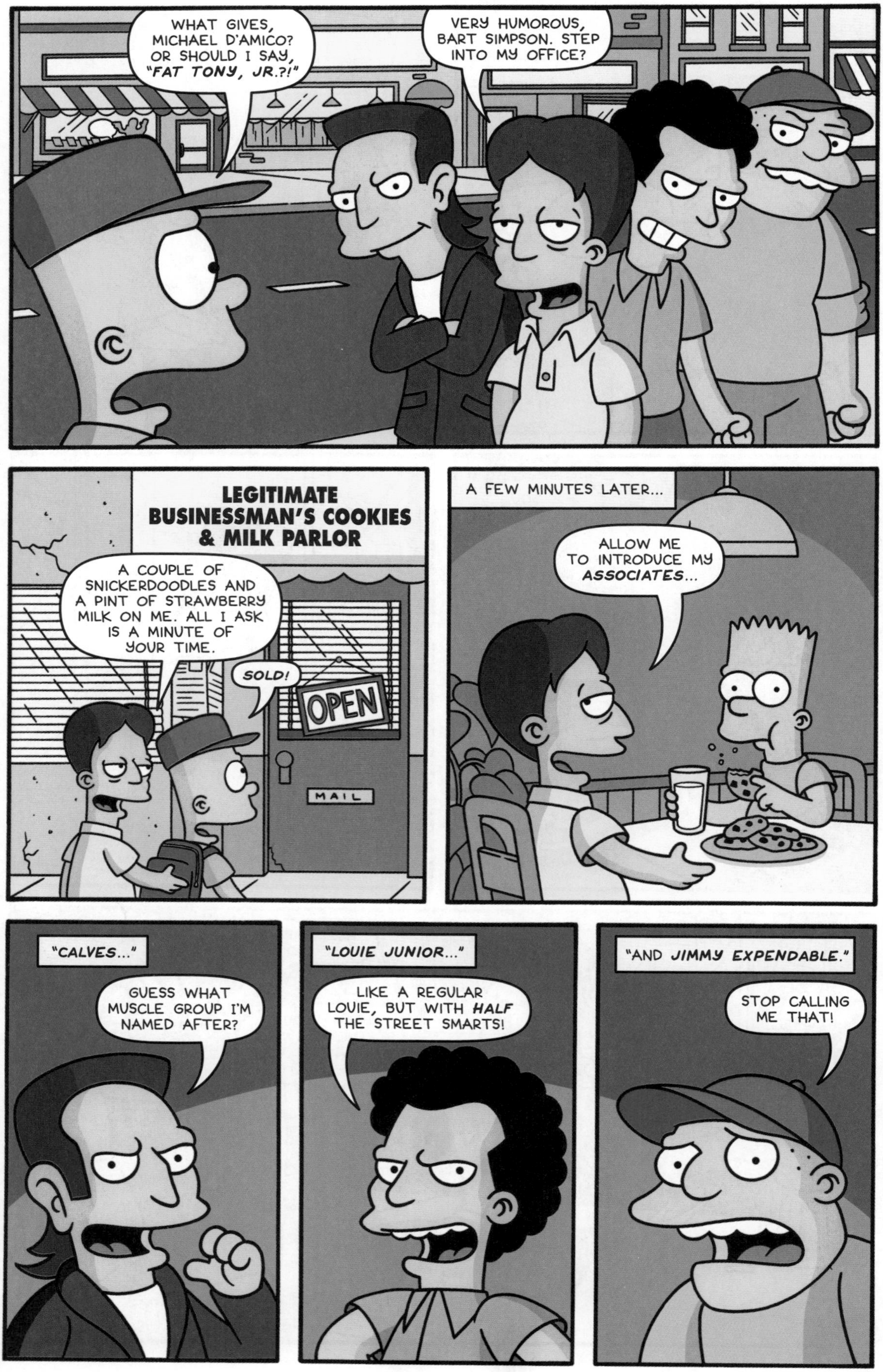

WHAT GIVES, MICHAEL D'AMICO? OR SHOULD I SAY, "FAT TONY, JR.?!"
VERY HUMOROUS, BART SIMPSON. STEP INTO MY OFFICE?
LEGITIMATE BUSINESSMAN'S COOKIES & MILK PARLOR
A COUPLE OF SNICKERDOODLES AND A PINT OF STRAWBERRY MILK ON ME. ALL I ASK IS A MINUTE OF YOUR TIME.
SOLD!
OPEN
MAIL
A FEW MINUTES LATER...
ALLOW ME TO INTRODUCE MY ASSOCIATES...
"CALVES..."
GUESS WHAT MUSCLE GROUP I'M NAMED AFTER?
"LOUIE JUNIOR..."
LIKE A REGULAR LOUIE, BUT WITH HALF THE STREET SMARTS!
"AND JIMMY EXPENDABLE."
STOP CALLING ME THAT!

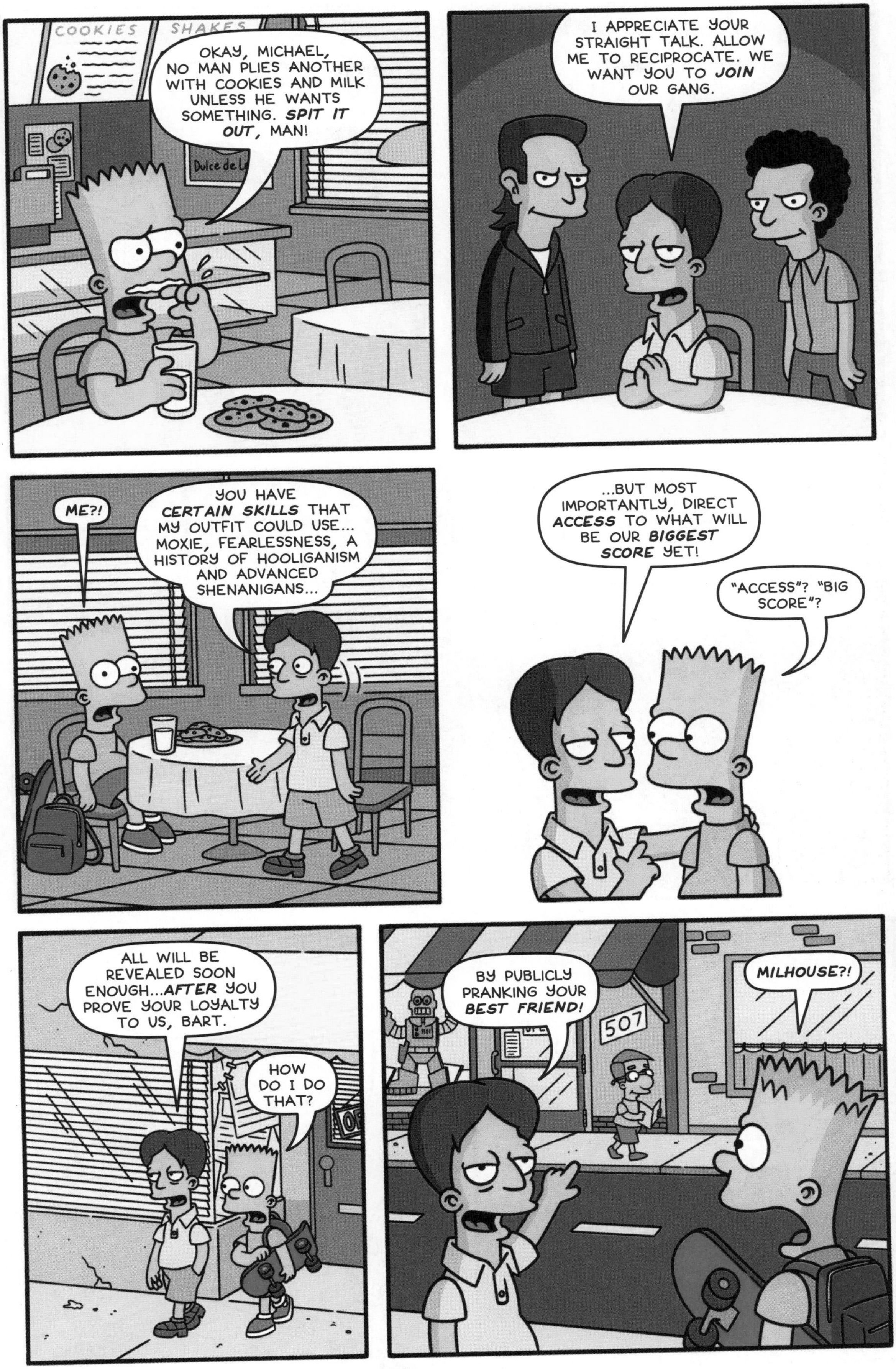
COOKIES
SHAKES
OKAY, MICHAEL, NO MAN PLIES ANOTHER WITH COOKIES AND MILK UNLESS HE WANTS SOMETHING. SPIT IT OUT, MAN!
I APPRECIATE YOUR STRAIGHT TALK. ALLOW ME TO RECIPROCATE. WE WANT YOU TO JOIN OUR GANG.
ME?!
YOU HAVE CERTAIN SKILLS THAT MY OUTFIT COULD USE... MOXIE, FEARLESSNESS, A HISTORY OF HOOLIGANISM AND ADVANCED SHENANIGANS...
...BUT MOST IMPORTANTLY, DIRECT ACCESS TO WHAT WILL BE OUR BIGGEST SCORE YET!
"ACCESS"? "BIG SCORE"?
ALL WILL BE REVEALED SOON ENOUGH...AFTER YOU PROVE YOUR LOYALTY TO US, BART.
HOW DO I DO THAT?
BY PUBLICLY PRANKING YOUR BEST FRIEND!
507
MILHOUSE?!

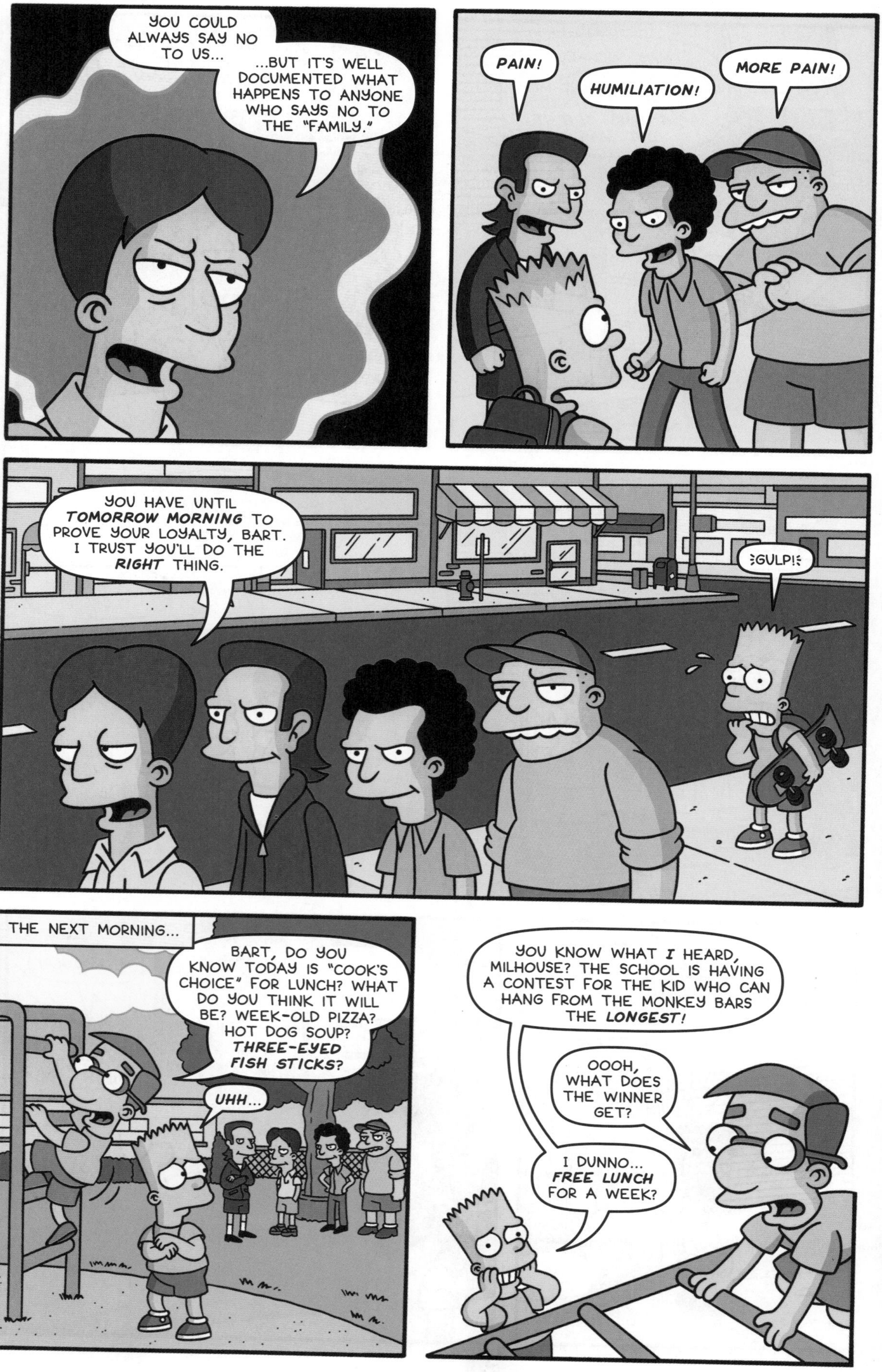
YOU COULD ALWAYS SAY NO TO US...
...BUT IT'S WELL DOCUMENTED WHAT HAPPENS TO ANYONE WHO SAYS NO TO THE "FAMILY."
PAIN!
HUMILIATION!
MORE PAIN!
YOU HAVE UNTIL TOMORROW MORNING TO PROVE YOUR LOYALTY, BART. I TRUST YOU'LL DO THE RIGHT THING.
GULP!
THE NEXT MORNING...
BART, DO YOU KNOW TODAY IS "COOK'S CHOICE" FOR LUNCH? WHAT DO YOU THINK IT WILL BE? WEEK-OLD PIZZA? HOT DOG SOUP? THREE-EYED FISH STICKS?
UHH...
YOU KNOW WHAT I HEARD, MILHOUSE? THE SCHOOL IS HAVING A CONTEST FOR THE KID WHO CAN HANG FROM THE MONKEY BARS THE LONGEST!
OOOH, WHAT DOES THE WINNER GET?
I DUNNO... FREE LUNCH FOR A WEEK?

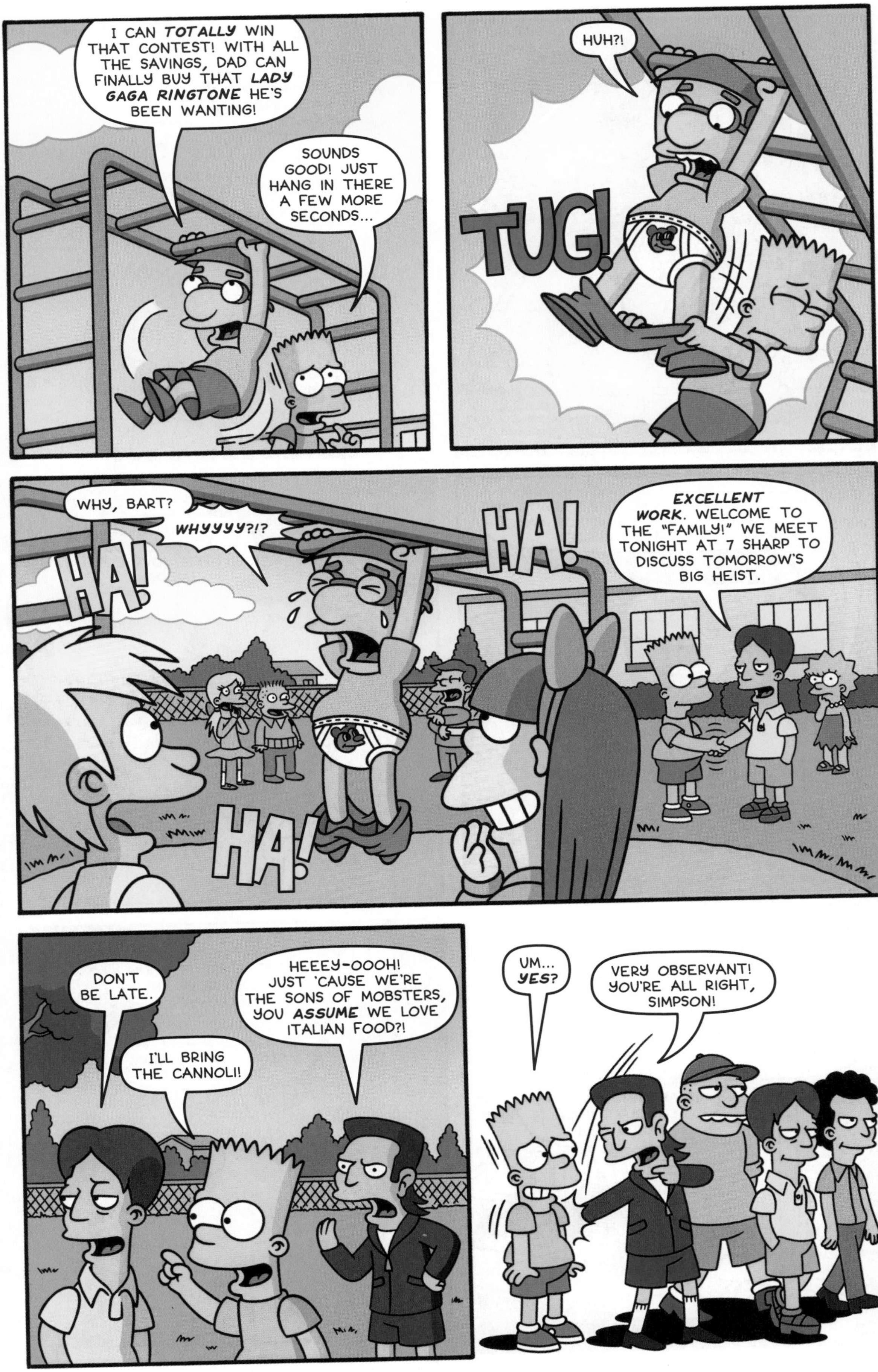
I CAN TOTALLY WIN THAT CONTEST! WITH ALL THE SAVINGS, DAD CAN FINALLY BUY THAT LADY GAGA RINGTONE HE'S BEEN WANTING!
SOUNDS GOOD! JUST HANG IN THERE A FEW MORE SECONDS...
HUH?!
TUG!
WHY, BART?
WHYYYY?!?
HA!
HA!
HA!
HA!
EXCELLENT WORK. WELCOME TO THE "FAMILY!" WE MEET TONIGHT AT 7 SHARP TO DISCUSS TOMORROW'S BIG HEIST.
DON'T BE LATE.
I'LL BRING THE CANNOLI!
HEEEY-OOOH! JUST 'CAUSE WE'RE THE SONS OF MOBSTERS, YOU ASSUME WE LOVE ITALIAN FOOD?!
UM... YES?
VERY OBSERVANT! YOU'RE ALL RIGHT, SIMPSON!

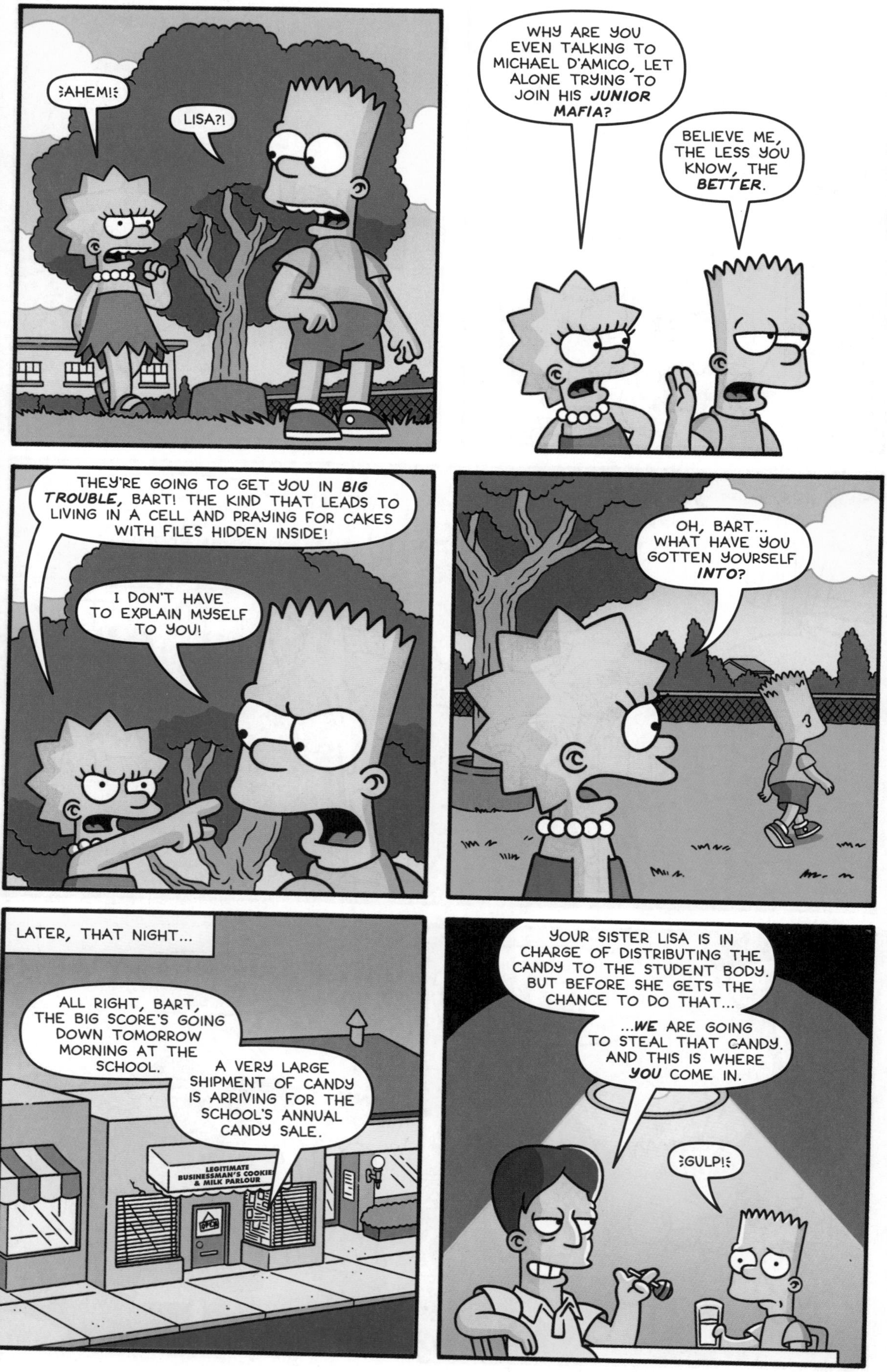

AHEM!
LISA?!
WHY ARE YOU EVEN TALKING TO MICHAEL D'AMICO, LET ALONE TRYING TO JOIN HIS *JUNIOR MAFIA*?
BELIEVE ME, THE LESS YOU KNOW, THE *BETTER*.
THEY'RE GOING TO GET YOU IN *BIG TROUBLE,* BART! THE KIND THAT LEADS TO LIVING IN A CELL AND PRAYING FOR CAKES WITH FILES HIDDEN INSIDE!
I DON'T HAVE TO EXPLAIN MYSELF TO YOU!
OH, BART... WHAT HAVE YOU GOTTEN YOURSELF *INTO*?
LATER, THAT NIGHT...
ALL RIGHT, BART, THE BIG SCORE'S GOING DOWN TOMORROW MORNING AT THE SCHOOL.
A VERY LARGE SHIPMENT OF CANDY IS ARRIVING FOR THE SCHOOL'S ANNUAL CANDY SALE.
LEGITIMATE BUSINESSMAN'S COOKIES & MILK PARLOUR
YOUR SISTER LISA IS IN CHARGE OF DISTRIBUTING THE CANDY TO THE STUDENT BODY. BUT BEFORE SHE GETS THE CHANCE TO DO THAT...
...*WE* ARE GOING TO STEAL THAT CANDY. AND THIS IS WHERE *YOU* COME IN.
GULP!

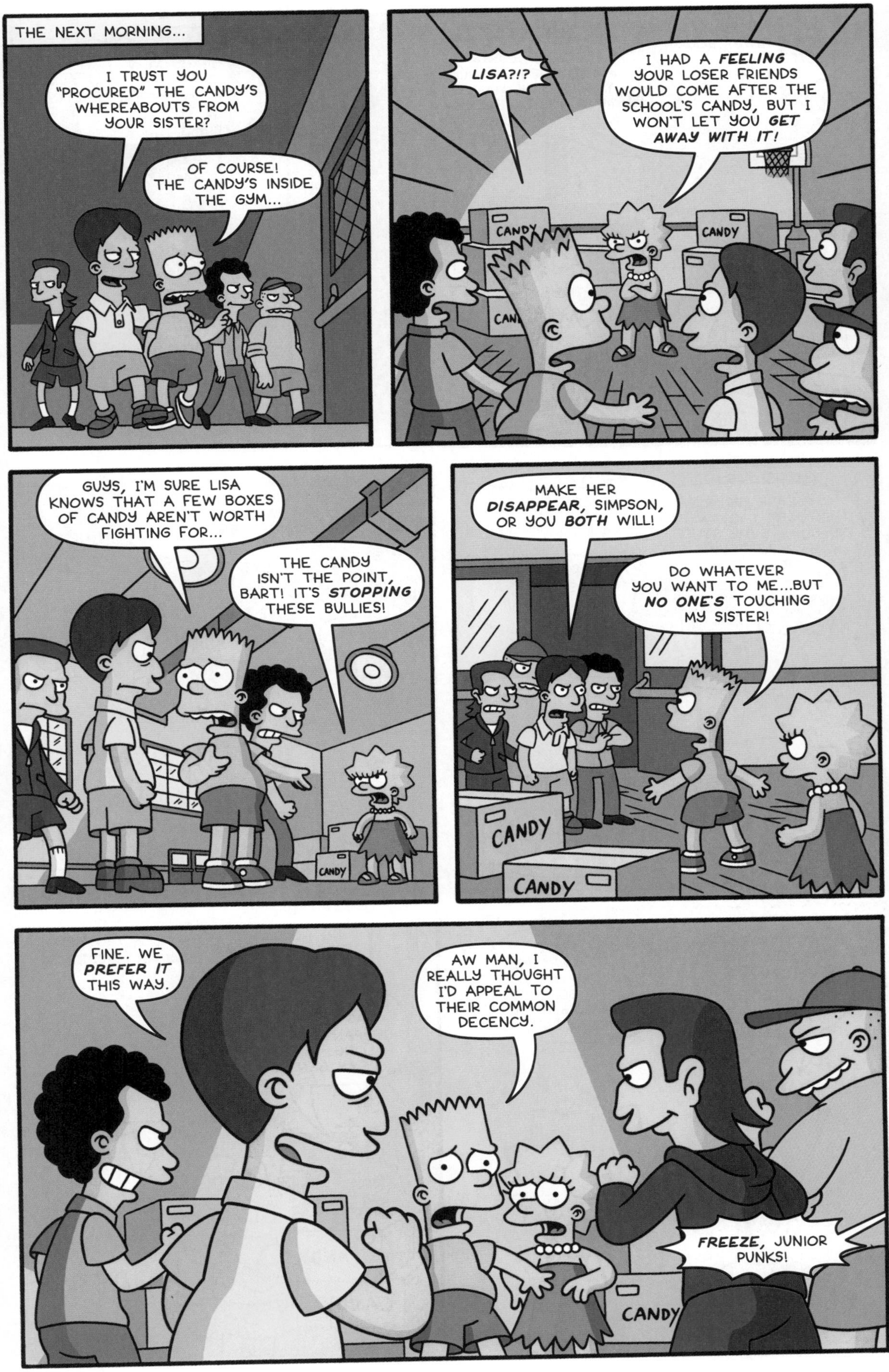
THE NEXT MORNING...
I TRUST YOU "PROCURED" THE CANDY'S WHEREABOUTS FROM YOUR SISTER?
OF COURSE! THE CANDY'S INSIDE THE GYM...
LISA?!?
I HAD A FEELING YOUR LOSER FRIENDS WOULD COME AFTER THE SCHOOL'S CANDY, BUT I WON'T LET YOU GET AWAY WITH IT!
CANDY
CANDY
GUYS, I'M SURE LISA KNOWS THAT A FEW BOXES OF CANDY AREN'T WORTH FIGHTING FOR...
THE CANDY ISN'T THE POINT, BART! IT'S STOPPING THESE BULLIES!
CANDY
MAKE HER DISAPPEAR, SIMPSON, OR YOU BOTH WILL!
DO WHATEVER YOU WANT TO ME...BUT NO ONE'S TOUCHING MY SISTER!
CANDY
CANDY
FINE. WE PREFER IT THIS WAY.
AW MAN, I REALLY THOUGHT I'D APPEAL TO THEIR COMMON DECENCY.
FREEZE, JUNIOR PUNKS!
CANDY

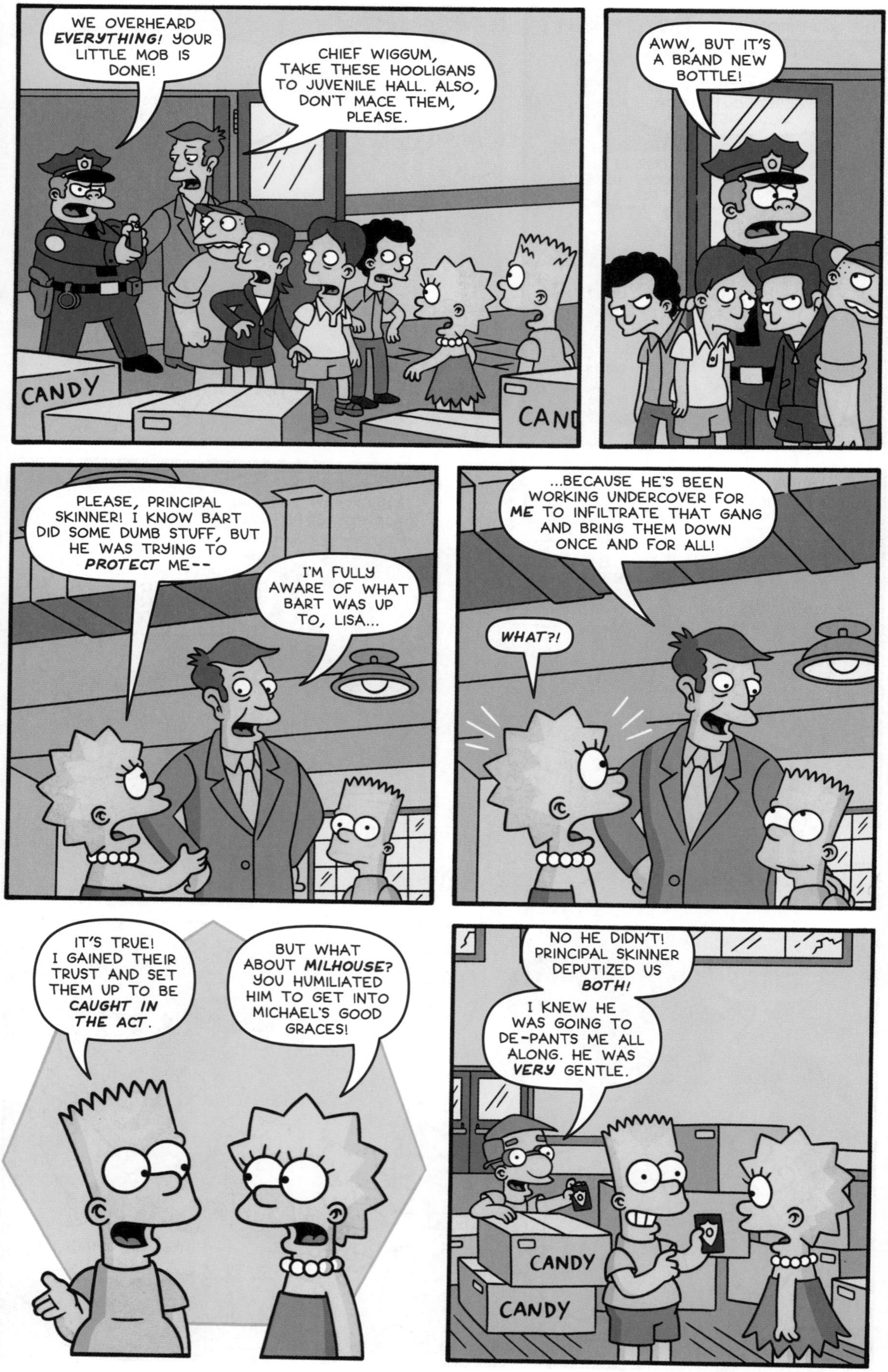
WE OVERHEARD EVERYTHING! YOUR LITTLE MOB IS DONE!
CHIEF WIGGUM, TAKE THESE HOOLIGANS TO JUVENILE HALL. ALSO, DON'T MACE THEM, PLEASE.
CANDY
CAND
AWW, BUT IT'S A BRAND NEW BOTTLE!
PLEASE, PRINCIPAL SKINNER! I KNOW BART DID SOME DUMB STUFF, BUT HE WAS TRYING TO PROTECT ME--
I'M FULLY AWARE OF WHAT BART WAS UP TO, LISA...
...BECAUSE HE'S BEEN WORKING UNDERCOVER FOR ME TO INFILTRATE THAT GANG AND BRING THEM DOWN ONCE AND FOR ALL!
WHAT?!
IT'S TRUE! I GAINED THEIR TRUST AND SET THEM UP TO BE CAUGHT IN THE ACT.
BUT WHAT ABOUT MILHOUSE? YOU HUMILIATED HIM TO GET INTO MICHAEL'S GOOD GRACES!
NO HE DIDN'T! PRINCIPAL SKINNER DEPUTIZED US BOTH!
I KNEW HE WAS GOING TO DE-PANTS ME ALL ALONG. HE WAS VERY GENTLE.
CANDY
CANDY

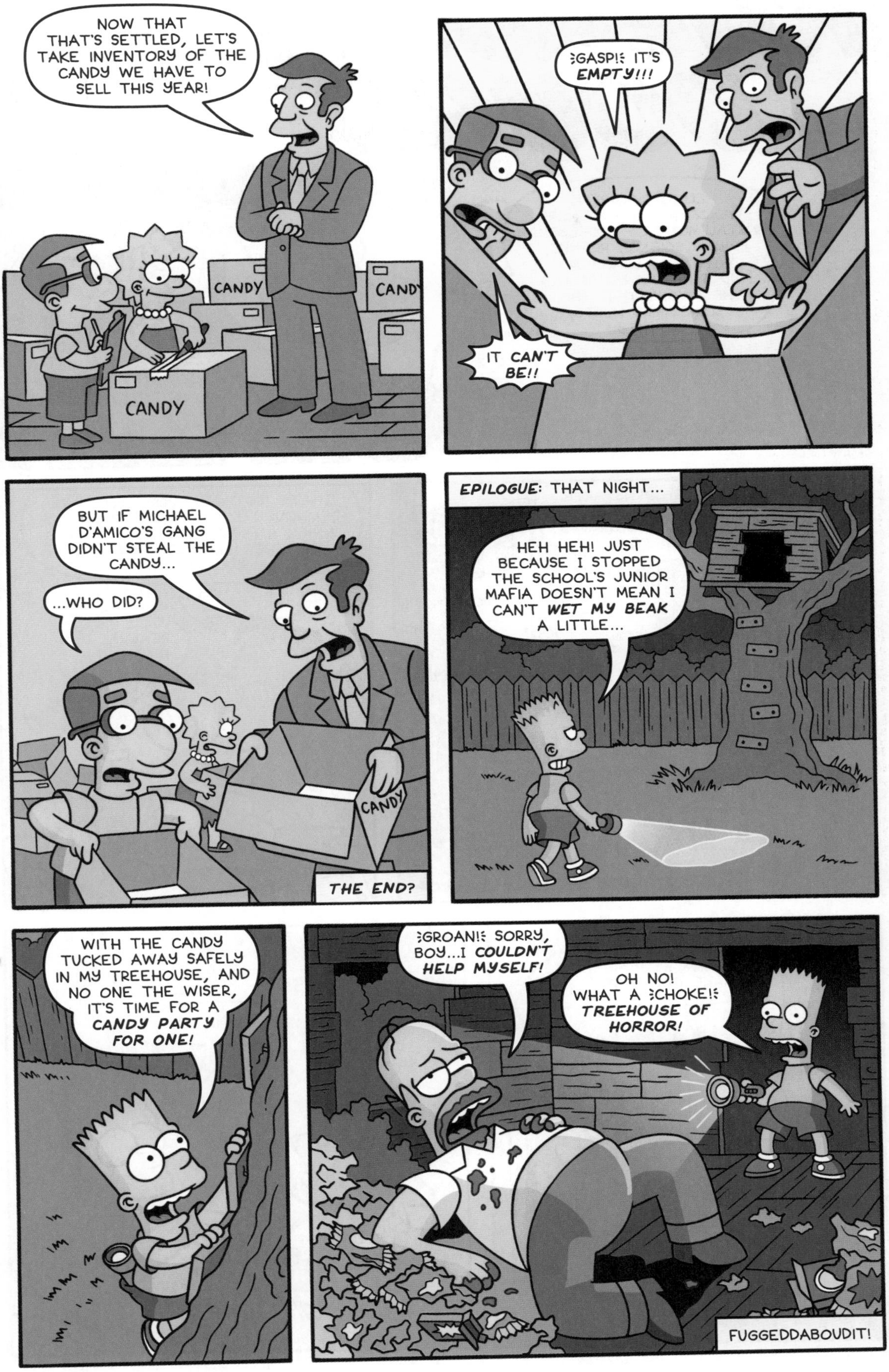

NOW THAT THAT'S SETTLED, LET'S TAKE INVENTORY OF THE CANDY WE HAVE TO SELL THIS YEAR!
CANDY
CANDY
CANDY
⁝GASP!⁝ IT'S EMPTY!!!
IT CAN'T BE!!
BUT IF MICHAEL D'AMICO'S GANG DIDN'T STEAL THE CANDY...
...WHO DID?
CANDY
THE END?
EPILOGUE: THAT NIGHT...
HEH HEH! JUST BECAUSE I STOPPED THE SCHOOL'S JUNIOR MAFIA DOESN'T MEAN I CAN'T WET MY BEAK A LITTLE...
WITH THE CANDY TUCKED AWAY SAFELY IN MY TREEHOUSE, AND NO ONE THE WISER, IT'S TIME FOR A CANDY PARTY FOR ONE!
⁝GROAN!⁝ SORRY, BOY...I COULDN'T HELP MYSELF!
OH NO! WHAT A ⁝CHOKE!⁝ TREEHOUSE OF HORROR!
FUGGEDDABOUDIT!

KNEADING DOUGH

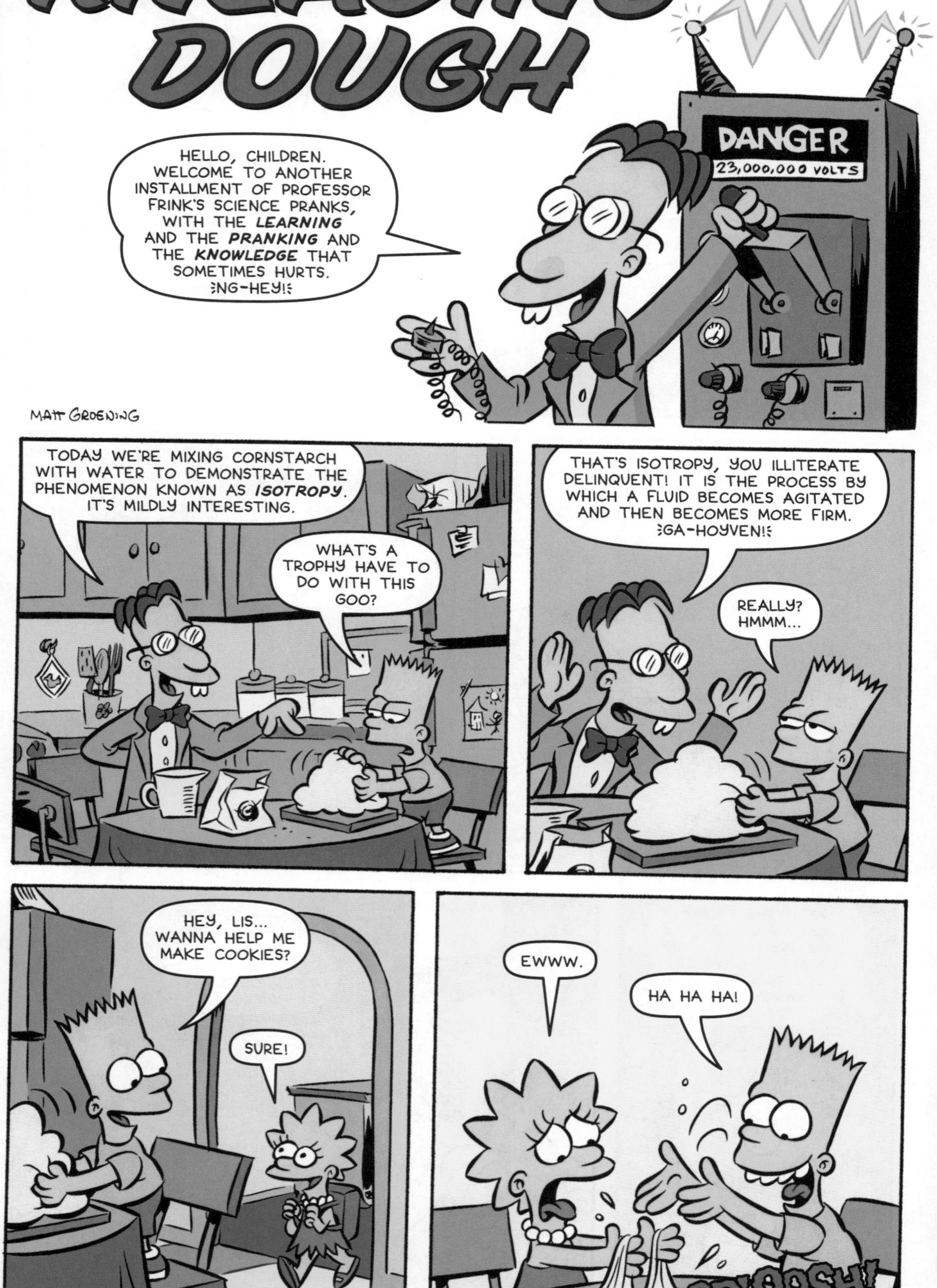
HELLO, CHILDREN. WELCOME TO ANOTHER INSTALLMENT OF PROFESSOR FRINK'S SCIENCE PRANKS, WITH THE LEARNING AND THE PRANKING AND THE KNOWLEDGE THAT SOMETIMES HURTS. NG-HEY!
DANGER
23,000,000 VOLTS
MATT GROENING
TODAY WE'RE MIXING CORNSTARCH WITH WATER TO DEMONSTRATE THE PHENOMENON KNOWN AS ISOTROPY. IT'S MILDLY INTERESTING.
WHAT'S A TROPHY HAVE TO DO WITH THIS GOO?
THAT'S ISOTROPY, YOU ILLITERATE DELINQUENT! IT IS THE PROCESS BY WHICH A FLUID BECOMES AGITATED AND THEN BECOMES MORE FIRM. GA-HOYVEN!
REALLY? HMMM...
HEY, LIS... WANNA HELP ME MAKE COOKIES?
SURE!
EWWW.
HA HA HA!
SPLOOSH!

TONY DIGEROLAMO SCRIPT

MIKE KAZALEH PENCILS & INKS

NATHAN HAMILL COLORS

KAREN BATES LETTERS

NATHAN KANE EDITOR

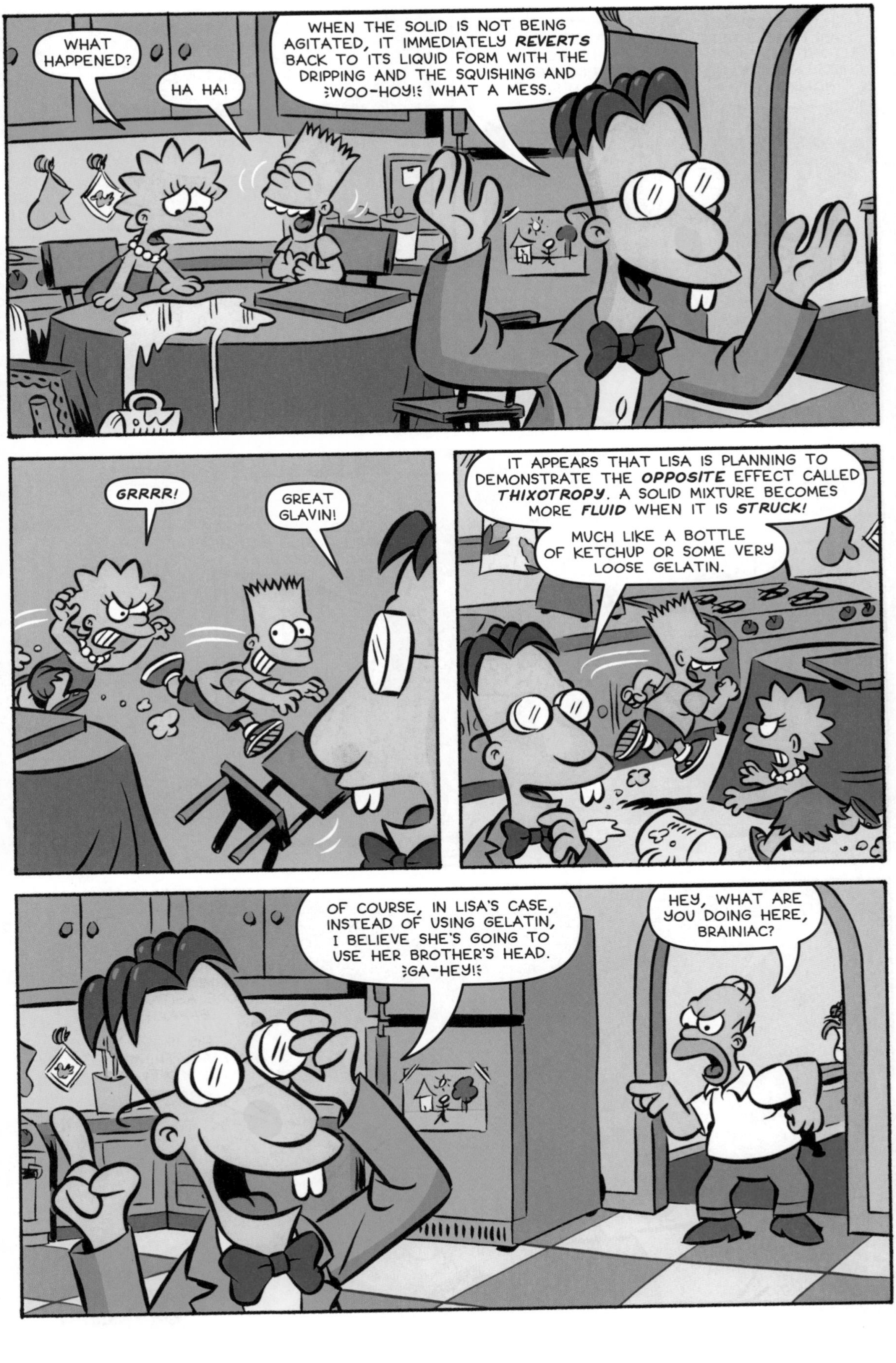
WHAT HAPPENED?
HA HA!
WHEN THE SOLID IS NOT BEING AGITATED, IT IMMEDIATELY ***REVERTS*** BACK TO ITS LIQUID FORM WITH THE DRIPPING AND THE SQUISHING AND ⁝WOO-HOY!⁝ WHAT A MESS.
GRRRR!
GREAT GLAVIN!
IT APPEARS THAT LISA IS PLANNING TO DEMONSTRATE THE ***OPPOSITE*** EFFECT CALLED ***THIXOTROPY***. A SOLID MIXTURE BECOMES MORE ***FLUID*** WHEN IT IS ***STRUCK!***
MUCH LIKE A BOTTLE OF KETCHUP OR SOME VERY LOOSE GELATIN.
OF COURSE, IN LISA'S CASE, INSTEAD OF USING GELATIN, I BELIEVE SHE'S GOING TO USE HER BROTHER'S HEAD. ⁝GA-HEY!⁝
HEY, WHAT ARE YOU DOING HERE, BRAINIAC?

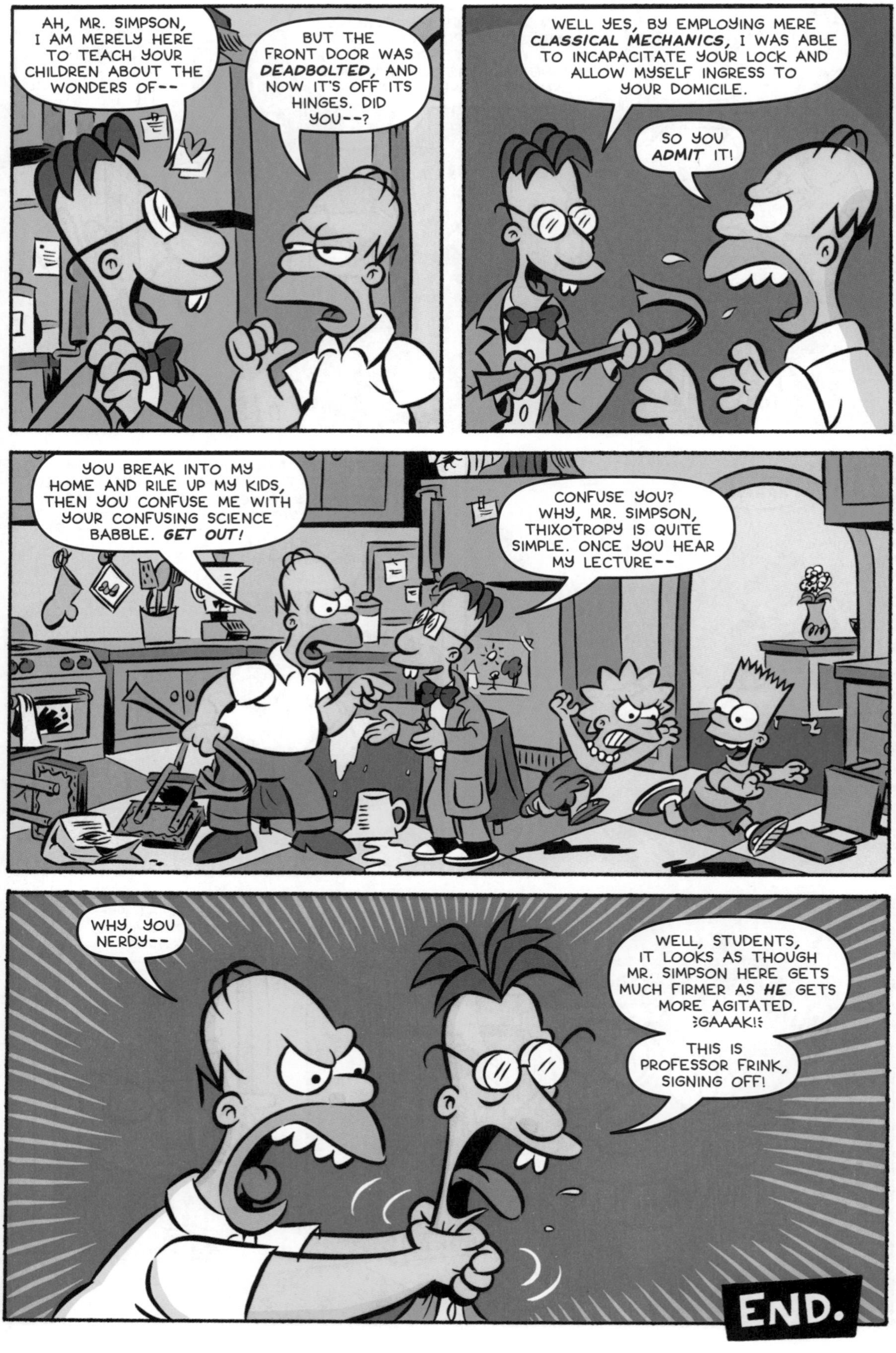
AH, MR. SIMPSON, I AM MERELY HERE TO TEACH YOUR CHILDREN ABOUT THE WONDERS OF--
BUT THE FRONT DOOR WAS DEADBOLTED, AND NOW IT'S OFF ITS HINGES. DID YOU--?
WELL YES, BY EMPLOYING MERE CLASSICAL MECHANICS, I WAS ABLE TO INCAPACITATE YOUR LOCK AND ALLOW MYSELF INGRESS TO YOUR DOMICILE.
SO YOU ADMIT IT!
YOU BREAK INTO MY HOME AND RILE UP MY KIDS, THEN YOU CONFUSE ME WITH YOUR CONFUSING SCIENCE BABBLE. GET OUT!
CONFUSE YOU? WHY, MR. SIMPSON, THIXOTROPY IS QUITE SIMPLE. ONCE YOU HEAR MY LECTURE--
WHY, YOU NERDY--
WELL, STUDENTS, IT LOOKS AS THOUGH MR. SIMPSON HERE GETS MUCH FIRMER AS HE GETS MORE AGITATED. GAAAK!
THIS IS PROFESSOR FRINK, SIGNING OFF!
END.

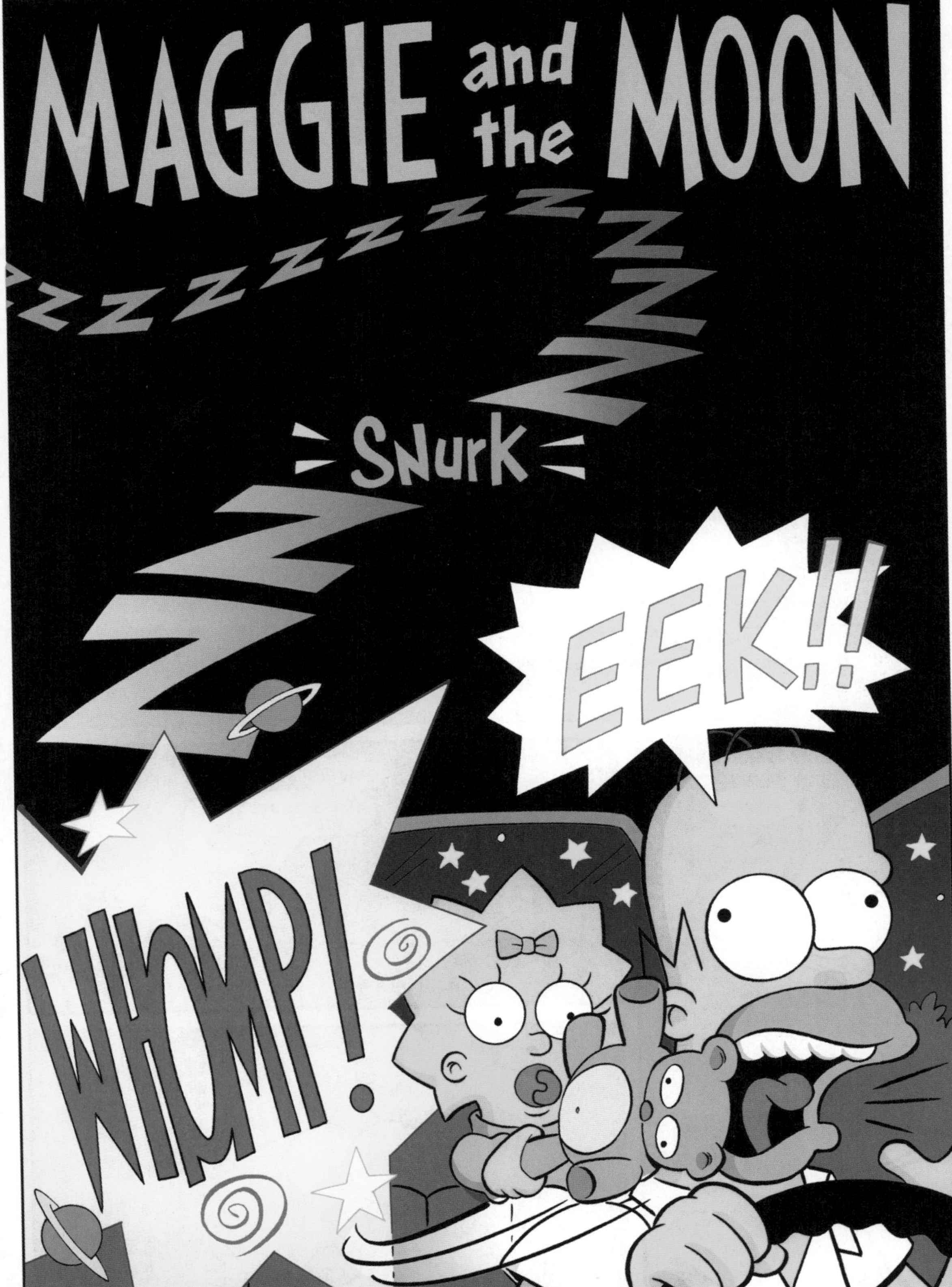
MAGGIE and the MOON
ZZZZZZZZZZZZZZ
SNURK
ZZZ
EEK!!
WHOMP!
MATT GROENING

CAROL LAY
SCRIPT & ART

NATHAN HAMILL
COLORS

KAREN BATES
LETTERS

NATHAN KANE
EDITOR

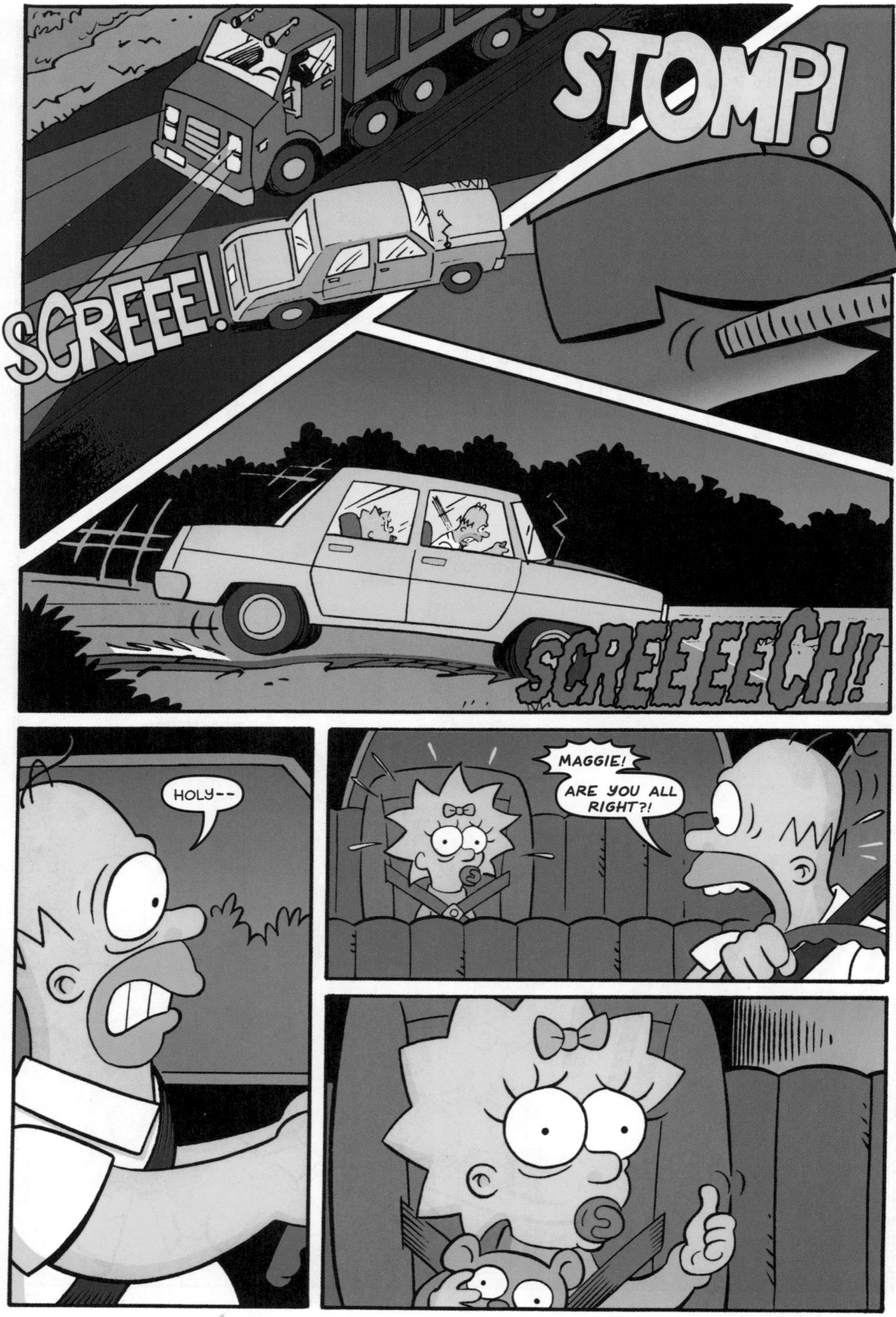
STOMP!
SCREEE!
SCREEEEECH!
HOLY--
MAGGIE!
ARE YOU ALL RIGHT?!

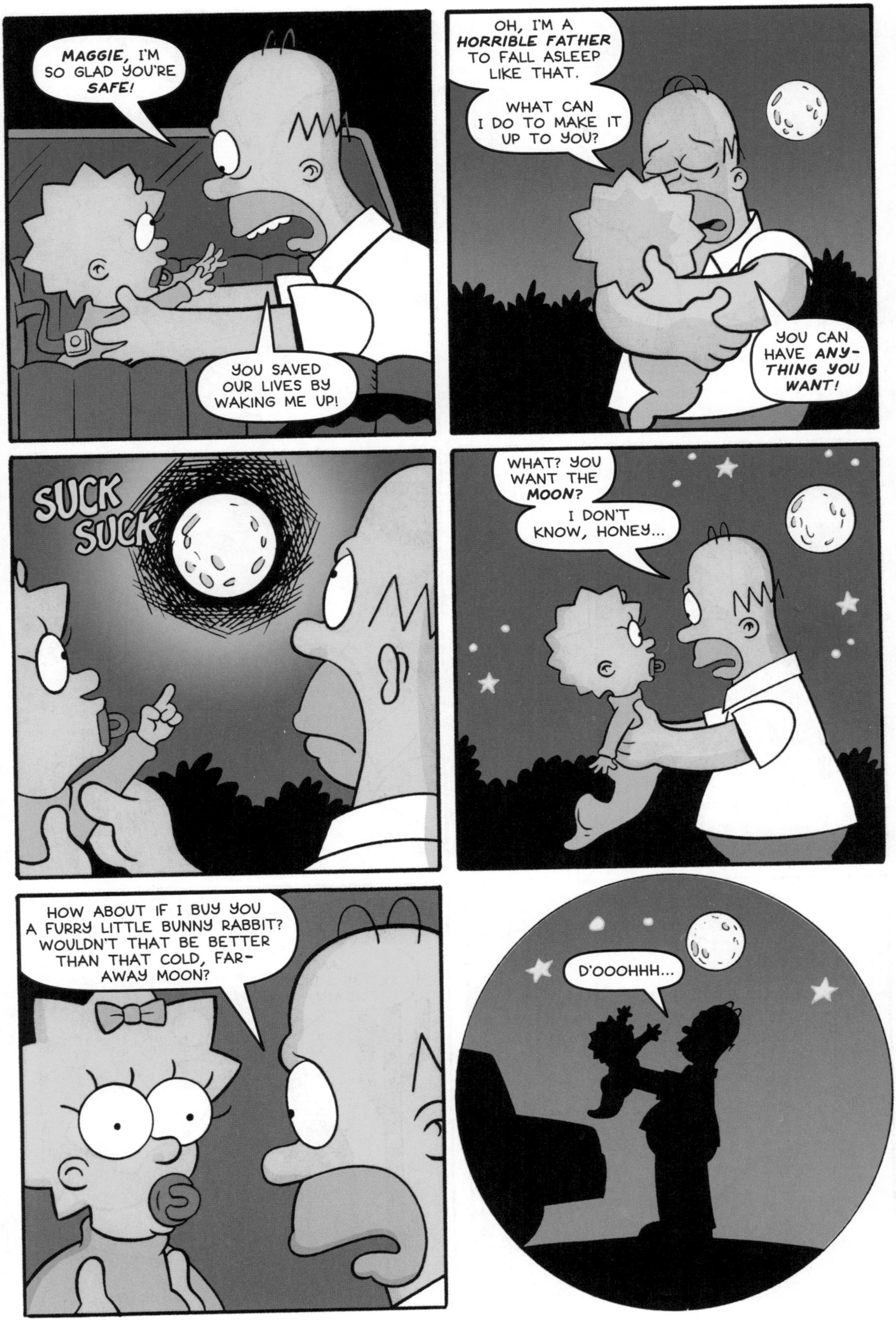
MAGGIE, I'M SO GLAD YOU'RE SAFE!
YOU SAVED OUR LIVES BY WAKING ME UP!
OH, I'M A HORRIBLE FATHER TO FALL ASLEEP LIKE THAT.
WHAT CAN I DO TO MAKE IT UP TO YOU?
YOU CAN HAVE ANY-THING YOU WANT!
SUCK SUCK
WHAT? YOU WANT THE MOON?
I DON'T KNOW, HONEY...
HOW ABOUT IF I BUY YOU A FURRY LITTLE BUNNY RABBIT? WOULDN'T THAT BE BETTER THAN THAT COLD, FAR-AWAY MOON?
D'OOOHHH...

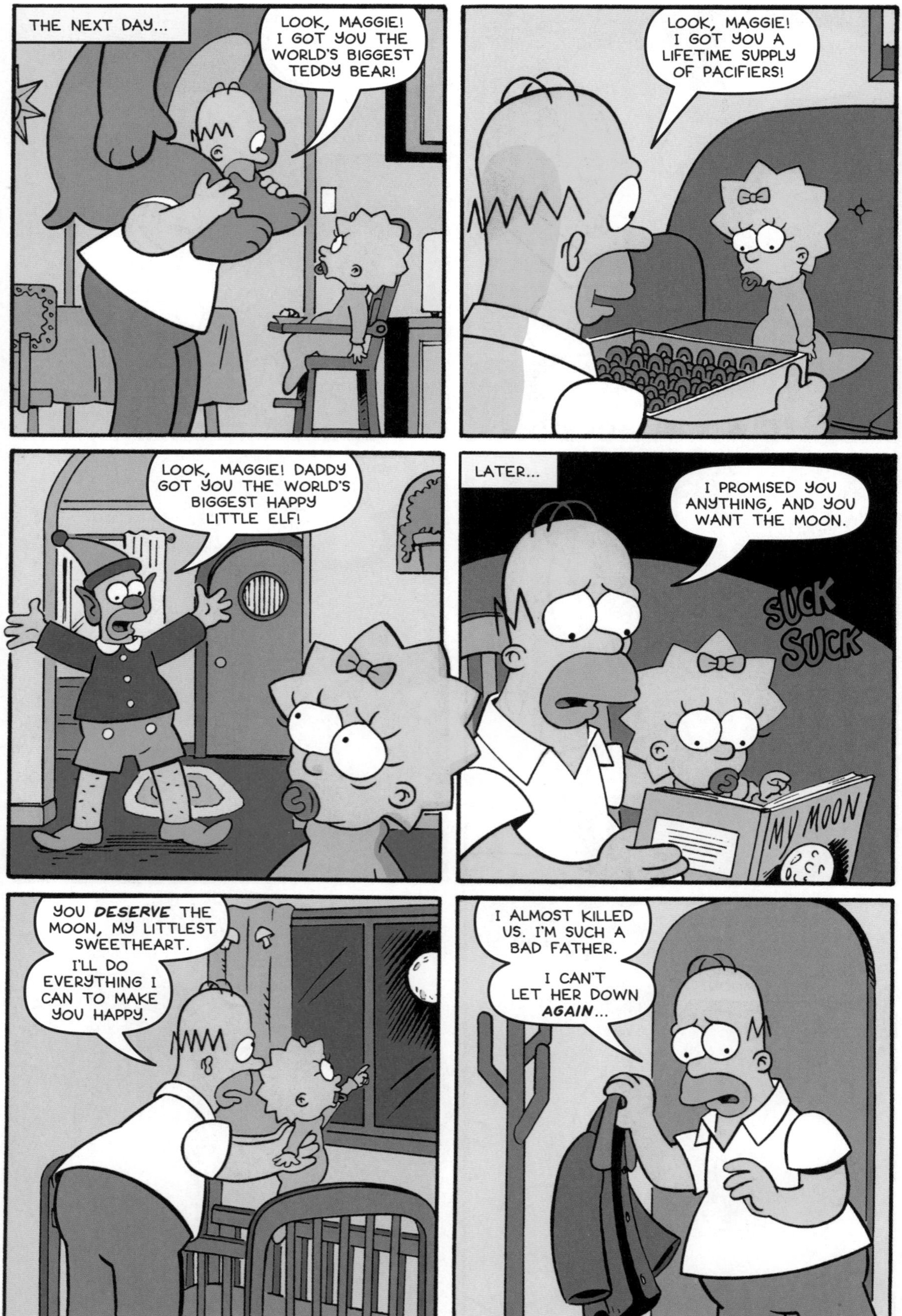
THE NEXT DAY...
LOOK, MAGGIE! I GOT YOU THE WORLD'S BIGGEST TEDDY BEAR!
LOOK, MAGGIE! I GOT YOU A LIFETIME SUPPLY OF PACIFIERS!
LOOK, MAGGIE! DADDY GOT YOU THE WORLD'S BIGGEST HAPPY LITTLE ELF!
LATER...
I PROMISED YOU ANYTHING, AND YOU WANT THE MOON.
SUCK SUCK
MY MOON
YOU DESERVE THE MOON, MY LITTLEST SWEETHEART.
I'LL DO EVERYTHING I CAN TO MAKE YOU HAPPY.
I ALMOST KILLED US. I'M SUCH A BAD FATHER.
I CAN'T LET HER DOWN AGAIN...

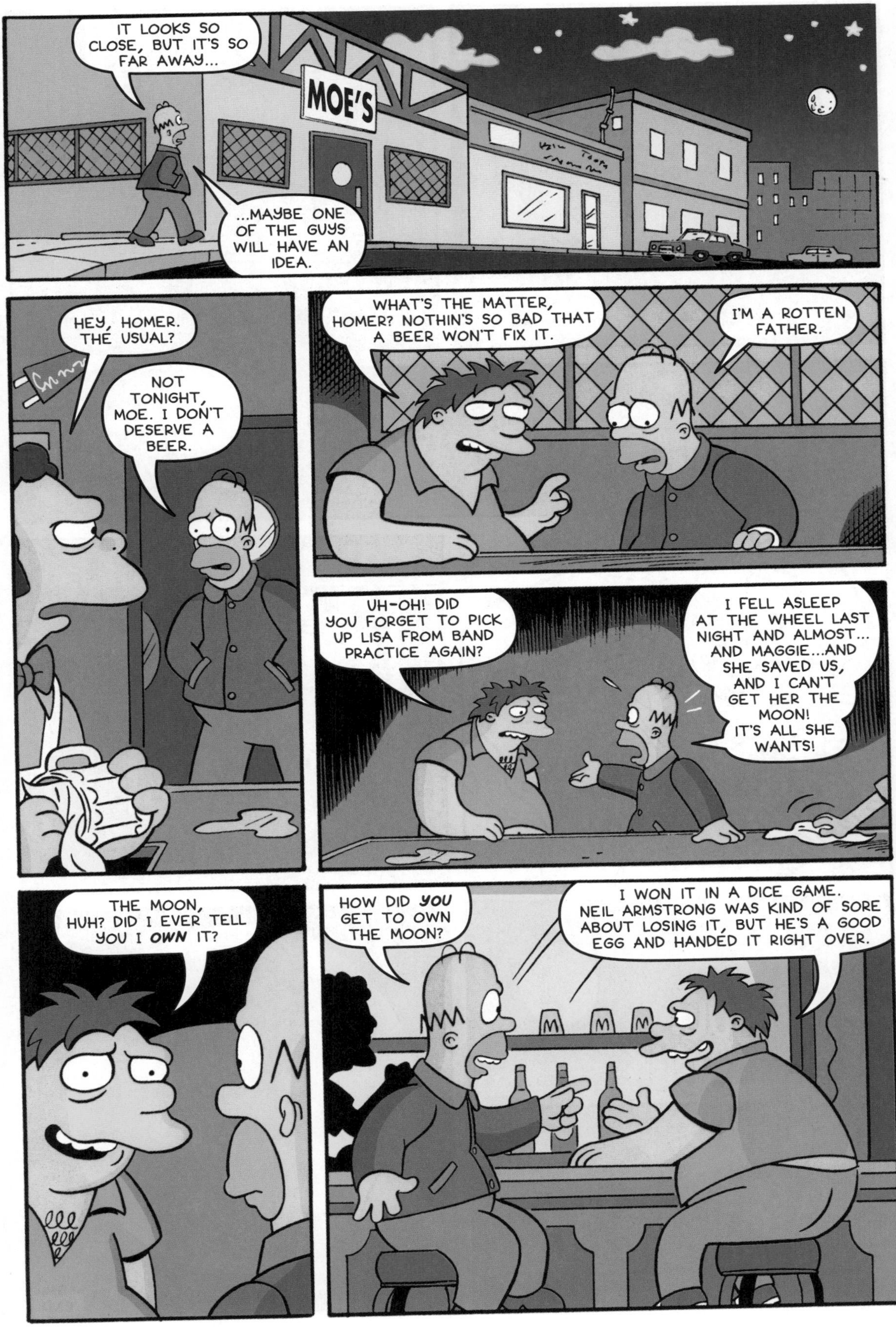
MOE'S
IT LOOKS SO CLOSE, BUT IT'S SO FAR AWAY...
...MAYBE ONE OF THE GUYS WILL HAVE AN IDEA.
HEY, HOMER. THE USUAL?
NOT TONIGHT, MOE. I DON'T DESERVE A BEER.
WHAT'S THE MATTER, HOMER? NOTHIN'S SO BAD THAT A BEER WON'T FIX IT.
I'M A ROTTEN FATHER.
UH-OH! DID YOU FORGET TO PICK UP LISA FROM BAND PRACTICE AGAIN?
I FELL ASLEEP AT THE WHEEL LAST NIGHT AND ALMOST... AND MAGGIE...AND SHE SAVED US, AND I CAN'T GET HER THE MOON! IT'S ALL SHE WANTS!
THE MOON, HUH? DID I EVER TELL YOU I ***OWN*** IT?
HOW DID ***YOU*** GET TO OWN THE MOON?
I WON IT IN A DICE GAME. NEIL ARMSTRONG WAS KIND OF SORE ABOUT LOSING IT, BUT HE'S A GOOD EGG AND HANDED IT RIGHT OVER.

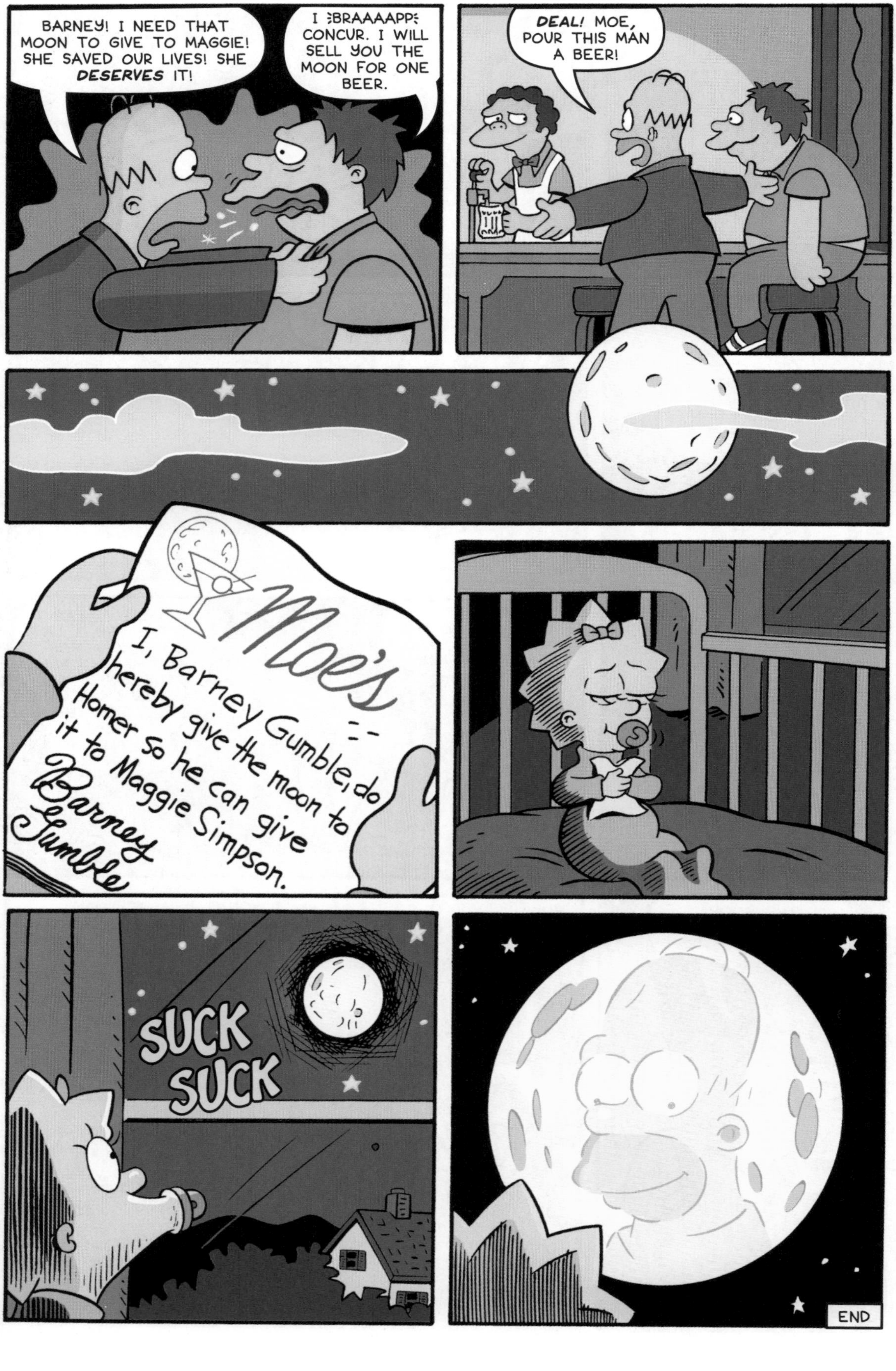

BARNEY! I NEED THAT MOON TO GIVE TO MAGGIE! SHE SAVED OUR LIVES! SHE DESERVES IT!
I BRAAAAPP CONCUR. I WILL SELL YOU THE MOON FOR ONE BEER.
DEAL! MOE, POUR THIS MAN A BEER!
Moe's
I, Barney Gumble, do hereby give the moon to Homer so he can give it to Maggie Simpson.
Barney Gumble
SUCK
SUCK
END

LISA'S LAUGHATORY

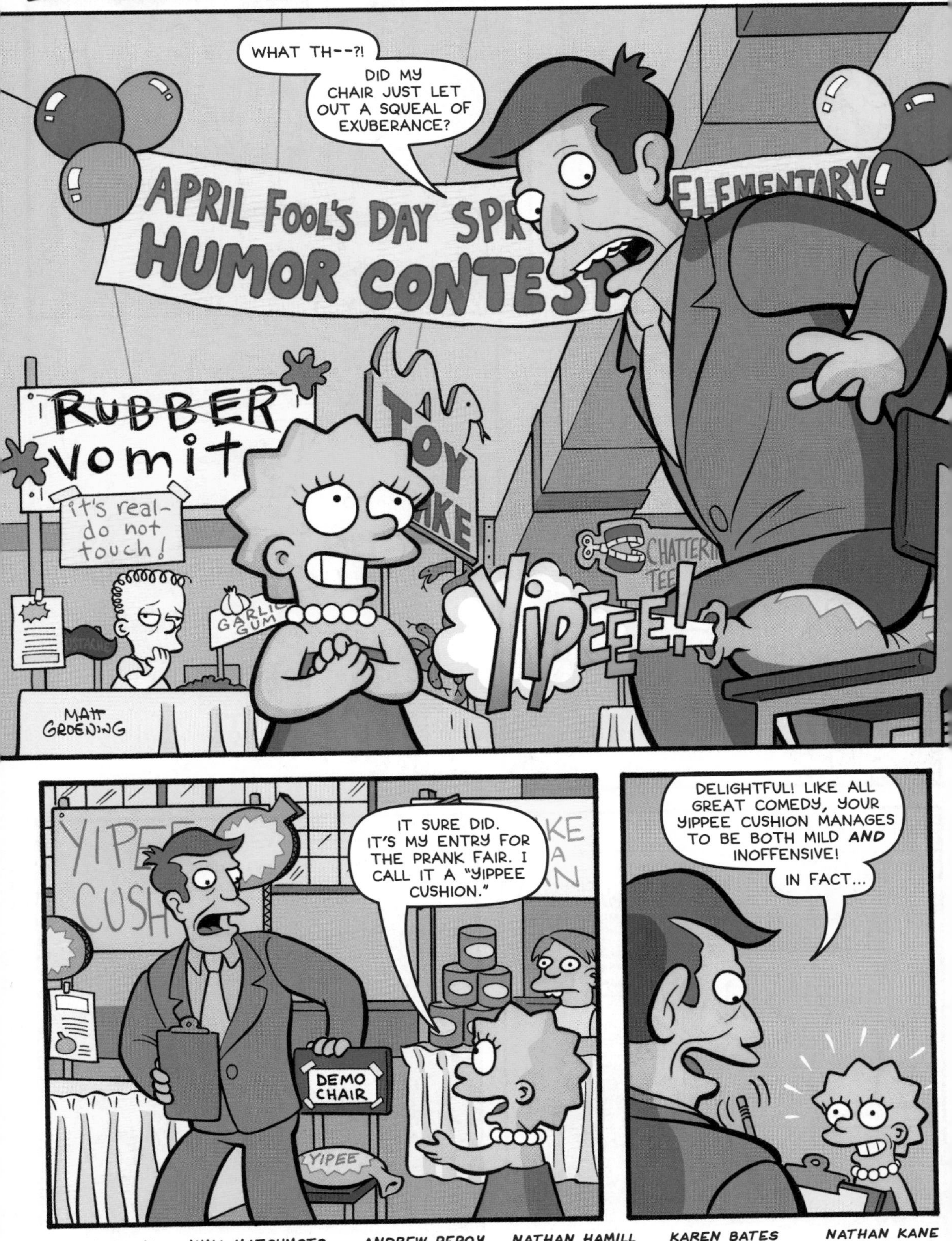
WHAT TH--?!
DID MY CHAIR JUST LET OUT A SQUEAL OF EXUBERANCE?
APRIL FOOL'S DAY SPR
ELEMENTARY!
HUMOR CONTEST
RUBBER
vomit
it's real- do not touch!
YIPEEE!
MATT GROENING
IT SURE DID. IT'S MY ENTRY FOR THE PRANK FAIR. I CALL IT A "YIPPEE CUSHION."
DEMO CHAIR
YIPEE
DELIGHTFUL! LIKE ALL GREAT COMEDY, YOUR YIPPEE CUSHION MANAGES TO BE BOTH MILD **AND** INOFFENSIVE!
IN FACT...

ARIE KAPLAN SCRIPT · ***NINA MATSUMOTO*** PENCILS · ***ANDREW PEPOY*** INKS · ***NATHAN HAMILL*** COLORS · ***KAREN BATES*** LETTERS · ***NATHAN KANE*** EDITOR

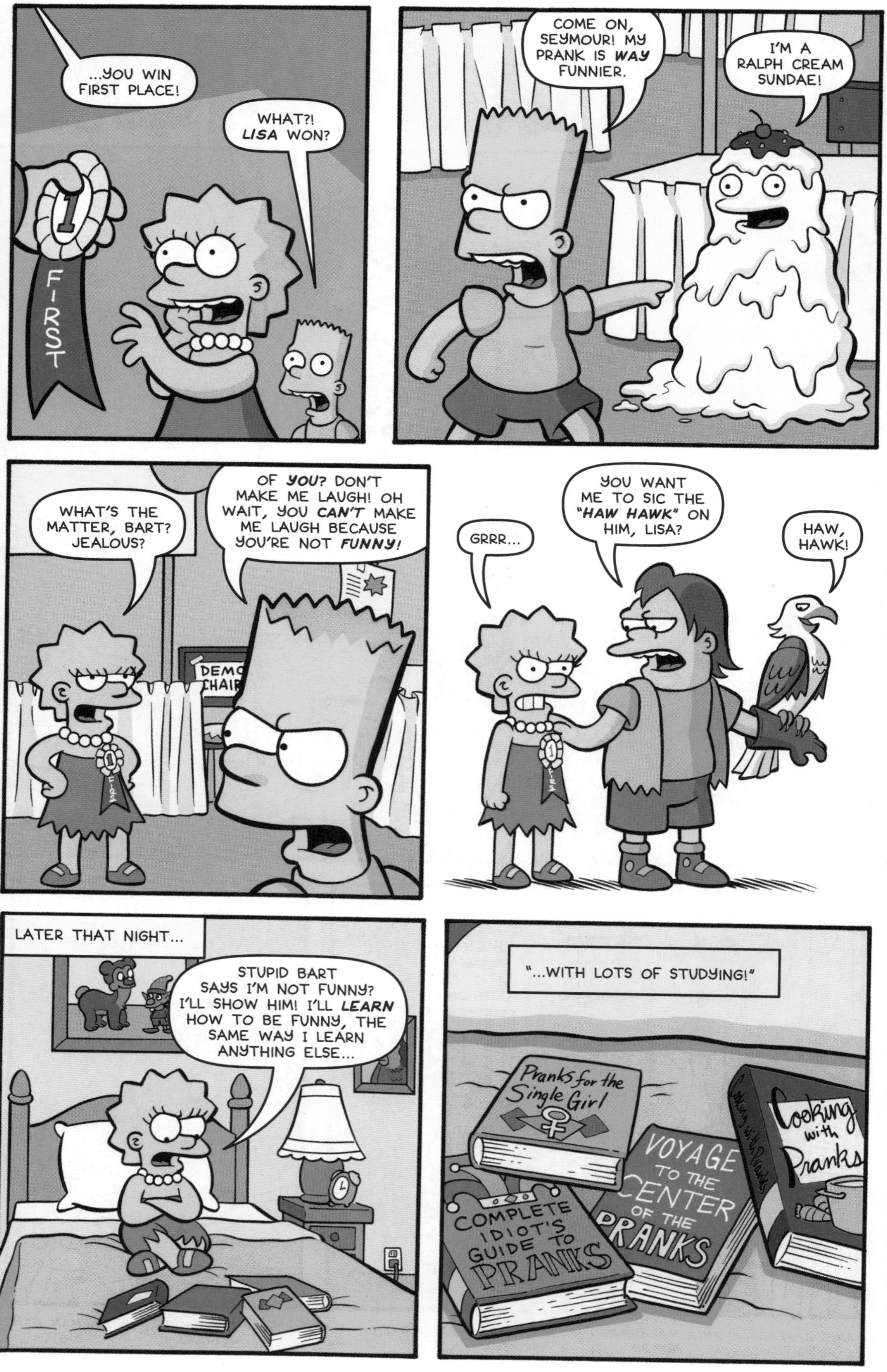

...YOU WIN FIRST PLACE!
FIRST
WHAT?! LISA WON?
COME ON, SEYMOUR! MY PRANK IS WAY FUNNIER.
I'M A RALPH CREAM SUNDAE!
WHAT'S THE MATTER, BART? JEALOUS?
OF YOU? DON'T MAKE ME LAUGH! OH WAIT, YOU CAN'T MAKE ME LAUGH BECAUSE YOU'RE NOT FUNNY!
GRRR...
YOU WANT ME TO SIC THE "HAW HAWK" ON HIM, LISA?
HAW, HAWK!
LATER THAT NIGHT...
STUPID BART SAYS I'M NOT FUNNY? I'LL SHOW HIM! I'LL LEARN HOW TO BE FUNNY, THE SAME WAY I LEARN ANYTHING ELSE...
"...WITH LOTS OF STUDYING!"
Pranks for the Single Girl
VOYAGE TO THE CENTER OF THE PRANKS
Cooking with Pranks
COMPLETE IDIOT'S GUIDE TO PRANKS

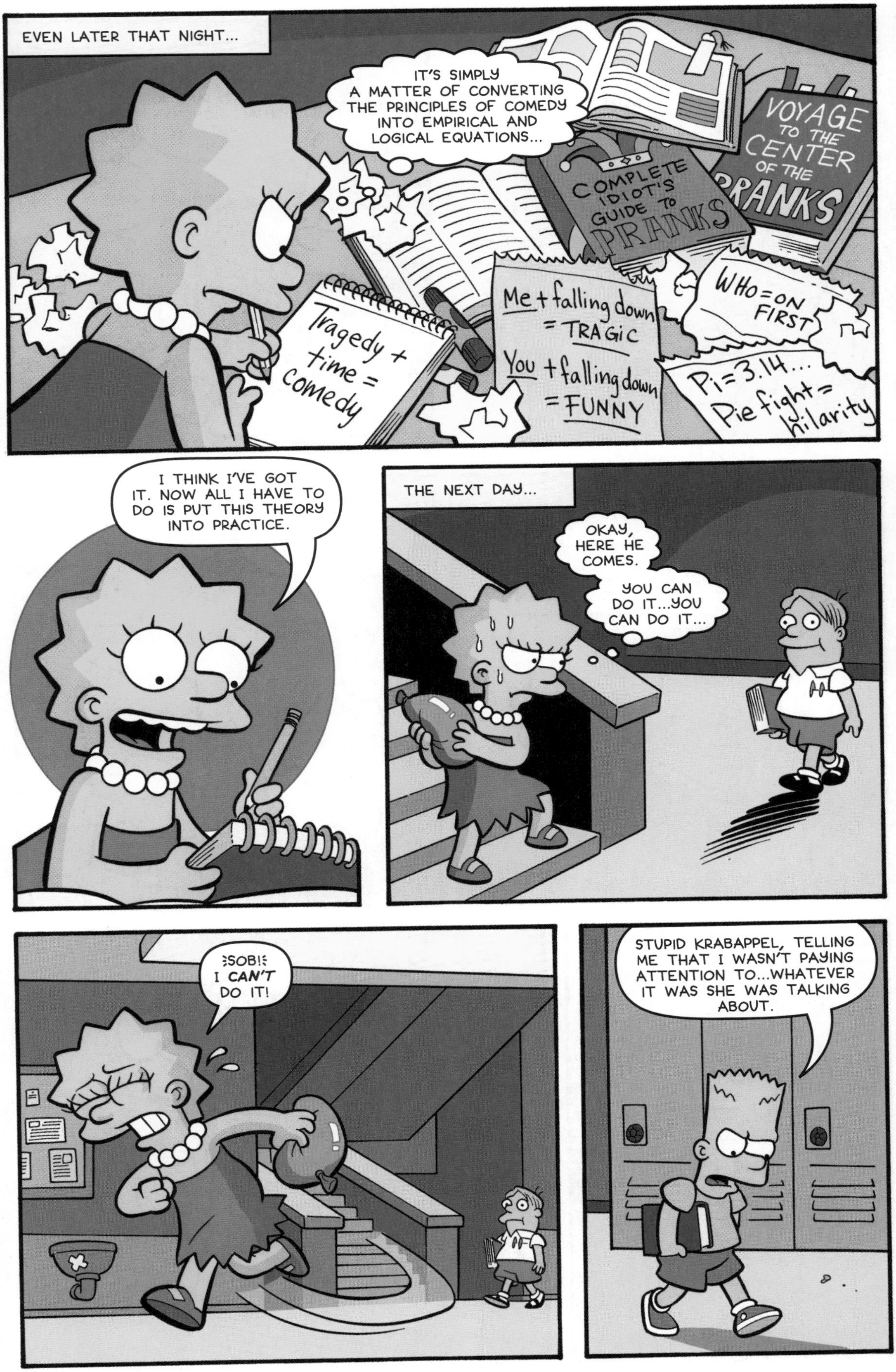
EVEN LATER THAT NIGHT...
IT'S SIMPLY A MATTER OF CONVERTING THE PRINCIPLES OF COMEDY INTO EMPIRICAL AND LOGICAL EQUATIONS...
VOYAGE TO THE CENTER OF THE PRANKS
COMPLETE IDIOT'S GUIDE TO PRANKS
Tragedy + time = comedy
Me + falling down = TRAGIC
You + falling down = FUNNY
WHO = ON FIRST
Pi = 3.14... Pie fight = hilarity
I THINK I'VE GOT IT. NOW ALL I HAVE TO DO IS PUT THIS THEORY INTO PRACTICE.
THE NEXT DAY...
OKAY, HERE HE COMES.
YOU CAN DO IT...YOU CAN DO IT...
SOB! I CAN'T DO IT!
STUPID KRABAPPEL, TELLING ME THAT I WASN'T PAYING ATTENTION TO...WHATEVER IT WAS SHE WAS TALKING ABOUT.

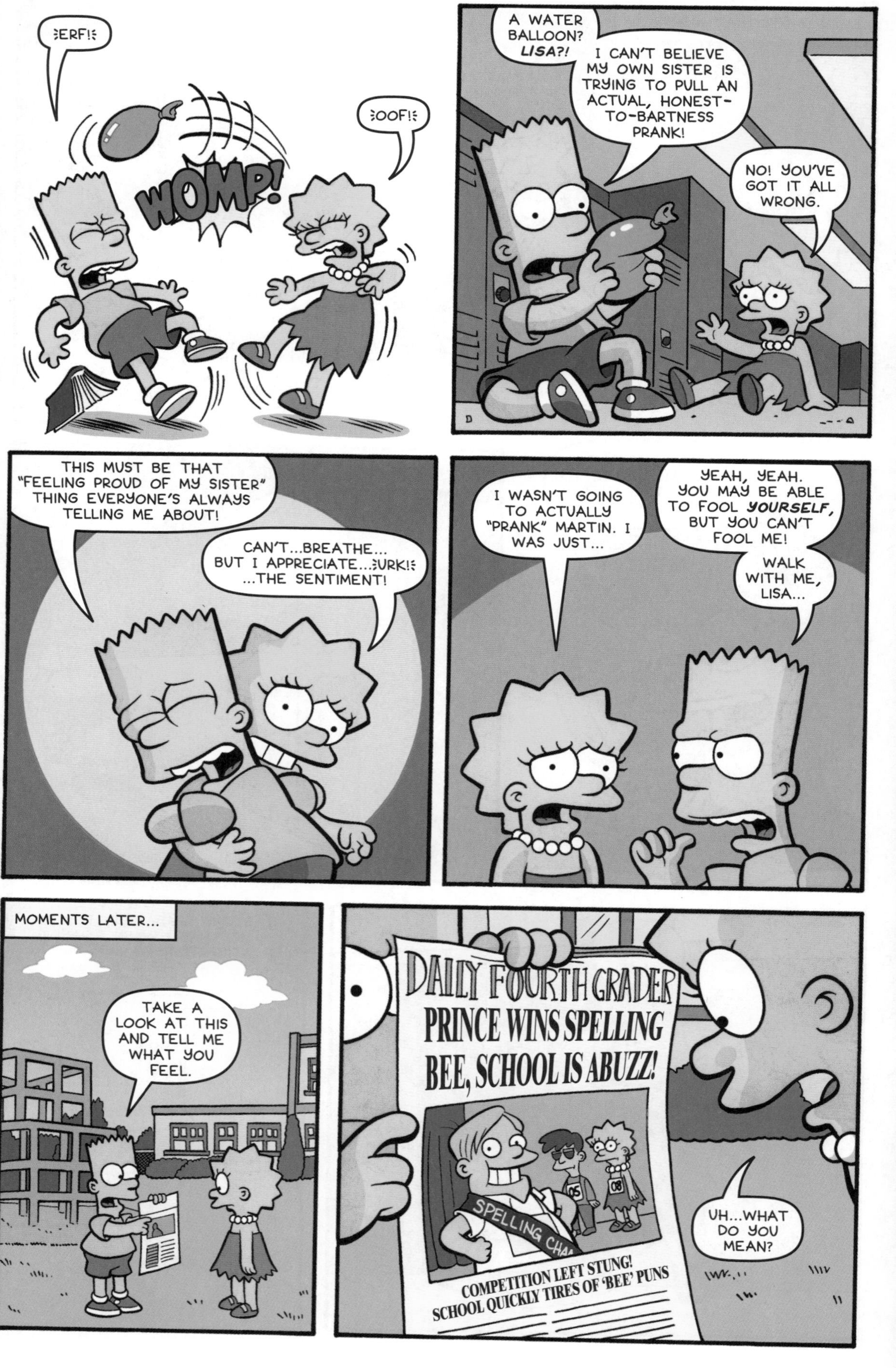
ERF!
WOMP!
OOF!
A WATER BALLOON? LISA?!
I CAN'T BELIEVE MY OWN SISTER IS TRYING TO PULL AN ACTUAL, HONEST-TO-BARTNESS PRANK!
NO! YOU'VE GOT IT ALL WRONG.
THIS MUST BE THAT "FEELING PROUD OF MY SISTER" THING EVERYONE'S ALWAYS TELLING ME ABOUT!
CAN'T...BREATHE... BUT I APPRECIATE...URK! ...THE SENTIMENT!
I WASN'T GOING TO ACTUALLY "PRANK" MARTIN. I WAS JUST...
YEAH, YEAH. YOU MAY BE ABLE TO FOOL YOURSELF, BUT YOU CAN'T FOOL ME!
WALK WITH ME, LISA...
MOMENTS LATER...
TAKE A LOOK AT THIS AND TELL ME WHAT YOU FEEL.
DAILY FOURTH GRADER
PRINCE WINS SPELLING BEE, SCHOOL IS ABUZZ!
SPELLING CHA
05
08
COMPETITION LEFT STUNG!
SCHOOL QUICKLY TIRES OF 'BEE' PUNS
UH...WHAT DO YOU MEAN?

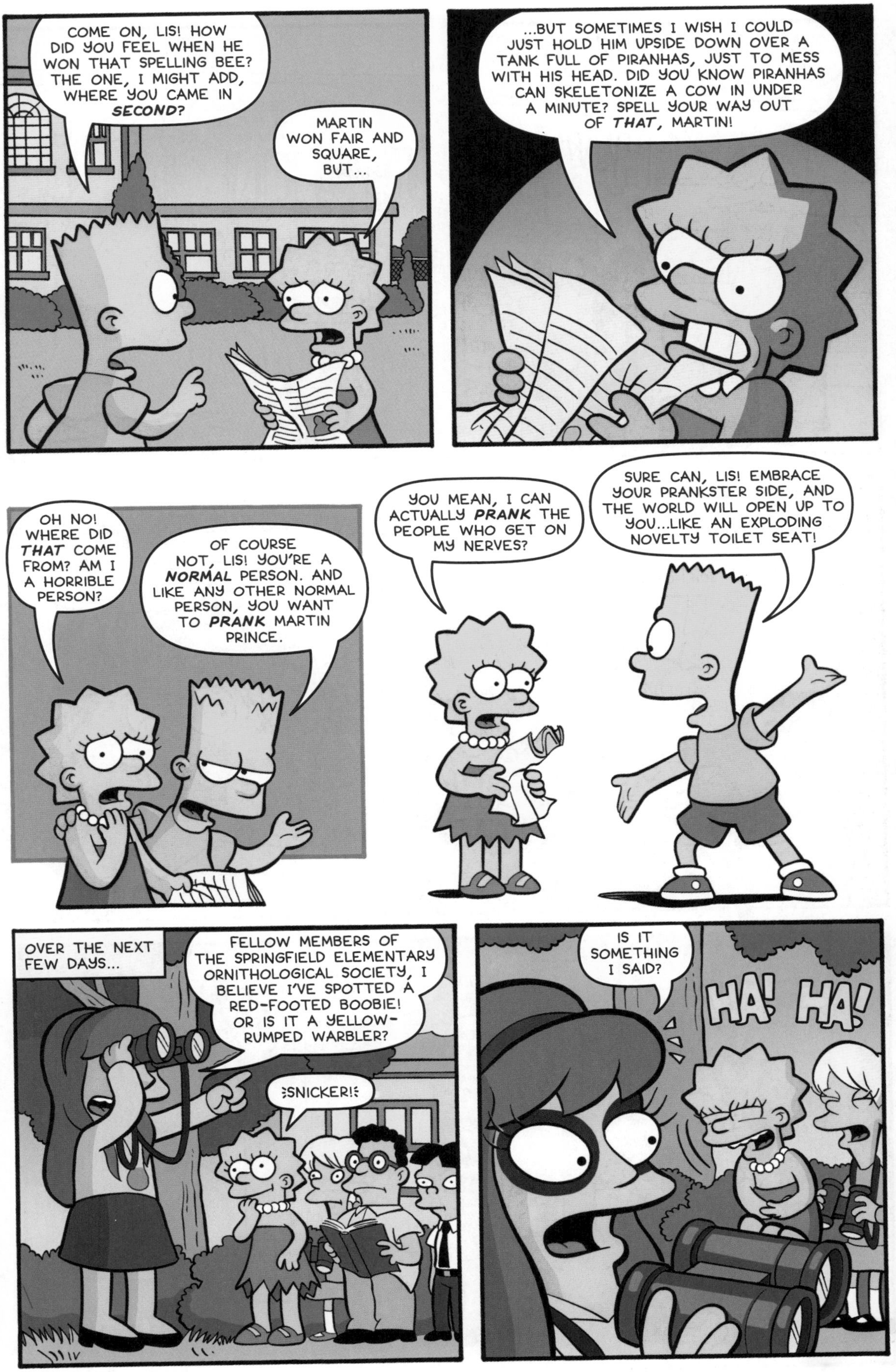
COME ON, LIS! HOW DID YOU FEEL WHEN HE WON THAT SPELLING BEE? THE ONE, I MIGHT ADD, WHERE YOU CAME IN *SECOND*?
MARTIN WON FAIR AND SQUARE, BUT...
...BUT SOMETIMES I WISH I COULD JUST HOLD HIM UPSIDE DOWN OVER A TANK FULL OF PIRANHAS, JUST TO MESS WITH HIS HEAD. DID YOU KNOW PIRANHAS CAN SKELETONIZE A COW IN UNDER A MINUTE? SPELL YOUR WAY OUT OF *THAT*, MARTIN!
OH NO! WHERE DID *THAT* COME FROM? AM I A HORRIBLE PERSON?
OF COURSE NOT, LIS! YOU'RE A *NORMAL* PERSON. AND LIKE ANY OTHER NORMAL PERSON, YOU WANT TO *PRANK* MARTIN PRINCE.
YOU MEAN, I CAN ACTUALLY *PRANK* THE PEOPLE WHO GET ON MY NERVES?
SURE CAN, LIS! EMBRACE YOUR PRANKSTER SIDE, AND THE WORLD WILL OPEN UP TO YOU...LIKE AN EXPLODING NOVELTY TOILET SEAT!
OVER THE NEXT FEW DAYS...
FELLOW MEMBERS OF THE SPRINGFIELD ELEMENTARY ORNITHOLOGICAL SOCIETY, I BELIEVE I'VE SPOTTED A RED-FOOTED BOOBIE! OR IS IT A YELLOW-RUMPED WARBLER?
SNICKER!
IS IT SOMETHING I SAID?
HA! HA!

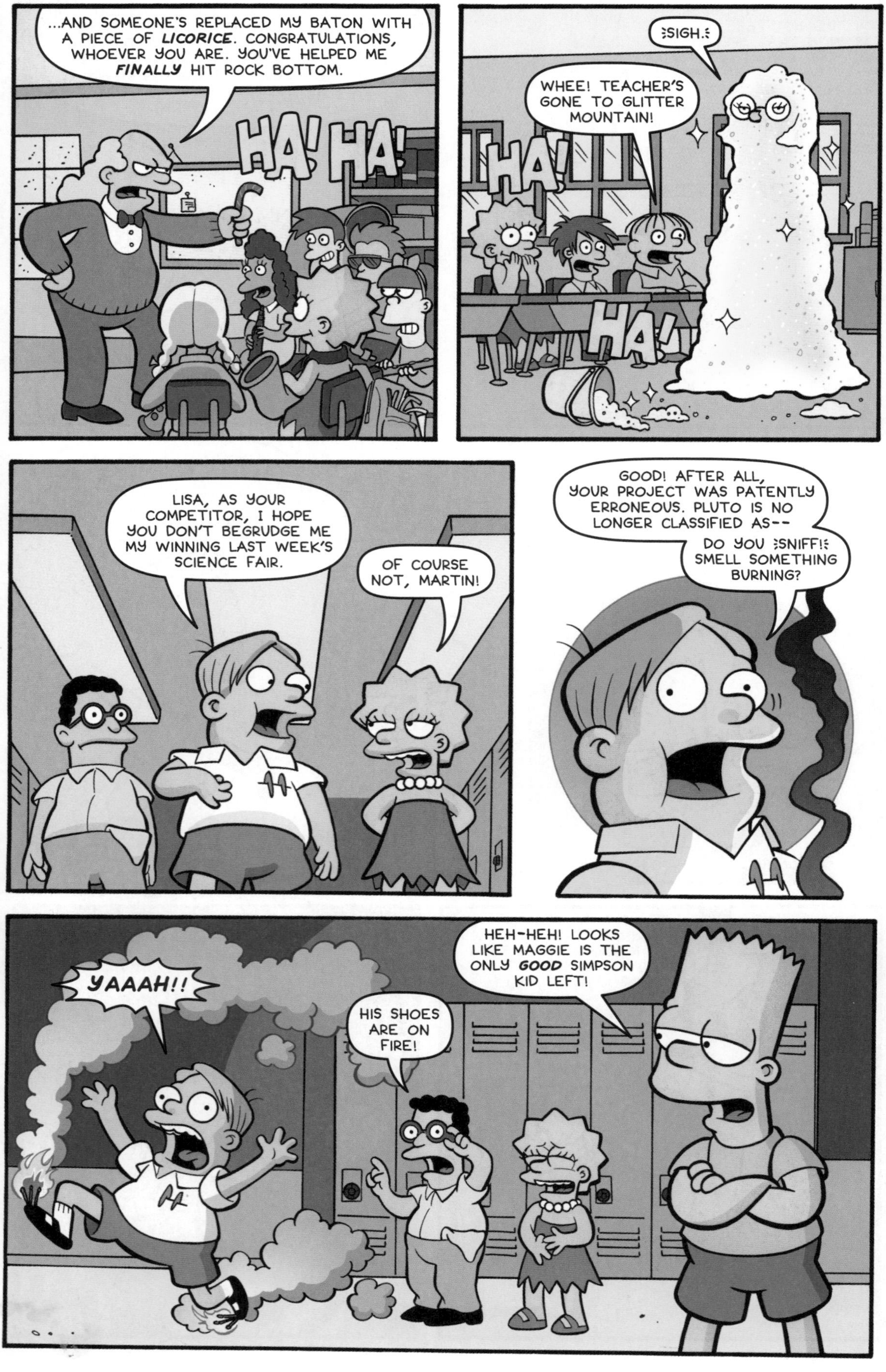
...AND SOMEONE'S REPLACED MY BATON WITH A PIECE OF *LICORICE*. CONGRATULATIONS, WHOEVER YOU ARE. YOU'VE HELPED ME *FINALLY* HIT ROCK BOTTOM.
HA! HA!
SIGH.
WHEE! TEACHER'S GONE TO GLITTER MOUNTAIN!
HA!
HA!
LISA, AS YOUR COMPETITOR, I HOPE YOU DON'T BEGRUDGE ME MY WINNING LAST WEEK'S SCIENCE FAIR.
OF COURSE NOT, MARTIN!
GOOD! AFTER ALL, YOUR PROJECT WAS PATENTLY ERRONEOUS. PLUTO IS NO LONGER CLASSIFIED AS--
DO YOU SNIFF! SMELL SOMETHING BURNING?
YAAAH!!
HIS SHOES ARE ON FIRE!
HEH-HEH! LOOKS LIKE MAGGIE IS THE ONLY *GOOD* SIMPSON KID LEFT!

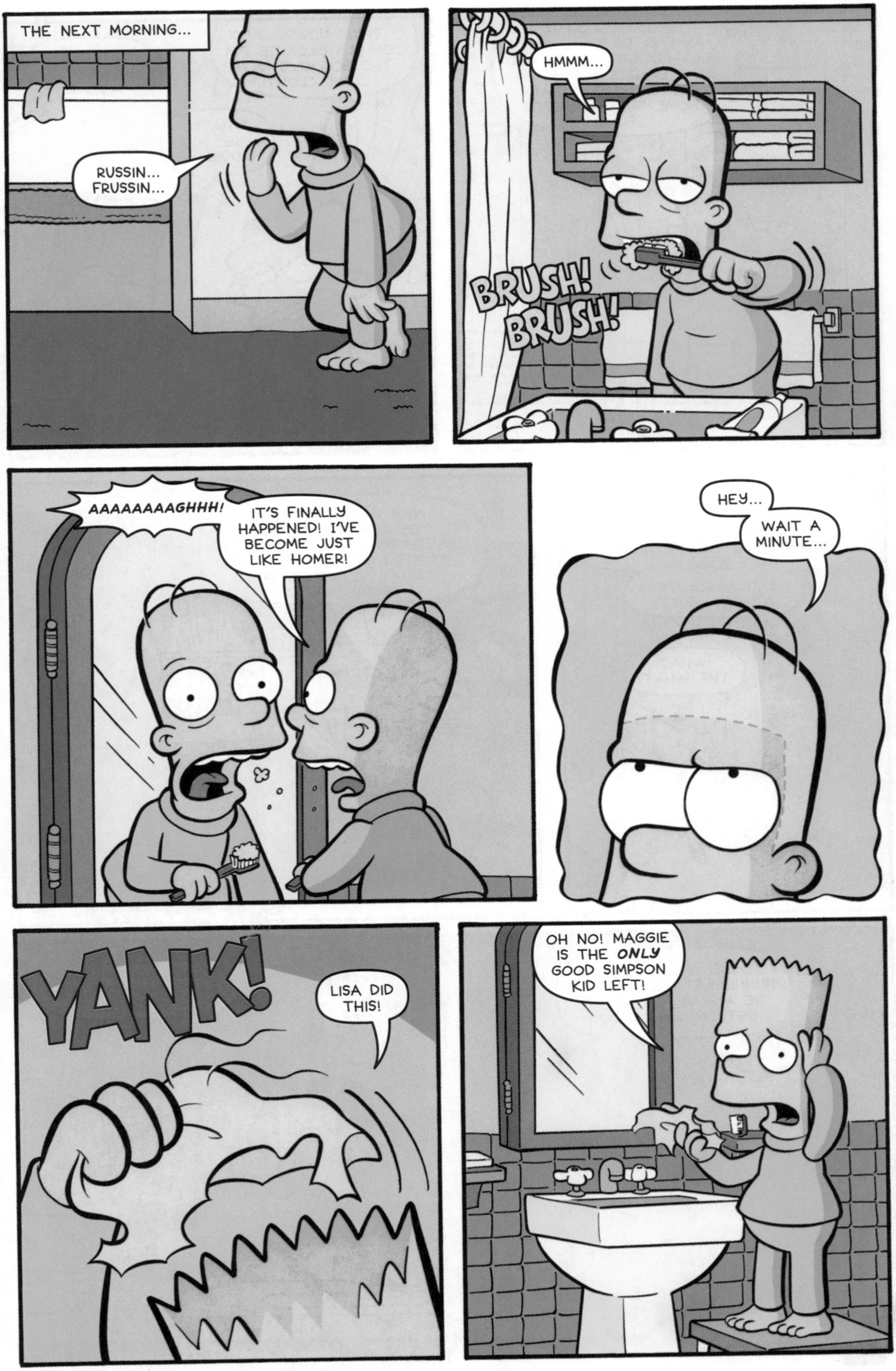
THE NEXT MORNING...
RUSSIN... FRUSSIN...
HMMM...
BRUSH! BRUSH!
AAAAAAAAGHHH!
IT'S FINALLY HAPPENED! I'VE BECOME JUST LIKE HOMER!
HEY...
WAIT A MINUTE...
YANK!
LISA DID THIS!
OH NO! MAGGIE IS THE ONLY GOOD SIMPSON KID LEFT!

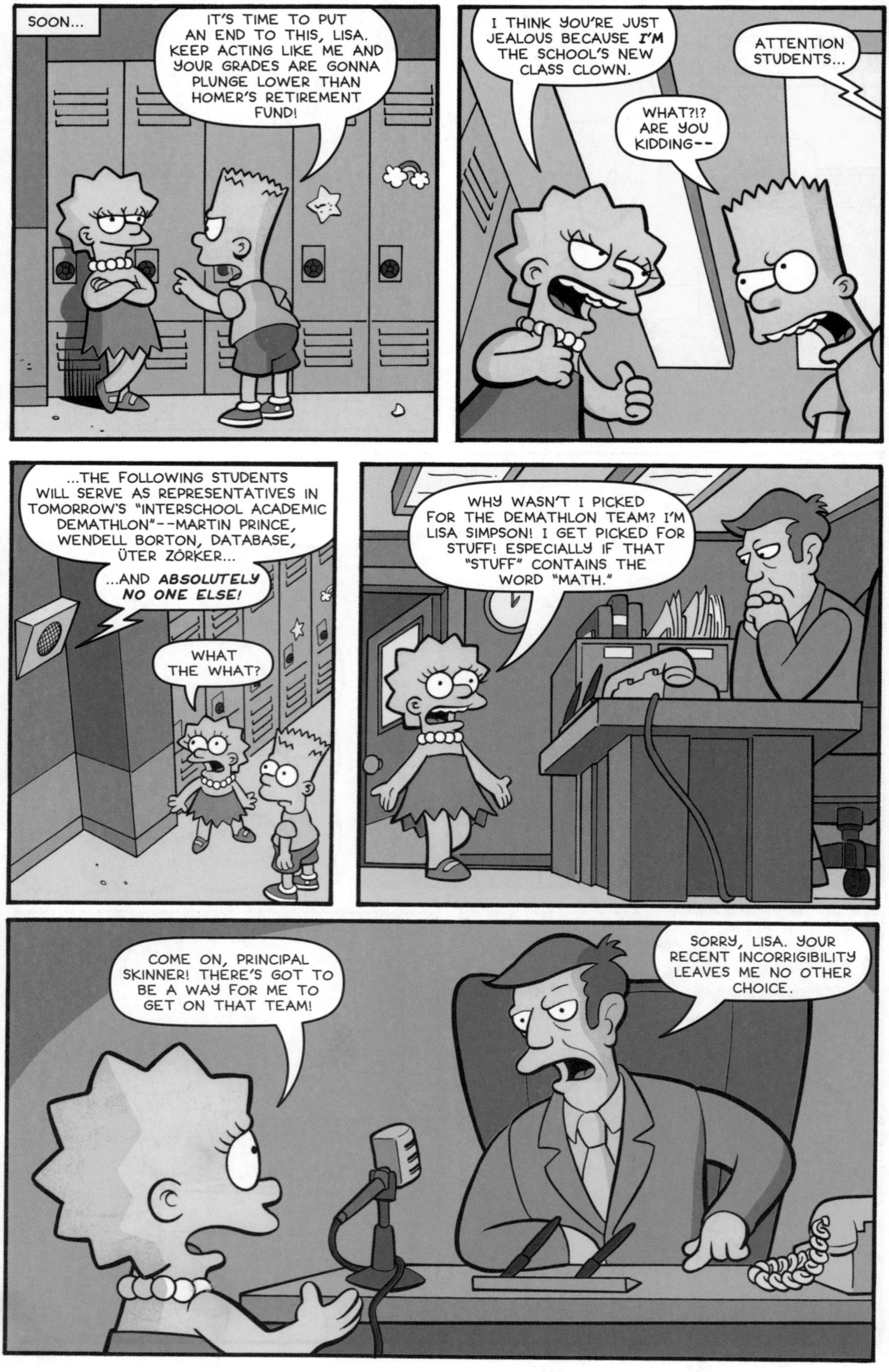
SOON...
IT'S TIME TO PUT AN END TO THIS, LISA. KEEP ACTING LIKE ME AND YOUR GRADES ARE GONNA PLUNGE LOWER THAN HOMER'S RETIREMENT FUND!
I THINK YOU'RE JUST JEALOUS BECAUSE I'M THE SCHOOL'S NEW CLASS CLOWN.
WHAT?!? ARE YOU KIDDING--
ATTENTION STUDENTS...
...THE FOLLOWING STUDENTS WILL SERVE AS REPRESENTATIVES IN TOMORROW'S "INTERSCHOOL ACADEMIC DEMATHLON"--MARTIN PRINCE, WENDELL BORTON, DATABASE, ÜTER ZÖRKER...
...AND ABSOLUTELY NO ONE ELSE!
WHAT THE WHAT?
WHY WASN'T I PICKED FOR THE DEMATHLON TEAM? I'M LISA SIMPSON! I GET PICKED FOR STUFF! ESPECIALLY IF THAT "STUFF" CONTAINS THE WORD "MATH."
COME ON, PRINCIPAL SKINNER! THERE'S GOT TO BE A WAY FOR ME TO GET ON THAT TEAM!
SORRY, LISA. YOUR RECENT INCORRIGIBILITY LEAVES ME NO OTHER CHOICE.

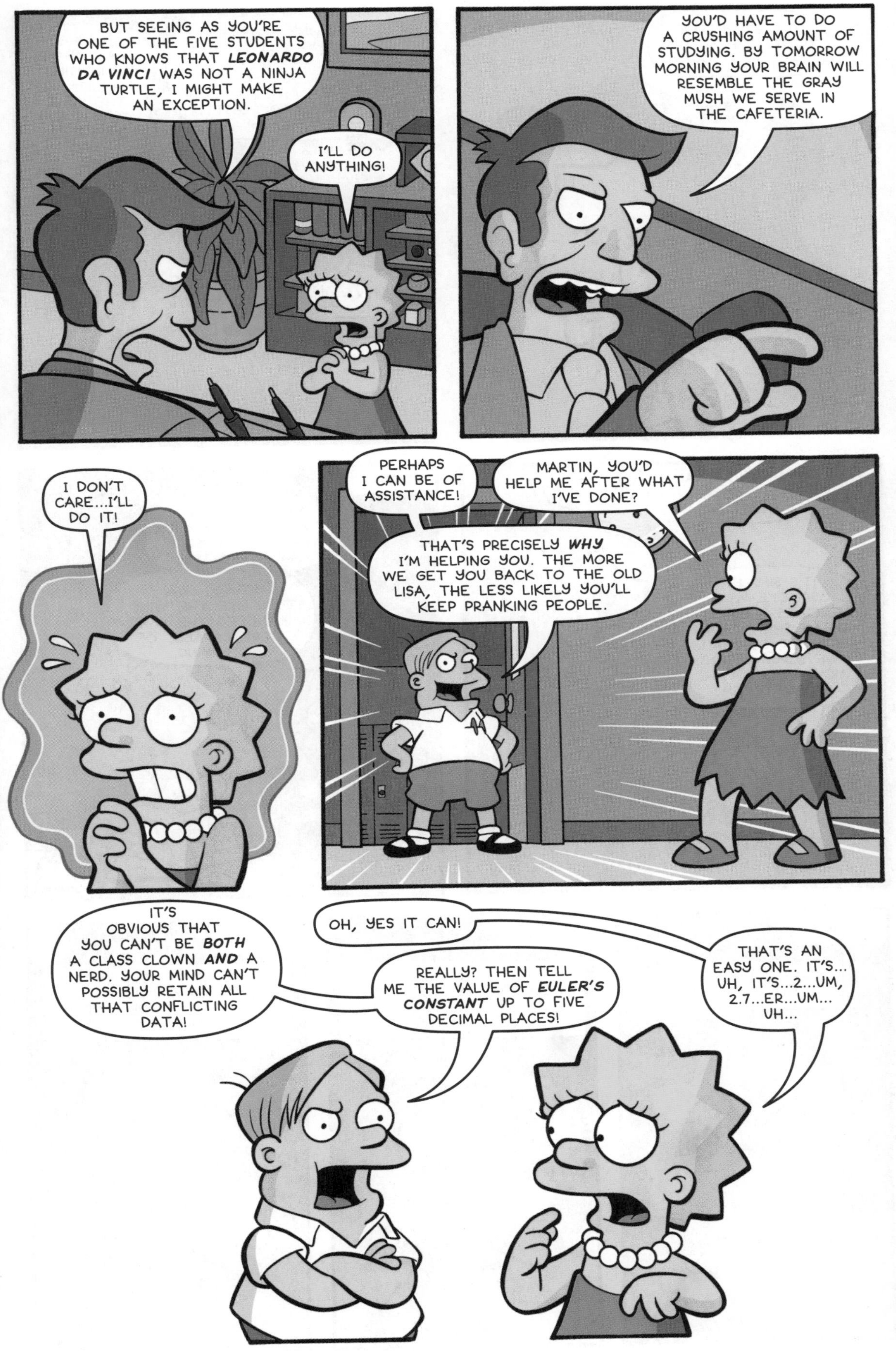

BUT SEEING AS YOU'RE ONE OF THE FIVE STUDENTS WHO KNOWS THAT *LEONARDO DA VINCI* WAS NOT A NINJA TURTLE, I MIGHT MAKE AN EXCEPTION.
I'LL DO ANYTHING!
YOU'D HAVE TO DO A CRUSHING AMOUNT OF STUDYING. BY TOMORROW MORNING YOUR BRAIN WILL RESEMBLE THE GRAY MUSH WE SERVE IN THE CAFETERIA.
I DON'T CARE...I'LL DO IT!
PERHAPS I CAN BE OF ASSISTANCE!
MARTIN, YOU'D HELP ME AFTER WHAT I'VE DONE?
THAT'S PRECISELY *WHY* I'M HELPING YOU. THE MORE WE GET YOU BACK TO THE OLD LISA, THE LESS LIKELY YOU'LL KEEP PRANKING PEOPLE.
IT'S OBVIOUS THAT YOU CAN'T BE *BOTH* A CLASS CLOWN *AND* A NERD. YOUR MIND CAN'T POSSIBLY RETAIN ALL THAT CONFLICTING DATA!
OH, YES IT CAN!
REALLY? THEN TELL ME THE VALUE OF *EULER'S CONSTANT* UP TO FIVE DECIMAL PLACES!
THAT'S AN EASY ONE. IT'S... UH, IT'S...2...UM, 2.7...ER...UM... UH...

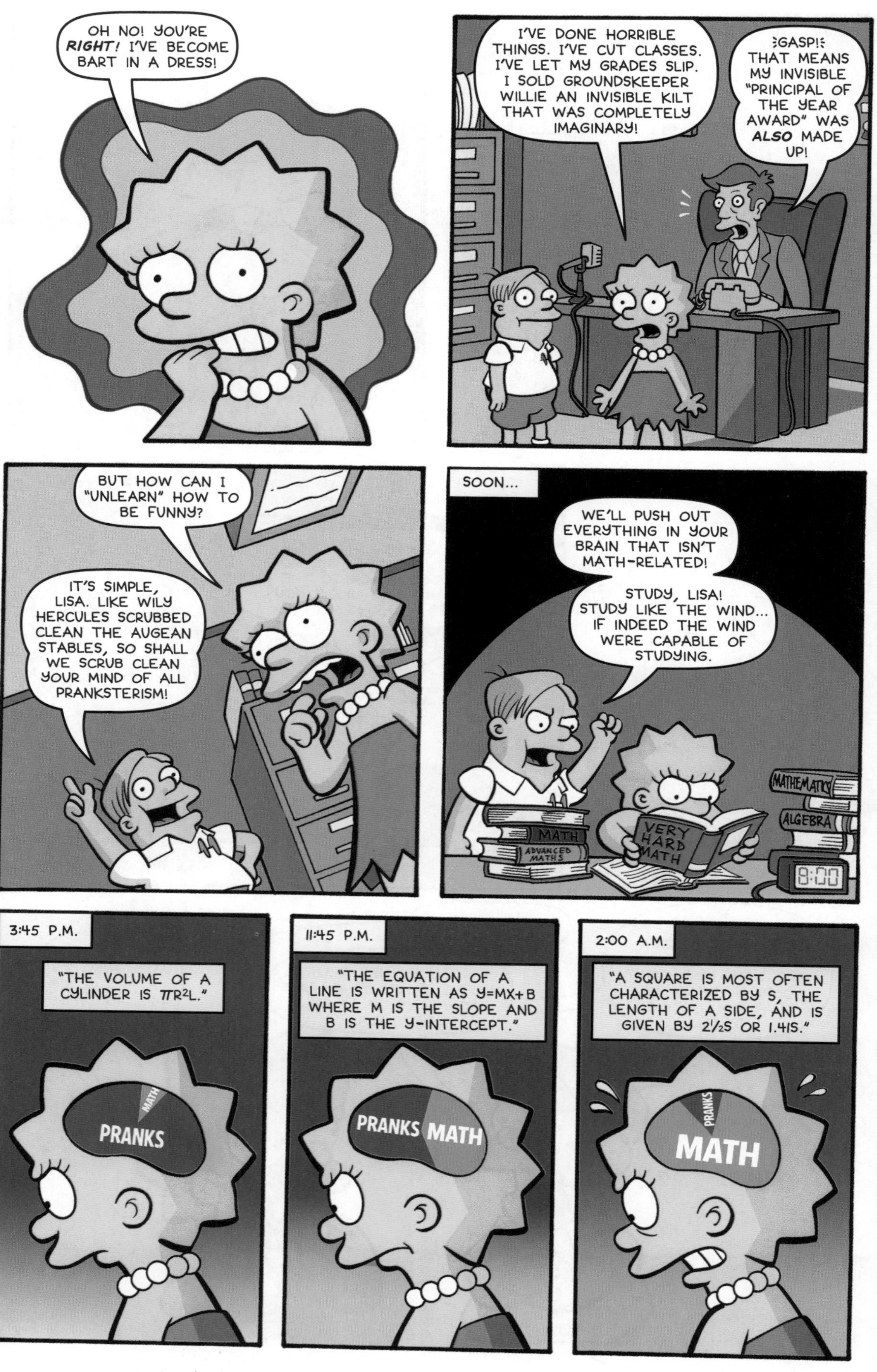
OH NO! YOU'RE *RIGHT!* I'VE BECOME BART IN A DRESS!
I'VE DONE HORRIBLE THINGS. I'VE CUT CLASSES. I'VE LET MY GRADES SLIP. I SOLD GROUNDSKEEPER WILLIE AN INVISIBLE KILT THAT WAS COMPLETELY IMAGINARY!
GASP! THAT MEANS MY INVISIBLE "PRINCIPAL OF THE YEAR AWARD" WAS ***ALSO*** MADE UP!
BUT HOW CAN I "UNLEARN" HOW TO BE FUNNY?
IT'S SIMPLE, LISA. LIKE WILY HERCULES SCRUBBED CLEAN THE AUGEAN STABLES, SO SHALL WE SCRUB CLEAN YOUR MIND OF ALL PRANKSTERISM!
SOON...
WE'LL PUSH OUT EVERYTHING IN YOUR BRAIN THAT ISN'T MATH-RELATED!
STUDY, LISA! STUDY LIKE THE WIND... IF INDEED THE WIND WERE CAPABLE OF STUDYING.
MATHEMATICS
ALGEBRA
MATH
ADVANCED MATHS
VERY HARD MATH
8:00
3:45 P.M.
"THE VOLUME OF A CYLINDER IS πR^2L."
MATH
PRANKS
11:45 P.M.
"THE EQUATION OF A LINE IS WRITTEN AS Y=MX+B WHERE M IS THE SLOPE AND B IS THE Y-INTERCEPT."
PRANKS
MATH
2:00 A.M.
"A SQUARE IS MOST OFTEN CHARACTERIZED BY S, THE LENGTH OF A SIDE, AND IS GIVEN BY $2^{1/2}S$ OR 1.41S."
PRANKS
MATH

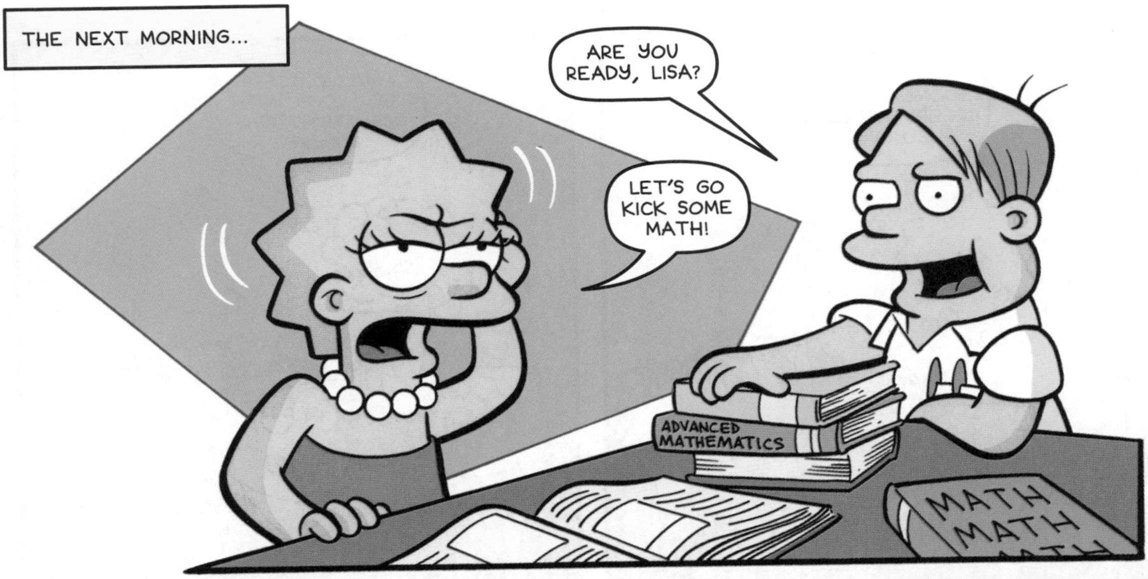
THE NEXT MORNING...
ARE YOU READY, LISA?
LET'S GO KICK SOME MATH!
ADVANCED MATHEMATICS
MATH MATH

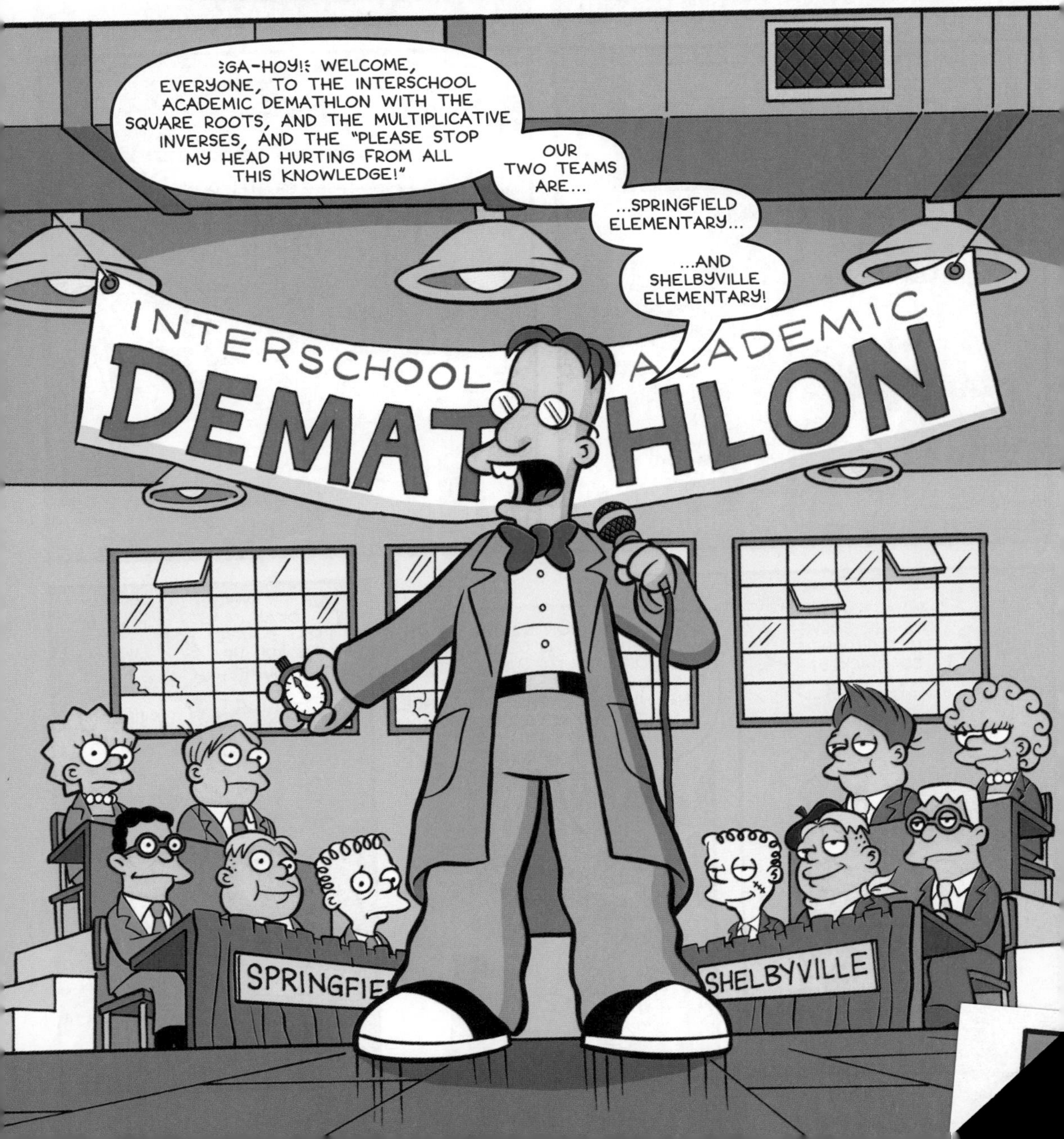
GA-HOY! WELCOME, EVERYONE, TO THE INTERSCHOOL ACADEMIC DEMATHLON WITH THE SQUARE ROOTS, AND THE MULTIPLICATIVE INVERSES, AND THE "PLEASE STOP MY HEAD HURTING FROM ALL THIS KNOWLEDGE!"
OUR TWO TEAMS ARE...
...SPRINGFIELD ELEMENTARY...
...AND SHELBYVILLE ELEMENTARY!
INTERSCHOOL ACADEMIC DEMATHLON
SPRINGFIE
SHELBYVILLE

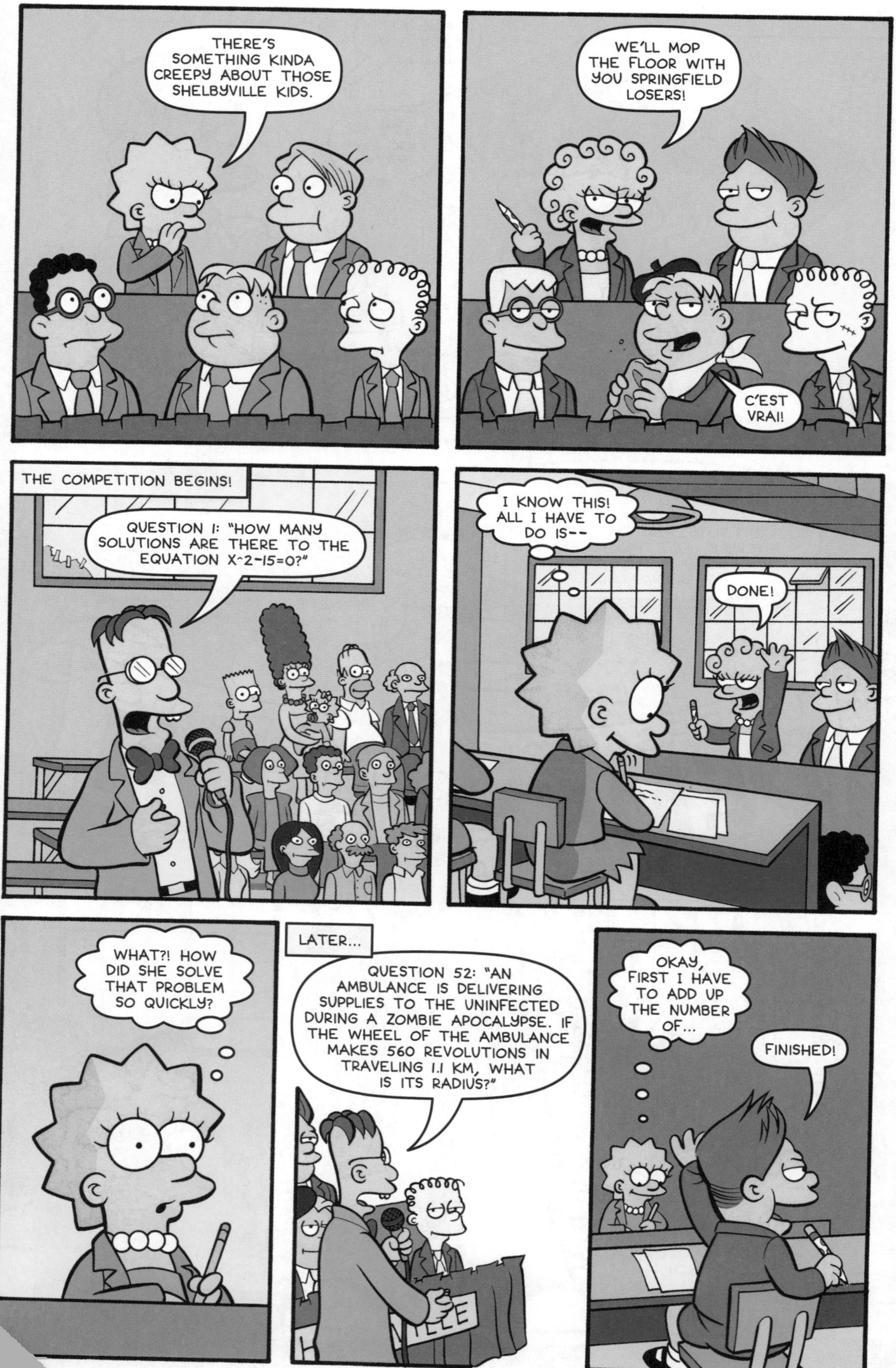
THERE'S SOMETHING KINDA CREEPY ABOUT THOSE SHELBYVILLE KIDS.
WE'LL MOP THE FLOOR WITH YOU SPRINGFIELD LOSERS!
C'EST VRAI!
THE COMPETITION BEGINS!
QUESTION 1: "HOW MANY SOLUTIONS ARE THERE TO THE EQUATION X^2-15=0?"
I KNOW THIS! ALL I HAVE TO DO IS--
DONE!
WHAT?! HOW DID SHE SOLVE THAT PROBLEM SO QUICKLY?
LATER...
QUESTION 52: "AN AMBULANCE IS DELIVERING SUPPLIES TO THE UNINFECTED DURING A ZOMBIE APOCALYPSE. IF THE WHEEL OF THE AMBULANCE MAKES 560 REVOLUTIONS IN TRAVELING 1.1 KM, WHAT IS ITS RADIUS?"
OKAY, FIRST I HAVE TO ADD UP THE NUMBER OF...
FINISHED!

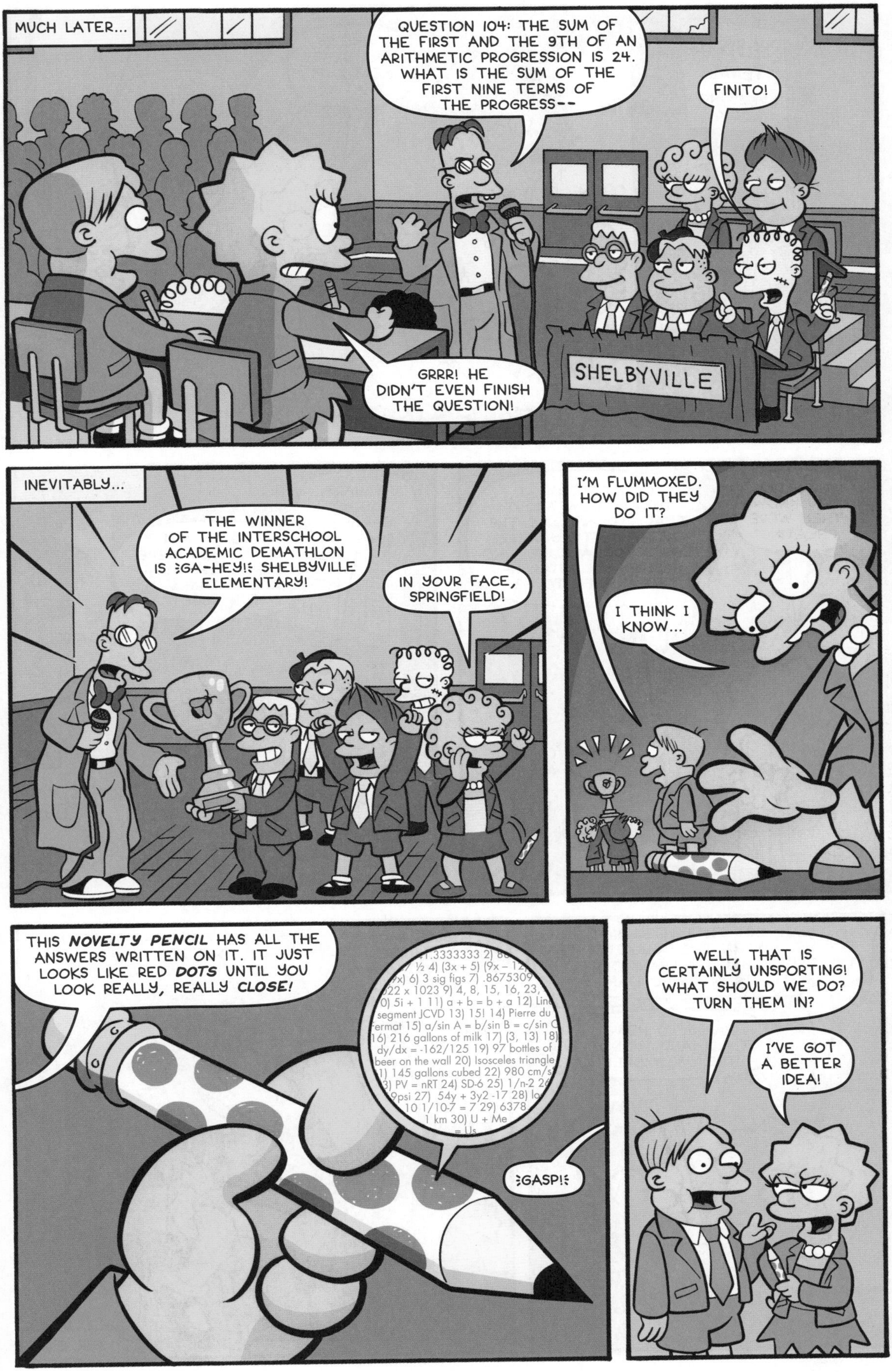
MUCH LATER...
QUESTION 104: THE SUM OF THE FIRST AND THE 9TH OF AN ARITHMETIC PROGRESSION IS 24. WHAT IS THE SUM OF THE FIRST NINE TERMS OF THE PROGRESS--
FINITO!
GRRR! HE DIDN'T EVEN FINISH THE QUESTION!
SHELBYVILLE
INEVITABLY...
THE WINNER OF THE INTERSCHOOL ACADEMIC DEMATHLON IS ⁝GA-HEY!⁝ SHELBYVILLE ELEMENTARY!
IN YOUR FACE, SPRINGFIELD!
I'M FLUMMOXED. HOW DID THEY DO IT?
I THINK I KNOW...
THIS NOVELTY PENCIL HAS ALL THE ANSWERS WRITTEN ON IT. IT JUST LOOKS LIKE RED DOTS UNTIL YOU LOOK REALLY, REALLY CLOSE!
1.3333333 2)
½ 4) (3x + 5) (9x – 12)
6) 3 sig figs 7) .8675309
22 x 1023 9) 4, 8, 15, 16, 23,
5i + 1 11) a + b = b + a 12) Line
segment JCVD 13) 15! 14) Pierre du
Fermat 15) a/sin A = b/sin B = c/sin C
16) 216 gallons of milk 17) (3, 13) 18)
dy/dx = -162/125 19) 97 bottles of
beer on the wall 20) Isosceles triangle
145 gallons cubed 22) 980 cm/s
PV = nRT 24) SD-6 25) 1/n-2
9psi 27) 54y + 3y2 -17 28)
10 1/10-7 = 7 29) 6378
1 km 30) U + Me
= Us
⁝GASP!⁝
WELL, THAT IS CERTAINLY UNSPORTING! WHAT SHOULD WE DO? TURN THEM IN?
I'VE GOT A BETTER IDEA!

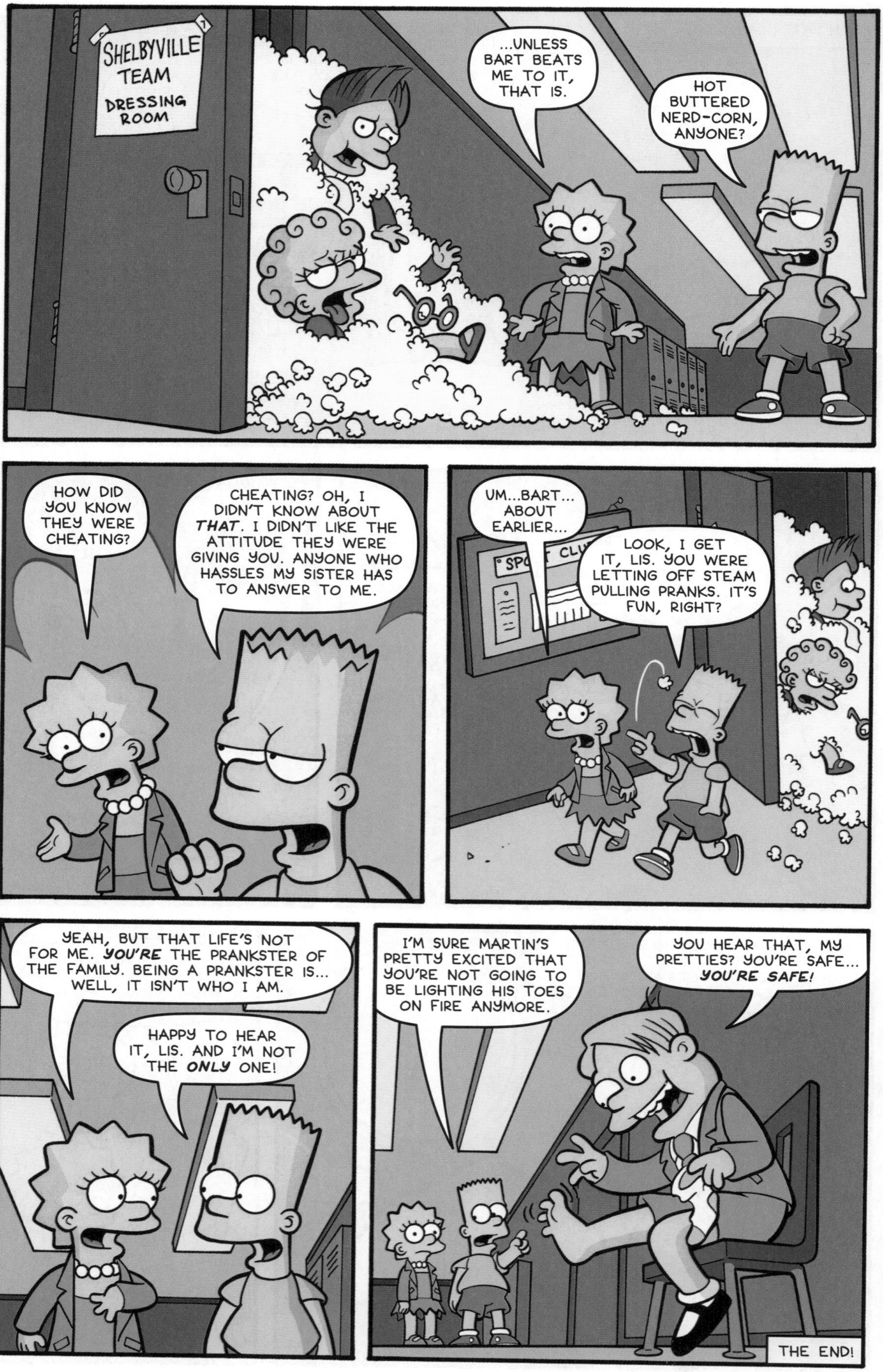
SHELBYVILLE TEAM DRESSING ROOM
...UNLESS BART BEATS ME TO IT, THAT IS.
HOT BUTTERED NERD-CORN, ANYONE?
HOW DID YOU KNOW THEY WERE CHEATING?
CHEATING? OH, I DIDN'T KNOW ABOUT THAT. I DIDN'T LIKE THE ATTITUDE THEY WERE GIVING YOU. ANYONE WHO HASSLES MY SISTER HAS TO ANSWER TO ME.
UM...BART... ABOUT EARLIER...
LOOK, I GET IT, LIS. YOU WERE LETTING OFF STEAM PULLING PRANKS. IT'S FUN, RIGHT?
YEAH, BUT THAT LIFE'S NOT FOR ME. YOU'RE THE PRANKSTER OF THE FAMILY. BEING A PRANKSTER IS... WELL, IT ISN'T WHO I AM.
HAPPY TO HEAR IT, LIS. AND I'M NOT THE ONLY ONE!
I'M SURE MARTIN'S PRETTY EXCITED THAT YOU'RE NOT GOING TO BE LIGHTING HIS TOES ON FIRE ANYMORE.
YOU HEAR THAT, MY PRETTIES? YOU'RE SAFE... YOU'RE SAFE!
THE END!

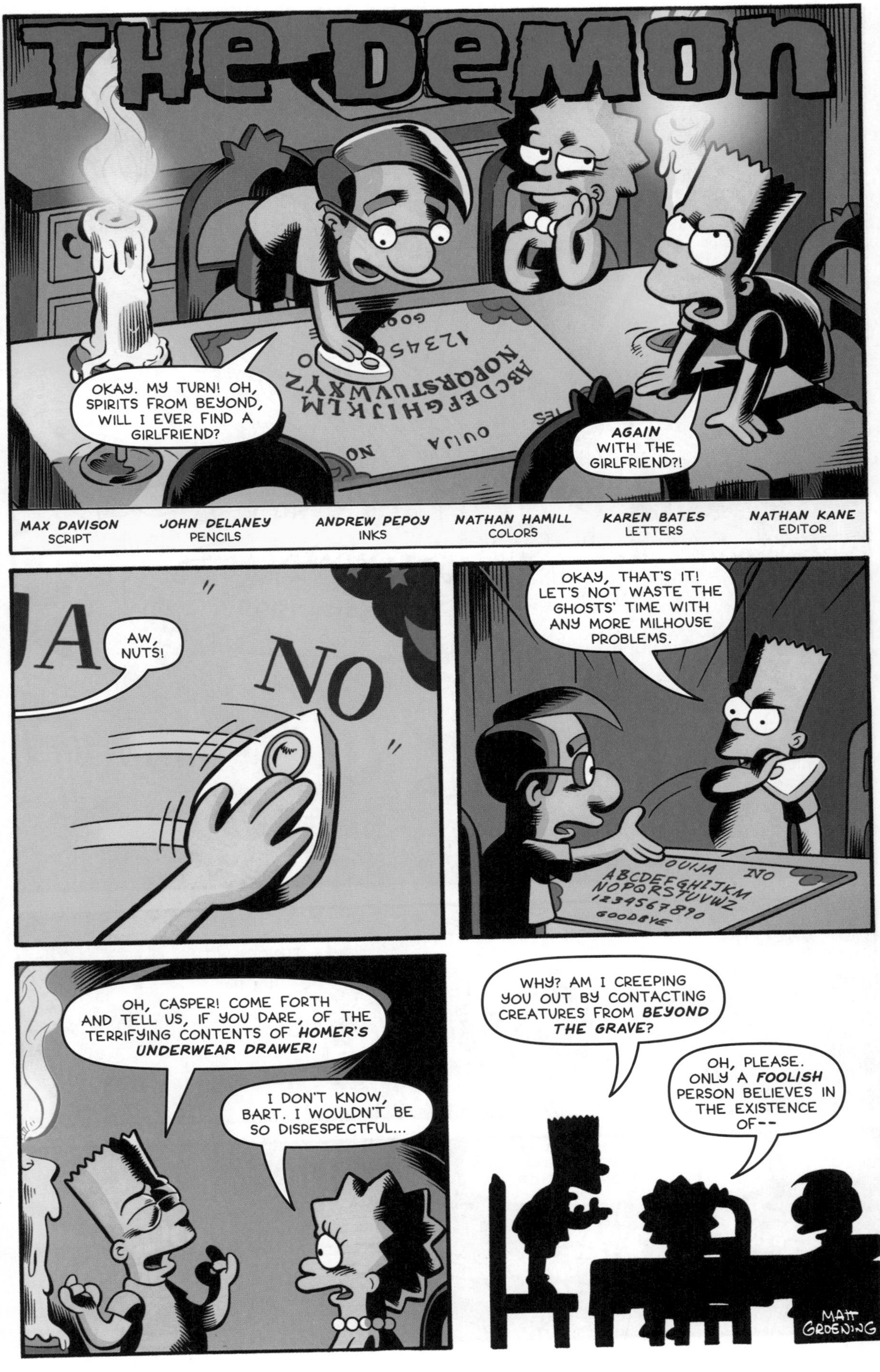

THE DEMON
OKAY. MY TURN! OH, SPIRITS FROM BEYOND, WILL I EVER FIND A GIRLFRIEND?
AGAIN WITH THE GIRLFRIEND?!
MAX DAVISON SCRIPT
JOHN DELANEY PENCILS
ANDREW PEPOY INKS
NATHAN HAMILL COLORS
KAREN BATES LETTERS
NATHAN KANE EDITOR
AW, NUTS!
NO
OKAY, THAT'S IT! LET'S NOT WASTE THE GHOSTS' TIME WITH ANY MORE MILHOUSE PROBLEMS.
OH, CASPER! COME FORTH AND TELL US, IF YOU DARE, OF THE TERRIFYING CONTENTS OF HOMER'S UNDERWEAR DRAWER!
I DON'T KNOW, BART. I WOULDN'T BE SO DISRESPECTFUL...
WHY? AM I CREEPING YOU OUT BY CONTACTING CREATURES FROM BEYOND THE GRAVE?
OH, PLEASE. ONLY A FOOLISH PERSON BELIEVES IN THE EXISTENCE OF--
MATT GROENING

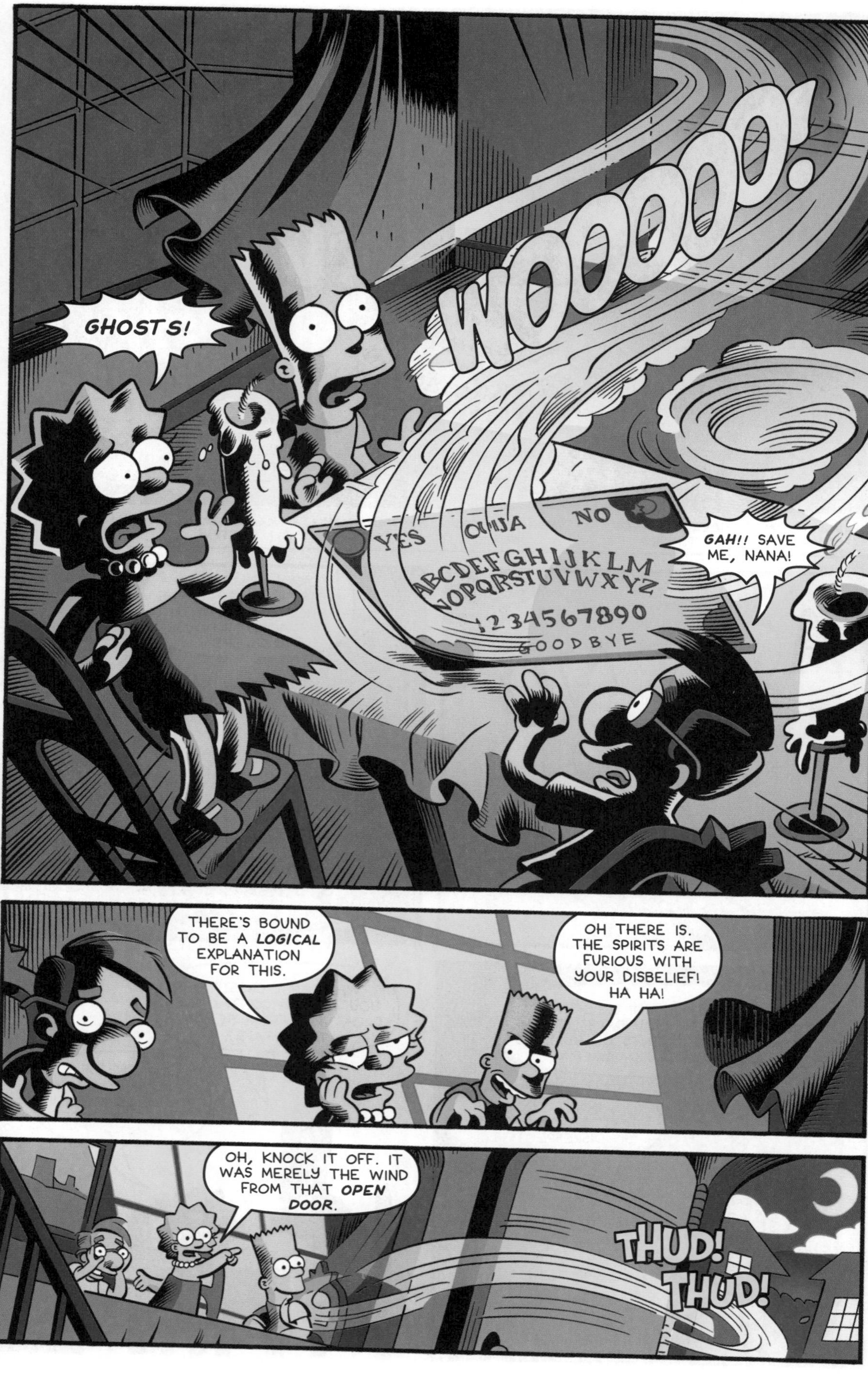
WOOOOOO!
GHOSTS!
YES
OUIJA
NO
ABCDEFGHIJKLM
NOPQRSTUVWXYZ
1234567890
GOODBYE
GAH!! SAVE ME, NANA!
THERE'S BOUND TO BE A LOGICAL EXPLANATION FOR THIS.
OH THERE IS. THE SPIRITS ARE FURIOUS WITH YOUR DISBELIEF! HA HA!
OH, KNOCK IT OFF. IT WAS MERELY THE WIND FROM THAT OPEN DOOR.
THUD! THUD!

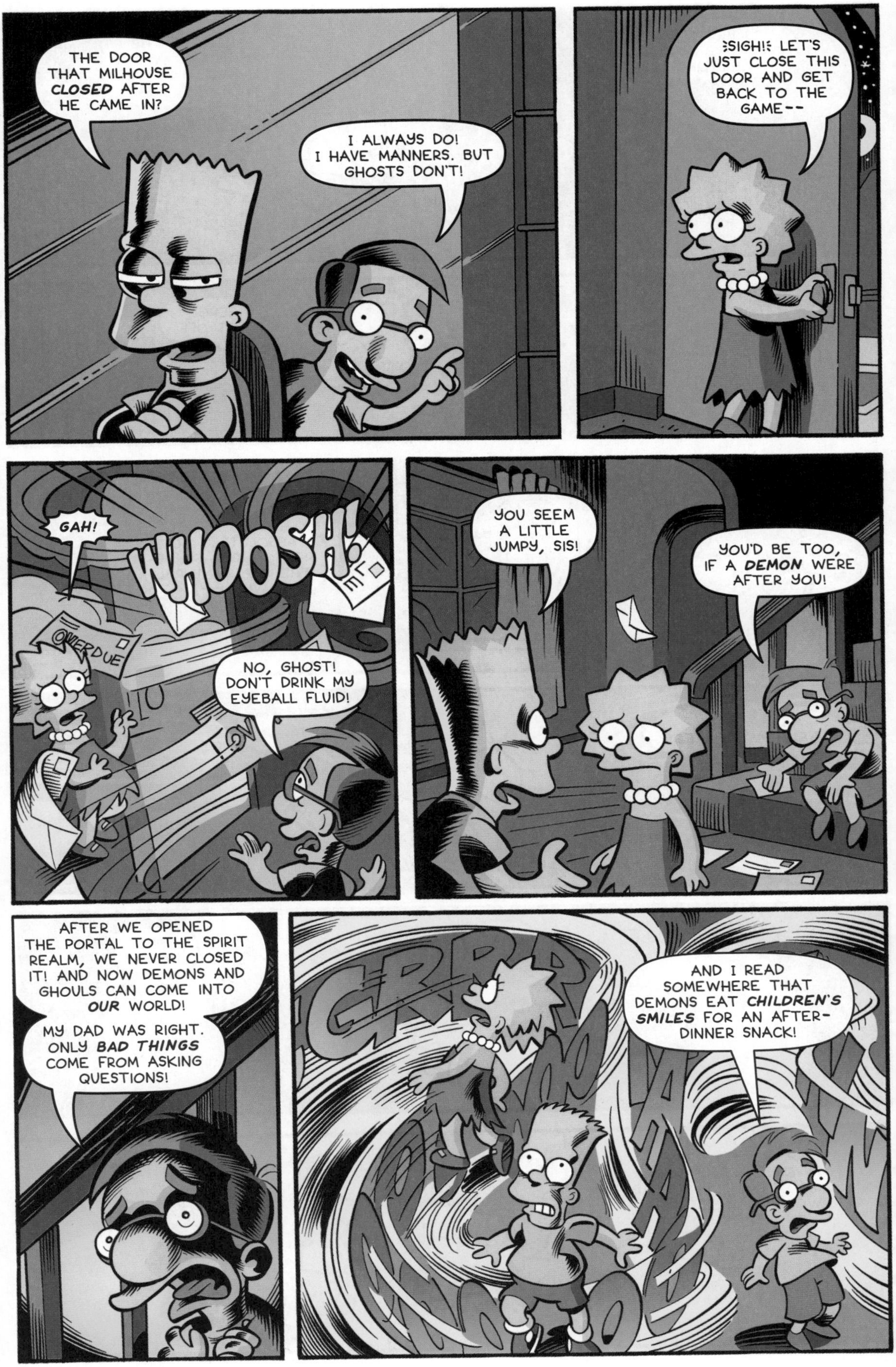
THE DOOR THAT MILHOUSE CLOSED AFTER HE CAME IN?
I ALWAYS DO! I HAVE MANNERS. BUT GHOSTS DON'T!
SIGH! LET'S JUST CLOSE THIS DOOR AND GET BACK TO THE GAME--
GAH!
WHOOSH!
OVERDUE
NO, GHOST! DON'T DRINK MY EYEBALL FLUID!
YOU SEEM A LITTLE JUMPY, SIS!
YOU'D BE TOO, IF A DEMON WERE AFTER YOU!
AFTER WE OPENED THE PORTAL TO THE SPIRIT REALM, WE NEVER CLOSED IT! AND NOW DEMONS AND GHOULS CAN COME INTO OUR WORLD!
MY DAD WAS RIGHT. ONLY BAD THINGS COME FROM ASKING QUESTIONS!
AND I READ SOMEWHERE THAT DEMONS EAT CHILDREN'S SMILES FOR AN AFTER-DINNER SNACK!

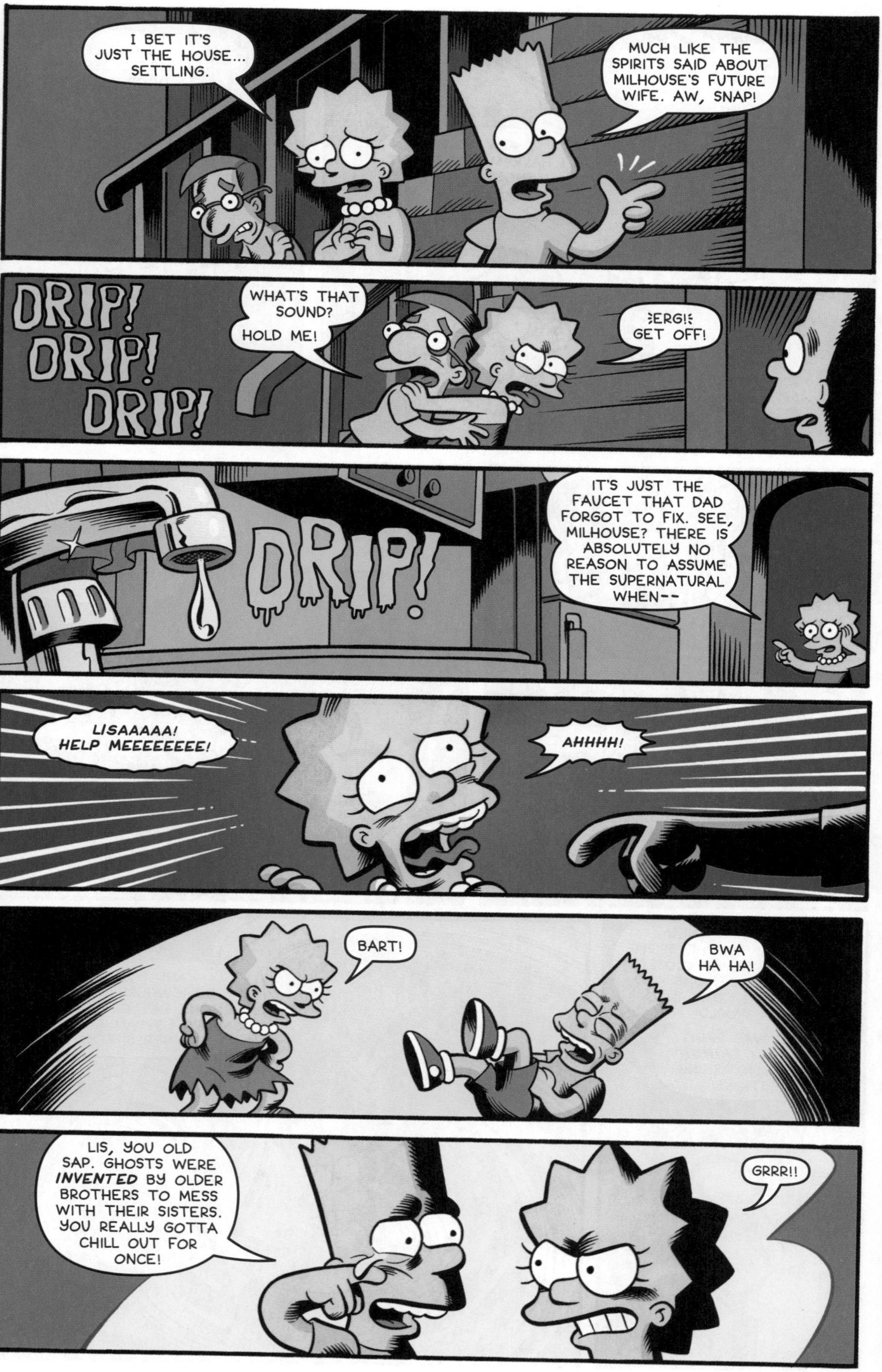

I BET IT'S JUST THE HOUSE... SETTLING.
MUCH LIKE THE SPIRITS SAID ABOUT MILHOUSE'S FUTURE WIFE. AW, SNAP!
DRIP! DRIP! DRIP!
WHAT'S THAT SOUND?
HOLD ME!
ERG!
GET OFF!
DRIP!
IT'S JUST THE FAUCET THAT DAD FORGOT TO FIX. SEE, MILHOUSE? THERE IS ABSOLUTELY NO REASON TO ASSUME THE SUPERNATURAL WHEN--
LISAAAAA! HELP MEEEEEEEE!
AHHHH!
BART!
BWA HA HA!
LIS, YOU OLD SAP. GHOSTS WERE *INVENTED* BY OLDER BROTHERS TO MESS WITH THEIR SISTERS. YOU REALLY GOTTA CHILL OUT FOR ONCE!
GRRR!!

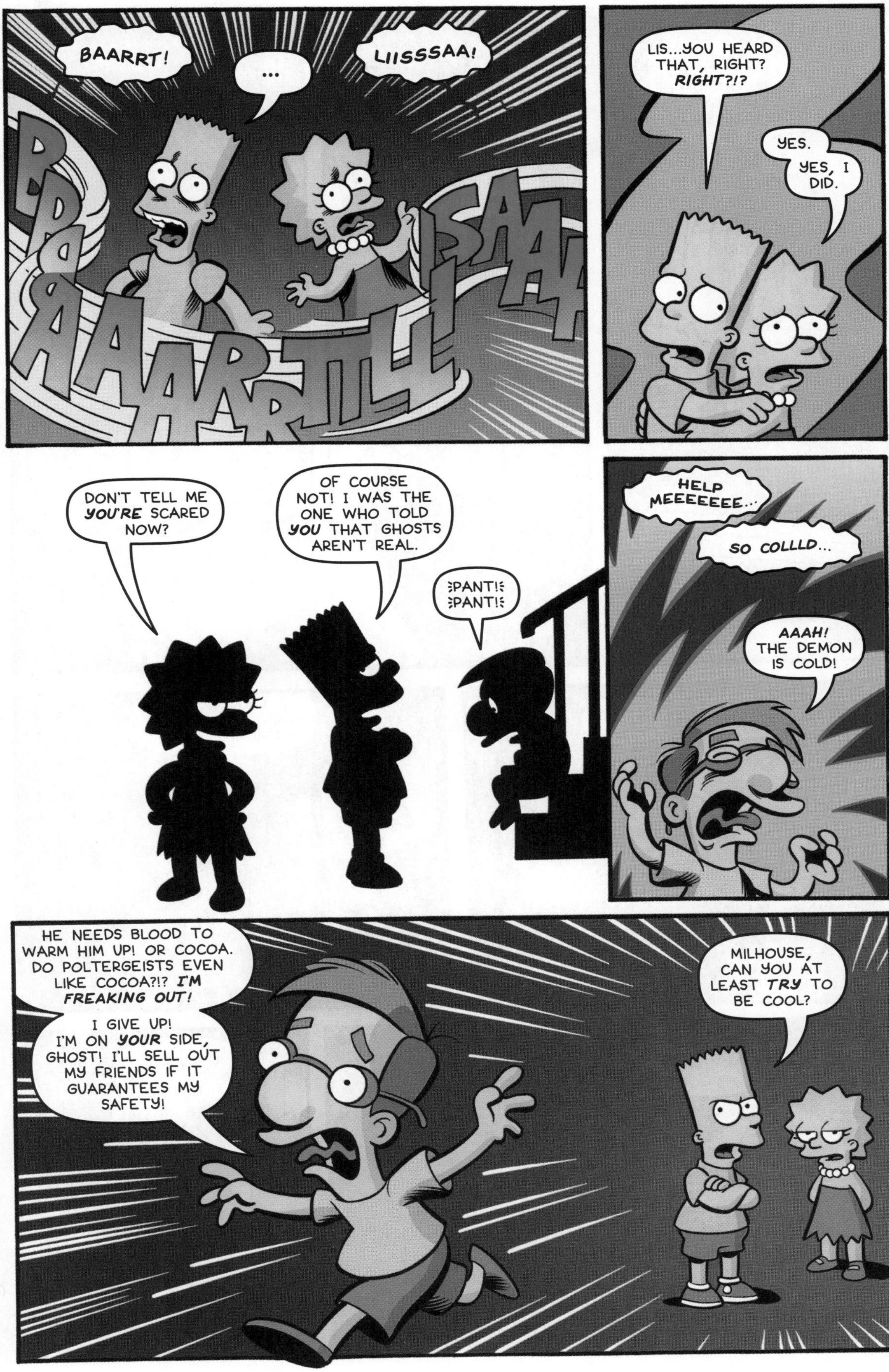
BAARRT!
...
LIISSSAA!
BAAARRT!!
LISAAA
LIS...YOU HEARD THAT, RIGHT? RIGHT?!?
YES. YES, I DID.
DON'T TELL ME YOU'RE SCARED NOW?
OF COURSE NOT! I WAS THE ONE WHO TOLD YOU THAT GHOSTS AREN'T REAL.
PANT! PANT!
HELP MEEEEEEE...
SO COLLLD...
AAAH! THE DEMON IS COLD!
HE NEEDS BLOOD TO WARM HIM UP! OR COCOA. DO POLTERGEISTS EVEN LIKE COCOA?!? I'M FREAKING OUT!
I GIVE UP! I'M ON YOUR SIDE, GHOST! I'LL SELL OUT MY FRIENDS IF IT GUARANTEES MY SAFETY!
MILHOUSE, CAN YOU AT LEAST TRY TO BE COOL?

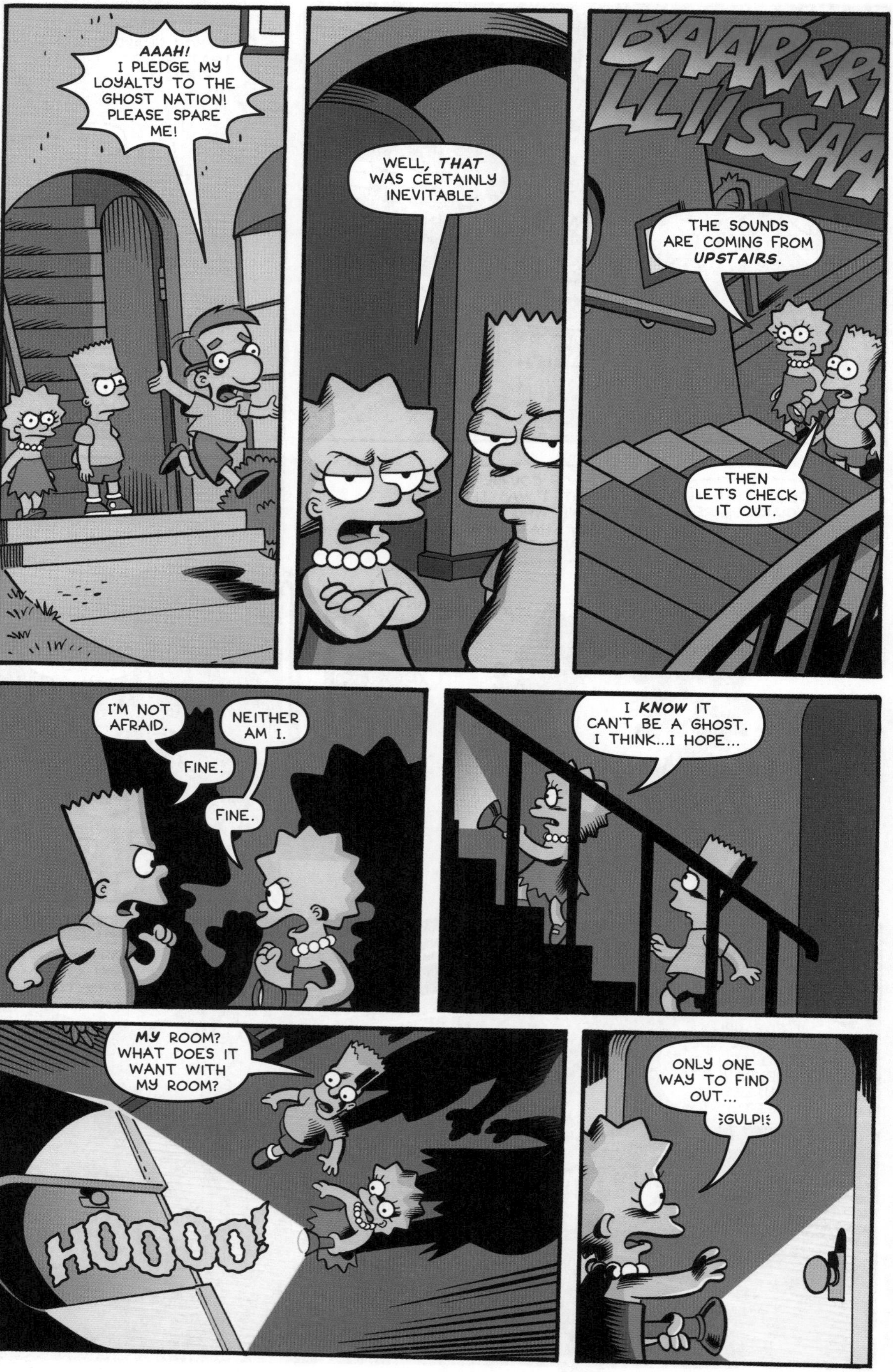
AAAH! I PLEDGE MY LOYALTY TO THE GHOST NATION! PLEASE SPARE ME!
WELL, THAT WAS CERTAINLY INEVITABLE.
BAARRRTT LLIISSAA
THE SOUNDS ARE COMING FROM UPSTAIRS.
THEN LET'S CHECK IT OUT.
I'M NOT AFRAID.
NEITHER AM I.
FINE.
FINE.
I KNOW IT CAN'T BE A GHOST. I THINK...I HOPE...
MY ROOM? WHAT DOES IT WANT WITH MY ROOM?
HOOOO!
ONLY ONE WAY TO FIND OUT...
GULP!

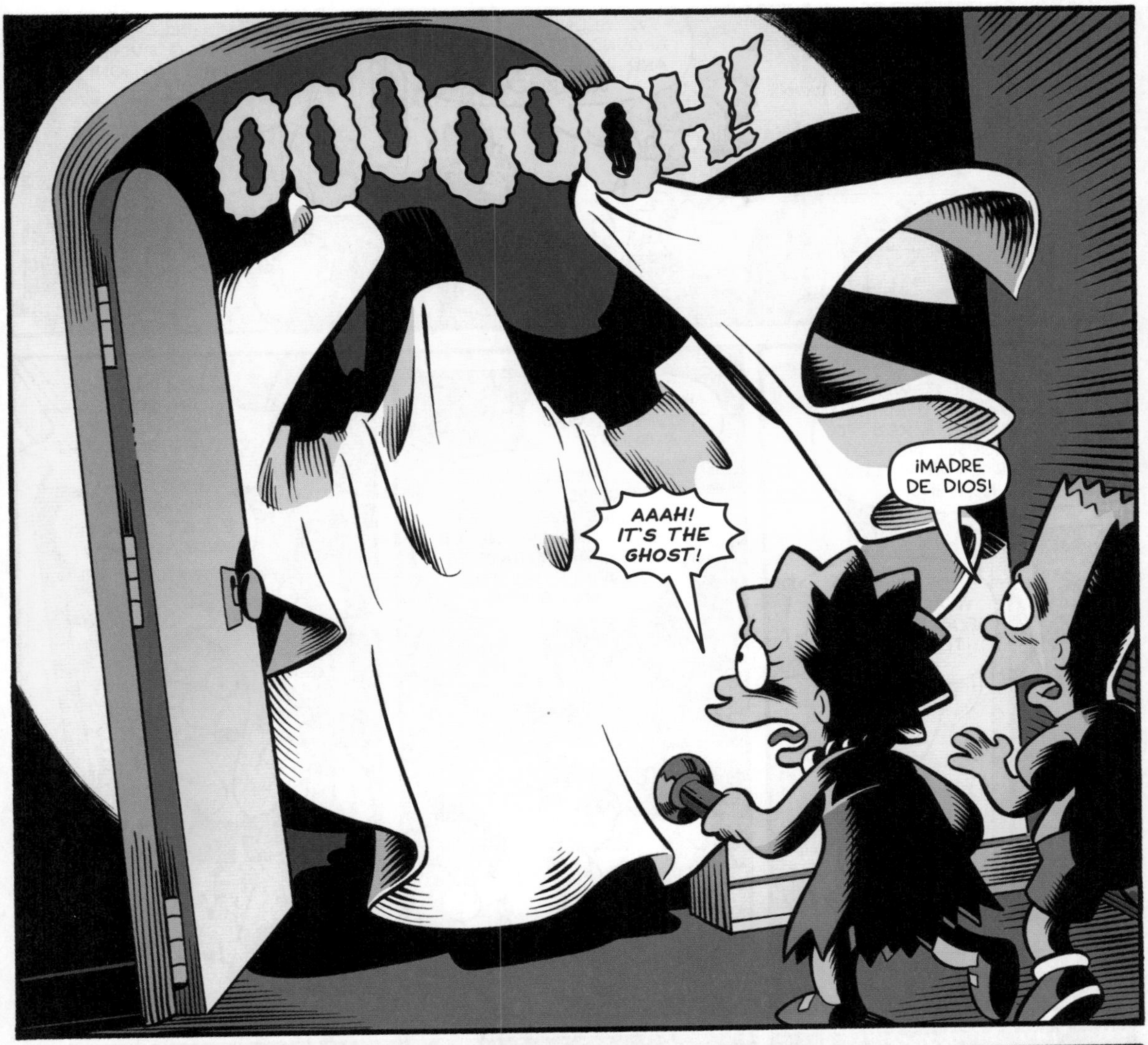
OOOOOOOH!
AAAH! IT'S THE GHOST!
¡MADRE DE DIOS!

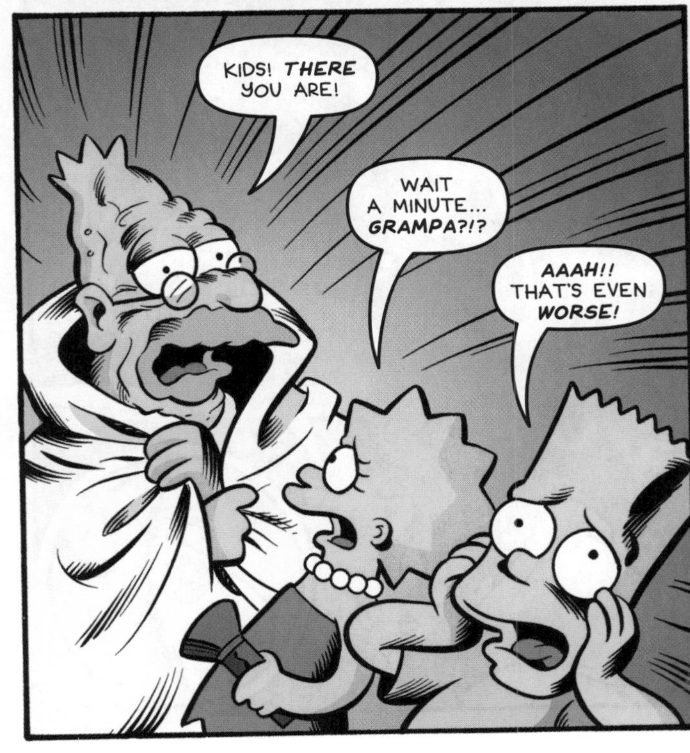
KIDS! THERE YOU ARE!
WAIT A MINUTE... GRAMPA?!?
AAAH!! THAT'S EVEN WORSE!

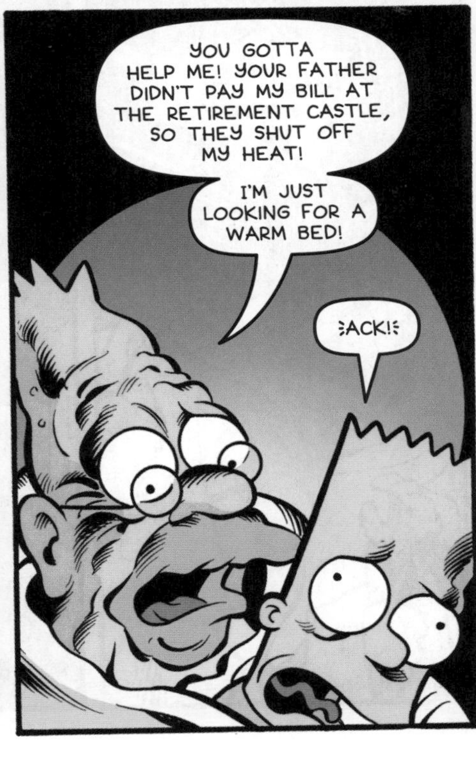
YOU GOTTA HELP ME! YOUR FATHER DIDN'T PAY MY BILL AT THE RETIREMENT CASTLE, SO THEY SHUT OFF MY HEAT!
I'M JUST LOOKING FOR A WARM BED!
ACK!

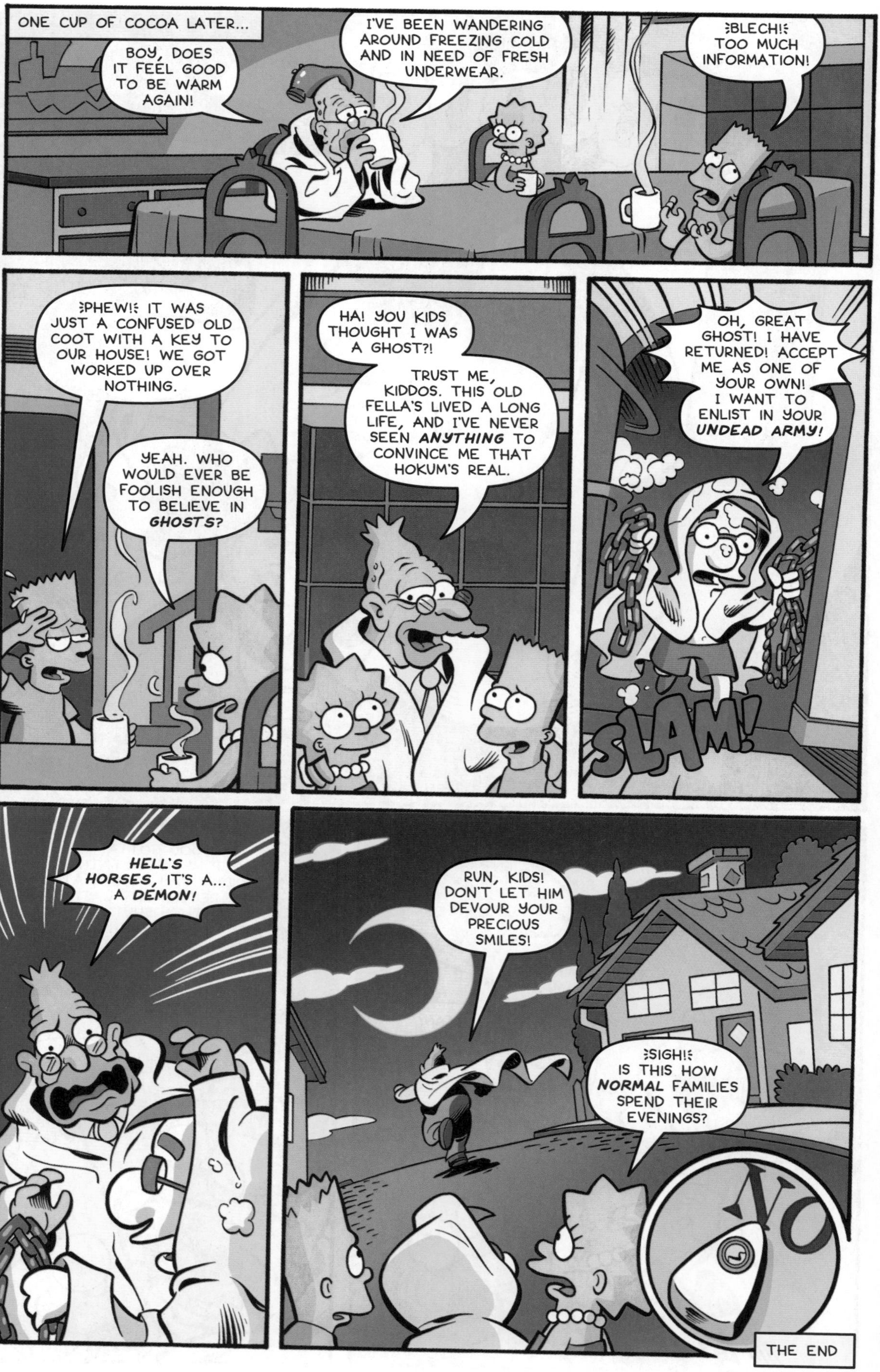
ONE CUP OF COCOA LATER...
BOY, DOES IT FEEL GOOD TO BE WARM AGAIN!
I'VE BEEN WANDERING AROUND FREEZING COLD AND IN NEED OF FRESH UNDERWEAR.
BLECH! TOO MUCH INFORMATION!
PHEW! IT WAS JUST A CONFUSED OLD COOT WITH A KEY TO OUR HOUSE! WE GOT WORKED UP OVER NOTHING.
YEAH. WHO WOULD EVER BE FOOLISH ENOUGH TO BELIEVE IN GHOSTS?
HA! YOU KIDS THOUGHT I WAS A GHOST?!
TRUST ME, KIDDOS. THIS OLD FELLA'S LIVED A LONG LIFE, AND I'VE NEVER SEEN ANYTHING TO CONVINCE ME THAT HOKUM'S REAL.
OH, GREAT GHOST! I HAVE RETURNED! ACCEPT ME AS ONE OF YOUR OWN! I WANT TO ENLIST IN YOUR UNDEAD ARMY!
SLAM!
HELL'S HORSES, IT'S A... A DEMON!
RUN, KIDS! DON'T LET HIM DEVOUR YOUR PRECIOUS SMILES!
SIGH! IS THIS HOW NORMAL FAMILIES SPEND THEIR EVENINGS?
THE END

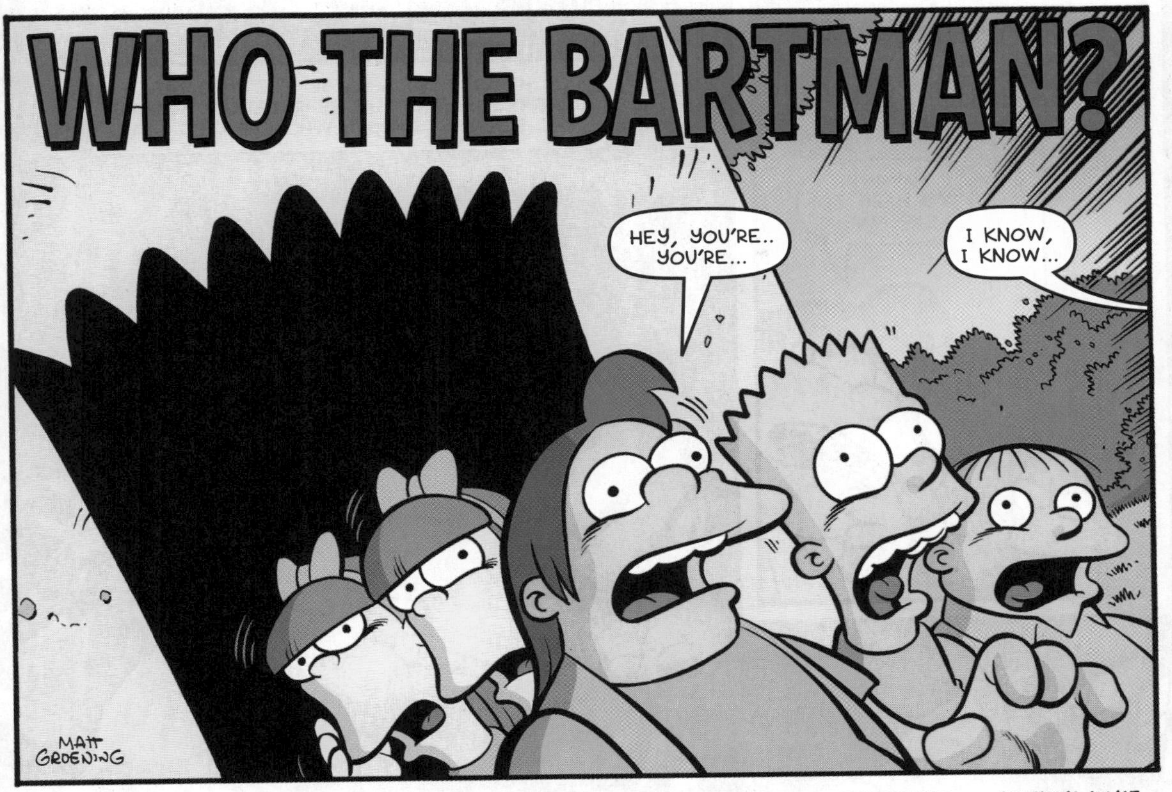
WHO THE BARTMAN?
HEY, YOU'RE.. YOU'RE...
I KNOW, I KNOW...
MATT GROENING

ARIE KAPLAN SCRIPT · **TONE RODRIGUEZ** PENCILS · **ANDREW PEPOY** INKS · **NATHAN HAMILL** COLORS · **KAREN BATES** LETTERS · **NATHAN KANE** EDITOR

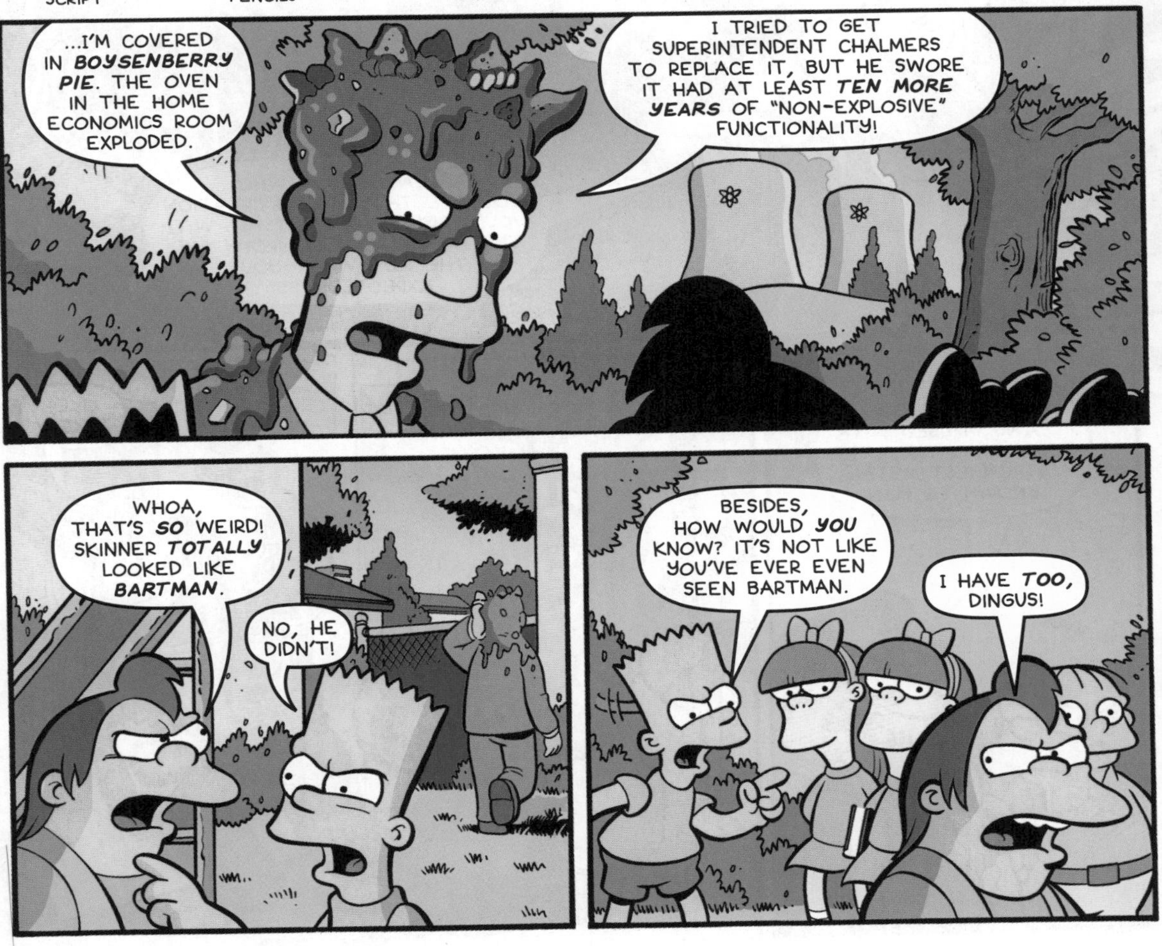
...I'M COVERED IN BOYSENBERRY PIE. THE OVEN IN THE HOME ECONOMICS ROOM EXPLODED.
I TRIED TO GET SUPERINTENDENT CHALMERS TO REPLACE IT, BUT HE SWORE IT HAD AT LEAST TEN MORE YEARS OF "NON-EXPLOSIVE" FUNCTIONALITY!
WHOA, THAT'S SO WEIRD! SKINNER TOTALLY LOOKED LIKE BARTMAN.
NO, HE DIDN'T!
BESIDES, HOW WOULD YOU KNOW? IT'S NOT LIKE YOU'VE EVER EVEN SEEN BARTMAN.
I HAVE TOO, DINGUS!

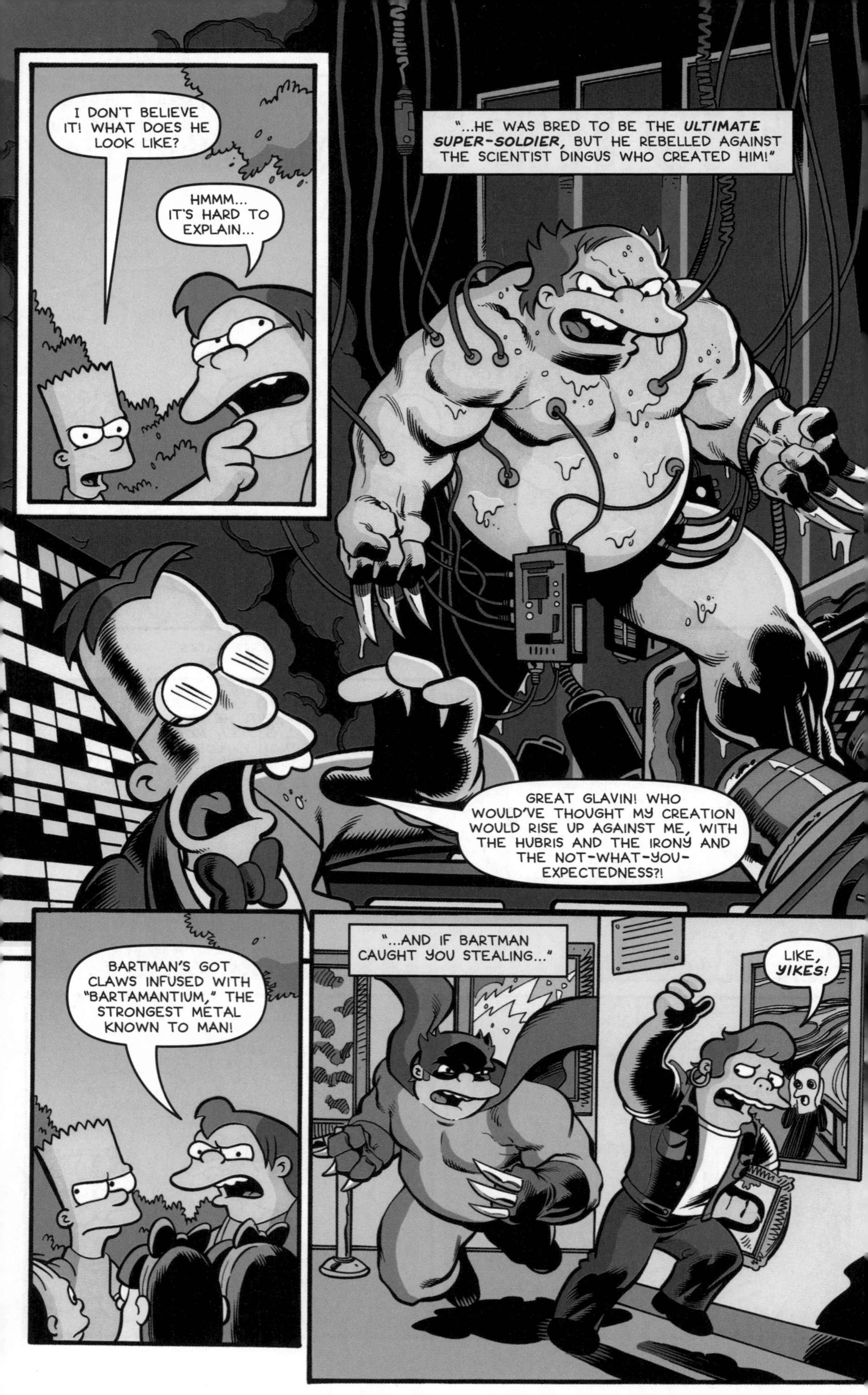
I DON'T BELIEVE IT! WHAT DOES HE LOOK LIKE?
HMMM... IT'S HARD TO EXPLAIN...
"...HE WAS BRED TO BE THE *ULTIMATE SUPER-SOLDIER,* BUT HE REBELLED AGAINST THE SCIENTIST DINGUS WHO CREATED HIM!"
GREAT GLAVIN! WHO WOULD'VE THOUGHT MY CREATION WOULD RISE UP AGAINST ME, WITH THE HUBRIS AND THE IRONY AND THE NOT-WHAT-YOU-EXPECTEDNESS?!
BARTMAN'S GOT CLAWS INFUSED WITH "BARTAMANTIUM," THE STRONGEST METAL KNOWN TO MAN!
"...AND IF BARTMAN CAUGHT YOU STEALING..."
LIKE, *YIKES!*

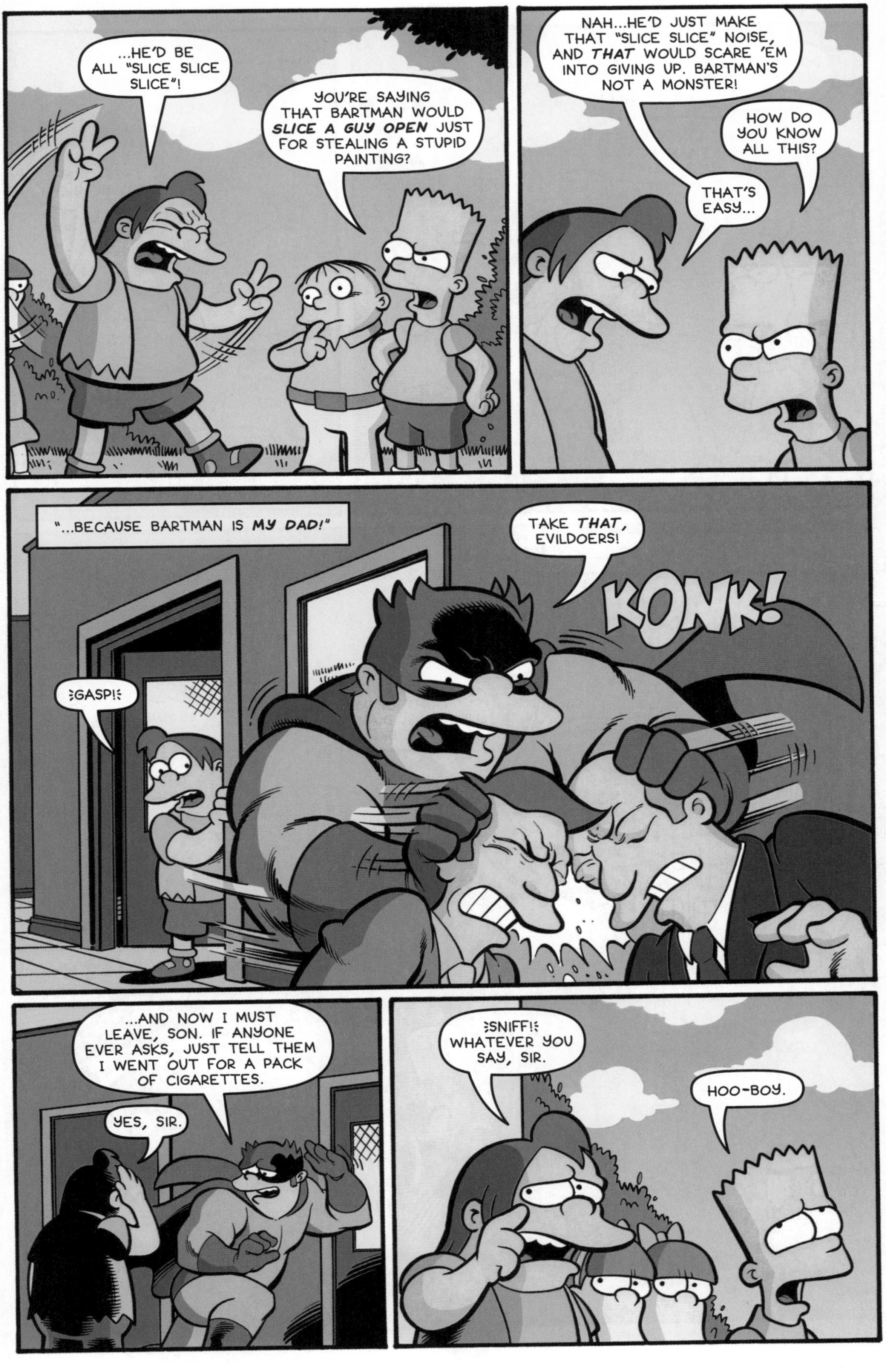
...HE'D BE ALL "SLICE SLICE SLICE"!
YOU'RE SAYING THAT BARTMAN WOULD *SLICE A GUY OPEN* JUST FOR STEALING A STUPID PAINTING?
NAH...HE'D JUST MAKE THAT "SLICE SLICE" NOISE, AND *THAT* WOULD SCARE 'EM INTO GIVING UP. BARTMAN'S NOT A MONSTER!
HOW DO YOU KNOW ALL THIS?
THAT'S EASY...
"...BECAUSE BARTMAN IS *MY DAD!*"
TAKE *THAT*, EVILDOERS!
KONK!
GASP!
...AND NOW I MUST LEAVE, SON. IF ANYONE EVER ASKS, JUST TELL THEM I WENT OUT FOR A PACK OF CIGARETTES.
YES, SIR.
SNIFF! WHATEVER YOU SAY, SIR.
HOO-BOY.

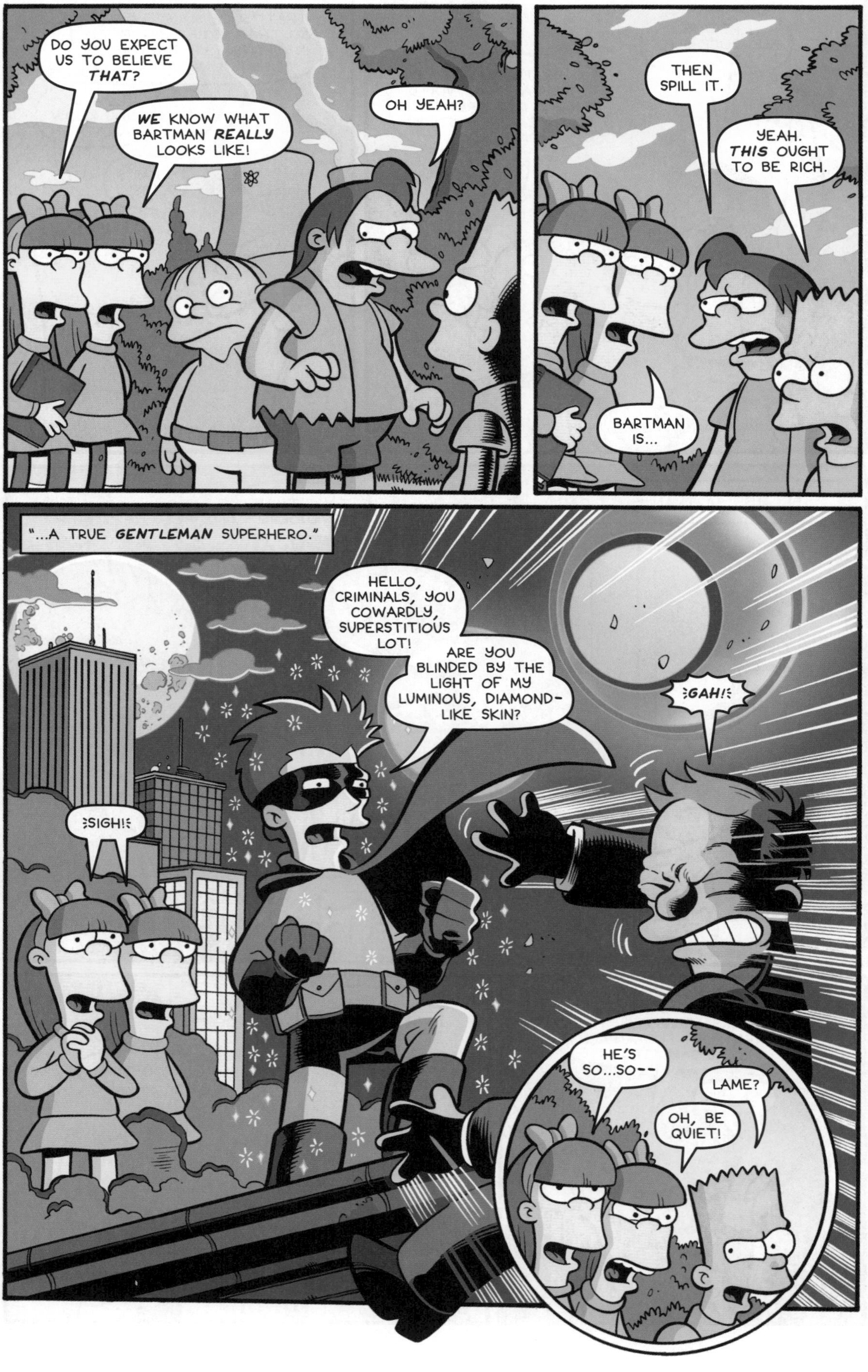
DO YOU EXPECT US TO BELIEVE *THAT?*
WE KNOW WHAT BARTMAN ***REALLY*** LOOKS LIKE!
OH YEAH?
THEN SPILL IT.
YEAH. ***THIS*** OUGHT TO BE RICH.
BARTMAN IS...
"...A TRUE ***GENTLEMAN*** SUPERHERO."
HELLO, CRIMINALS, YOU COWARDLY, SUPERSTITIOUS LOT!
ARE YOU BLINDED BY THE LIGHT OF MY LUMINOUS, DIAMOND-LIKE SKIN?
GAH!
SIGH!
HE'S SO...SO--
LAME?
OH, BE QUIET!

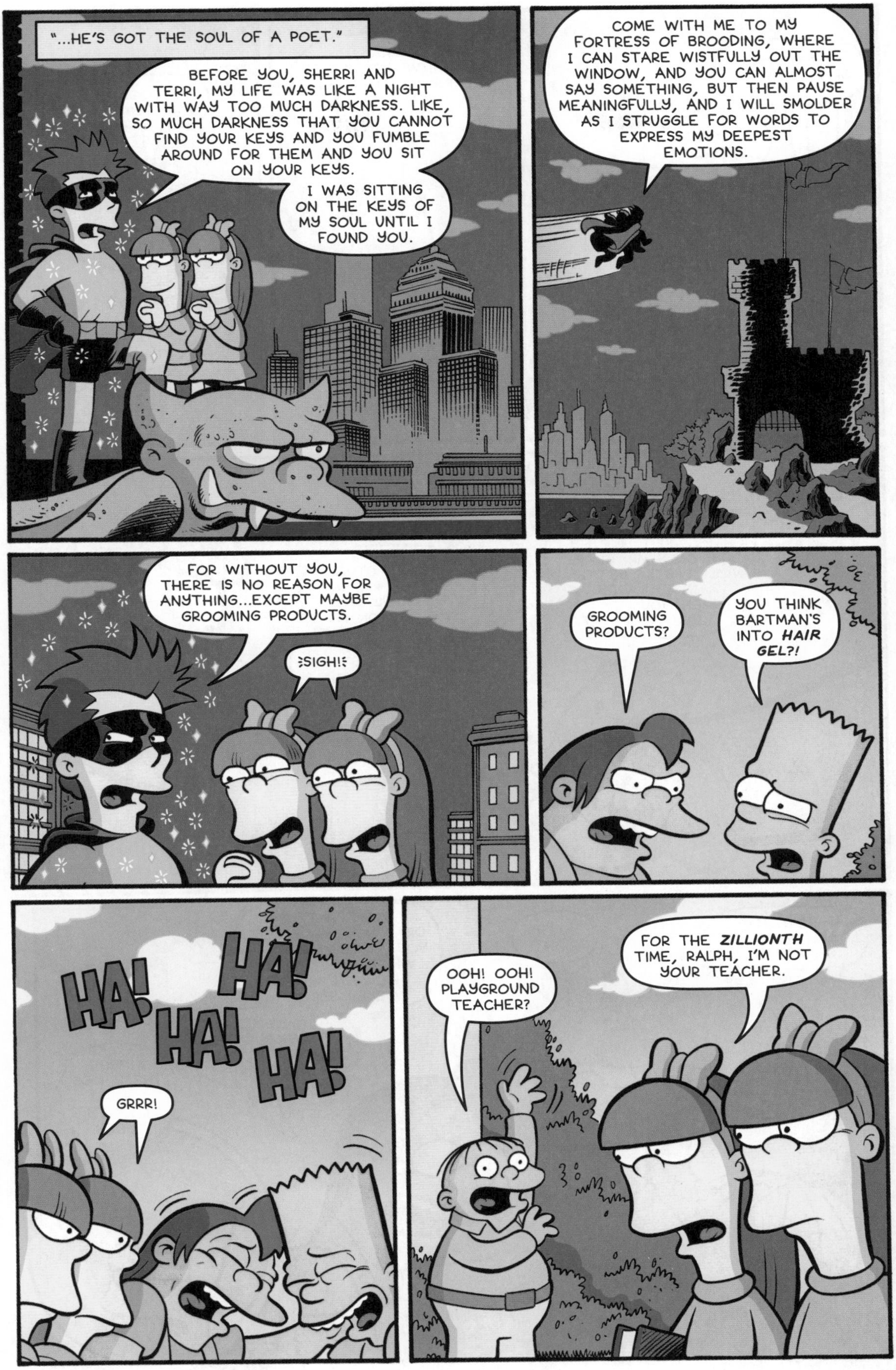
"...HE'S GOT THE SOUL OF A POET."
BEFORE YOU, SHERRI AND TERRI, MY LIFE WAS LIKE A NIGHT WITH WAY TOO MUCH DARKNESS. LIKE, SO MUCH DARKNESS THAT YOU CANNOT FIND YOUR KEYS AND YOU FUMBLE AROUND FOR THEM AND YOU SIT ON YOUR KEYS.
I WAS SITTING ON THE KEYS OF MY SOUL UNTIL I FOUND YOU.
COME WITH ME TO MY FORTRESS OF BROODING, WHERE I CAN STARE WISTFULLY OUT THE WINDOW, AND YOU CAN ALMOST SAY SOMETHING, BUT THEN PAUSE MEANINGFULLY, AND I WILL SMOLDER AS I STRUGGLE FOR WORDS TO EXPRESS MY DEEPEST EMOTIONS.
FOR WITHOUT YOU, THERE IS NO REASON FOR ANYTHING...EXCEPT MAYBE GROOMING PRODUCTS.
SIGH!
GROOMING PRODUCTS?
YOU THINK BARTMAN'S INTO **HAIR GEL**?!
HA! HA! HA! HA!
GRRR!
OOH! OOH! PLAYGROUND TEACHER?
FOR THE **ZILLIONTH** TIME, RALPH, I'M NOT YOUR TEACHER.

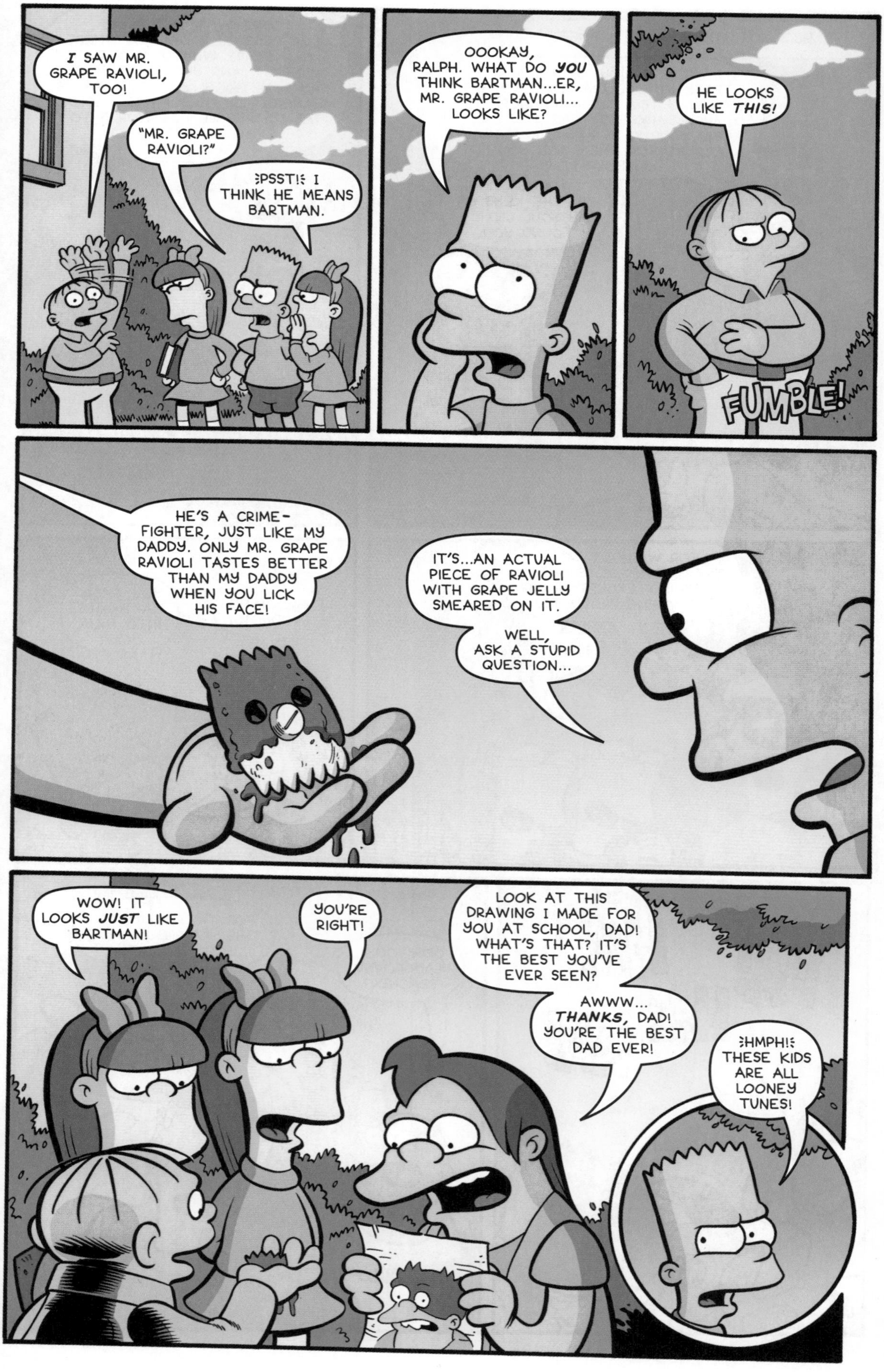
I SAW MR. GRAPE RAVIOLI, TOO!
"MR. GRAPE RAVIOLI?"
PSST! I THINK HE MEANS BARTMAN.
OOOKAY, RALPH. WHAT DO YOU THINK BARTMAN...ER, MR. GRAPE RAVIOLI... LOOKS LIKE?
HE LOOKS LIKE THIS!
FUMBLE!
HE'S A CRIME-FIGHTER, JUST LIKE MY DADDY. ONLY MR. GRAPE RAVIOLI TASTES BETTER THAN MY DADDY WHEN YOU LICK HIS FACE!
IT'S...AN ACTUAL PIECE OF RAVIOLI WITH GRAPE JELLY SMEARED ON IT.
WELL, ASK A STUPID QUESTION...
WOW! IT LOOKS JUST LIKE BARTMAN!
YOU'RE RIGHT!
LOOK AT THIS DRAWING I MADE FOR YOU AT SCHOOL, DAD! WHAT'S THAT? IT'S THE BEST YOU'VE EVER SEEN?
AWWW... THANKS, DAD! YOU'RE THE BEST DAD EVER!
HMPH! THESE KIDS ARE ALL LOONEY TUNES!

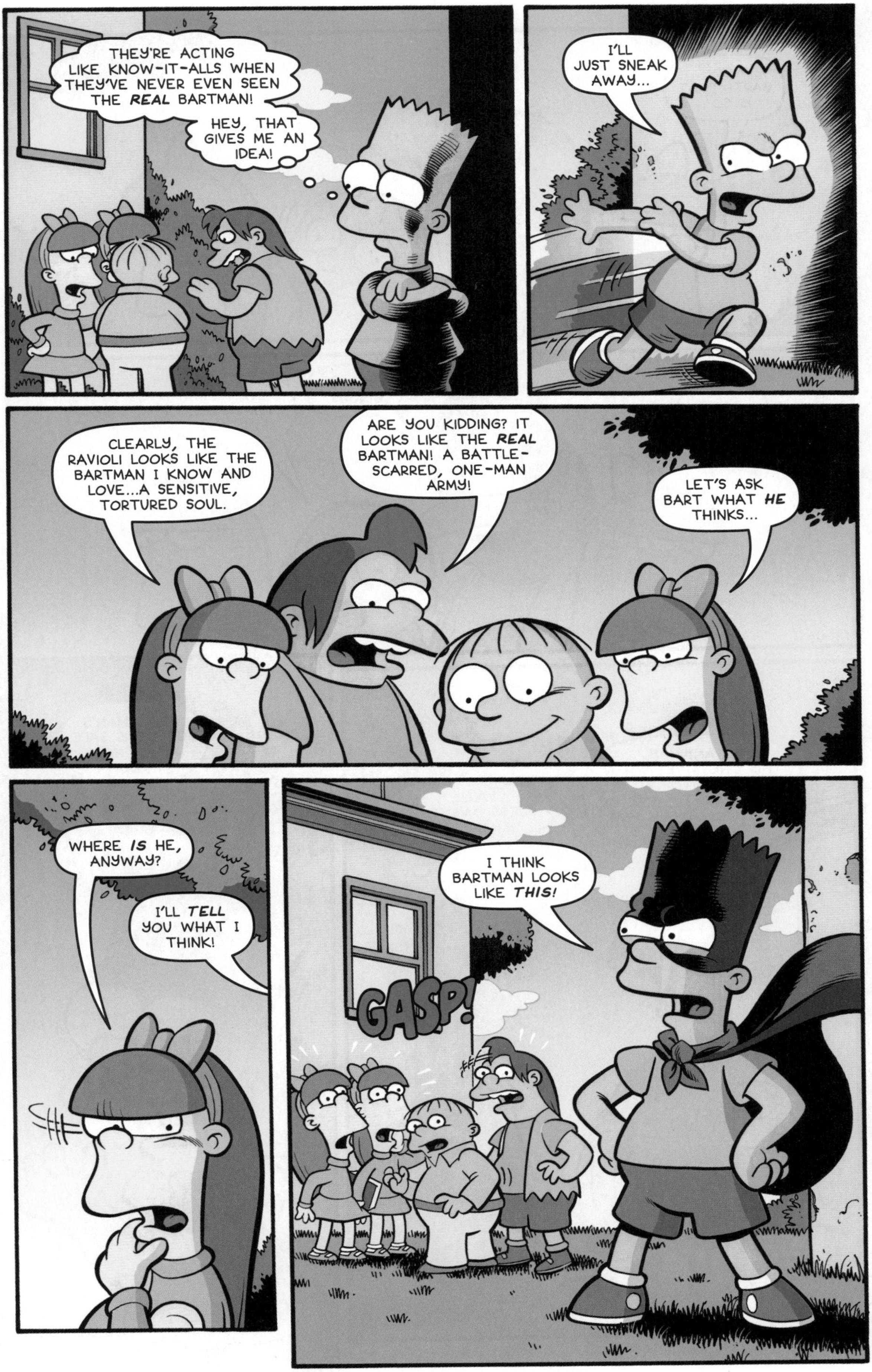
THEY'RE ACTING LIKE KNOW-IT-ALLS WHEN THEY'VE NEVER EVEN SEEN THE *REAL* BARTMAN!
HEY, THAT GIVES ME AN IDEA!
I'LL JUST SNEAK AWAY...
CLEARLY, THE RAVIOLI LOOKS LIKE THE BARTMAN I KNOW AND LOVE...A SENSITIVE, TORTURED SOUL.
ARE YOU KIDDING? IT LOOKS LIKE THE *REAL* BARTMAN! A BATTLE-SCARRED, ONE-MAN ARMY!
LET'S ASK BART WHAT *HE* THINKS...
WHERE *IS* HE, ANYWAY?
I'LL *TELL* YOU WHAT I THINK!
I THINK BARTMAN LOOKS LIKE *THIS*!
GASP!

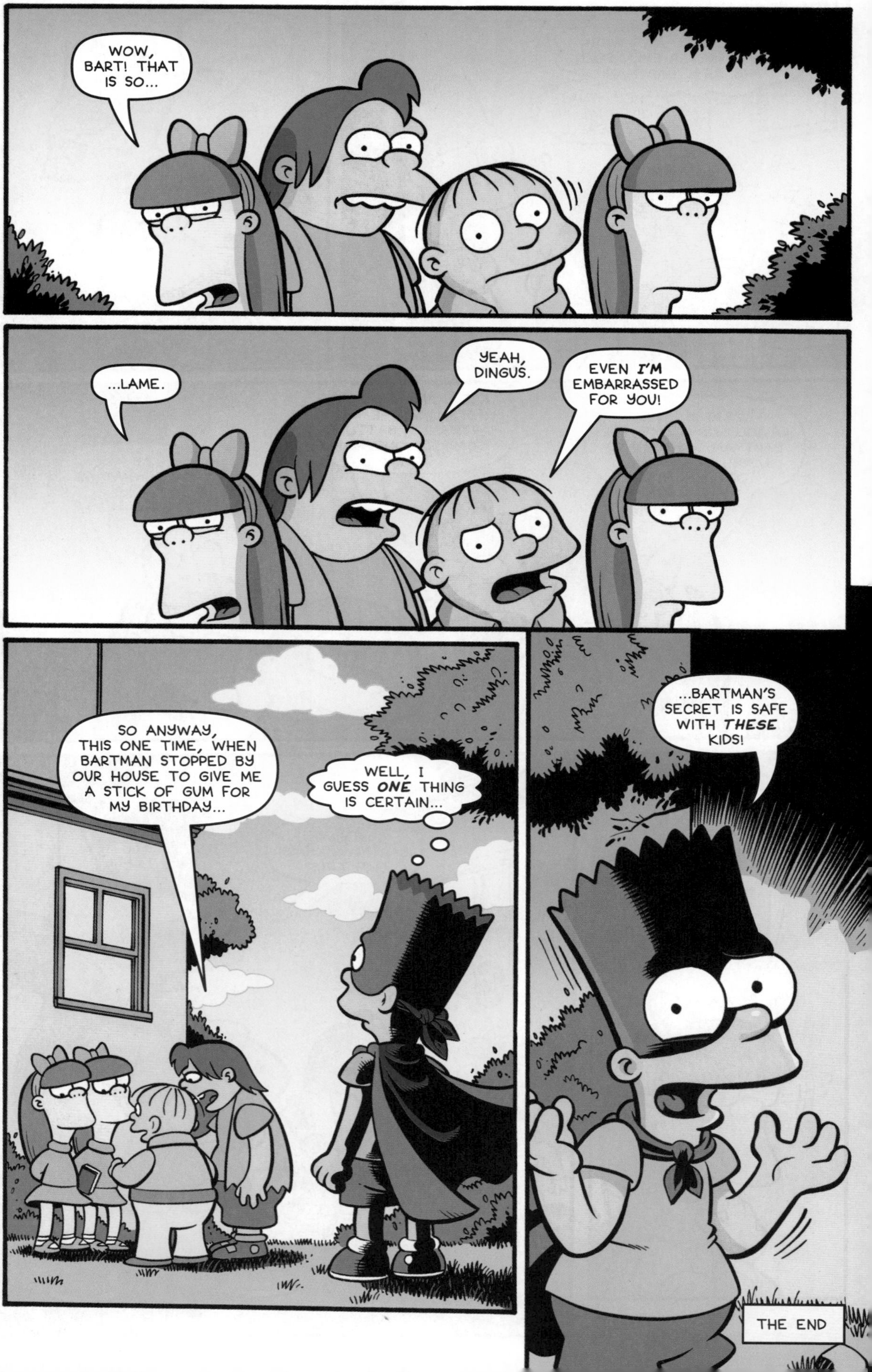
WOW, BART! THAT IS SO...
...LAME.
YEAH, DINGUS.
EVEN I'M EMBARRASSED FOR YOU!
SO ANYWAY, THIS ONE TIME, WHEN BARTMAN STOPPED BY OUR HOUSE TO GIVE ME A STICK OF GUM FOR MY BIRTHDAY...
WELL, I GUESS ONE THING IS CERTAIN...
...BARTMAN'S SECRET IS SAFE WITH THESE KIDS!
THE END

THE TODD & RODYSSEY

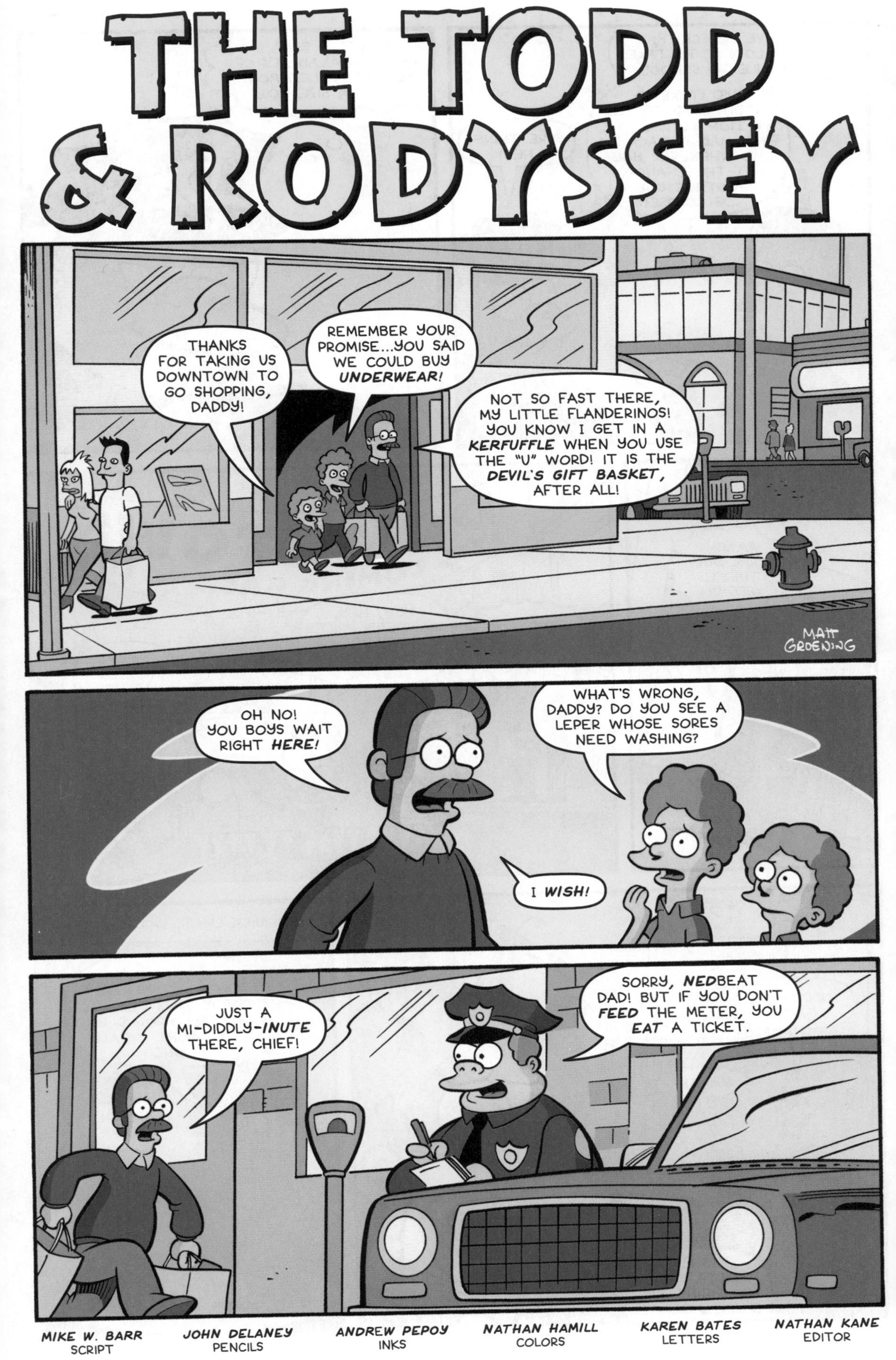
THANKS FOR TAKING US DOWNTOWN TO GO SHOPPING, DADDY!
REMEMBER YOUR PROMISE...YOU SAID WE COULD BUY **UNDERWEAR**!
NOT SO FAST THERE, MY LITTLE FLANDERINOS! YOU KNOW I GET IN A **KERFUFFLE** WHEN YOU USE THE "U" WORD! IT IS THE **DEVIL'S GIFT BASKET**, AFTER ALL!
MATT GROENING
OH NO! YOU BOYS WAIT RIGHT **HERE**!
WHAT'S WRONG, DADDY? DO YOU SEE A LEPER WHOSE SORES NEED WASHING?
I **WISH**!
JUST A MI-DIDDLY-**INUTE** THERE, CHIEF!
SORRY, **NED**BEAT DAD! BUT IF YOU DON'T **FEED** THE METER, YOU **EAT** A TICKET.

MIKE W. BARR SCRIPT | **JOHN DELANEY** PENCILS | **ANDREW PEPOY** INKS | **NATHAN HAMILL** COLORS | **KAREN BATES** LETTERS | **NATHAN KANE** EDITOR

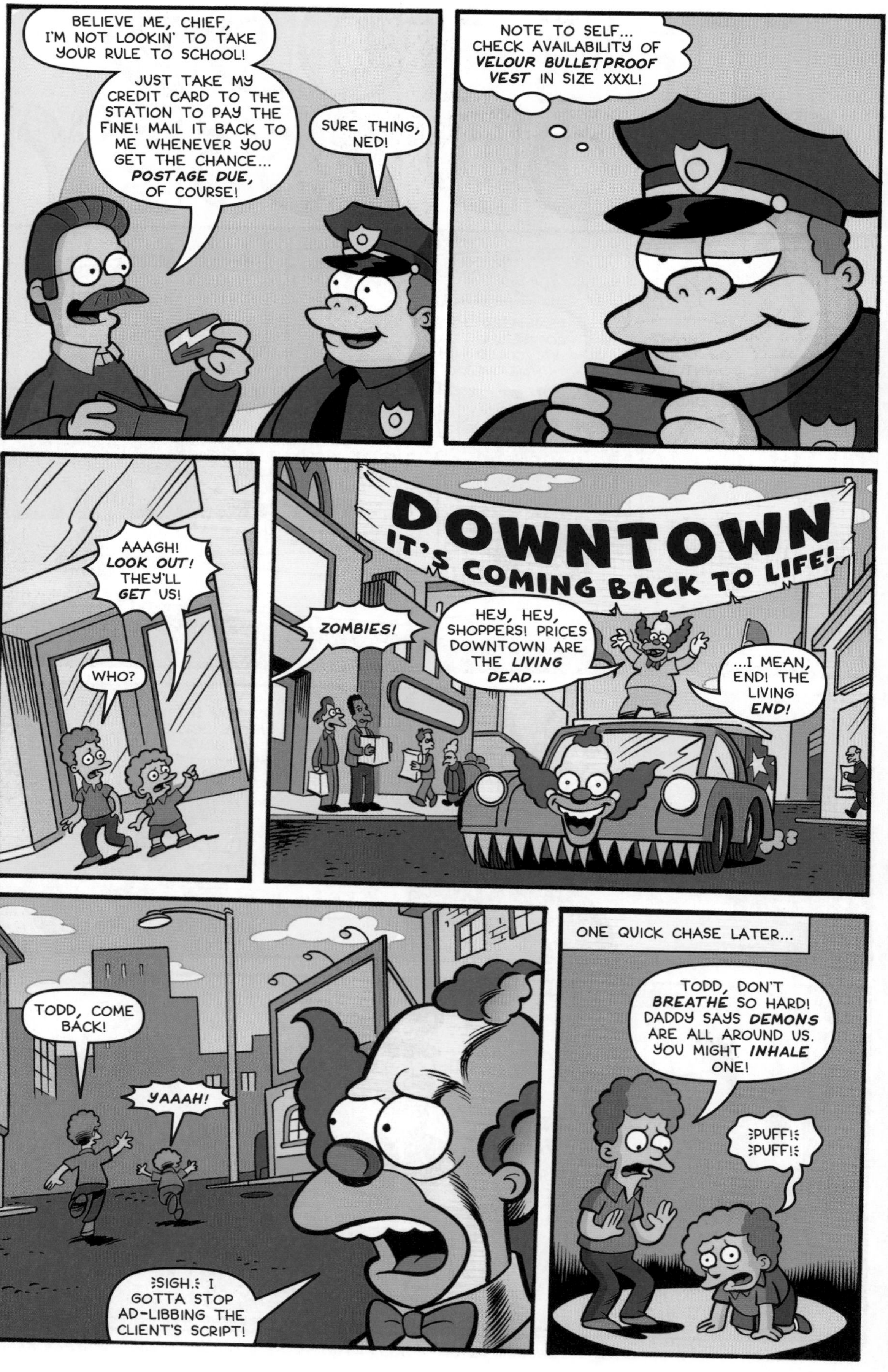
BELIEVE ME, CHIEF, I'M NOT LOOKIN' TO TAKE YOUR RULE TO SCHOOL!
JUST TAKE MY CREDIT CARD TO THE STATION TO PAY THE FINE! MAIL IT BACK TO ME WHENEVER YOU GET THE CHANCE... POSTAGE DUE, OF COURSE!
SURE THING, NED!
NOTE TO SELF... CHECK AVAILABILITY OF VELOUR BULLETPROOF VEST IN SIZE XXXL!
AAAGH! LOOK OUT! THEY'LL GET US!
WHO?
ZOMBIES!
DOWNTOWN IT'S COMING BACK TO LIFE!
HEY, HEY, SHOPPERS! PRICES DOWNTOWN ARE THE LIVING DEAD...
...I MEAN, END! THE LIVING END!
TODD, COME BACK!
YAAAH!
SIGH. I GOTTA STOP AD-LIBBING THE CLIENT'S SCRIPT!
ONE QUICK CHASE LATER...
TODD, DON'T BREATHE SO HARD! DADDY SAYS DEMONS ARE ALL AROUND US. YOU MIGHT INHALE ONE!
PUFF! PUFF!

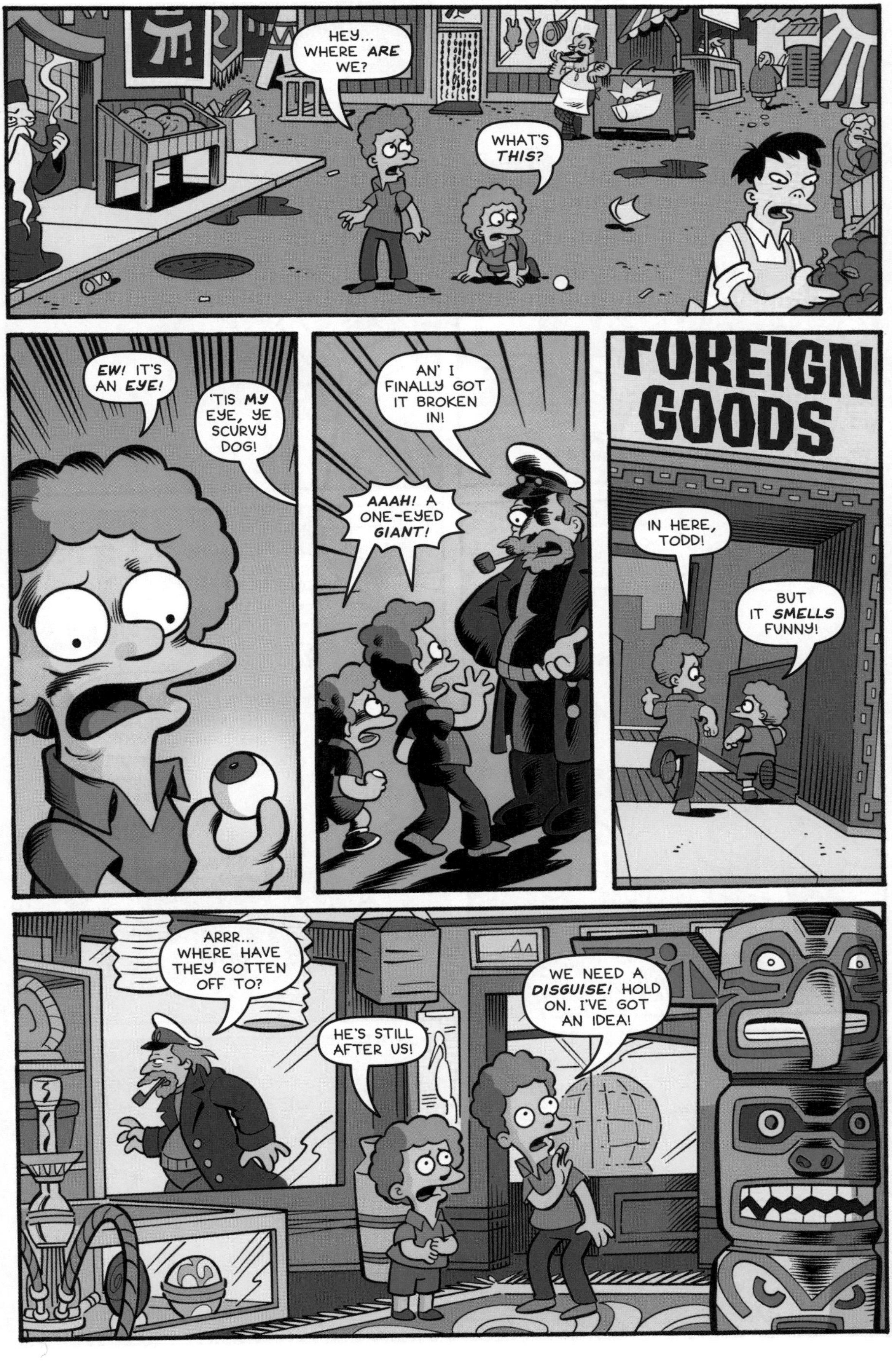
HEY... WHERE ARE WE?
WHAT'S THIS?
EW! IT'S AN EYE!
'TIS MY EYE, YE SCURVY DOG!
AN' I FINALLY GOT IT BROKEN IN!
AAAH! A ONE-EYED GIANT!
FOREIGN GOODS
IN HERE, TODD!
BUT IT SMELLS FUNNY!
ARRR... WHERE HAVE THEY GOTTEN OFF TO?
HE'S STILL AFTER US!
WE NEED A DISGUISE! HOLD ON. I'VE GOT AN IDEA!

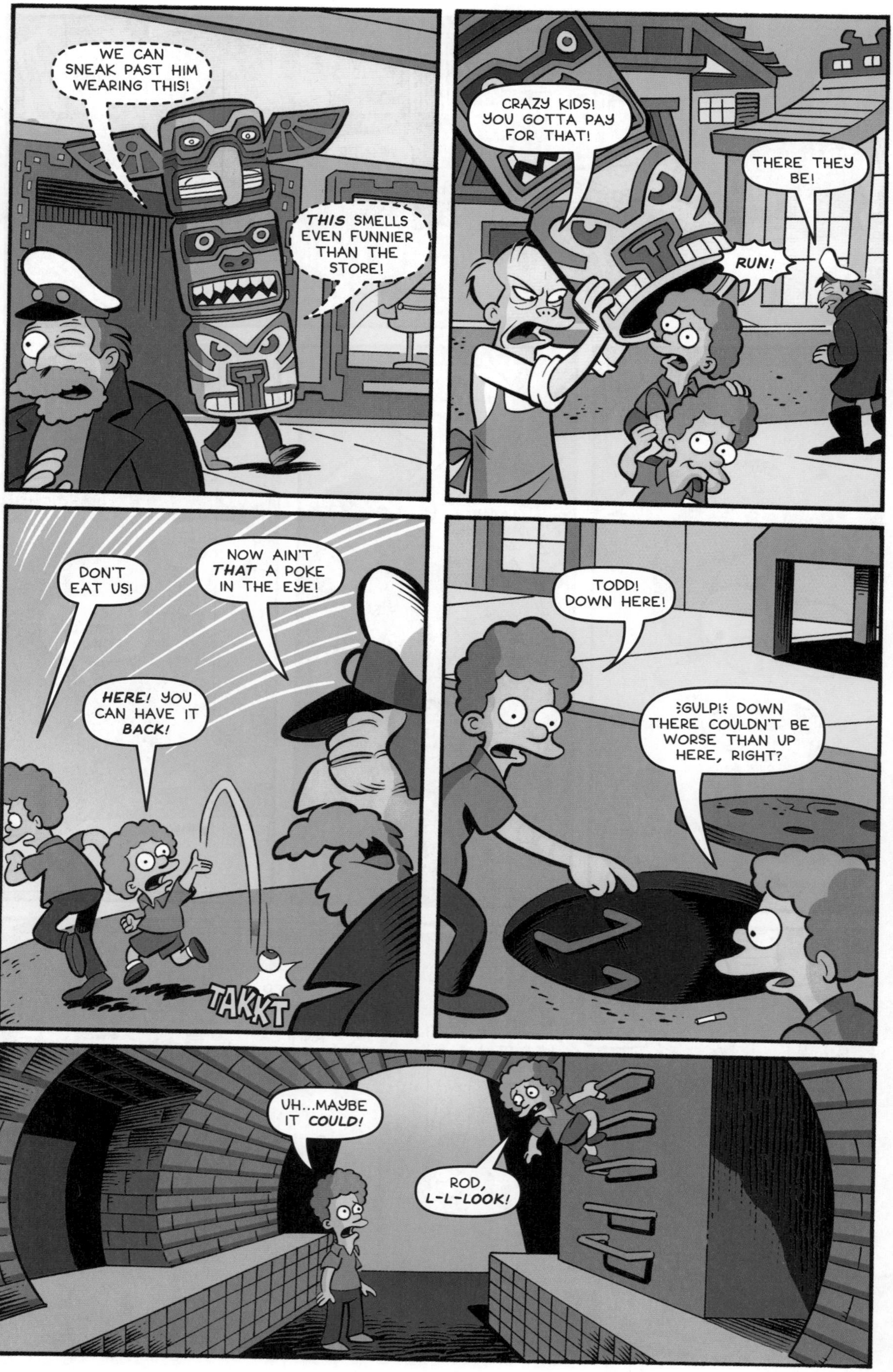
WE CAN SNEAK PAST HIM WEARING THIS!
THIS SMELLS EVEN FUNNIER THAN THE STORE!
CRAZY KIDS! YOU GOTTA PAY FOR THAT!
THERE THEY BE!
RUN!
DON'T EAT US!
NOW AIN'T THAT A POKE IN THE EYE!
HERE! YOU CAN HAVE IT BACK!
TAKKT
TODD! DOWN HERE!
GULP! DOWN THERE COULDN'T BE WORSE THAN UP HERE, RIGHT?
UH...MAYBE IT COULD!
ROD, L-L-LOOK!

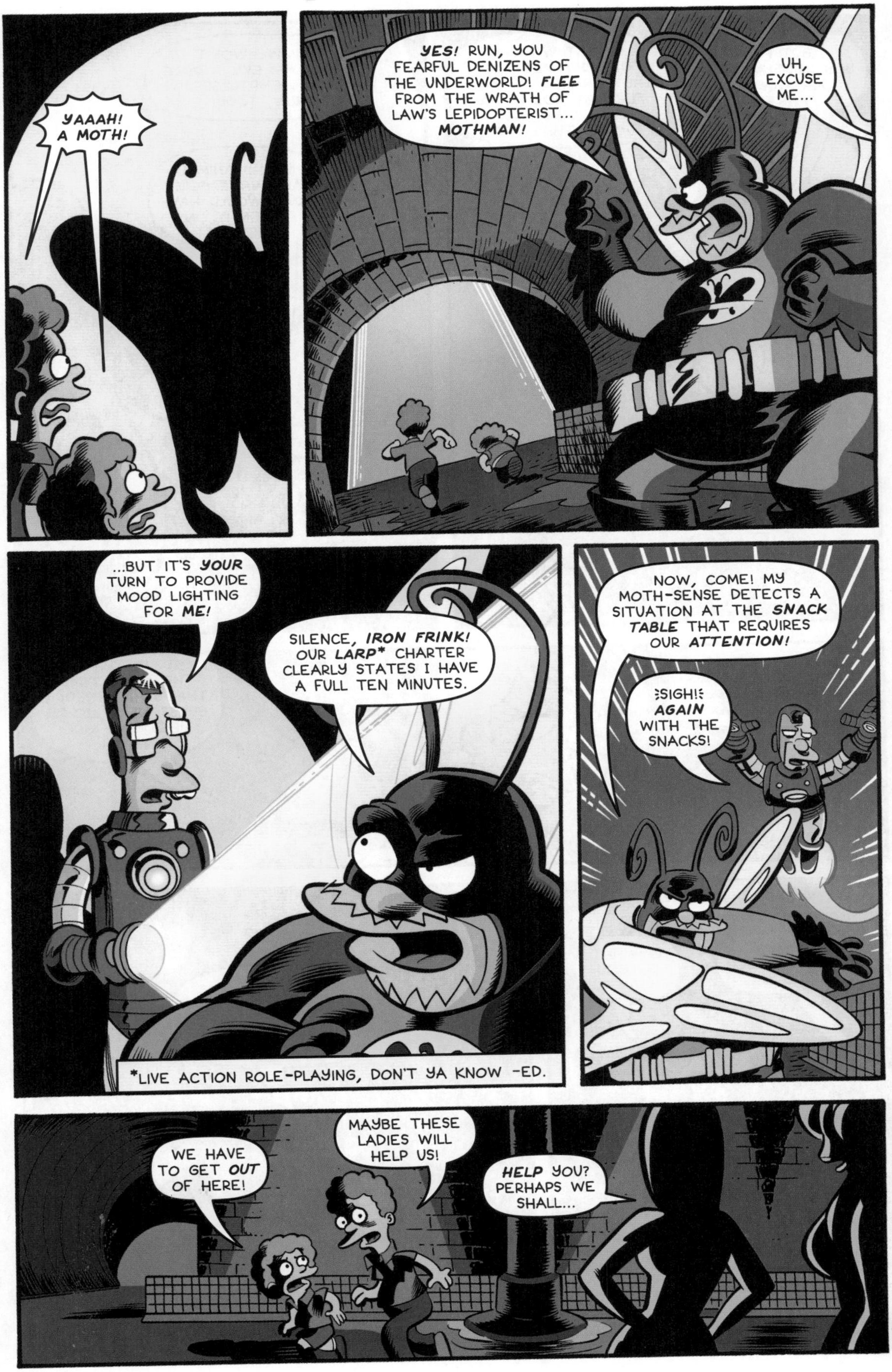
YAAAH! A MOTH!
YES! RUN, YOU FEARFUL DENIZENS OF THE UNDERWORLD! FLEE FROM THE WRATH OF LAW'S LEPIDOPTERIST... MOTHMAN!
UH, EXCUSE ME...
...BUT IT'S YOUR TURN TO PROVIDE MOOD LIGHTING FOR ME!
SILENCE, IRON FRINK! OUR LARP* CHARTER CLEARLY STATES I HAVE A FULL TEN MINUTES.
*LIVE ACTION ROLE-PLAYING, DON'T YA KNOW -ED.
NOW, COME! MY MOTH-SENSE DETECTS A SITUATION AT THE SNACK TABLE THAT REQUIRES OUR ATTENTION!
SIGH! AGAIN WITH THE SNACKS!
WE HAVE TO GET OUT OF HERE!
MAYBE THESE LADIES WILL HELP US!
HELP YOU? PERHAPS WE SHALL...

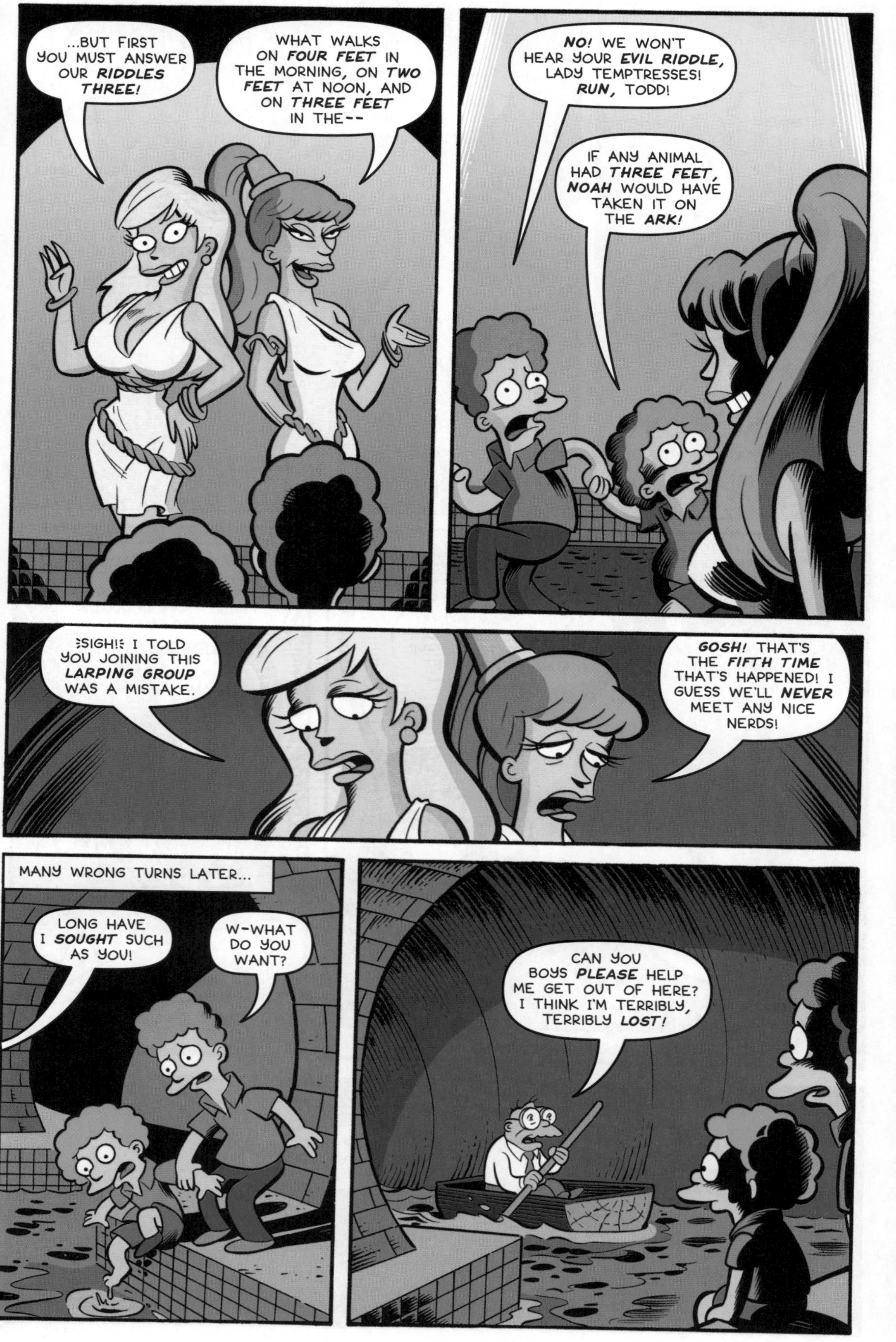
...BUT FIRST YOU MUST ANSWER OUR RIDDLES THREE!
WHAT WALKS ON FOUR FEET IN THE MORNING, ON TWO FEET AT NOON, AND ON THREE FEET IN THE--
NO! WE WON'T HEAR YOUR EVIL RIDDLE, LADY TEMPTRESSES! RUN, TODD!
IF ANY ANIMAL HAD THREE FEET, NOAH WOULD HAVE TAKEN IT ON THE ARK!
:SIGH!: I TOLD YOU JOINING THIS LARPING GROUP WAS A MISTAKE.
GOSH! THAT'S THE FIFTH TIME THAT'S HAPPENED! I GUESS WE'LL NEVER MEET ANY NICE NERDS!
MANY WRONG TURNS LATER...
LONG HAVE I SOUGHT SUCH AS YOU!
W-WHAT DO YOU WANT?
CAN YOU BOYS PLEASE HELP ME GET OUT OF HERE? I THINK I'M TERRIBLY, TERRIBLY LOST!

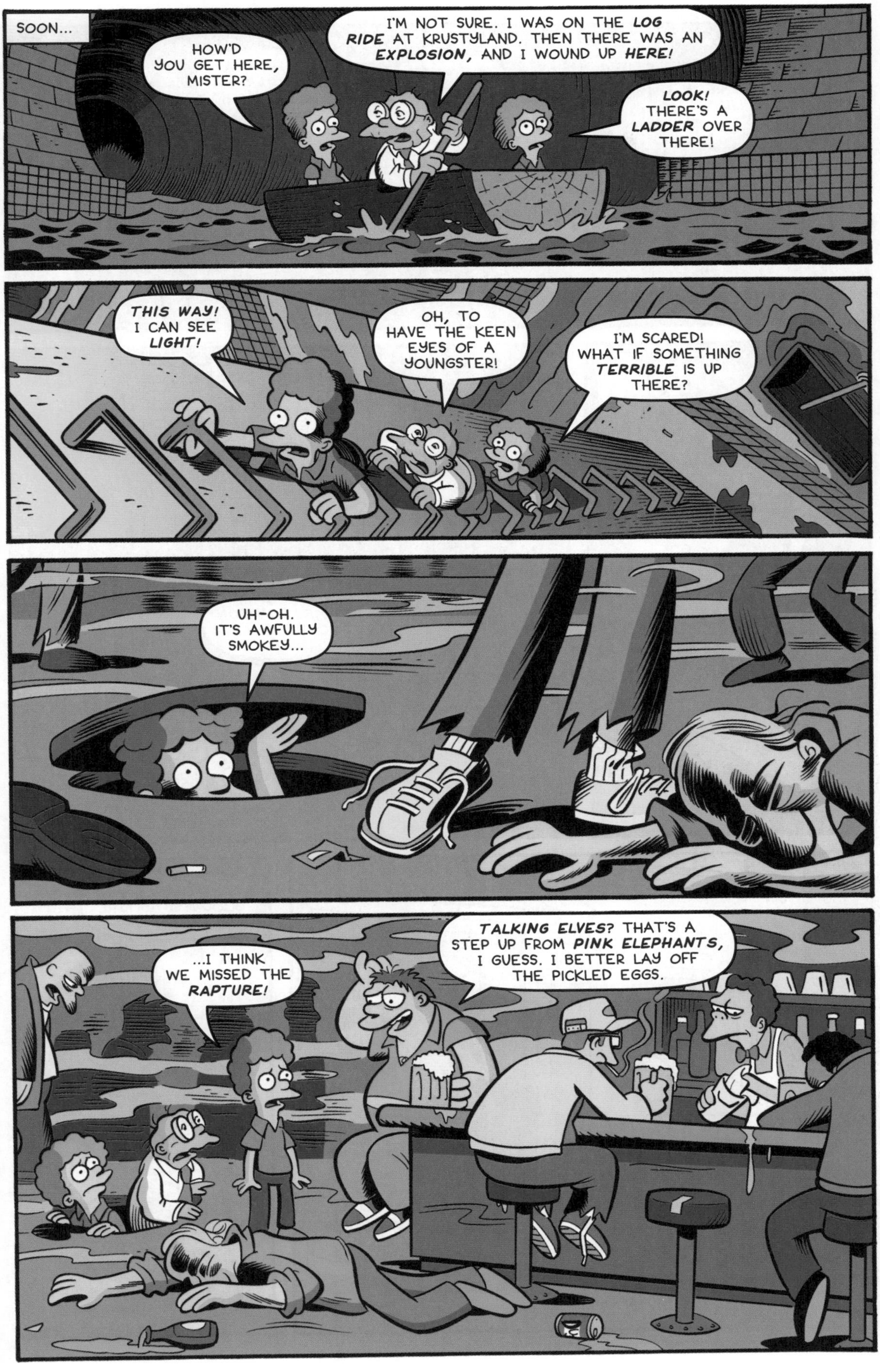
SOON...
HOW'D YOU GET HERE, MISTER?
I'M NOT SURE. I WAS ON THE LOG RIDE AT KRUSTYLAND. THEN THERE WAS AN EXPLOSION, AND I WOUND UP HERE!
LOOK! THERE'S A LADDER OVER THERE!
THIS WAY! I CAN SEE LIGHT!
OH, TO HAVE THE KEEN EYES OF A YOUNGSTER!
I'M SCARED! WHAT IF SOMETHING TERRIBLE IS UP THERE?
UH-OH. IT'S AWFULLY SMOKEY...
...I THINK WE MISSED THE RAPTURE!
TALKING ELVES? THAT'S A STEP UP FROM PINK ELEPHANTS, I GUESS. I BETTER LAY OFF THE PICKLED EGGS.

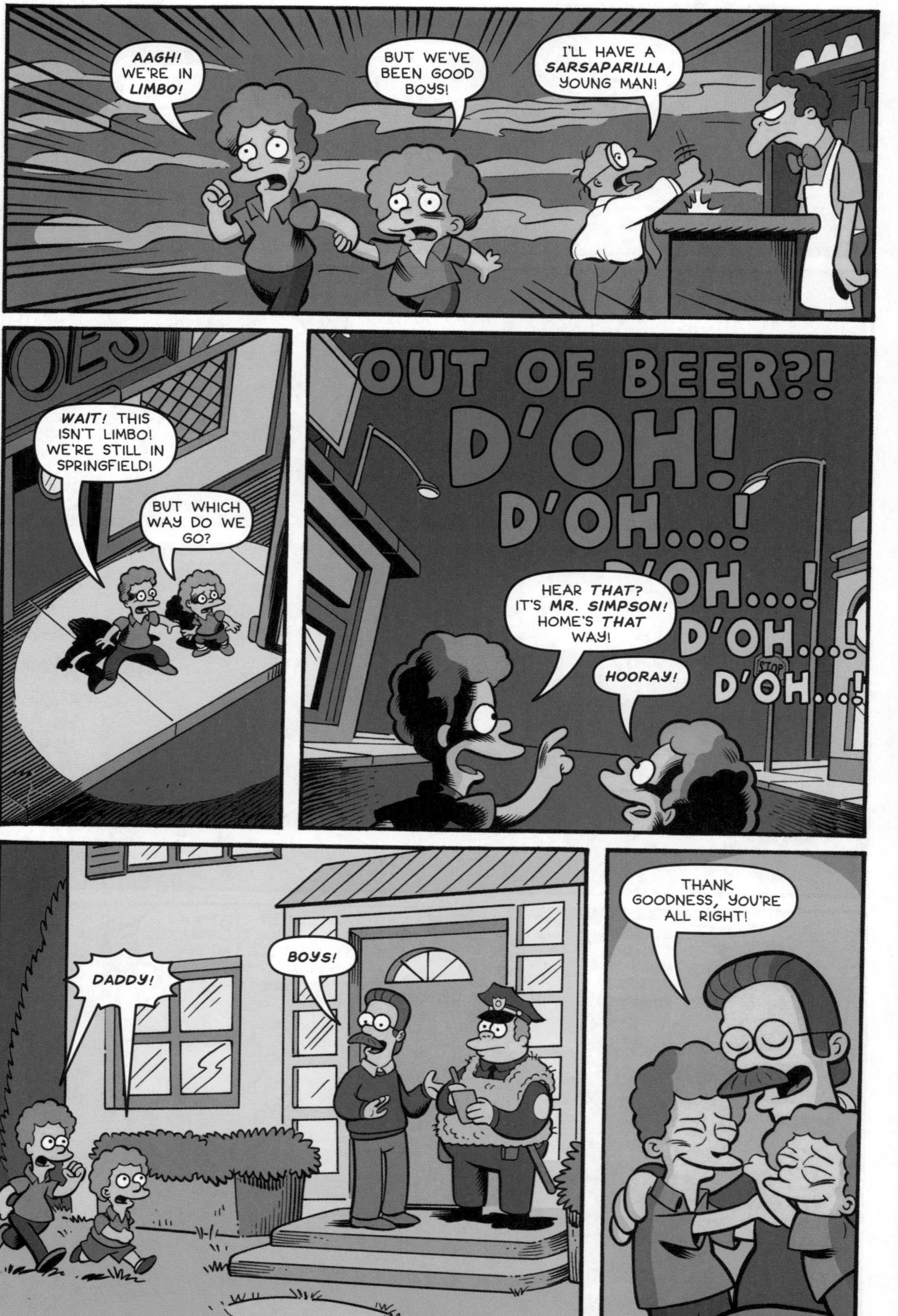
AAGH! WE'RE IN LIMBO!
BUT WE'VE BEEN GOOD BOYS!
I'LL HAVE A SARSAPARILLA, YOUNG MAN!
WAIT! THIS ISN'T LIMBO! WE'RE STILL IN SPRINGFIELD!
BUT WHICH WAY DO WE GO?
OUT OF BEER?!
D'OH!
D'OH...!
D'OH...!
D'OH...!
D'OH...!
HEAR THAT? IT'S MR. SIMPSON! HOME'S THAT WAY!
HOORAY!
STOP
DADDY!
BOYS!
THANK GOODNESS, YOU'RE ALL RIGHT!

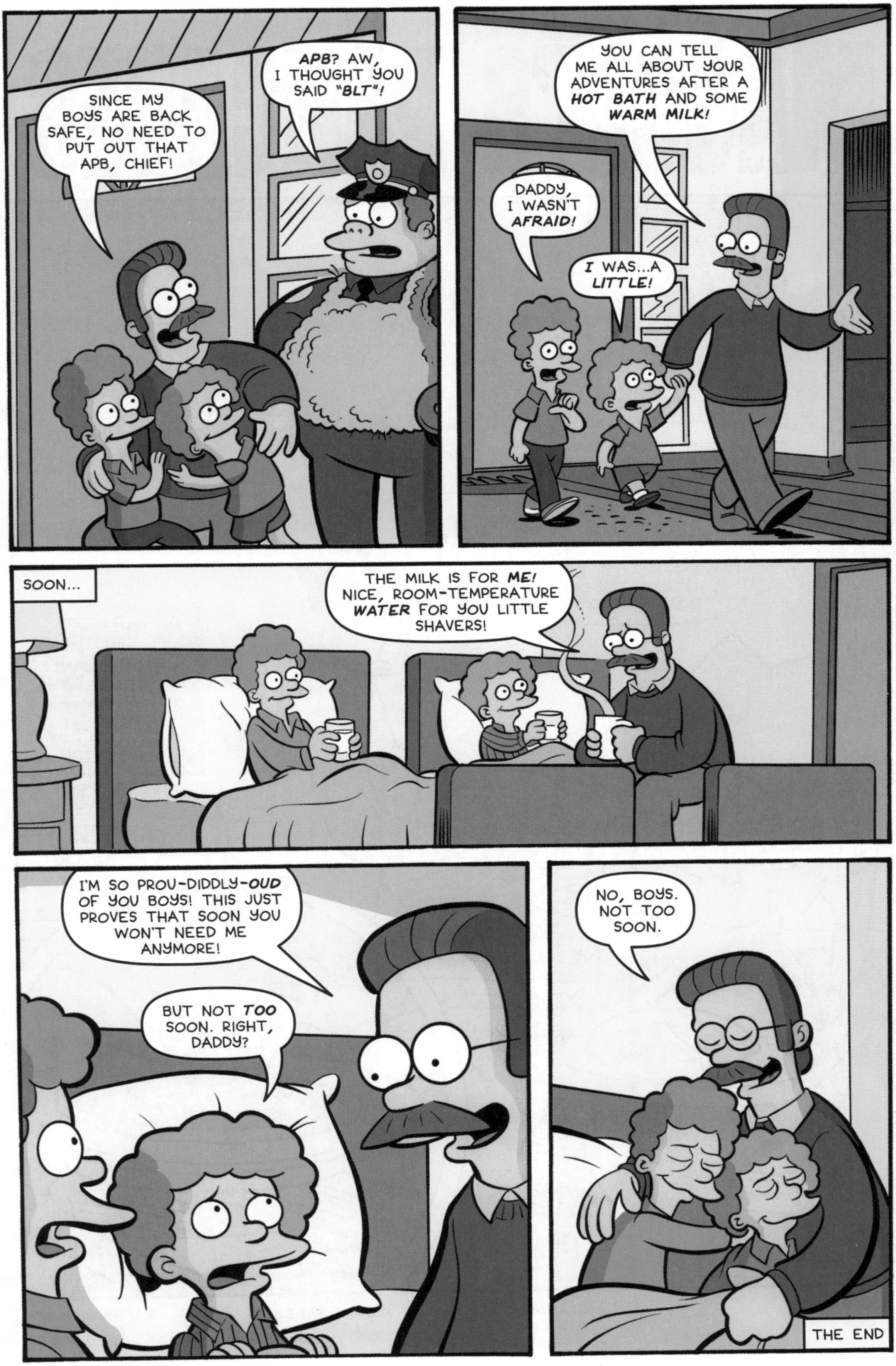
SINCE MY BOYS ARE BACK SAFE, NO NEED TO PUT OUT THAT APB, CHIEF!
APB? AW, I THOUGHT YOU SAID "BLT"!
YOU CAN TELL ME ALL ABOUT YOUR ADVENTURES AFTER A HOT BATH AND SOME WARM MILK!
DADDY, I WASN'T AFRAID!
I WAS...A LITTLE!
SOON...
THE MILK IS FOR ME! NICE, ROOM-TEMPERATURE WATER FOR YOU LITTLE SHAVERS!
I'M SO PROU-DIDDLY-OUD OF YOU BOYS! THIS JUST PROVES THAT SOON YOU WON'T NEED ME ANYMORE!
BUT NOT TOO SOON. RIGHT, DADDY?
NO, BOYS. NOT TOO SOON.
THE END

MAGGIE'S PANCAKES

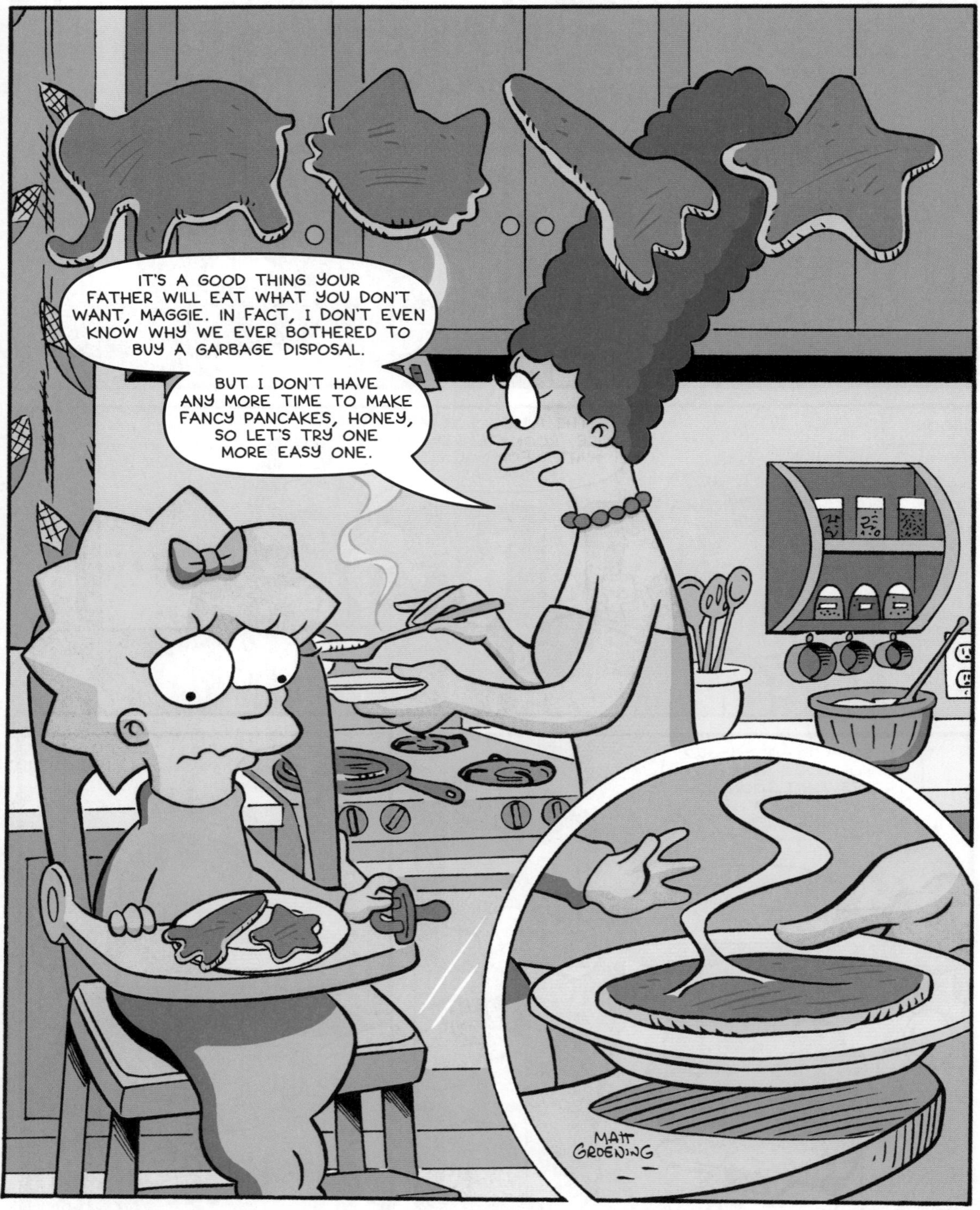
IT'S A GOOD THING YOUR FATHER WILL EAT WHAT YOU DON'T WANT, MAGGIE. IN FACT, I DON'T EVEN KNOW WHY WE EVER BOTHERED TO BUY A GARBAGE DISPOSAL.
BUT I DON'T HAVE ANY MORE TIME TO MAKE FANCY PANCAKES, HONEY, SO LET'S TRY ONE MORE EASY ONE.
MATT GROENING

CAROL LAY STORY & ART

ART VILLANUEVA COLORS

KAREN BATES LETTERS

NATHAN KANE EDITOR

SUCK! SUCK!

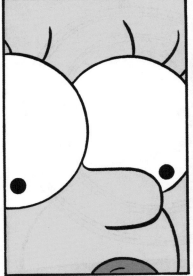

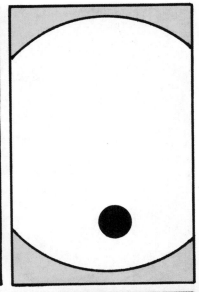

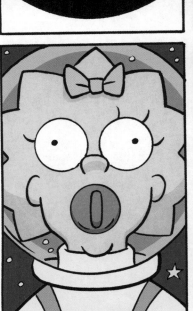

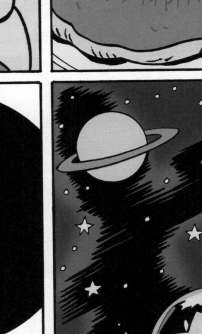

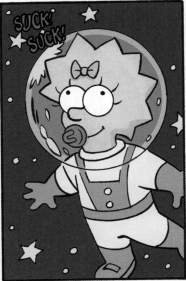

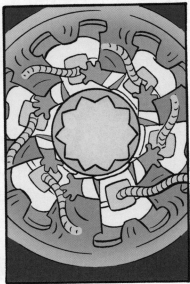

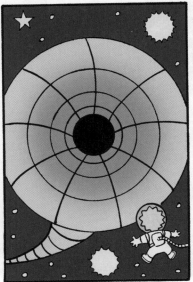

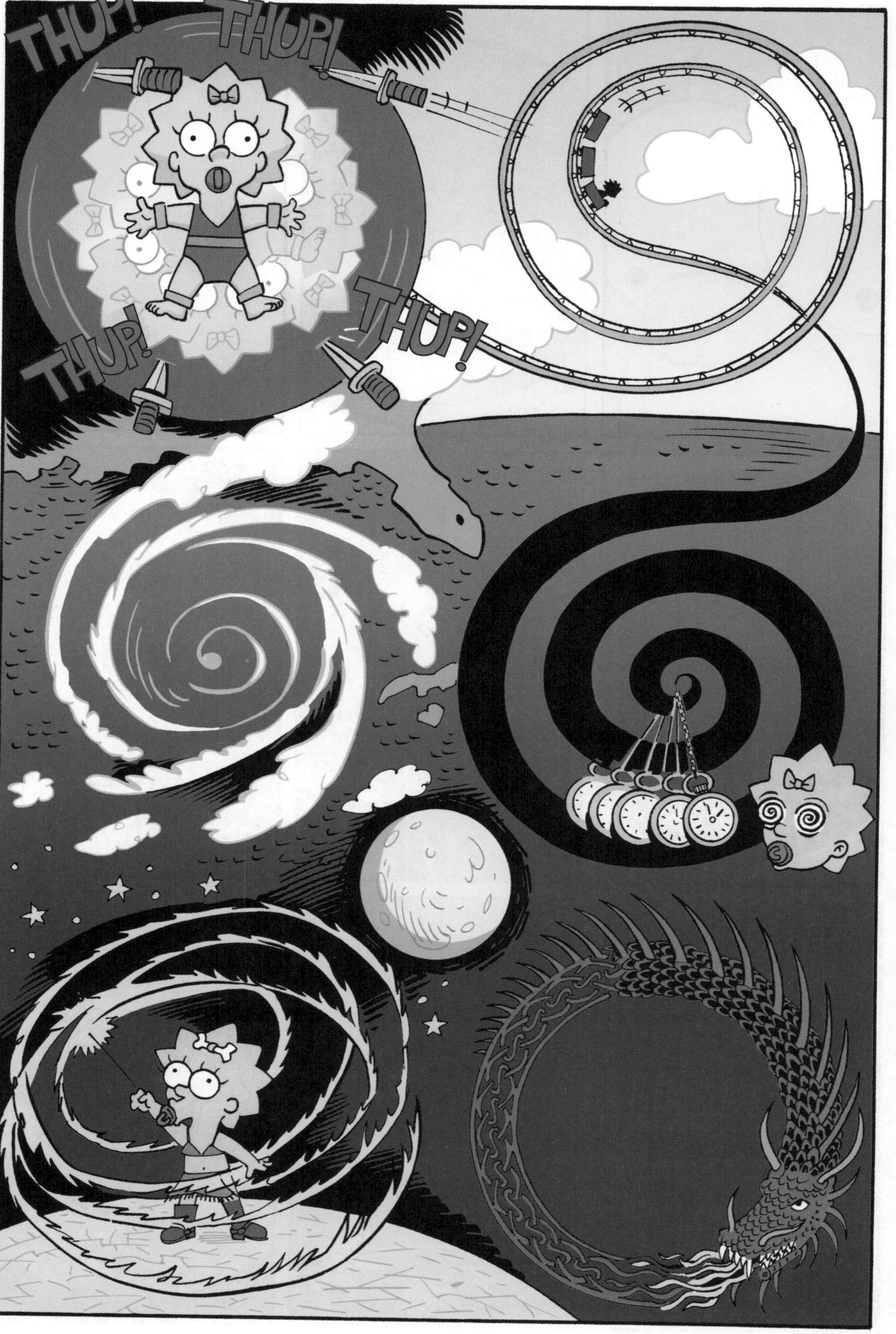
THUP!
THUP!
THUP!
THUP!

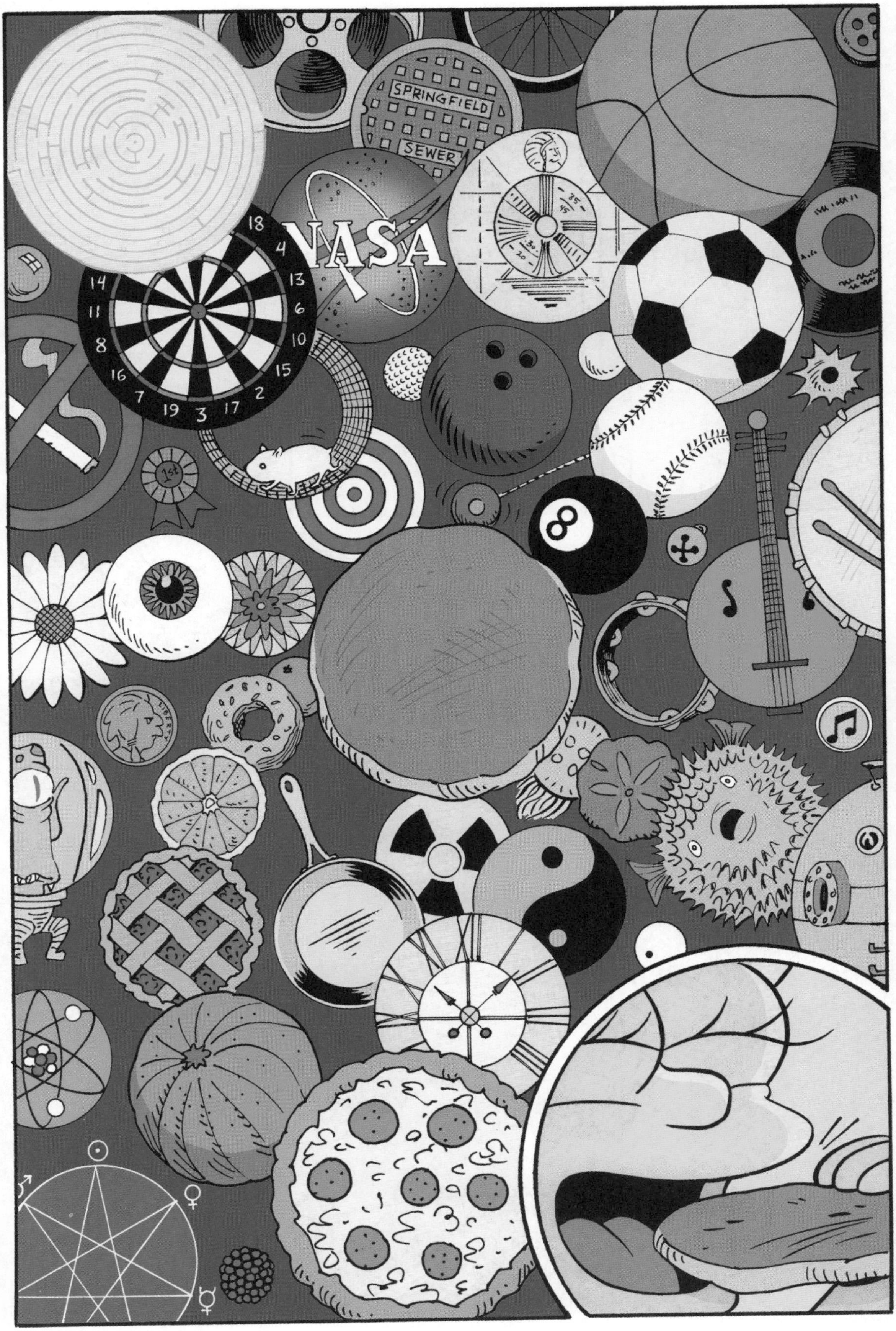

SPRINGFIELD
SEWER
NASA

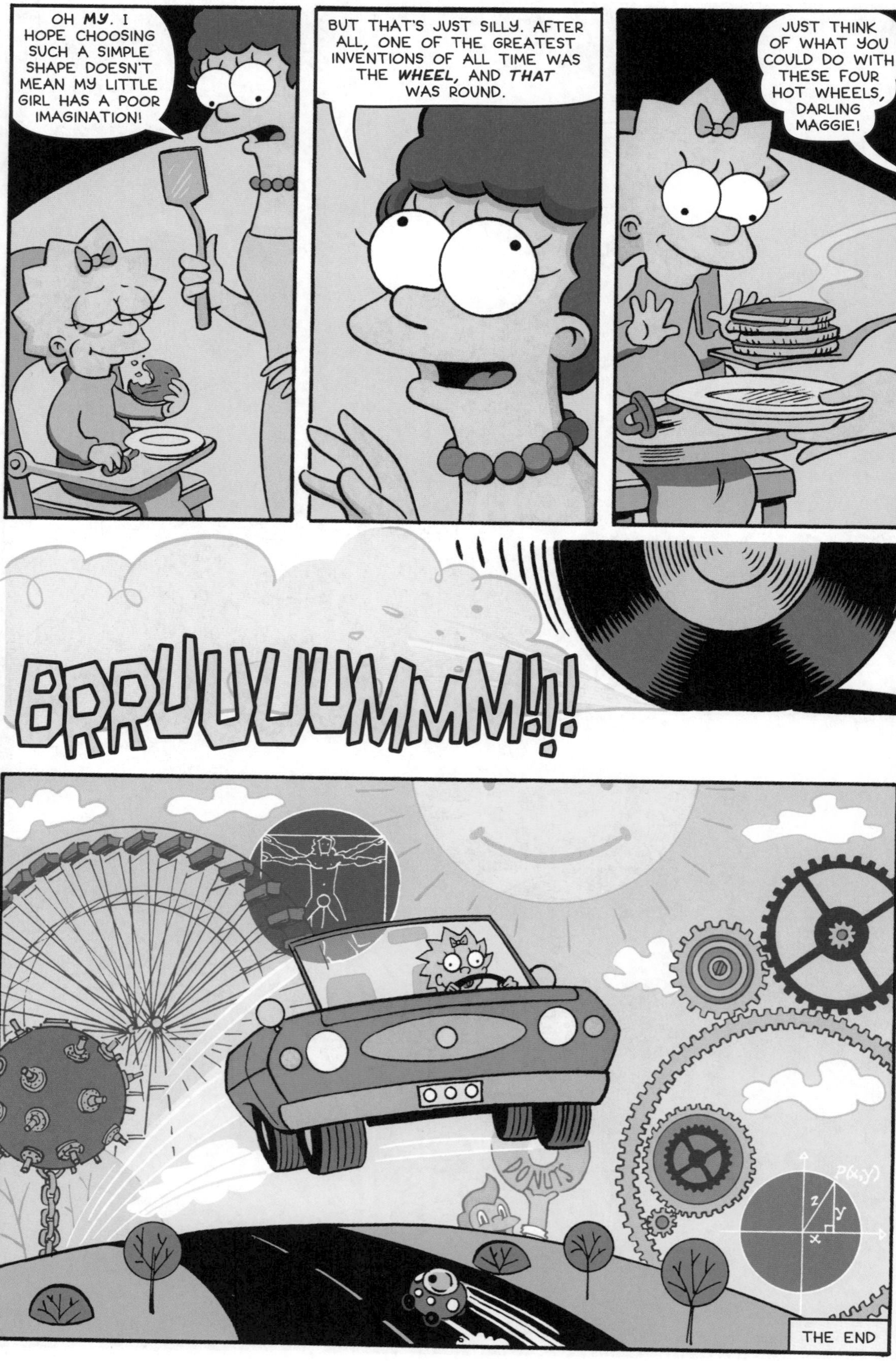
OH MY. I HOPE CHOOSING SUCH A SIMPLE SHAPE DOESN'T MEAN MY LITTLE GIRL HAS A POOR IMAGINATION!
BUT THAT'S JUST SILLY. AFTER ALL, ONE OF THE GREATEST INVENTIONS OF ALL TIME WAS THE WHEEL, AND THAT WAS ROUND.
JUST THINK OF WHAT YOU COULD DO WITH THESE FOUR HOT WHEELS, DARLING MAGGIE!
BRRUUUUMMM!!!
DONUTS
P(x,y)
z
y
x
THE END

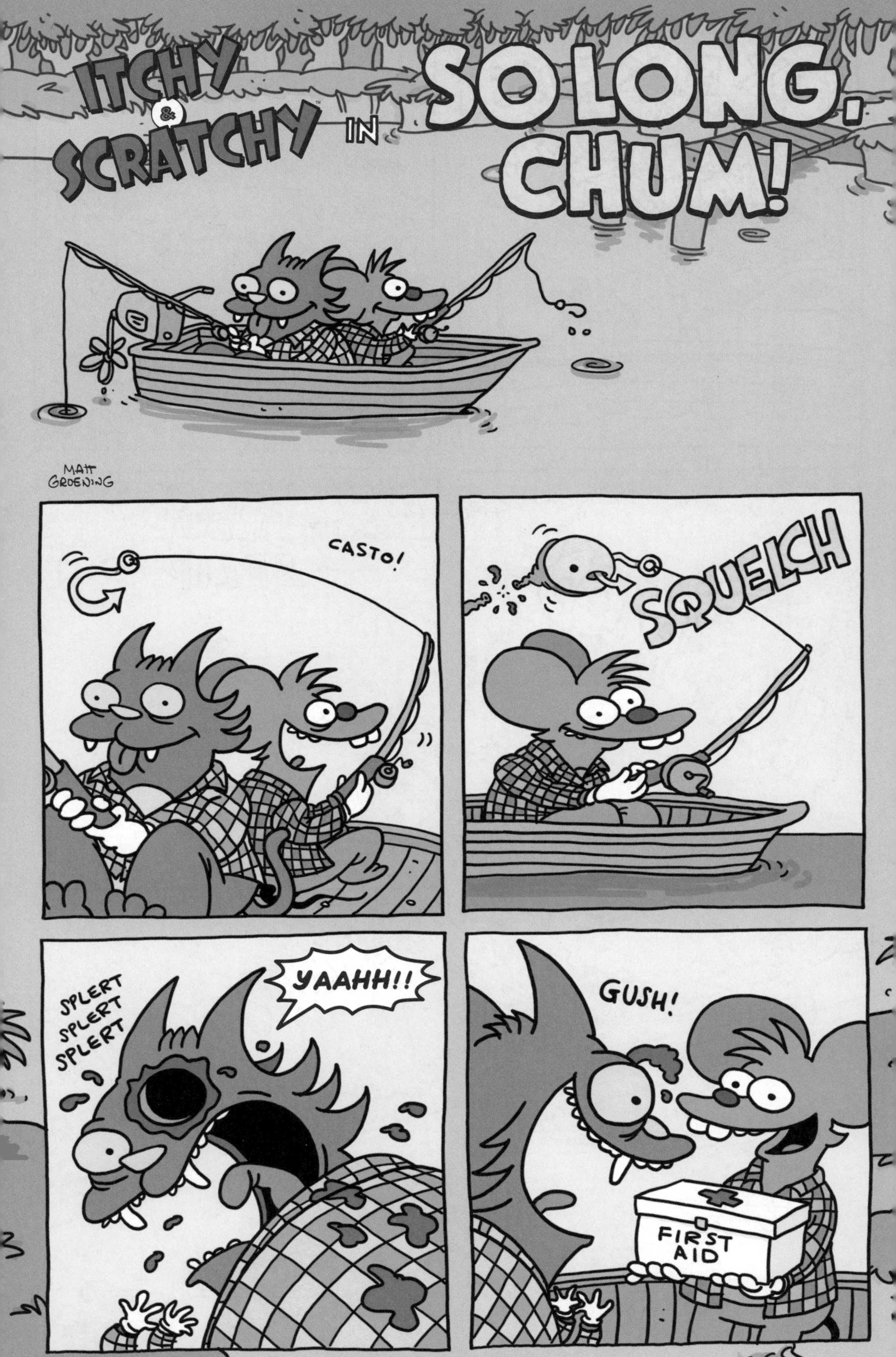
ITCHY & SCRATCHY™ IN
SO LONG, CHUM!
MATT GROENING
CASTO!
SQUELCH
SPLERT SPLERT SPLERT
YAAHH!!
GUSH!
FIRST AID

DEAN RANKINE STORY & ART

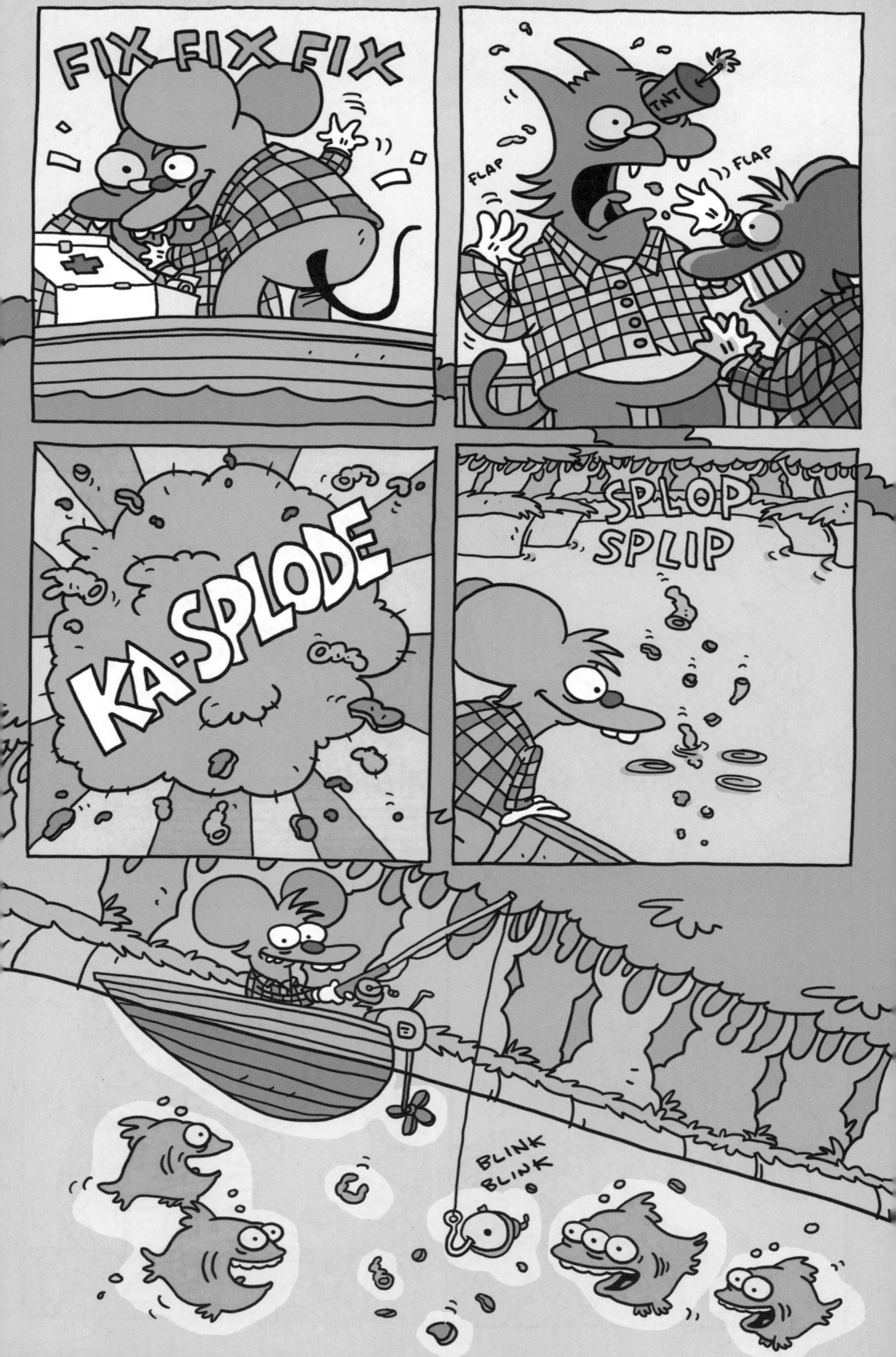

FIX FIX FIX
TNT
FLAP
FLAP
KA-SPLODE
SPLOP
SPLIP
BLINK
BLINK

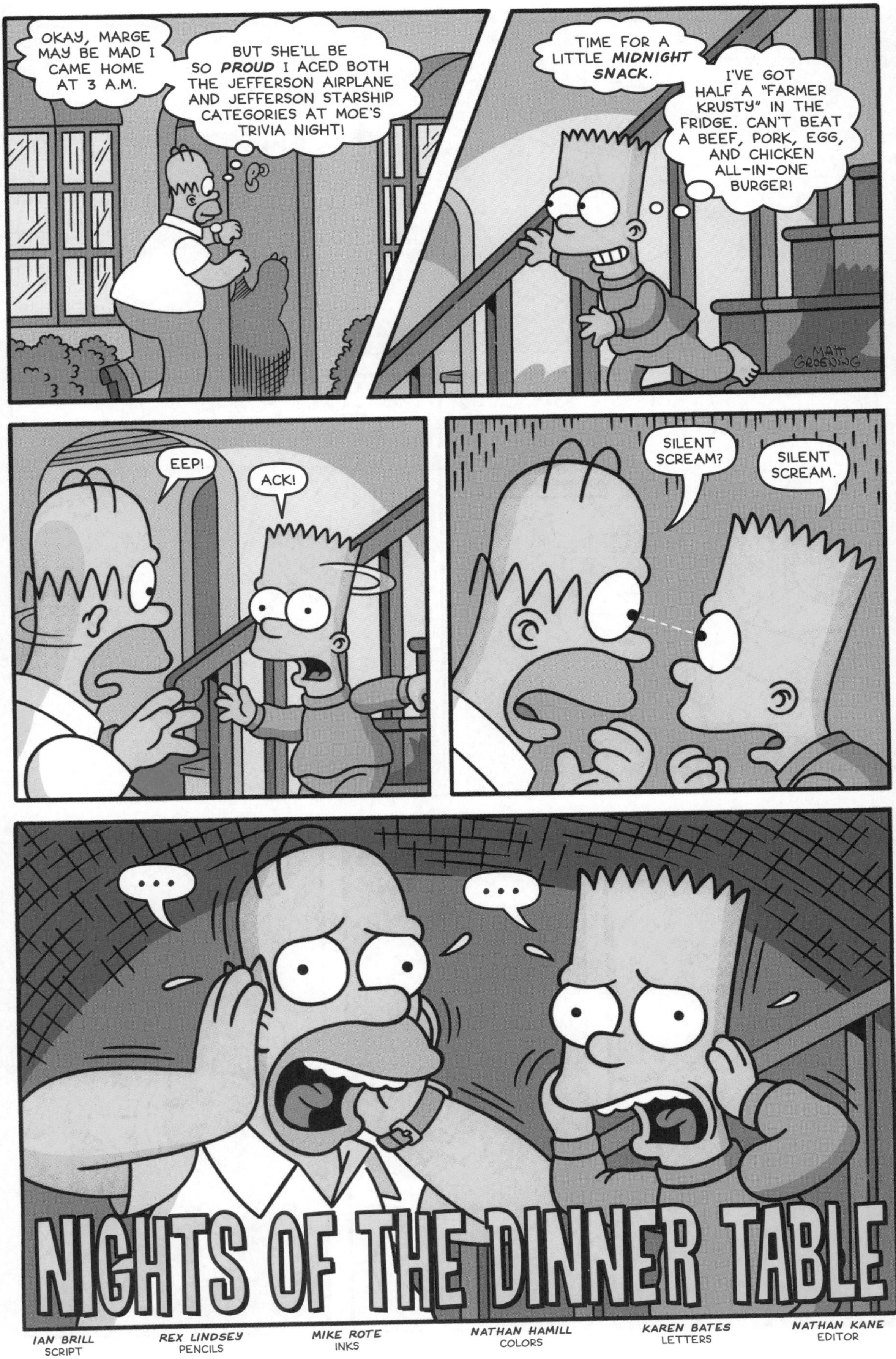
OKAY, MARGE MAY BE MAD I CAME HOME AT 3 A.M.
BUT SHE'LL BE SO PROUD I ACED BOTH THE JEFFERSON AIRPLANE AND JEFFERSON STARSHIP CATEGORIES AT MOE'S TRIVIA NIGHT!
TIME FOR A LITTLE MIDNIGHT SNACK.
I'VE GOT HALF A "FARMER KRUSTY" IN THE FRIDGE. CAN'T BEAT A BEEF, PORK, EGG, AND CHICKEN ALL-IN-ONE BURGER!
MATT GROENING
EEP!
ACK!
SILENT SCREAM?
SILENT SCREAM.
...
...
NIGHTS OF THE DINNER TABLE

IAN BRILL
SCRIPT

REX LINDSEY
PENCILS

MIKE ROTE
INKS

NATHAN HAMILL
COLORS

KAREN BATES
LETTERS

NATHAN KANE
EDITOR

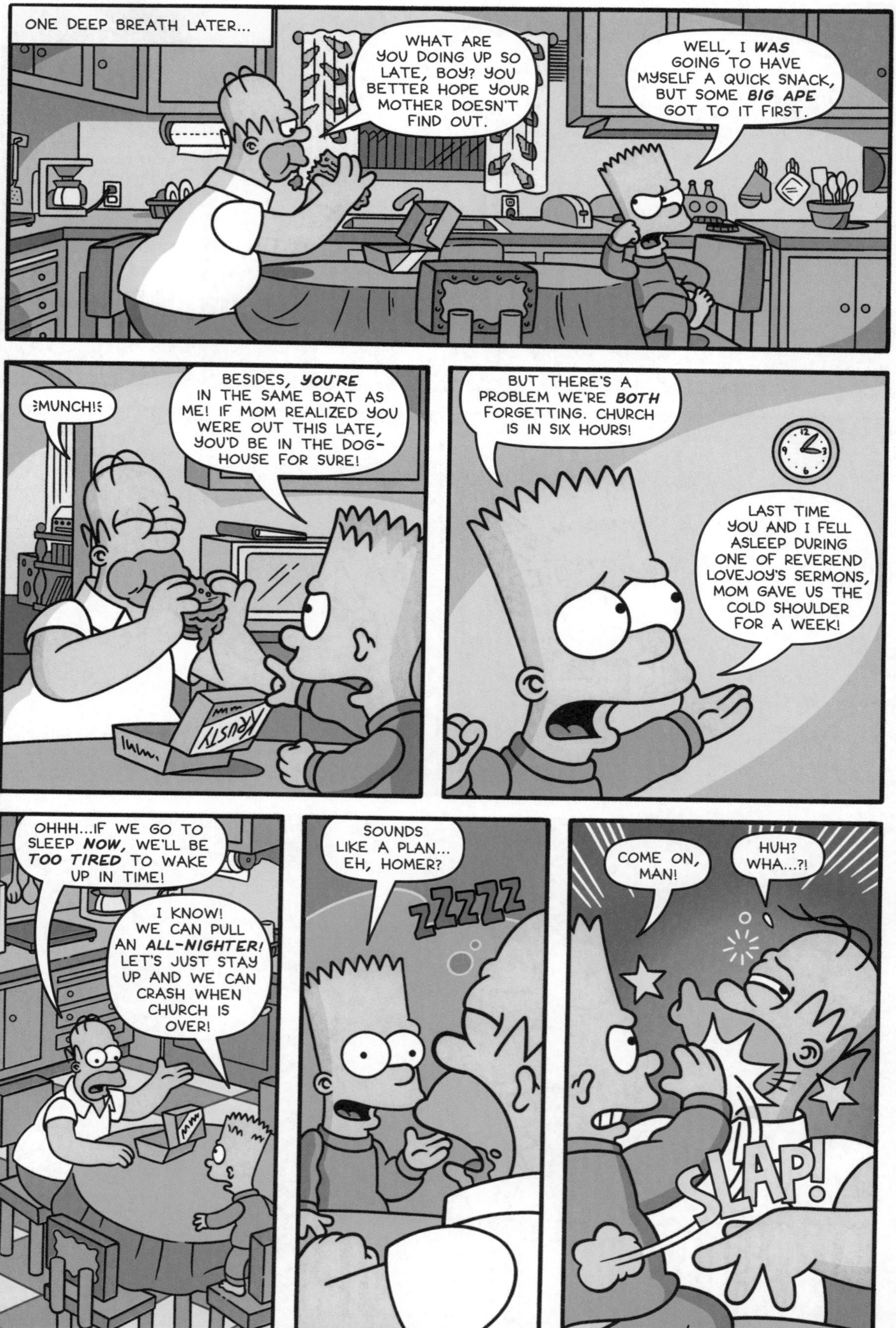
ONE DEEP BREATH LATER...
WHAT ARE YOU DOING UP SO LATE, BOY? YOU BETTER HOPE YOUR MOTHER DOESN'T FIND OUT.
WELL, I WAS GOING TO HAVE MYSELF A QUICK SNACK, BUT SOME BIG APE GOT TO IT FIRST.
MUNCH!
BESIDES, YOU'RE IN THE SAME BOAT AS ME! IF MOM REALIZED YOU WERE OUT THIS LATE, YOU'D BE IN THE DOG-HOUSE FOR SURE!
KRUSTY
BUT THERE'S A PROBLEM WE'RE BOTH FORGETTING. CHURCH IS IN SIX HOURS!
LAST TIME YOU AND I FELL ASLEEP DURING ONE OF REVEREND LOVEJOY'S SERMONS, MOM GAVE US THE COLD SHOULDER FOR A WEEK!
OHHH...IF WE GO TO SLEEP NOW, WE'LL BE TOO TIRED TO WAKE UP IN TIME!
I KNOW! WE CAN PULL AN ALL-NIGHTER! LET'S JUST STAY UP AND WE CAN CRASH WHEN CHURCH IS OVER!
SOUNDS LIKE A PLAN... EH, HOMER?
ZZZZZ
COME ON, MAN!
HUH? WHA...?!
SLAP!

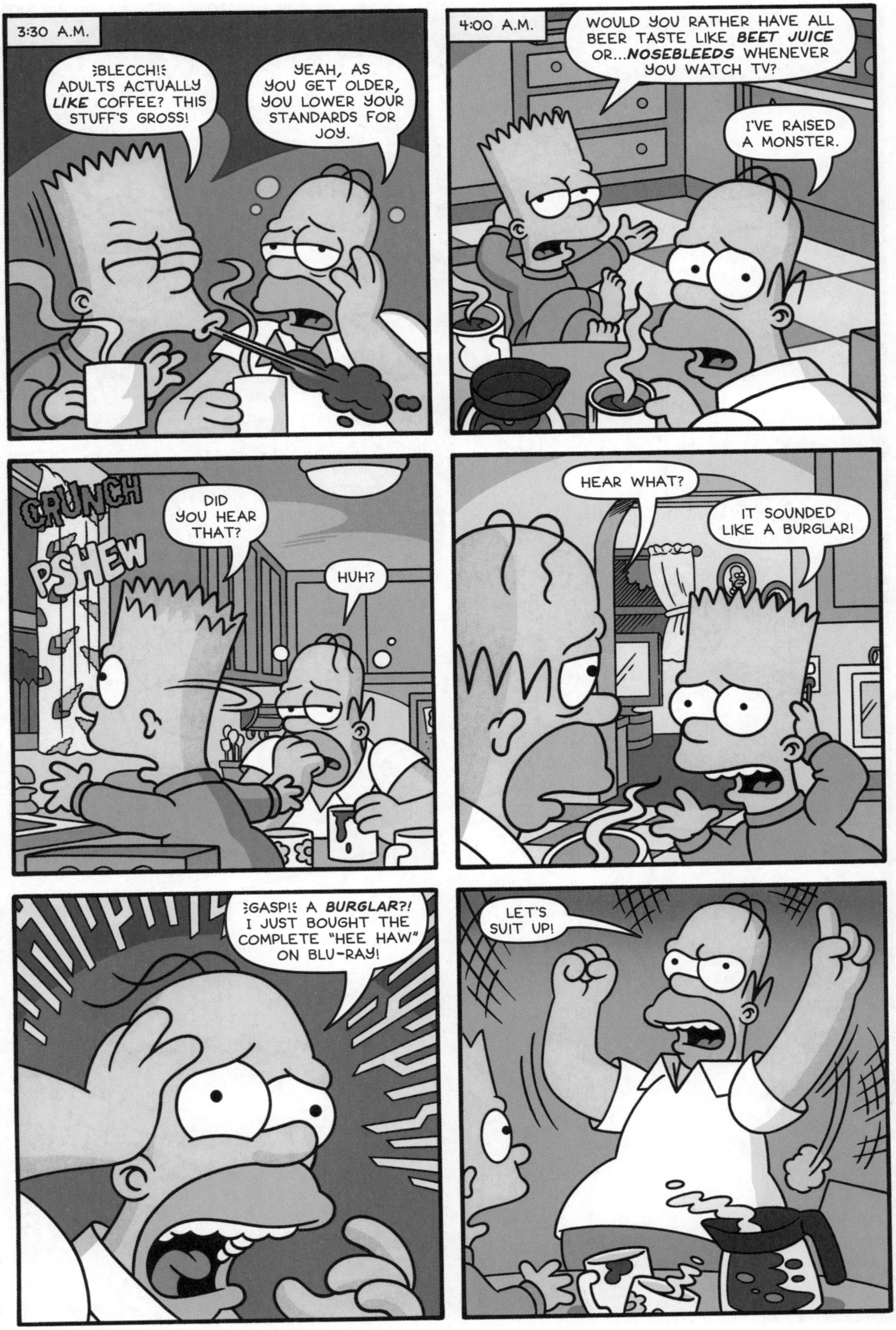
3:30 A.M.
⁝BLECCH!⁝ ADULTS ACTUALLY *LIKE* COFFEE? THIS STUFF'S GROSS!
YEAH, AS YOU GET OLDER, YOU LOWER YOUR STANDARDS FOR JOY.
4:00 A.M.
WOULD YOU RATHER HAVE ALL BEER TASTE LIKE ***BEET JUICE*** OR...***NOSEBLEEDS*** WHENEVER YOU WATCH TV?
I'VE RAISED A MONSTER.
CRUNCH
PSHEW
DID YOU HEAR THAT?
HUH?
HEAR WHAT?
IT SOUNDED LIKE A BURGLAR!
⁝GASP!⁝ A ***BURGLAR?!*** I JUST BOUGHT THE COMPLETE "HEE HAW" ON BLU-RAY!
LET'S SUIT UP!

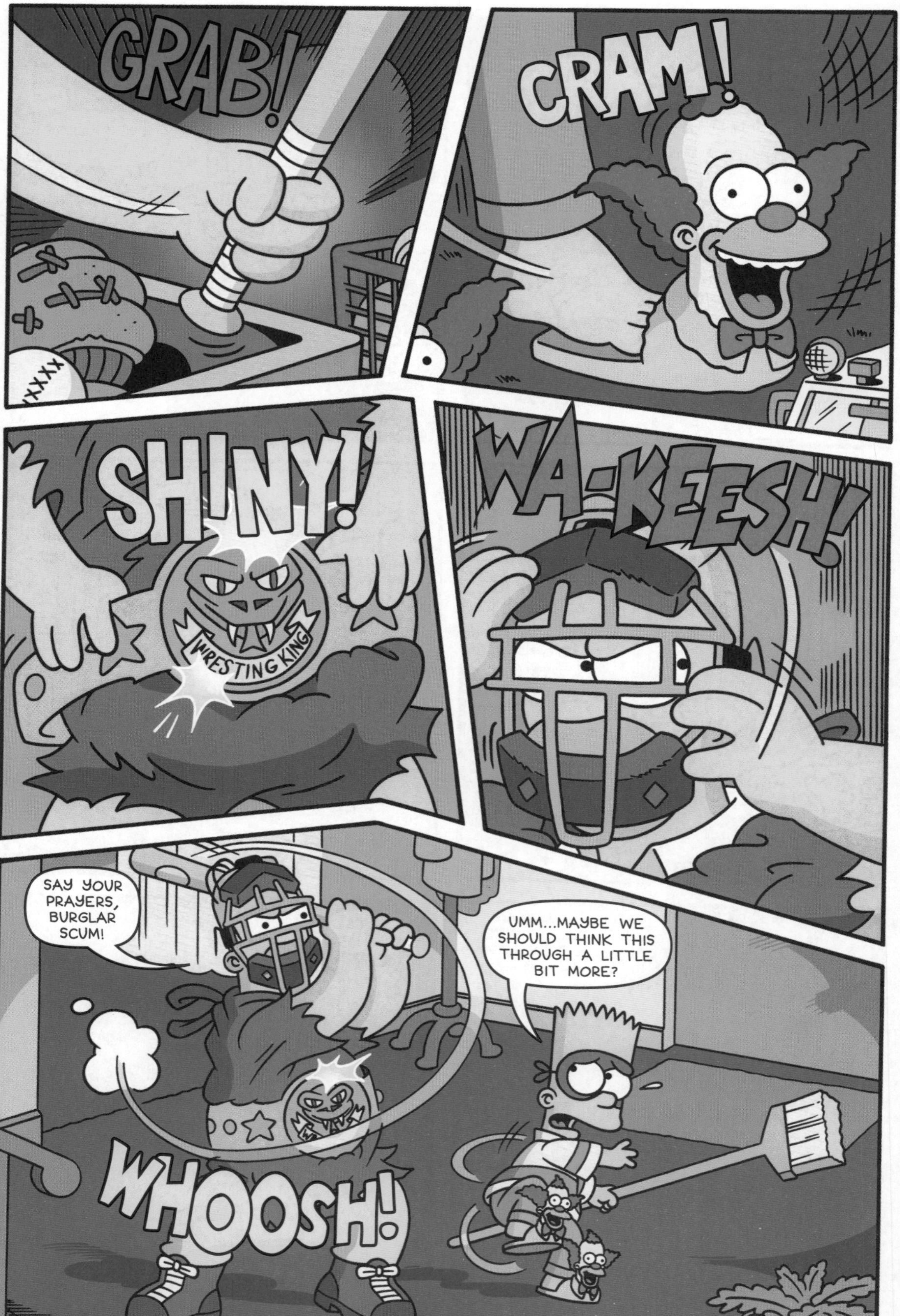
GRAB!
CRAM!
SHINY!
WRESTING KING
WA-KEESH!
SAY YOUR PRAYERS, BURGLAR SCUM!
UMM...MAYBE WE SHOULD THINK THIS THROUGH A LITTLE BIT MORE?
WHOOSH!

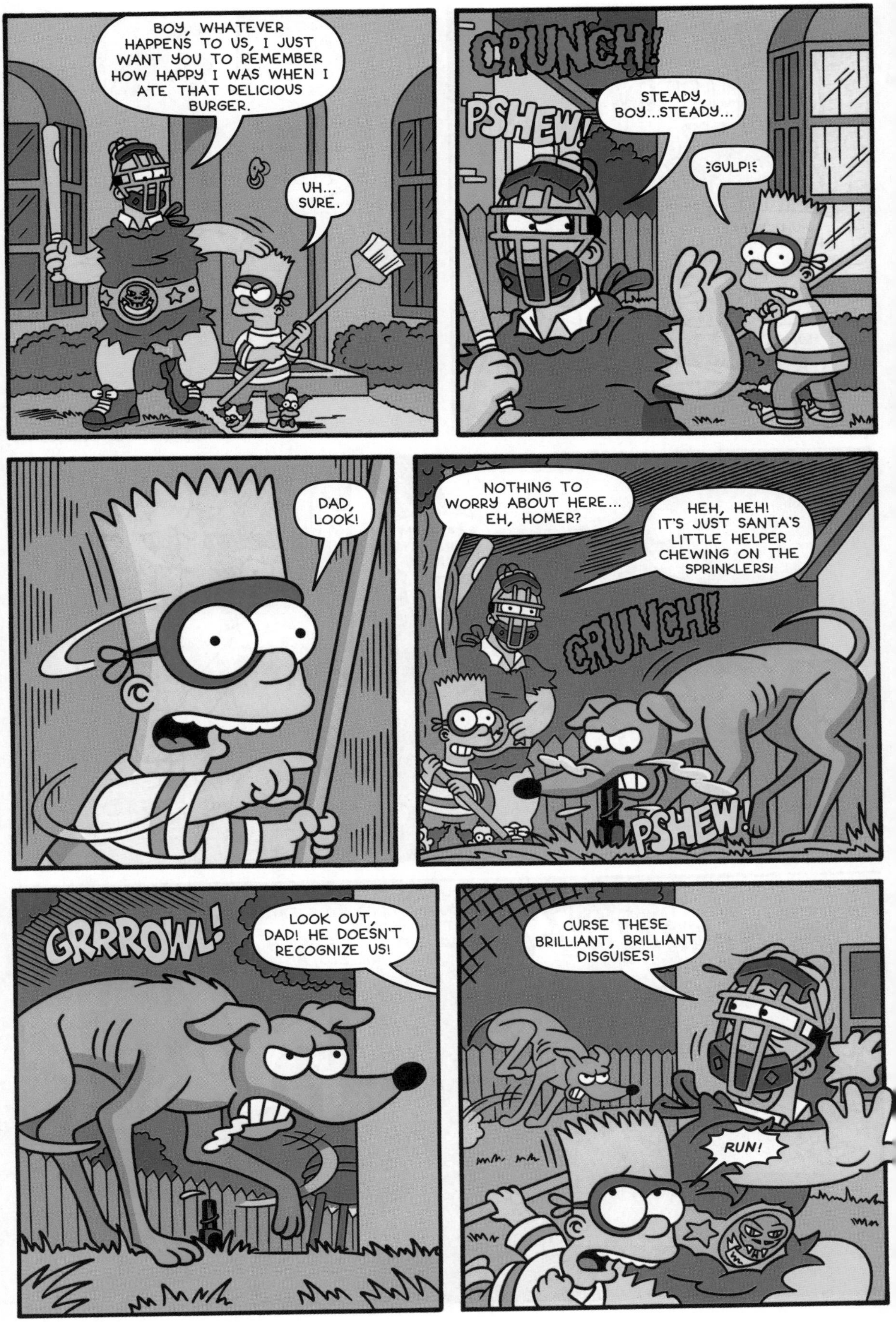
BOY, WHATEVER HAPPENS TO US, I JUST WANT YOU TO REMEMBER HOW HAPPY I WAS WHEN I ATE THAT DELICIOUS BURGER.
UH... SURE.
CRUNCH!
PSHEW!
STEADY, BOY...STEADY...
GULP!
DAD, LOOK!
NOTHING TO WORRY ABOUT HERE... EH, HOMER?
HEH, HEH! IT'S JUST SANTA'S LITTLE HELPER CHEWING ON THE SPRINKLERS!
CRUNCH!
PSHEW!
GRRROWL!
LOOK OUT, DAD! HE DOESN'T RECOGNIZE US!
CURSE THESE BRILLIANT, BRILLIANT DISGUISES!
RUN!

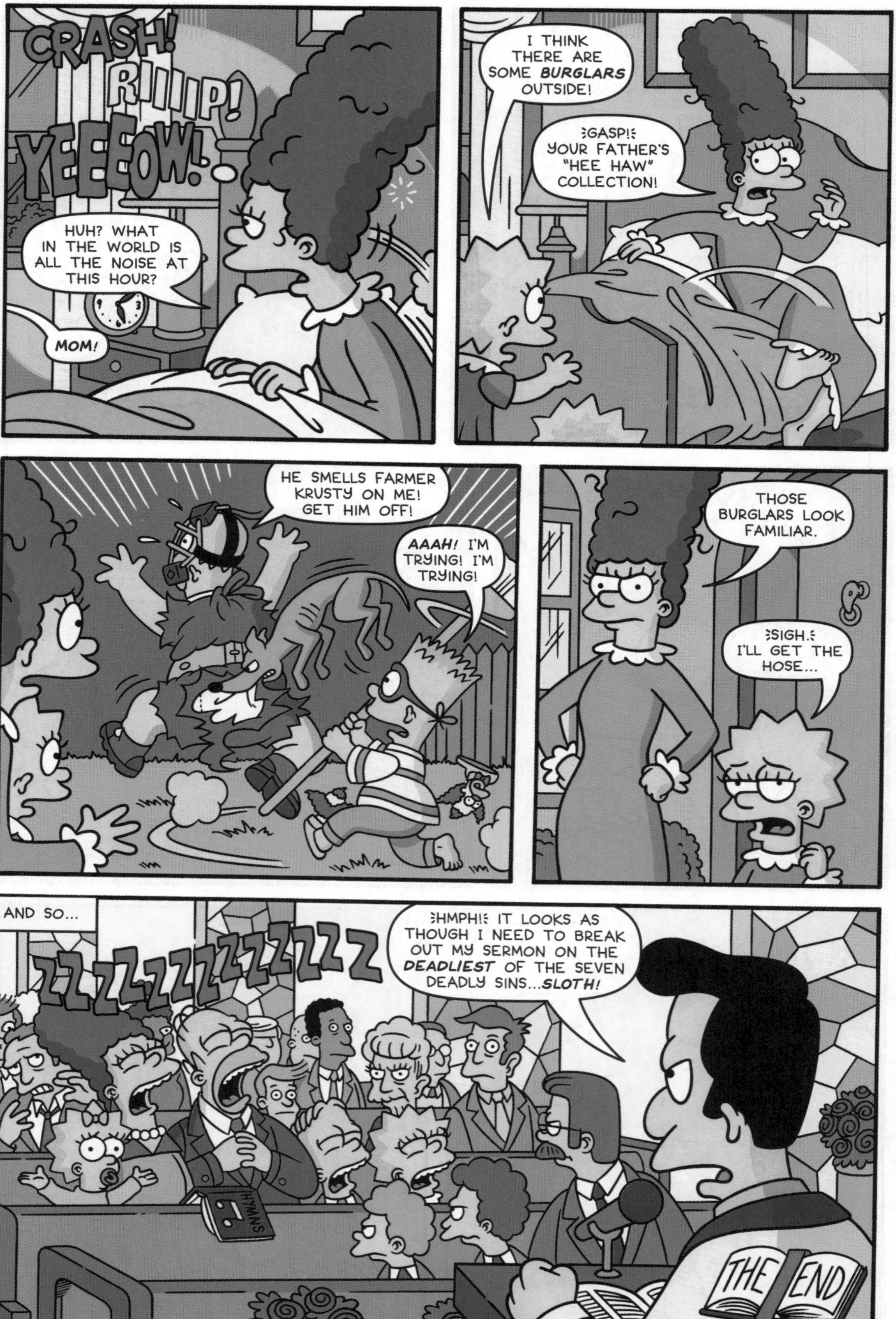

CRASH!
RIIIIP!
YEEEOW!
HUH? WHAT IN THE WORLD IS ALL THE NOISE AT THIS HOUR?
MOM!
I THINK THERE ARE SOME BURGLARS OUTSIDE!
GASP! YOUR FATHER'S "HEE HAW" COLLECTION!
HE SMELLS FARMER KRUSTY ON ME! GET HIM OFF!
AAAH! I'M TRYING! I'M TRYING!
THOSE BURGLARS LOOK FAMILIAR.
SIGH. I'LL GET THE HOSE...
AND SO...
ZZZZZZZZZZZZZZZ
HMPH! IT LOOKS AS THOUGH I NEED TO BREAK OUT MY SERMON ON THE DEADLIEST OF THE SEVEN DEADLY SINS...SLOTH!
HYMNS
THE END

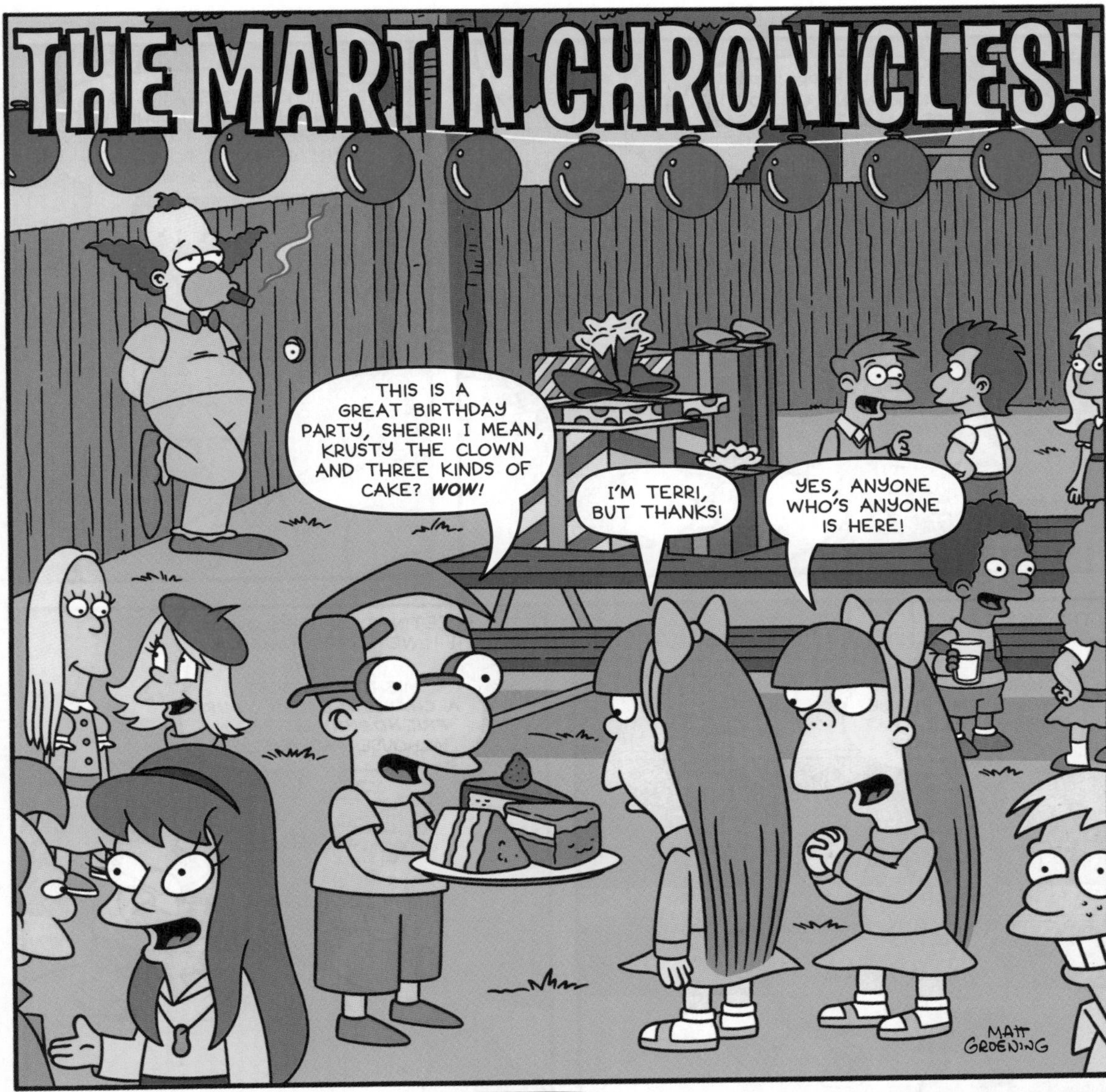
THE MARTIN CHRONICLES!
THIS IS A GREAT BIRTHDAY PARTY, SHERRI! I MEAN, KRUSTY THE CLOWN AND THREE KINDS OF CAKE? WOW!
I'M TERRI, BUT THANKS!
YES, ANYONE WHO'S ANYONE IS HERE!
MATT GROENING

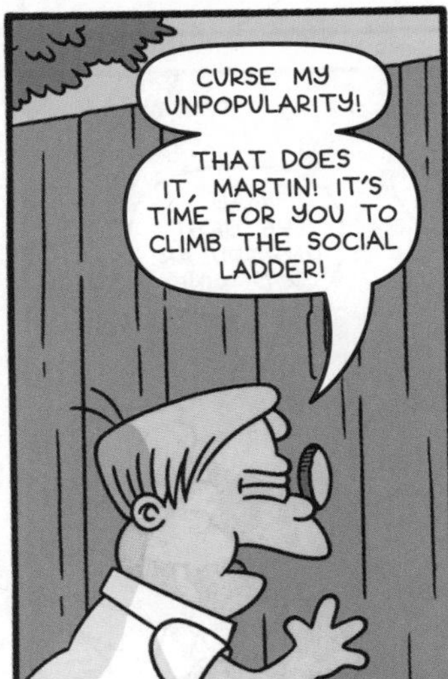
CURSE MY UNPOPULARITY!
THAT DOES IT, MARTIN! IT'S TIME FOR YOU TO CLIMB THE SOCIAL LADDER!

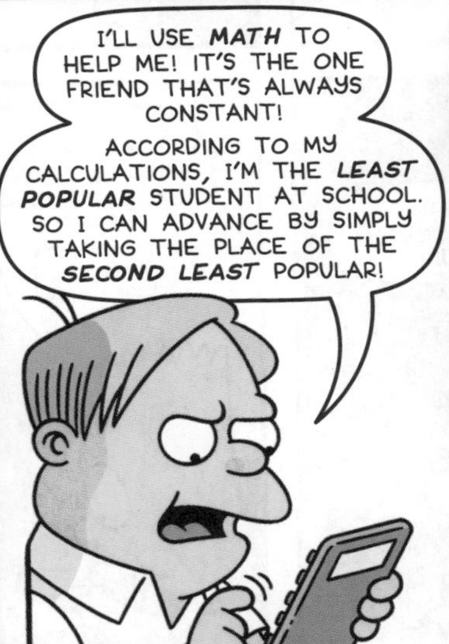
I'LL USE MATH TO HELP ME! IT'S THE ONE FRIEND THAT'S ALWAYS CONSTANT!
ACCORDING TO MY CALCULATIONS, I'M THE LEAST POPULAR STUDENT AT SCHOOL. SO I CAN ADVANCE BY SIMPLY TAKING THE PLACE OF THE SECOND LEAST POPULAR!

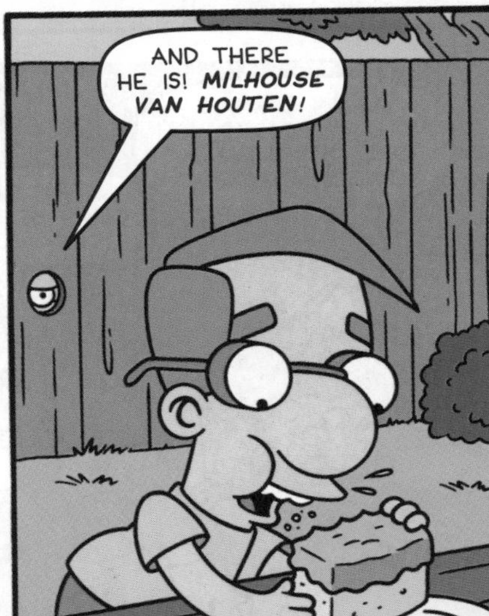
AND THERE HE IS! MILHOUSE VAN HOUTEN!

IAN BOOTHBY SCRIPT · *PHIL ORTIZ* PENCILS · *MIKE ROTE* INKS · *NATHAN HAMILL* COLORS · *KAREN BATES* LETTERS · *NATHAN KANE* EDITOR

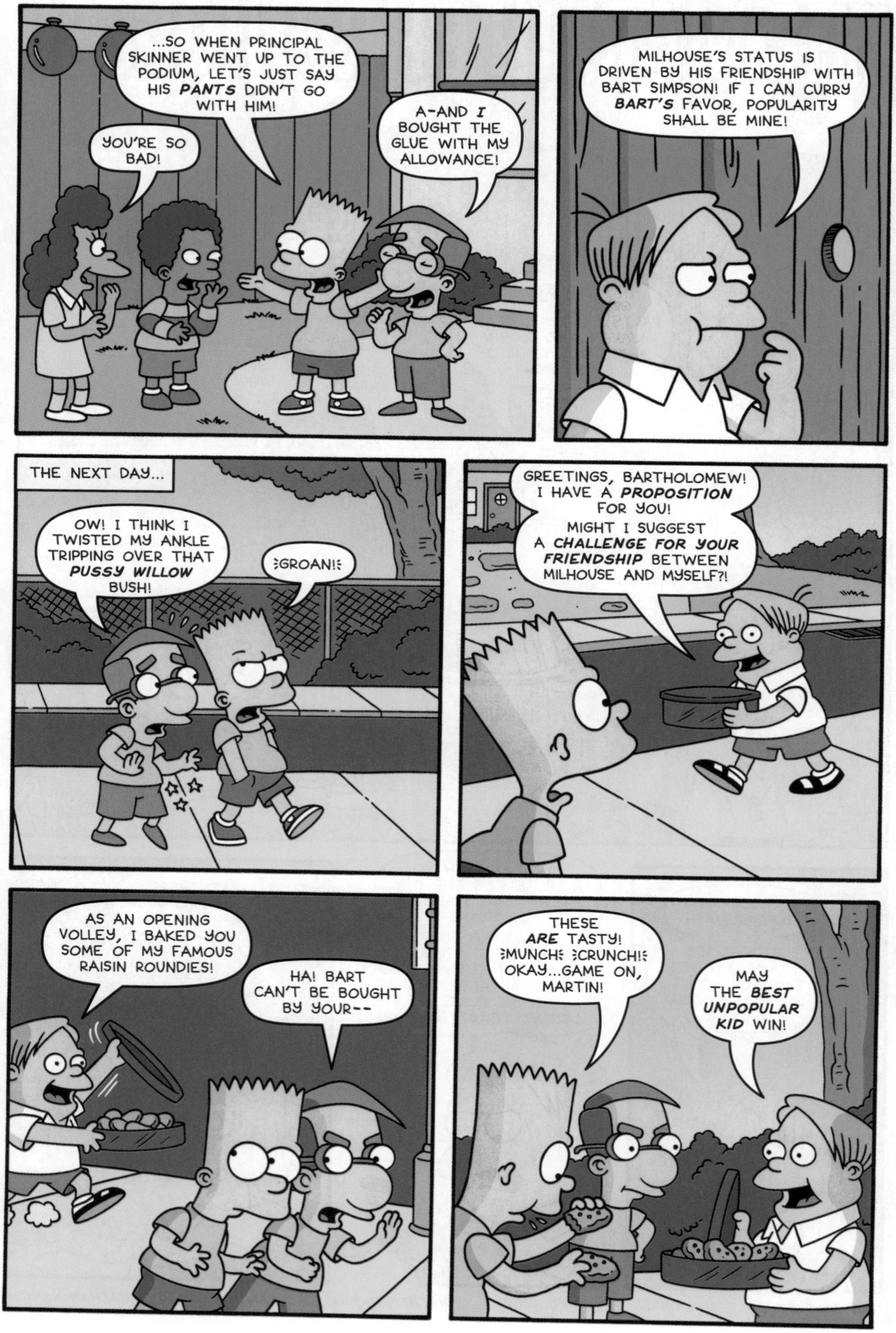
...SO WHEN PRINCIPAL SKINNER WENT UP TO THE PODIUM, LET'S JUST SAY HIS PANTS DIDN'T GO WITH HIM!
YOU'RE SO BAD!
A-AND I BOUGHT THE GLUE WITH MY ALLOWANCE!
MILHOUSE'S STATUS IS DRIVEN BY HIS FRIENDSHIP WITH BART SIMPSON! IF I CAN CURRY BART'S FAVOR, POPULARITY SHALL BE MINE!
THE NEXT DAY...
OW! I THINK I TWISTED MY ANKLE TRIPPING OVER THAT PUSSY WILLOW BUSH!
GROAN!
GREETINGS, BARTHOLOMEW! I HAVE A PROPOSITION FOR YOU!
MIGHT I SUGGEST A CHALLENGE FOR YOUR FRIENDSHIP BETWEEN MILHOUSE AND MYSELF?!
AS AN OPENING VOLLEY, I BAKED YOU SOME OF MY FAMOUS RAISIN ROUNDIES!
HA! BART CAN'T BE BOUGHT BY YOUR--
THESE ARE TASTY! MUNCH! CRUNCH! OKAY...GAME ON, MARTIN!
MAY THE BEST UNPOPULAR KID WIN!

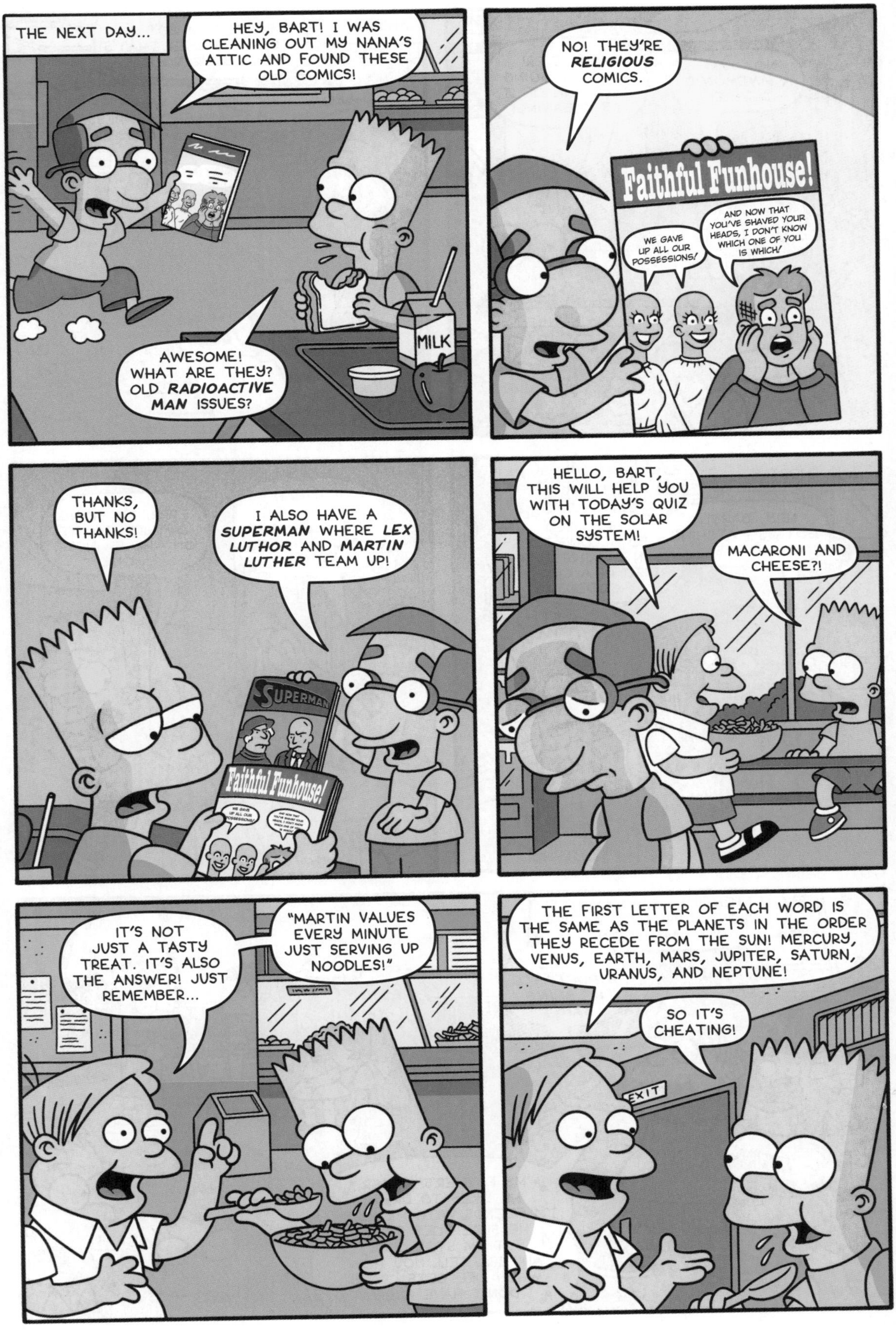
THE NEXT DAY...
HEY, BART! I WAS CLEANING OUT MY NANA'S ATTIC AND FOUND THESE OLD COMICS!
AWESOME! WHAT ARE THEY? OLD RADIOACTIVE MAN ISSUES?
NO! THEY'RE RELIGIOUS COMICS.
Faithful Funhouse!
WE GAVE UP ALL OUR POSSESSIONS!
AND NOW THAT YOU'VE SHAVED YOUR HEADS, I DON'T KNOW WHICH ONE OF YOU IS WHICH!
THANKS, BUT NO THANKS!
I ALSO HAVE A SUPERMAN WHERE LEX LUTHOR AND MARTIN LUTHER TEAM UP!
SUPERMAN
Faithful Funhouse!
HELLO, BART, THIS WILL HELP YOU WITH TODAY'S QUIZ ON THE SOLAR SYSTEM!
MACARONI AND CHEESE?!
IT'S NOT JUST A TASTY TREAT. IT'S ALSO THE ANSWER! JUST REMEMBER...
"MARTIN VALUES EVERY MINUTE JUST SERVING UP NOODLES!"
THE FIRST LETTER OF EACH WORD IS THE SAME AS THE PLANETS IN THE ORDER THEY RECEDE FROM THE SUN! MERCURY, VENUS, EARTH, MARS, JUPITER, SATURN, URANUS, AND NEPTUNE!
SO IT'S CHEATING!
EXIT

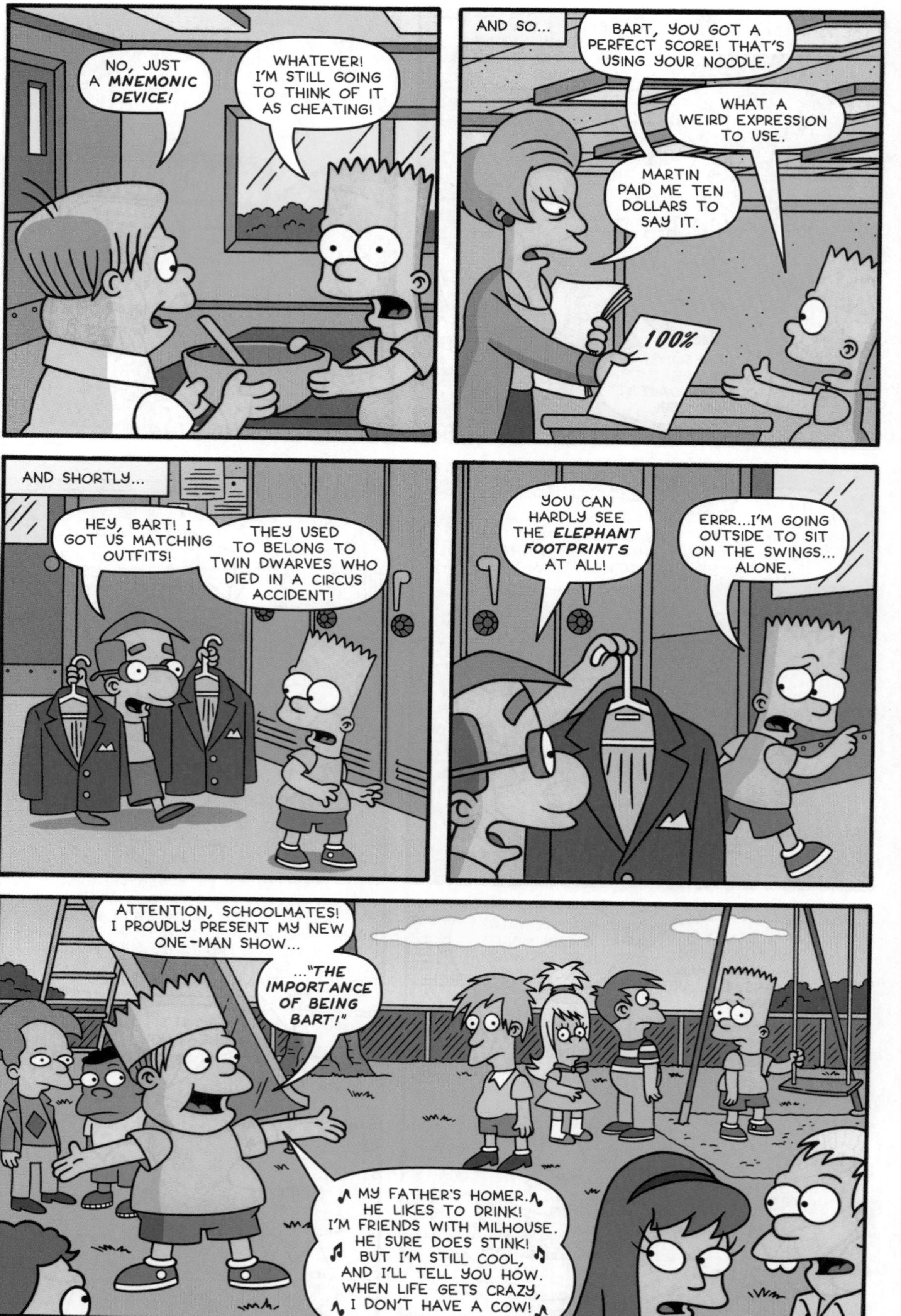
NO, JUST A MNEMONIC DEVICE!
WHATEVER! I'M STILL GOING TO THINK OF IT AS CHEATING!
AND SO...
BART, YOU GOT A PERFECT SCORE! THAT'S USING YOUR NOODLE.
WHAT A WEIRD EXPRESSION TO USE.
MARTIN PAID ME TEN DOLLARS TO SAY IT.
100%
AND SHORTLY...
HEY, BART! I GOT US MATCHING OUTFITS!
THEY USED TO BELONG TO TWIN DWARVES WHO DIED IN A CIRCUS ACCIDENT!
YOU CAN HARDLY SEE THE ELEPHANT FOOTPRINTS AT ALL!
ERRR...I'M GOING OUTSIDE TO SIT ON THE SWINGS... ALONE.
ATTENTION, SCHOOLMATES! I PROUDLY PRESENT MY NEW ONE-MAN SHOW...
..."THE IMPORTANCE OF BEING BART!"
MY FATHER'S HOMER. HE LIKES TO DRINK! I'M FRIENDS WITH MILHOUSE. HE SURE DOES STINK! BUT I'M STILL COOL, AND I'LL TELL YOU HOW. WHEN LIFE GETS CRAZY, I DON'T HAVE A COW!

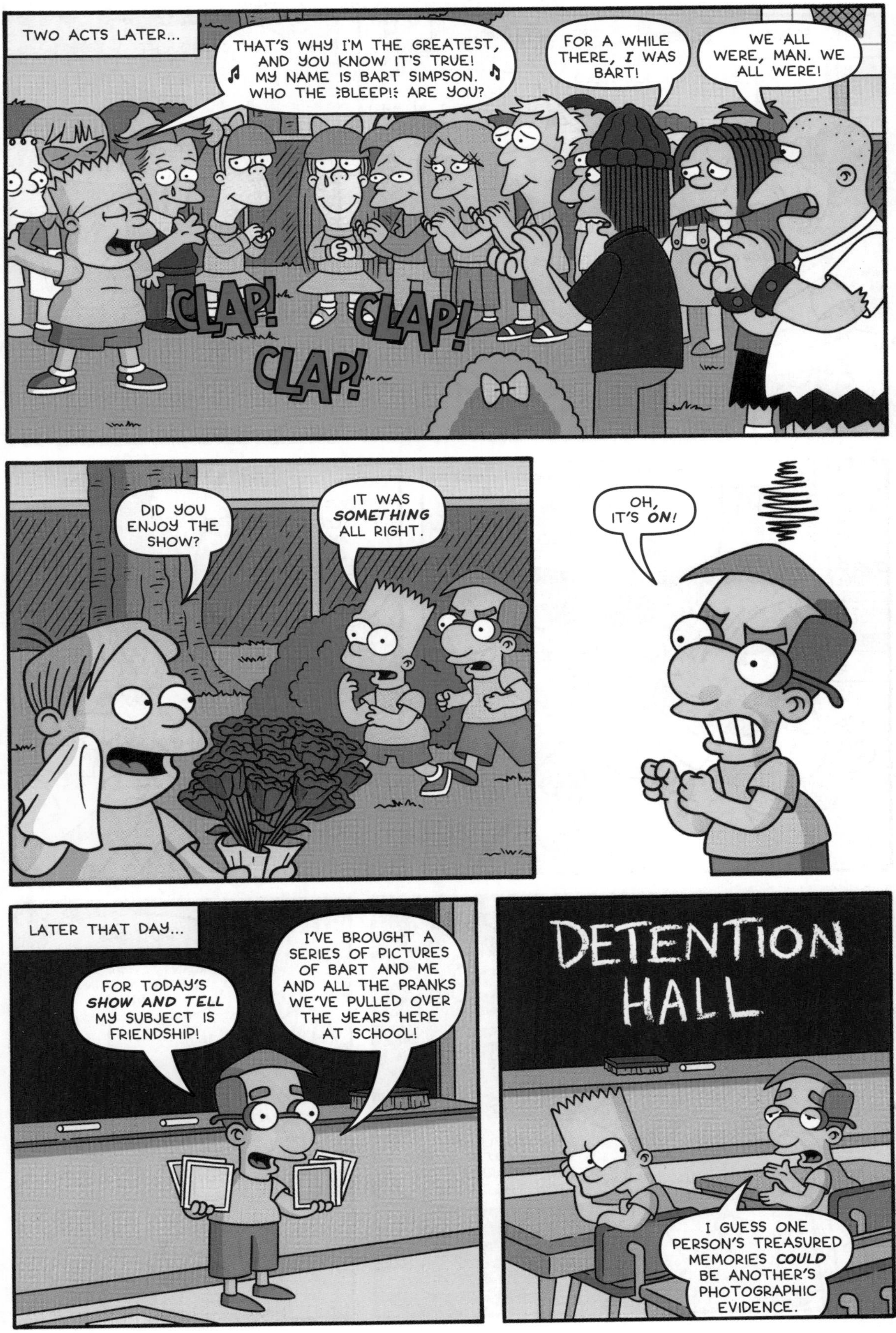
TWO ACTS LATER...
THAT'S WHY I'M THE GREATEST, AND YOU KNOW IT'S TRUE! MY NAME IS BART SIMPSON. WHO THE ⁝BLEEP!⁝ ARE YOU?
FOR A WHILE THERE, *I* WAS BART!
WE ALL WERE, MAN. WE ALL WERE!
CLAP!
CLAP!
CLAP!
DID YOU ENJOY THE SHOW?
IT WAS *SOMETHING* ALL RIGHT.
OH, IT'S *ON*!
LATER THAT DAY...
FOR TODAY'S *SHOW AND TELL* MY SUBJECT IS FRIENDSHIP!
I'VE BROUGHT A SERIES OF PICTURES OF BART AND ME AND ALL THE PRANKS WE'VE PULLED OVER THE YEARS HERE AT SCHOOL!
DETENTION HALL
I GUESS ONE PERSON'S TREASURED MEMORIES *COULD* BE ANOTHER'S PHOTOGRAPHIC EVIDENCE.

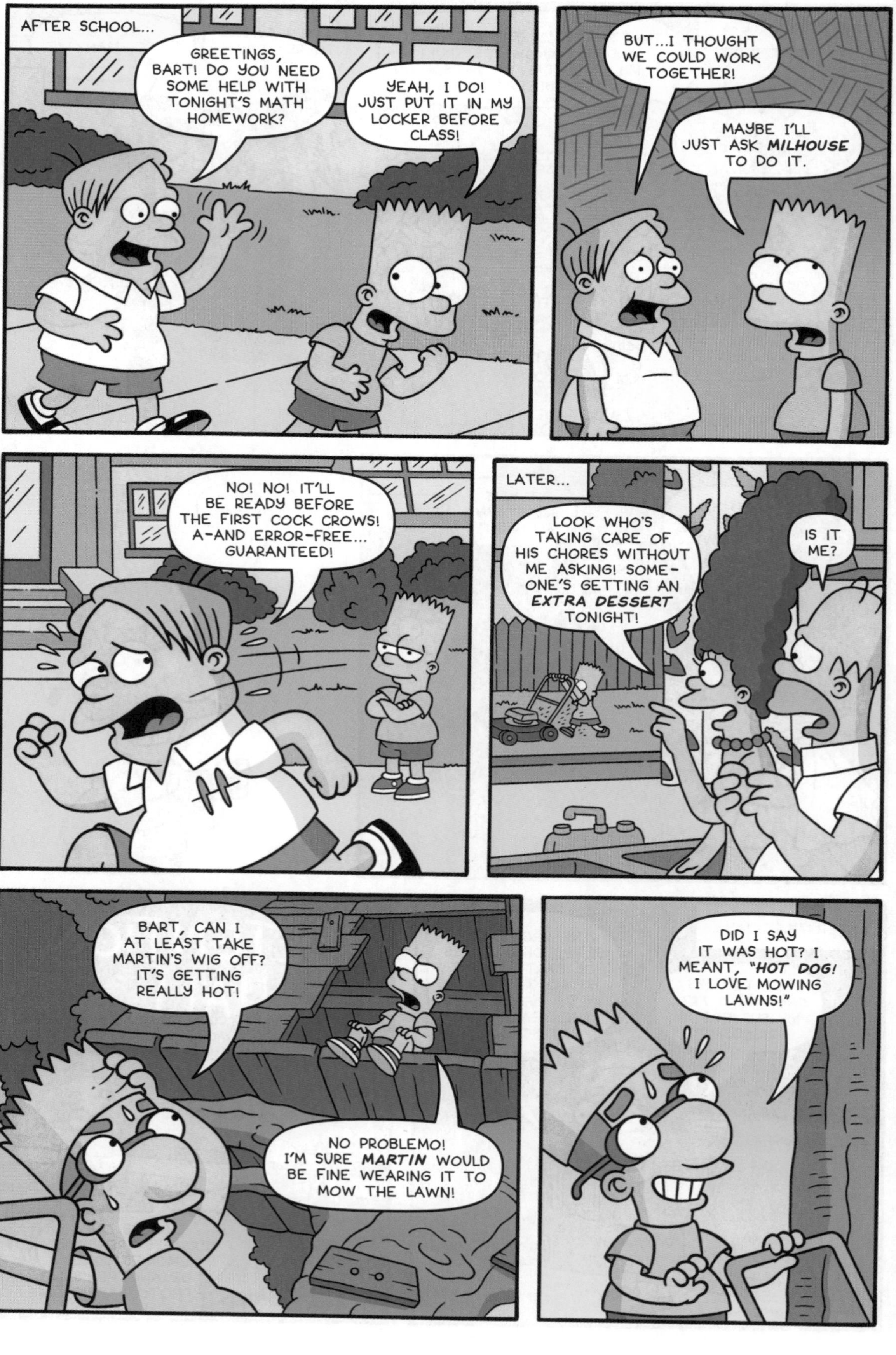
AFTER SCHOOL...
GREETINGS, BART! DO YOU NEED SOME HELP WITH TONIGHT'S MATH HOMEWORK?
YEAH, I DO! JUST PUT IT IN MY LOCKER BEFORE CLASS!
BUT...I THOUGHT WE COULD WORK TOGETHER!
MAYBE I'LL JUST ASK MILHOUSE TO DO IT.
NO! NO! IT'LL BE READY BEFORE THE FIRST COCK CROWS! A-AND ERROR-FREE... GUARANTEED!
LATER...
LOOK WHO'S TAKING CARE OF HIS CHORES WITHOUT ME ASKING! SOME-ONE'S GETTING AN EXTRA DESSERT TONIGHT!
IS IT ME?
BART, CAN I AT LEAST TAKE MARTIN'S WIG OFF? IT'S GETTING REALLY HOT!
NO PROBLEMO! I'M SURE MARTIN WOULD BE FINE WEARING IT TO MOW THE LAWN!
DID I SAY IT WAS HOT? I MEANT, "HOT DOG! I LOVE MOWING LAWNS!"

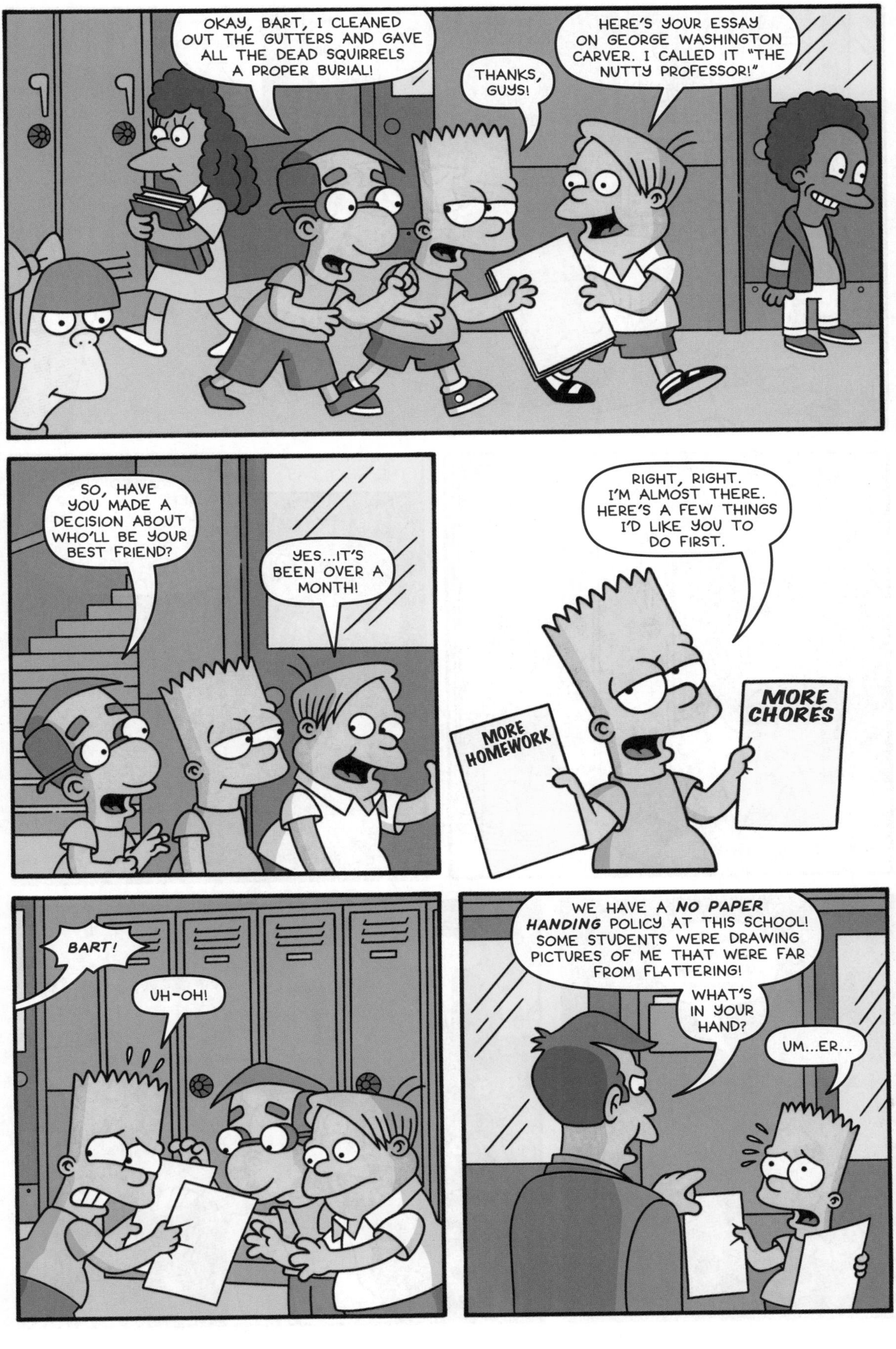
OKAY, BART, I CLEANED OUT THE GUTTERS AND GAVE ALL THE DEAD SQUIRRELS A PROPER BURIAL!
THANKS, GUYS!
HERE'S YOUR ESSAY ON GEORGE WASHINGTON CARVER. I CALLED IT "THE NUTTY PROFESSOR!"
SO, HAVE YOU MADE A DECISION ABOUT WHO'LL BE YOUR BEST FRIEND?
YES...IT'S BEEN OVER A MONTH!
RIGHT, RIGHT. I'M ALMOST THERE. HERE'S A FEW THINGS I'D LIKE YOU TO DO FIRST.
MORE HOMEWORK
MORE CHORES
BART!
UH-OH!
WE HAVE A NO PAPER HANDING POLICY AT THIS SCHOOL! SOME STUDENTS WERE DRAWING PICTURES OF ME THAT WERE FAR FROM FLATTERING!
WHAT'S IN YOUR HAND?
UM...ER...

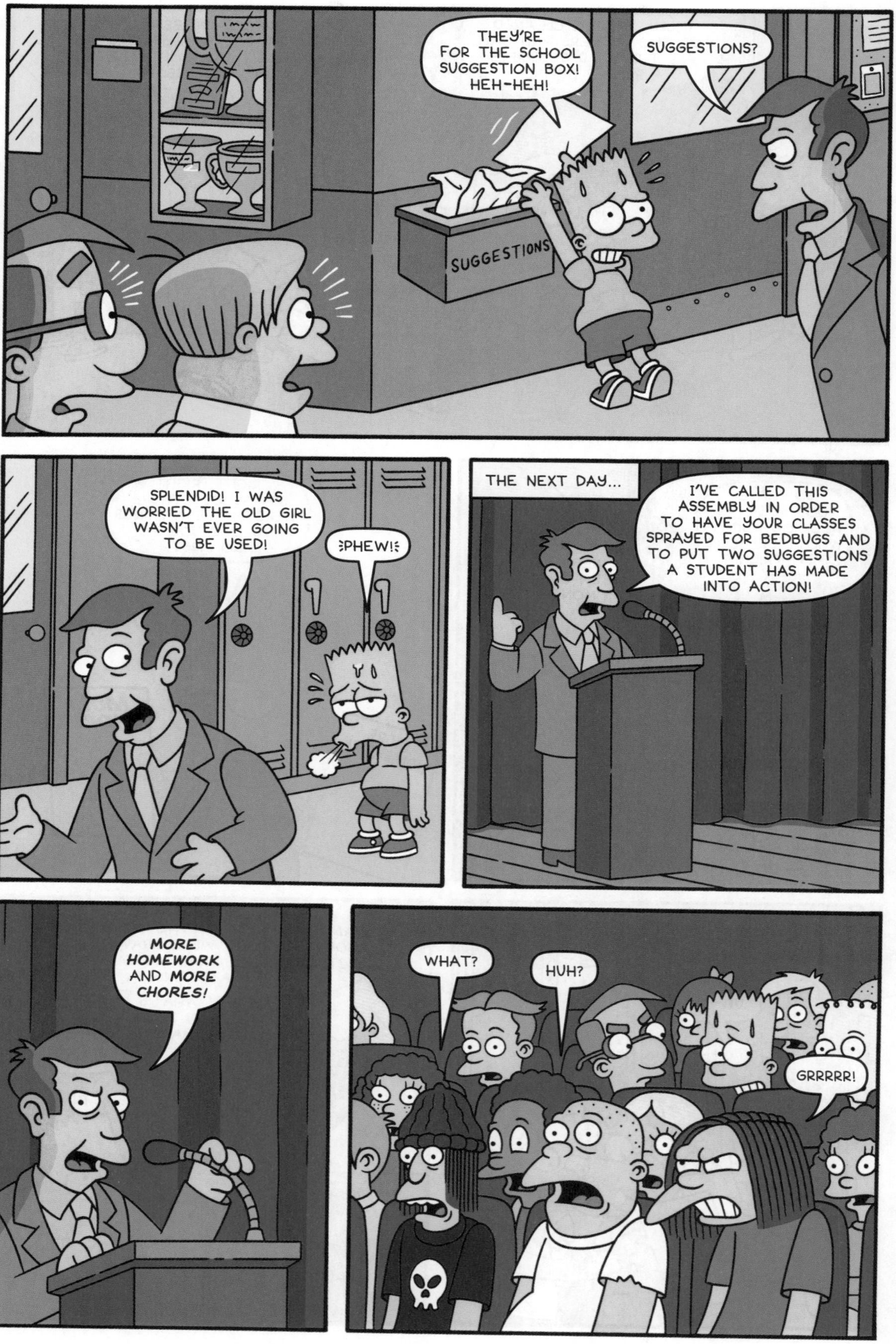
THEY'RE FOR THE SCHOOL SUGGESTION BOX! HEH-HEH!
SUGGESTIONS?
SUGGESTIONS
SPLENDID! I WAS WORRIED THE OLD GIRL WASN'T EVER GOING TO BE USED!
PHEW!
THE NEXT DAY...
I'VE CALLED THIS ASSEMBLY IN ORDER TO HAVE YOUR CLASSES SPRAYED FOR BEDBUGS AND TO PUT TWO SUGGESTIONS A STUDENT HAS MADE INTO ACTION!
MORE HOMEWORK AND MORE CHORES!
WHAT?
HUH?
GRRRRR!

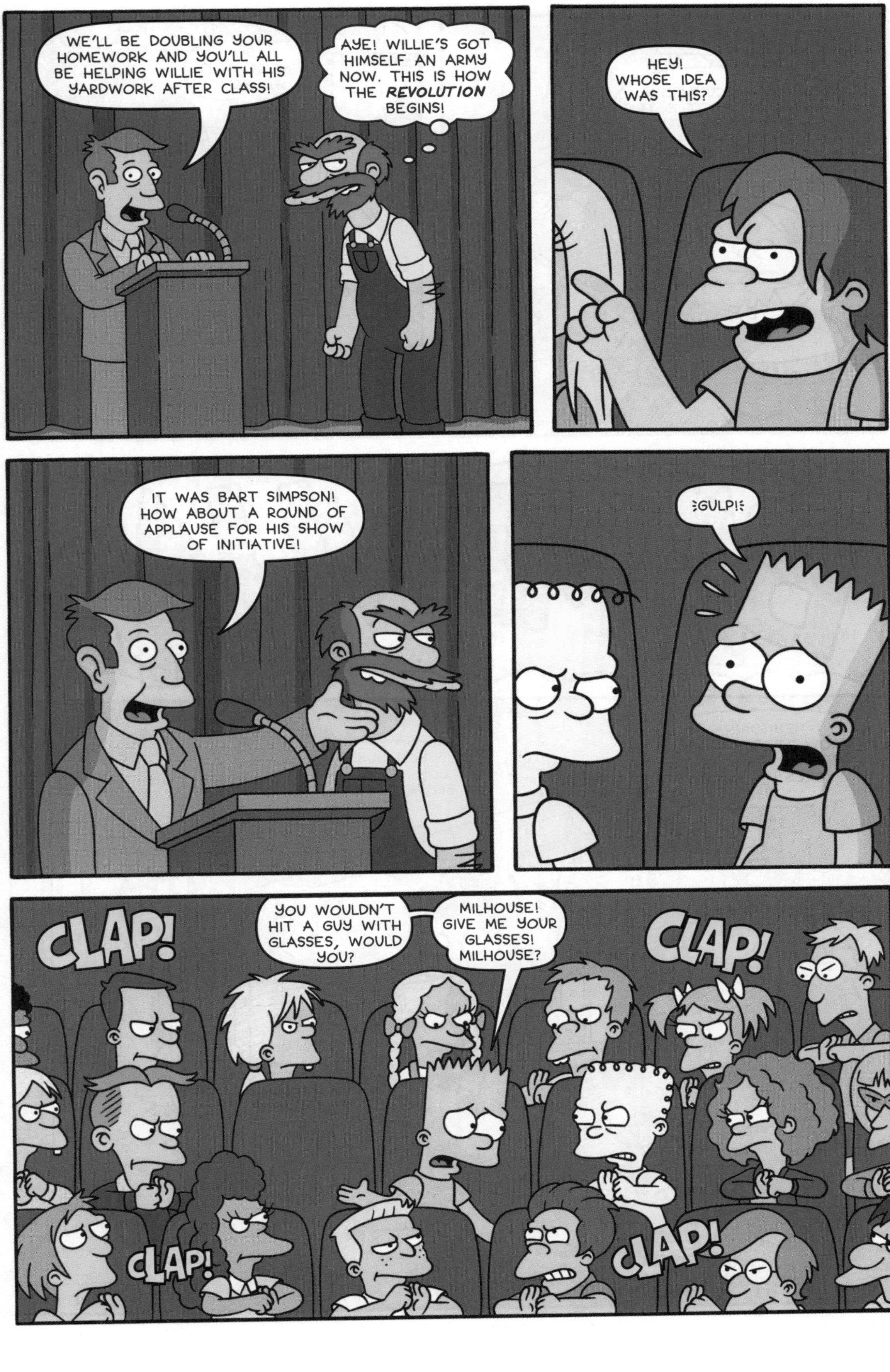
WE'LL BE DOUBLING YOUR HOMEWORK AND YOU'LL ALL BE HELPING WILLIE WITH HIS YARDWORK AFTER CLASS!
AYE! WILLIE'S GOT HIMSELF AN ARMY NOW. THIS IS HOW THE *REVOLUTION* BEGINS!
HEY! WHOSE IDEA WAS THIS?
IT WAS BART SIMPSON! HOW ABOUT A ROUND OF APPLAUSE FOR HIS SHOW OF INITIATIVE!
GULP!
CLAP!
YOU WOULDN'T HIT A GUY WITH GLASSES, WOULD YOU?
MILHOUSE! GIVE ME YOUR GLASSES! MILHOUSE?
CLAP!
CLAP!
CLAP!

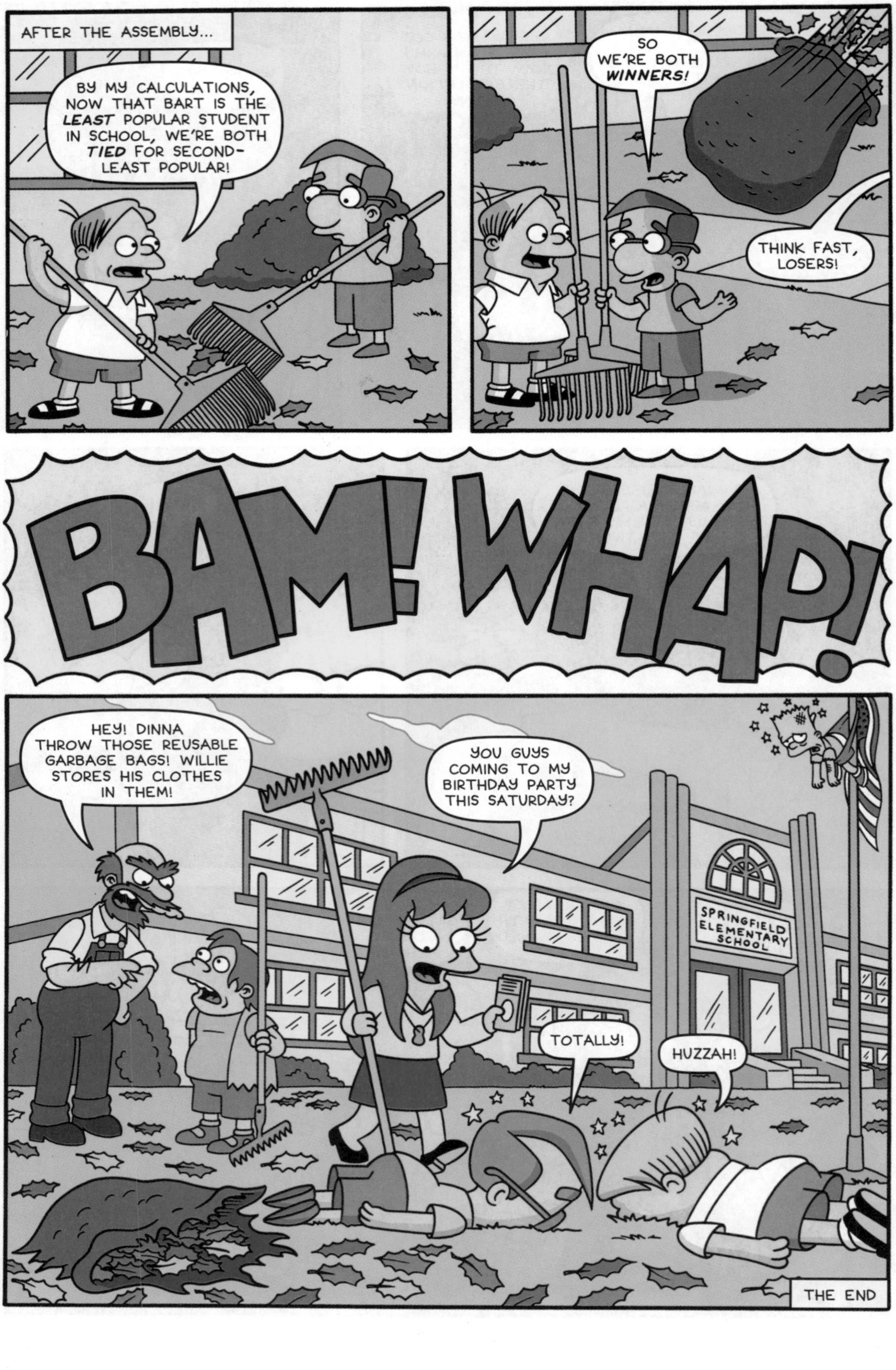
AFTER THE ASSEMBLY...
BY MY CALCULATIONS, NOW THAT BART IS THE LEAST POPULAR STUDENT IN SCHOOL, WE'RE BOTH TIED FOR SECOND-LEAST POPULAR!
SO WE'RE BOTH WINNERS!
THINK FAST, LOSERS!
BAM! WHAP!
HEY! DINNA THROW THOSE REUSABLE GARBAGE BAGS! WILLIE STORES HIS CLOTHES IN THEM!
YOU GUYS COMING TO MY BIRTHDAY PARTY THIS SATURDAY?
SPRINGFIELD ELEMENTARY SCHOOL
TOTALLY!
HUZZAH!
THE END